CROSSED

Visit us at www.boldstrokesbooks.com

CROSSED

by

Meredith Doench

2015

Handwritten inscription:

To Molly —
You are a great
friend! Thanks
so much for your
support!

Meredith Doench

CROSSED
© 2015 BY MEREDITH DOENCH. ALL RIGHTS RESERVED.

ISBN 13: 978-1-62639-377-6

THIS TRADE PAPERBACK ORIGINAL IS PUBLISHED BY
BOLD STROKES BOOKS, INC.
P.O. BOX 249
VALLEY FALLS, NY 12185

FIRST EDITION: AUGUST 2015

CREDITS
EDITOR: RUTH STERNGLANTZ
PRODUCTION DESIGN: STACIA SEAMAN
COVER DESIGN BY GABRIELLE PENDERGRAST

Acknowledgments

This novel would not have been possible without the testimonies and narratives of ex-gay ministries and conversion therapy survivors. Thanks to all of you who took the time to speak with me or allowed me to read your writings about a deeply personal period in your lives. Please know that your courage, your words, and your pain touched me deeply. These characters would not have been possible without you.

If you are a survivor of ex-gay ministries and/or conversion therapy, please visit Beyond Ex-gay for resources that may be helpful. #everylifematters.

I strongly support President Barack Obama's 2015 call to end the use of conversion therapy for minors throughout the United States. In memory of Leelah Alcorn and the multitudes of other LGBT youth struggling with conversion therapies, a ban on such devastating practices cannot come soon enough.

Thank you a million times over to my family for all of your support of my writing endeavors. Mom, without your home and the space to write, these words would never have been written. Many thanks to Brian and Alana for offering advice on everything from the book cover to titles. Dad, thank you for always believing that my work would one day be published.

Many thanks to Geeta Kothari, Man Martin, Christiane Buuck, and other Kenyon workshoppers who offered feedback and guidance on the direction of this novel. A special thank you to Nancy Zafris for her belief in these characters and stellar advice on plot. I still have my plot string.

Many thanks to Stephen Graham Jones, who first heard the idea for this novel in the English department hallway at Texas Tech University. His response—Cool idea. Write it.—gave me the courage to begin.

Many thanks to Liz Mackay, officemate extraordinaire, whose support has never wavered. Those writing boot camps and cell phone timers helped this novel come alive.

Last but certainly not least, many thanks to Bold Strokes Books, particularly Len Barot, for taking a chance on me; Ruth Sternglantz, my editor, for your sharp eye; and G.S. Pendergrast for the cover art.

Dad: This one's for you.

PROLOGUE

He wasn't a stranger. She knew him from somewhere; this was her first sensation. The girl had been sitting with her back against the cool limestone wall, flip-flops kicked off, while she drew hearts and stars inside her journal. He'd already filled the entrance of the cave before she realized anyone was there. The bright sun obscured his face and the girl's eyes moved down the length of his dark shadow and stopped at his midsection—hips that narrowed so thin. Recognition flashed in her eyes, and with a deep breath, relief washed through her.

"Lose your way?" the girl asked. When he didn't answer, she added, "It's easy to get turned around inside these caves." Her voice carried along the belly of the cavern and rolled out to the shadow.

When he didn't respond, she spoke again. This time her voice was a bit too loud and her words came out like a helpless bleat toward the stranger. "Most people don't come around here."

His shadow crept farther and farther over her. She saw the outline of something large and heavy clenched inside his right hand. There was nowhere for her to go but to retreat deeper inside the cave. The girl hurled at him the only thing she could, the journal, and scrambled away on her hands and knees.

The first blow came hard and quick to the crown of the girl's head. The dark shadow worked quickly near her feet. He lined his tools against the limestone wall: duct tape, a thick rag, an oversized camera lens pulled from the bag. She lay stone-still in a pool of her own blood and listened as he screwed together the pieces of a tripod near her feet.

"Damn it to hell," he grumbled under his breath when one of the legs slipped from his hands.

He bent over to collect the steel beam and the girl took her opportunity. She rolled over and curled her legs against her chest. The shadow turned just as she kicked her feet into his right hip. She held the strength of a seasoned soccer player in those thighs and knocked him down to the ground, the steel leg of the tripod banging against the stone floor. The girl was up and past him before he realized what had happened.

The early August humidity drenched the limestone quarry, thick with summer life. Roping vines wound haphazardly through trees and across the paths. Branches that had once been winter barren now screamed with green leaves and offshoots of growth that clawed at her naked legs, leaving swollen scarlet welts. Bits of jagged stone jutted through the mud-hardened and rocky path that was cockeyed and unpredictable. She left smatterings of blood with each frantic step of her shredded bare feet. The world began to spin about the girl as her thick, hot, wet blood seeped between her shoulder blades and trickled down her lower back.

Ragged, shallow breaths whistled as though a stone had been shoved deep inside her windpipe. She raced on while the shadow gained on her. There was still a good half mile to go before she would reach the entrance to the quarry, before she could reach safety.

The girl panicked and moved too fast; one foot churned over the next, her arms pumping out of sync with her legs. A stray branch whipped across her left cheek, gouging high on the cheekbone and ripping the skin back to the ear. It was the protruding edge of a large chunk of limestone, though, that caught her toes and threw her forward. Twigs and pebbles bit the heels of her open palms and ground deep below the skin. Her hips jutted out in a travesty of a downward dog position, and for a few seconds her body threatened to collapse beneath her. She shook her head to fight off the sudden flood of oncoming unconsciousness. Cold, gripping fear rocketed through the girl until she was up on her feet. She struggled to keep some semblance of balance and fought to regain speed. She'd only been down a matter of seconds, but it was enough.

The shadow lunged for her, and the swipe of his fingertips grazed the back of her flannel shirt. When she stumbled again, he hooked his thick elbow around her throat and yanked her against his heaving, sweating chest. The girl's legs flew into the air, much like a rag doll's. She kicked wildly, occasionally making contact with his legs, but her efforts were futile. The shadow's vise-grip chokehold slowly closed until everything went black.

CHAPTER ONE

Wednesday, January 9

Rowan, my life partner, believes there is a universal truth we all must face: our past never dies. Like a giant wheel, everything circles back around.

Meet everything head-on, Rowan always says. *Leave every person and experience with gratitude and peace overflowing inside your heart.*

I've insisted on doing things my way, not Rowan's, which is probably the entire reason why I'm back in a town I never wanted to return to. And why I still dream of the man with thin hips.

The town's name, Willow's Ridge, sends my stomach into a burning roil that fills the back of my throat with a bubbly acid. The universe must be playing some sort of cosmic joke on me. Why else would my very first serial case be located in the same town I swore I'd left forever? White breath clouds escape from my mouth in the cold and I slam my truck door closed. The sky is a dull winter gray with low, thick clouds that seem to rest not far above the tree line. I kick the toes of my lucky Frye boots against the back tire—right, left—knocking loose snow from the intricate and worn treads. Nothing on earth would sound more appealing than to be able to rewind the clock three hours, to go back to when I was nestled in bed with Rowan, safe and so ignorant of what the daylight would bring.

I've worked as a special agent for the Ohio Bureau of Criminal Investigation, the BCI, for the past two years. In that time, I've worked a few murder cases and a spree killing, but never a serial. I was trained at the academy for serial murders and profiling, but Ohio isn't exactly a hotbed of Jack the Rippers. Like my dad always said, you have to start somewhere. So my training has been put to work in a number of serial sex crimes and robberies since I landed the job at BCI. I'm always aware, though, that it would only take one serial murder case to write my ticket to the FBI.

Director Colby Sanders's call woke me just after four this morning, his voice as gruff and demanding as he normally is at four in the afternoon. "You got one shot here, Hansen. Understand?" He paused long enough to draw in a deep pull from his cigarette. "Blow this and I'll see to it you land on street patrol with the county cops."

"Yes, sir."

Sanders talks a good game, but I've seen the softer side of him on occasion. He'd been a federal agent, and earlier in his career, he'd worked a number of serial murder cases across the country. Sanders left the Bureau and came to London, Ohio, to direct the BCI when he turned fifty-five. He has a grown daughter in Columbus and grandkids to keep up with. Sanders knew my father, and I will always be grateful that he hand-selected me upon graduation from the academy.

"I always go with my gut, Hansen. Right now it's screaming you're perfect for this gig—experience or not. Pack for a few days. We've got a third murder in a little over a year."

"A serial."

"Looks that way. The third victim managed to get away from our guy last night but died in surgery about an hour ago."

"Did they get a statement before…?"

"Afraid not." He took another draw on the cigarette. I imagined his leathery face that shows the many hatched lines of sleepless nights and relentless detective duty. His voice carried the weight of years of hard living. "Report to Willow's Ridge station by zero eight hundred hours."

"Willow's Ridge?"

I heard the soft but audible sigh on the other end of the phone and imagined his grit-yellow fingertips grinding out the cigarette butt inside his tin ashtray. "Do I need to assign someone else?"

I kneaded my forehead, the oncoming headache only a few breaths away. "No, sir."

"I'm faxing the files now." There was a shuffling of papers on the other end of the phone. "Good luck, Agent. You're going to need it."

The snow-covered steps lead me up to the entrance of the McCraken County courthouse and police department while nerves pull at my stomach. Performance anxiety has been my constant companion over the last few years; Rowan says I live in a constant and elevated state of agitation. It doesn't help my nerves to know that the only reason Sanders chose me to work this case over a dozen other agents with many more years of experience is because of my history in Willow's Ridge. My past, not my skill, has landed me a serial—something I never could have seen coming. The wind whips the surrounding flagpoles as metal bangs against frozen metal. A strong gust threatens to plunder the US and Ohio state flags, both nothing more than a flurry of red, white, and blue. Somewhere in the near distance, there is the haunting wail of a train whistle.

Once inside the double glass doors, I drop my satchel on the X-ray belt and dig through layers of clothing for the badge attached to my belt. I flip it open for the young security guard at the checkpoint.

"I can't make the ID. Your head's covered."

I suddenly realize how unofficial I must look. My body is cocooned within my heaviest black coat, one of those puffy ski jackets that always remind me of inflated trash bags. My gray scarf, complete with black dog hair, has been wound repeatedly around my neck and over my mouth. I wouldn't be dressed for this winter weather without my black, Russian-style, faux-fur lined hat with the ear coverings flipped down, a Christmas gift from Rowan. In short, I look a heck of a lot like the Unabomber.

I unwind and uncap myself. "I hate the cold. I just got back from vacation in Maui."

The officer's face softens around the edges of his mouth and eyes as he compares the ID photo to my face. "Welcome to Willow's Ridge. Tonight will be the coldest we've had in years." He flips through a daily log. "Agent Luce Hansen, Captain Frank Davis is waiting for you in the morgue."

❖

The basement's wide corridors feature a line of enormous plate-glass windows with their taupe blinds closed to hide what actually goes on inside the coroner's office. Between the windows, the core values of the Willow's Ridge police and court system have been painted in ornate letters: *honesty*, *safety*, *integrity*, and *self-discipline*.

No matter how you decorate it, though, a morgue is still a morgue. Formaldehyde assaults my nostrils as soon as I push through its glass doors. The lights hum above and cast the quiet lab with an eerie glow of silver and metal. Stryker saws, hammers, scalpels, and other instruments line the counter next to the double sink. Two silver body trays sit side by side in the center of the large room. One holds a white-sheeted body with only the arms, shoulders, and head exposed, while the other holds a stack of case files and evidence bags. Scrapes and multiple bruising appear on the female body. She's fresh. This must be Emma Parks, the young woman that has brought me to Willow's Ridge.

A tall African American man steps out of an office doorway to greet me. "Agent Hansen? Captain Frank Davis." His grip on my hand is strong and engulfing, his palm probably twice the size of mine. The captain's face looks haggard but kind with smile lines that crease around his hazel eyes and wide mouth. Davis is dressed smart in a crisp white oxford, a navy tie, and pants that have been pressed to show the creases. He can't be much older than forty-five.

Davis introduces me to Dr. John Mitchell, the medical examiner for McCraken and two neighboring counties. What's left of Mitchell's red hair hangs in tight curls around his ears. In the bright lighting, Mitchell looks as though he's in a state of constant blush. "We're sure glad to see you, Hansen."

"How is Willow's Ridge holding up under all this pressure?"

"It shuts down after five, more or less." Davis takes my satchel and coat to hang behind the door. His movements are confident and fluid, which tells me he's a man comfortable leading others. "We've implemented a seven p.m. curfew for everyone under the age of eighteen." Davis finger-brushes his short gray-peppered hair. "There's a lot of panic out there."

As I stand beside the body, I tie my hair into a low ponytail. Davis hands me a mask and a pair of powder-blue latex gloves that are too large for me, the excess rubber pooling in my palms. Although I'm built muscular and probably stronger than most of the law enforcement officers I meet, I'm short—my boot heels push me just over the five-four mark. I've always wanted to be able to palm a basketball and slam-dunk that ball through the hoop. It won't happen for me in this lifetime without a ladder.

Mitchell struggles to snap the latex gloves over his red, meaty hands, then pulls the white sheet down to Emma Parks's waist. The puckered blue skin of death shows the jigsaw stitching from the autopsy's Y incision, which starts under each of her collarbones. I immediately begin breathing through my mouth, a lifesaving trick I learned early in my training.

I take Parks's cold hand in my own to examine the fingers and the cut of each nail. Sometimes killers will cut the victim's fingernails very short in order to get rid of any DNA evidence. It's hard *not* to be aware of these tricks in our *CSI* television culture. Her nails and hands, though, are a haphazard collection of ripped nails, scrapes, and torn fingertips that indicate she fought her killer. I gently place her hand on the table and lean in closer to her face. She looks so young with her long red-blond hair thrown over one shoulder. Parks turned twenty only a few weeks ago.

"The previous victims had their nails cut and filed after death," Mitchell says.

I nod. "Part of the killer's process of posing." I run my fingertip along Parks's jawline to a large swollen area that had been in the process of bruising at death. "This one ruined his plans when she got away."

Parks, according to the report Sanders sent, had been jogging last evening and was brutally attacked inside the limestone quarry. Somehow she got away from her attacker and gathered the strength to walk out of the forest and into the path of oncoming traffic on the bordering highway. It must have been like a scene out of a slasher horror film for the motorist who slammed on his brakes for the young, naked, staggering woman at three in the morning in subzero weather. He helped Parks into his car and drove her to the ER. She was taken immediately into surgery and had been resuscitated twice, but eventually she died in surgery. I make a note of the tiny pinprick on her jugular, a possible needle entry point.

"Toxicology came back with strong traces of benzodiazepine," Mitchell says.

"Roofies."

Mitchell nods. "Our killer mixed the drug with saline and injected it into the jugular for fast results," Mitchell explains. "He used minimal amounts so that the victims would be aware of what was happening but couldn't fight. He wanted to hear these girls scream—the sadistic fuck."

I let my open hands hover along Parks's body and move slowly over her shoulders and breasts. When I was in the academy, I was told I look like I'm reading braille. In a way, I guess I am reading the victim and her story. Rowan always says I am unconsciously evaluating the body's field, pulling information and clues from the residual energy that lingers around the corpse. I'm not sure about all that. All I know is it works for me and I rarely forget a mark on a body because of it.

"He had to have been very close," I mumble as I inspect a wound on her rib cage with my fingertips. "She trusted him. No other needle entry points?"

Davis shakes his head.

I scan back up to the entry point on the neck. Parks has a relatively thick neck for a young female. It would have been difficult in the rush and the panic of the attack to find the exact location of her jugular. Such precision on a flailing victim in the center of a forest would be difficult at best.

Roofies are a man's drug. Forensic psychiatrists have found that some male killers prefer this drug because it makes them feel all-powerful against a woman. She becomes the damsel in distress, making him the prince who must save her. Twisted, but it mirrors our culture's beliefs that women are physically weak and need a strong hero of a man for protection.

"No DNA found on the body? No semen?" I ask.

"Nothing." Mitchell rolls the white sheet down to Parks's kneecaps. "The cause of death was exsanguination. She bled out from the wounds to her genitals."

Before I can catch myself, I step back from the body. Parks's vagina looks like it has burst open. Her genitals have been not only stabbed, but sliced lengthwise.

"It looks to us like he was not able to finish with Parks for whatever reason. He started the mutilation and we think he intended to do what he's done to the other girls." He opens a file and places autopsy photographs of the other two victims' vaginas. "Looks like a flower to us."

Mitchell points to Hannerting's vagina where it has been cut into six quadrants. Each piece of skin has been pulled back and splayed out like the petals of a blooming flower, with the labia in the center. A long cut below the base of the vagina runs to the rectum as if to replicate a stem. Within each incision are the flashes of white bone. The breath catches in my throat. Although I read about this wound in the chart, nothing could have prepared me for the reality. I've never heard of such a severe wound to the female genitalia before. Sanders has worked on cases where the male victim's penis has been removed, but never one with such severe mutilation to a female.

"The other victim has this cutting to the genitals?"

"Yes," Davis says. "We believe it's some sort of signature."

"Were the victims conscious for the abuse?" I ask.

Mitchell shrugs. "We can't be sure. Most likely they were in and out. Given the level of benzodiazepine, they were certainly groggy and powerless against their attacker. Parks and the others knew something terrible was happening to them."

Davis hands me an evidence bag. "Doctors found this clutched in Parks's fist when she arrived at the hospital."

A gold-colored cross fills my open hand. It is heavy, certainly not pure gold, but some sort of brushed metal. I hold the cross up to the light. The back reads: *May the Lord be the savior of your soul.*

"We found a similar cross with each of the victims." Davis hands me the evidence report. No prints or DNA were found on this cross or the others.

I flip the bagged cross over to study the front of it. Engraved in the lower end of the cross: *Vatican '98.*

"The land of the pope." The cross thumps against the steel table as I lay it down.

"The cross could indicate the killer felt remorse for the murders," Davis says. "He possibly offered a prayer or a final good-bye for each of the victims."

"How generous of our killer," I say. Only Mitchell laughs.

"What do you make of the posed bodies?" Davis asks.

I fall back into professional mode. "Posing usually indicates some sort of ritual that the killer does in order to pay homage to someone or something. He's very precise, a perfectionist. The crosses suggest a possible religious motivation."

Mitchell hands me the other two files. "We may not be in the Bible Belt," he says, "but we have more than our fair share of churches around here."

"There was no sign of recent sexual intercourse on any of the bodies?"

Mitchell shakes his head and then ghosts Parks's body with the white sheet.

"These might not have been sexually motivated killings," I say, "but there are sexual components. The killer might not have raped these young women with his penis, but he used other methods of penetration: the needle to inject the roofies, the knife to the vagina. This suggests possible sexual dysfunction in the killer."

Mitchell chuckles. "Our man can't get it up."

"And he's pissed." It takes a lot of uncontrolled rage to destroy a human body in this manner, years and years of pent-up anger.

One of the files on the stack is filled with notes on the first victim,

Vivian Hannerting, whose case has since gone cold. She was killed in December, about thirteen months ago. Hannerting, twenty-three at the time of her death, was a second-year student at the community college about thirty miles from Willow's Ridge. She was last seen by her roommate leaving their rental house on foot to meet some friends at a nearby bar and grill. She never arrived. Hannerting's body was found three days later by a sanitation worker inside the Willow's Ridge limestone quarry, near the eastern edge of the town. The crime-scene photos show her posed in a seated position, her back against a stone wall inside the quarry, with her arms fully extended and draped over tree branches. Her pale, naked skin gleams against the snow that surrounds her. Hannerting's head is rolled to her right shoulder and tilted down, her eyes wide open as though death had sneaked up on her.

Davis hands me a second file for the next victim, Chandler Jones. "We knew the cases had to be connected, but there's close to a year between the murders. We thought this one might be a copycat."

"Because of the genital wounds?"

Davis nods. "They are very different."

Chandler Jones disappeared a week before Christmas and was found by a jogger with his dog inside the Willow's Ridge limestone quarry on Boxing Day. She was an active member of her Baptist church and was last seen leaving the church parking lot with her car loaded full of food for members of the church who were shut-ins. No one received the food. Her car was found on Christmas Eve in the Miller's Grocery parking lot.

The first crime-scene photograph haunts me: her abandoned car with the backseat of the sedan neatly lined with pink and green plastic containers of food, plastic silverware wrapped in the same colors, along with a crate full of individual milk cartons. The next photograph shows Jones's naked body sprawled out on a snowy wooded patch along the shoulder of the highway near the limestone quarry. Jones's body pose looks like a person placed inside a coffin, flat on her back with her hands crossed at the belly button. Her intertwined fingers aim down at her genitals. Rather than flowering the skin, Jones's genitals were cut out, leaving a gaping hole in her body. Her long hair had been spread away from her scalp in long red waves, a halo surrounding her face. The coroner found a small cross embedded deep inside her uterus.

I lay out the posed Hannerting and Jones crime-scene photographs beside Parks's body. All three victims were killed around the holiday season, maybe some sort of trigger for the killer.

"The killer's pattern has been broken."

"Meaning?" Davis asks.

I turn away from the body and lean up against the wall. "The killer doesn't know exactly when Parks died, right?"

Davis nods. His long, ropey arms cross over his chest as he rocks forward and back on the balls of his feet. Davis strikes me as athletic, as if always on the cusp of working out.

"He only knows what the media has reported, that Parks managed to flag down a motorist who rushed her to the hospital, and later she died in surgery. He has no idea if Parks was conscious and able to make a statement before her death. We need to use this to our advantage."

"What do you suggest?"

"The media is our strongest ally right now," I say. "We need to craft statements that suggest we know more than we do. We need the media to inflame him with regular reports and statements about the case."

Davis nods again, the furrow of his thick brow knotted in thought. "He is very particular in the way he leaves his crime scenes. The mistakes he made last night must be driving him crazy."

"He'll need to fix it," I tell Davis and Mitchell. "He'll kill again and soon. Let's hope the added pressure of the media causes him to make more errors." Time to start the legwork, so I shift from the killer to his victims. "Are there any indications the women knew each other or are connected in some way?"

Davis shrugs. "Willow's Ridge is a small town. These young women must have crossed paths at some point, but they didn't seem to know each other well. They weren't friends or any of the other social connections that we usually see."

The parents had supplied the police with high school graduation pictures. All three look out at me from their files: smiling, competent young women on the verge of life. Were these women selected at random? Could it be as simple as being in the wrong place at the wrong time? My gut tells me nothing about this case will be that simple.

"Catch me up to speed on the investigation."

Davis says, "Two men have been questioned. Both had alibis at the time of the crimes." He turns to me and rests his hands on the thick belt around his slim waist. "One we're still looking at pretty hard— Nicholas Sambino. He's an embalmer at Eldridge Funeral Home here in Willow's Ridge."

"Why Sambino?"

Davis rubs the corner of a bloodshot eye; it's clear he hasn't slept. "Sambino has had a number of interactions with us, disturbance calls and speeding, you know, minor arrests. Except for one. We like him for this based on a rape charge from last year. He was arrested for sexual assault of a fourteen-year-old female. The victim had numerous injuries and was attacked while jogging inside the limestone quarry. Based on the high publicity of the case and the young woman's unstable mental health, the family dropped the charges against Sambino. He walked."

I lean into the wall again, reading Davis's body language closely. My shoulder holster pulls tight against my back. I hate wearing one, but I've got the hips of a twelve-year-old. There's nothing there to hold up the weight of my service weapon. The only cop bling my low-slung waist holds is a badge looped through the belt. "You're not convinced he's our killer."

Captain Davis gives me a quick smile. "You're good," he says. "There are other circumstances to consider."

"Such as?"

He riffles through the stack of files and pulls one from the bottom. It is worn and splitting, thick with notes and crime-scene information. The very first photograph grabs my heart; it is of the navy eyes of my past. The depth of those eyes strikes me first, an old soul so wise and crippled with sadness. The clarity of those eyes beneath the dark lashes that once seemed to understand everything and knew me much better than I knew myself. I've been trained not to reveal emotions in a case, and I've mastered the ability to stuff them down with my poker face intact. I turn away with a fake cough.

"You all right?" Davis asks.

Although I can't breathe, I manage to nod. It's that feeling again—I'm being pushed underwater, held down, and choked. I fight, kick, and claw at the hand forcing me down, to no avail. When I finally surrender to its strength and take my first breath, the water gushes in and my underwater grave grows silent. Safe. Sheltered. I'm cradled by the watery arms that hold me.

"You don't seem all right." Davis's words make their way to me through these cloudy depths.

"Damn allergies," I manage to say. Whether or not he believes such a sorry excuse, it gives us both an escape from this embarrassing moment.

His words gurgle toward me. "Marci Tucker. Murdered in July

of 1989. She is the piece I can't place. Tucker was found bludgeoned inside the limestone quarry, though a different section of the park. She'd been killed near the caves and it looked like an attempted rape gone wrong. The case went cold almost immediately."

I hear the bubbles of oxygen float up as the water slips over the top of my head. I'm sinking deeper and deeper.

"There are ties between Tucker and the present cases—age, gender, and location. As far as we know, there wasn't a cross found on or near Tucker. Cause of death was multiple blows to the back of the head with some sort of pipe. A basic drug screen was run on Tucker and came up clear."

Mitchell says, "We didn't routinely test for date-rape drugs in 1989, so it's possible the victim could have been drugged with it. No needle entry points are listed on the autopsy." The incessant click of Mitchell's pen echoes inside the dead room and brings me rushing up through the water's surface.

To catch my breath, I look down at my feet—black boots that are as much a part of me as my left hand. They're in need of resoling and who knows how many gold-tinted laces I've been through. I wiggle my toes and think of my father; the boots were a gift from him when I was accepted into the academy. They were the last gift he gave me. Thoughts of my father always have a way of grounding me and bringing me back to the case at hand.

"If these cases are truly connected," Davis says, "that knocks out Sambino as a suspect. He would have been about nine years old at the time of the Tucker killing."

"It could be someone he knows well," I say, slowly returning to the game. "Sambino's father. An uncle or an older cousin. Someone he had regular contact with who he admired and made him vow to keep the secret."

Mitchell rubs his temples that bloom neon. I don't doubt his Irish descent and wonder if Mitchell has the temper to match as he pulls the white sheet up over Parks's head. "You mean that Sambino may be carrying on the crimes for someone else?"

I shrug. "We can't rule out any possibility at this point."

Work. It's always been my refuge when my emotions erupt. The obsessive side of me takes over with any case, occupying all my thoughts, puzzling out the details and various crime scenarios in my mind. I'm like a pit bull that clamps down and locks its jaw on a

Frisbee—you can pick the case up and swing it around all you want, but I won't let go until it's solved. It is the mystery of each case that hooks me in, all those unanswered questions. I want the answers. I want it all to make sense. Most of all, I want justice for those who can no longer speak for themselves. Victims just like Parks, Hannerting, Jones, and Tucker.

CHAPTER TWO

My dad always told me that in order to have a successful career in law enforcement you have to be able to bend and not break. Until his fatal heart attack that came out of nowhere, he'd been the Chief of Police for Chesterton County, not more than ninety miles west of Willow's Ridge. He's the only person I've ever met who could bend, bend, bend, and then bend some more without shattering.

Early on in my life, my dad was the one to define my strong instincts as a cop gut. "You've got a strong sensitivity to the truth," he always told me during my training. "Remember, it's all in the breath. When you're calm in the midst of a crisis, you can see the opening into the chaos. Once you're inside, everything begins to make sense." I breathe deep, drive on, and hope that my dad knew what he was talking about. I'm taking him at his word as I step into the center of this chaos.

The two-lane highway known as State Route 55 works as a thoroughfare for Willow's Ridge and connects the small town to the outlying limestone quarry. The highway splits the forest and enormous trees canopy the road. During the summer, there is nothing quite like driving along the rolling hills of State Route 55. If you're lucky enough to have a sunroof or convertible, it's difficult to see anything above your head other than a sea of green foliage.

"Breathe," I tell myself. "Just breathe." I feel as though I'm driving directly into a mouth of madness where everything feels so out of control.

Davis drew a map to the location where Emma Parks emerged from the forest and flagged down the motorist. In order to build a formal profile, I need to set the scene visually in my mind. Most of all, though, I want the time alone. Solitude is how I collect my strength and think through the inner workings of a crime. Thankfully, Davis stayed behind at the station to work with a media consultant on a statement he'll be reading at a six o'clock press conference.

Willow's Ridge is the quintessential small Midwestern town of maybe 5,000. It grew around the limestone quarry with caves that honeycomb the soft stone. The town map shows the almost seventy square miles of wooded forest that make up the limestone quarry along the western edge of the town. A residential area borders a portion of the quarry. It's the flux of the limestone, the unsteadiness of the rock that keeps people from building too close. Many come to Willow's Ridge for its small-town charm and to see the fall colors in the forested quarry. You can always find photographers hiking the trails to capture the old wood-covered bridges, and children collecting small pieces of limestone in their pockets even though signs clearly state: *Do Not Take the Rocks*. It's the charm and isolation of Willow's Ridge that draws so many visitors in and drives so many of its local teenagers out because of the complete lack of nightlife. With one road through town and few stoplights along its famous brick-lined Main Street, fast food chains and huge grocery stores have been zoned outside of the town limits.

Tourists, however, are nowhere in sight now that the town is coated with the hardness of winter. Despite its small population, Willow's Ridge has a lot of money; some members of its community easily clear $500,000 a year. A high-tech heart hospital and research center was built a few years ago outside of Willow's Ridge and quickly gained the reputation of the best in the Midwest. It is money that generally insulates Willow's Ridge from the harsh crimes that occur in the bigger cities of Ohio. That is, until recently.

Yellow crime-scene tape cordons off the entire section of State Route 55. An officer sits parked on the shoulder beside the location where it's been estimated that Emma Parks emerged from the forest. I kill the engine behind the cruiser. With a quick glance in the rearview mirror, I re-knot my hair in a messy bun and pull on my Russian cap. Cold seeps in through the edges of the car door and wind gusts gently rock the car back and forth. I brace myself for the assault of frigid weather.

The officer rolls down his window. The stubble of no shave in the last twenty-four hours pocks his face and his lips are windburned. I show my badge and then hold my arms tight around my body for some attempt at warmth.

"I need to walk the crime scene. How much longer will you be here?"

"Until Davis releases me." His face cringes against the blast of cold. "Won't be much longer. The scene has already been processed."

I slip under the yellow tape. I look back over my shoulder at the officer for a few seconds and then step forward into my past. There is hardly any shoulder to the highway, and I walk into the wall of winter-bare trees sooner than I expect.

"I'm okay." These words are meant to convince myself, but my voice breaks. The tall trees answer with creaks and moans from the bone-chilling wind.

Shafts of sunlight flicker in and out of the clouds as if attempting to generate warmth. I wrap the scarf over my face, leaving only my watery eyes exposed. Everything around me looks suspended, like an iced-over winter scene from a calendar. I follow the ditch along the side to a clearing into the woods carved out of trees as tall and thick as God.

In the distance, plumes of smoke twist up and away from what must be chimneys. In the last twenty years or so, the land around the limestone ravine has become coveted, and a house overlooking the dense forest had become a status symbol in the Willow's Ridge community. A neighborhood of huge homes has been built, each with five to ten acres of land. A creek snakes along the ravine at the base of the limestone cliffs and floods regularly, preventing further development in the area. Officers have interviewed all the people who own homes on the exclusive Willow's Ridge Lane, but no one reported seeing or hearing anything. Judging from the dense woods and the space between the houses and the road, it would be difficult to hear much at those homes, not to mention that most residents would have been sound asleep at three a.m. Besides, these private types, I've learned, tend to mind their own business. They'd be the least likely to report activity to us even if they saw something out of the ordinary.

This clearing hardly leads to what I would call a path, but the brush is thinner and I'm able to maneuver better. The snow covering is scattered because of the naked, billowing branches. Farther inside the forest, the crime-scene team has roped an area off. Small branches have been snapped off recently; I examine the end of one in my gloved hand, the white of the exposed inner wood. There is a fallen tree that blocks the wooded path. Snow and foliage around the trunk have been moved. Blood covers the ground near the tree trunk, the place where he most likely cut Parks's genitals. I drop to a squat for some quick photographs with my cell phone. The bloodstain is not as large as I expect, given exsanguination. Beside the bloody area, what looks like the slide of a boot marks the icy ground.

This was not a quick dump-and-drive crime scene. The killer or killers would have to be familiar with the tough terrain of the quarry. While it's easy access from the highway, the killer had to carry or drag Parks deep into these woods. He planned it, scoping out the exact location to leave the body. Outdoor crime scenes are notoriously difficult to process and this killer had the snow and foliage to help cover up any evidence. I imagine the killer so pleased with his plan: *Scream your head off, honey. You're mine now.* With a gloved hand, I trace the partial track. Parks had been found naked. This is the killer's footprint. He's never left anything close to a print before.

"What spooked you?" I ask out loud.

I push beyond the crime-scene tape a few yards deeper into the woods. There is a change in the landscape, denser pines with thicker underbrush so wiry it grabs at my ankles. *And this is winter.* I follow the thin trail of blood, an area already processed by the crime-scene team. Eventually I stumble upon a rocky cut in the land. My breath catches in my throat and my boot toes hang over the edge of the deep ravine. At least forty feet below rests a round pocket of water that runs so deep within the quarry it's rumored to never have completely frozen. It's a part of the chunky flow of icy water, through a ravine not much more than a deep creek, that shoots off from the quarry and snakes along the bottom of this cut in the land for miles.

When I look up, my father is there beside me, suddenly, the way he always appears these days. Dressed in his police chief regalia, he winks. "You caught a tough one, Lucy-girl."

I smile up at this familiar ghost who haunts my life. "Could use your help here, Pop. Can we talk through it?"

His nod says that he'd have it no other way.

I take two steps back and analyze the scene once more. From my initial observations of the land, I assumed the water ran perpendicular to State Route 55. Instead it runs parallel to the road. "If the water surprised me, it also surprised Parks."

My father nods and scans the terrain. This has always been his favorite part of a case, climbing inside the victim's and killer's heads to determine their every move. I've never met another cop better at it than my dad.

"She couldn't have gotten around this quarry, especially with the darkness of night," I say.

"Unless the killer only used this side of the ravine."

"Risky move," I say. Even though it had been the dead of the night, the drop site wasn't a foolproof distance from the highway and the winter-stripped land made visibility a bit easier. If he wanted to be sure she couldn't get away, he'd have put her on the *other* side of the ravine.

"He counted on the drugs to keep her from running."

"You think he miscalculated the dosage? Seems out of character for our guy."

My dad shrugs. "The frostbite on her hands and feet indicates that she'd been left in the freezing temperatures for some time."

"Something scared him off before he could finish the job. He left her, certain that she would die out here in the cold or from her wounds."

He nods. "We aren't far from the highway, are we?"

Suddenly it's clear: we've only found the body drop site, and he *wanted* her to be found. We still need to find the location where at least some of the mutilation took place and the killer cleaned the bodies. We're missing at least half of this grand puzzle.

Together, we head back toward the highway. I need to see the forest from the other end. I need to examine other entrance points in the area, perhaps from the neighboring properties' backyards. My father's large body pulls through the snow beside me. In these quiet moments alone with him, I'm always tempted to ask questions about where he is now. But Dad's adamant—his ghostly presence is only here to help me with cases. I reach out to take hold of his hand, but my fingers close on nothing but cold air. *This, whatever it is*, I remind myself, *has to be enough.*

There are literally hundreds of possible entrance and exit points to the limestone quarry, leaving thousands of potential drop sites. This begs the question, why this particular spot? Why would the killer leave his victims out in the open not more than three-fourths of a mile from major entrances to the quarry? An image of Vivian Hannerting flashes in my mind, a photograph of her positioned with a cross clenched in white-death hands, positioned not far from the main entrance to the limestone quarry park.

"We have ourselves a self-proclaimed prophet," I say to my father. "A messenger of some kind."

CHAPTER THREE

Since Emma Parks didn't own a car, she walked to and from her shifts at Wilson's Photography Shop. Her mile-and-a-half path home created a prime opportunity for abduction. In a town where most people know everyone else, it seems highly unlikely that a passing motorist wouldn't have seen a struggle and recognized Parks. That leaves only one other possibility: she went willingly with her killer.

Earlier, Davis's team scoured the shop and neighboring stores for any witnesses. They talked to Parks's coworkers and managers, but I want to follow up. Sometimes it's amazing what people can remember when a state badge is flashed at them.

The heater blasts on high as I drive the surroundings of Wilson's. Although the business is located on Main Street and next to a relatively active bank, it looks to be the only store open past six p.m. Main Street would be dark and deserted when Emma started her walk home. Especially in January, when the sky darkens shortly after five p.m.

"Same old story," I say aloud and pull on my hat. We hear these comments from young people all the time: nothing will happen to me, crime doesn't happen in my town, I can take care of myself. No one wants to believe that crime could actually happen to her. This is exactly what Parks told herself every night when she walked home from her job at the camera shop. Even though the previous murders in the area had been publicized, Parks would have reasoned that nothing could happen to her, that she was different from those victims.

Jasper Morgan, the manager who had been on duty with Parks last night, ignores my presence and works with the only customer in the small store. His monotonous drone about a camera's features is enough to put anybody to sleep. The displays around me feature many framed photographs against the backdrop of black velvet. Portraits and landscapes are most prominent, a kid with an oversized yellow Lab and a newborn cradled in their mother's arms. One framed print isn't like all the other family or nature themes, but a black and white of a woman lying partially nude in a wooded area. A leafy branch covers her crotch and fresh-cut daisies cover her chest. Long dark hair is brushed over the model's shoulder, and her eyes are shut as if she's fallen into a deep sleep. There's something odd about the angle of the camera, though, a fish-eye view that gives the model an ethereal look. This is a work of art rather than a family portrait.

Could it be Parks's work? According to the file, she told friends and family members that she wanted to go to an art school to study photography. She'd even applied to the Art Institute a month ago and was waiting to hear whether she'd been accepted or not. Davis mentioned that Parks's photography had been featured in a few local shows. There is no signature in the corner of this print.

"That's one of my favorites. I could stare at it for hours and still not see everything in the photo."

I turn to find a young woman standing behind me in a long white lab coat. Her name tag reads *Kaitlin*. Gothed out, she pulls with black-painted fingernails at her earlobe that holds a large ear stretcher. "It is amazing. Are you one of the lab techs?"

She nods. "Are you a cop?"

"The Ohio BCI."

"Is that like the FBI?" She has a habit of biting on her lower lip ring, leaving the skin red and swollen.

"Sort of, but on a state level. I work for the Ohio Bureau of Criminal Investigation."

"That's really cool," she says, twisting the ends of her flared black skirt around her knees. She wears black tights and neon-green leg warmers, the only color on her dark outfit. "I love *CSI* and *Criminal Minds*."

"Hollywood has a way of making everything look glamorous."

Kaitlin flashes me a near-perfect white smile. Underneath all those piercings and black painted makeup, she's quite attractive. Her blue eyes and high cheekbones are quite startling. And that body—curves, curves, curves everywhere.

Morgan, the manager, points to Kaitlin and slits his eyes at her. "Get back to work!"

She doesn't answer but tucks a stringy lock of dyed-black hair behind her ear. I catch the tip of her head that tells me to follow her while she stocks the shelves.

"Did you work many shifts with Emma Parks?"

"Not many. We're rarely busy and even less so at night. Only one cashier is scheduled after five." She lines the film boxes up in neat rows as she talks. "Emma and I did go on a few photo shoots together."

"Did she mention any customers that may have been bothering her? Anyone who came in regularly on her shifts?"

Before she can answer, Morgan ushers his only customer out of the store. Morgan's a heavy man, and his polyester pants swish each time his thighs rub together. He turns to me with his pale, doughy face. "You have questions about Emma? Speak to me. I'm the manager."

Kaitlin gives a dramatically loud sigh and when her eyes meet mine, I give her a quick wink. Jasper Morgan clearly imagines himself to be very important. I flip my badge at him. "When was the last time you worked with Emma?"

"Last night." Morgan finger-combs his mouse-brown thinning hair. "I already talked to the detectives."

"Just a few questions. You were the manager on duty last night. What time did Emma leave the store?"

Morgan fidgets with his belt, then hikes his worn pants up over his basketball belly. "The thing is," he says, "we don't always have a manager on duty. Most of our employees, like Emma, have been with us awhile and can act as managers."

"Was there supposed to be a manager here?"

He pushes up his thick glasses on the bridge of his nose. "Like I told the other detective, it was a Tuesday night."

"Tuesday? Is that significant?"

Morgan shakes his head. "Tuesday's our dead night so I went home early. Emma had closed on her own a hundred times. She locked up and counted the till before she left."

"Did she have a store key?"

"Emma had mine. She left it on the ridge above the door. I got it this morning. Nothing happened to her here, Agent. I promise you."

"Since you weren't here, there's no way for you to know that for sure."

Morgan shifts his weight. His beady eyes dart from one corner of the sales floor to the other. "It was only an hour! I wasn't feeling well."

I jot down the timeline.

"It's not a big deal," Morgan reasons. "There were no customers during that time." Morgan shrugs. "She closed down the till at seven fifty-eight p.m." He leads me to the register and shows me the close-out tape with the stamped time.

"Mr. Morgan, can anyone vouch for your whereabouts last night from seven to midnight?"

"I told you, I felt sick! I went home."

"Anyone there with you? A neighbor who might have seen you come in?"

"My girlfriend." Morgan plants a fist on his meaty hip. "She cooked me chicken noodle soup and stayed with me all night."

He gives me his address along with his girlfriend's. I tell him I'll be contacting her, but there is no nervous response. Judging from his direct answers, I'd say Morgan's telling the truth.

He scans the floor and finds Kaitlin listening to us. "Get busy! I want to leave here at eight oh-two!"

Kaitlin mumbles back something like "Eat shit," but Morgan either doesn't hear it or pretends not to.

"I need a few minutes with Kaitlin. I just have a few questions for her." Before Morgan can offer much of a refusal, Kaitlin is at my side and leads me to the break room away from his watchful eyes.

Kaitlin's a nervous type with fingernails bitten down to the quick. Her skin's near flawless—no zit or blemish to speak of—and she has a cute, tiny drop of a nose. Her torn, vintage clothing screams art chic; she can't be older than nineteen or twenty. And there is something else: Kaitlin is a lesbian. Sitting across from her at a small table in the break room, I can't help but read the strong vibes. I've been known to have an incredibly accurate gaydar and it's spinning round and round like an antenna on overload.

She tells me the officers who questioned the other workers at Wilson's didn't interview her. No one came to her home, as far as she knows. If that's true, this is the sort of sloppiness that could get Davis and his department crucified by the media.

Kaitlin pulls back her long hair into a ponytail showing off the fleshy planes of her face and her pouty black-painted lips. "This is about Emma's date, isn't it?"

"Date?"

She picks at the remainder of black polish on her nails and avoids eye contact with me.

"Kaitlin, we need your help. Emma needs your help."

Eventually she nods. "I want you to catch this creepster."

"Tell me what you saw."

"I stopped in the other night to buy some supplies. Emma was working alone. That's when he stopped in to see her."

"Have you seen him before?"

"Yeah. We both sort of know Tristan." Kaitlin doesn't look at me. She continues to pick at her chipping nail polish. "Emma said they got to know each other better a few weeks back at Bledsoe's in Columbus. Tristan is from here, too."

"What do you mean *sort of know*?"

Kaitlin shrugs and slumps back in her wooden-backed chair. "I've seen him around. If you live in Willow's Ridge, you sort of know everyone else."

"What's Tristan's last name?"

"Not sure. He's older than us. We didn't go to school together."

I wait for Kaitlin's eyes to meet mine. "Bledsoe's? The gay club?"

Kaitlin gives me a stone-cold glare. "I'm not a lesbian."

Who does she think she's kidding? Surely not me. "Okay." I tread lightly for the sake of the interview. "I'm not asking about you. Only Emma."

"I just want to clarify." Kaitlin's sudden defensiveness tells me that sexuality is an issue for her. "Emma never really dated guys and she wanted to meet a great girl. Tristan was with what Emma called a hottie at the club last week. He promised to set them up last night. He picked Emma up from work and the plan was the hottie would be at his apartment waiting for her. Emma was stoked."

That's why no one was alerted to Emma getting into someone's car. She'd gotten in willingly and with the promise of meeting a girl.

"Tristan was acting kind of creepy."

"Creepy how?"

"He has this dyed-black hair and like six or seven lip rings." She waves her hands, as if to say *start over*. "That didn't creep me out. I mean, *I* have dyed-black hair and a lip ring! It was that he kept telling us about dead bodies. He even said he'd tasted blood. I figured he was one of those vampire-wannabes, you know, *Twilight* shit?" She shivers and hugs herself. "*Twilight* is one thing, drinking blood is another."

"It sure is. Did you have plans to talk with Emma after this big date?"

"She was supposed to text, but I never heard from her." Kaitlin's eyes fill with sudden tears.

I reach into my coat pocket for the supply of tissues that are mandatory equipment for any investigator. "Why didn't you report this information to the police?"

She busies herself wiping away tears with smears of dark eye makeup. "I wasn't here when the cops came to do questioning."

"You could have called. I mean, the story is all over the news. Why tell me?"

Fresh tears spout from her eyes again. "You're cooler than I expected."

I laugh. "Thanks. I'll tell my superiors that." We sit in silence for a few minutes as she wipes away the tears. "Do you have a record, Kaitlin?"

"Just tickets for speeding. Is that a record?"

I shake my head. Where is this avoidance of the police coming from?

"Besides, I don't want anyone to think that Emma and I are more than friends. Sometimes that happens."

"People think you and Emma are a couple?"

"Sometimes."

"Were you sexually involved with Emma?"

Kaitlin shakes her head, but I'm not convinced. I'm suddenly filled with compassion for Kaitlin. Not only has she lost a friend and possibly a partner, but she is also clearly struggling with herself. It's not easy to come out in a small town, and I want to tell her everything will be okay, to be herself no matter what. This is what I wish someone would have said to me when I was coming out. But this is my personal reaction, not my professional response. Kaitlin's personal struggles have nothing to do with Emma. *Focus.*

"You're doing Emma a favor by talking to me." I reach out and squeeze Kaitlin's hand. "What else can you tell me about Tristan's features? Any tattoos? Race?"

"White. Really pale. I mean, he had to have on some kind of white powder or paint to be that white. He looked the way vampires do in all the movies. Jet-black hair and black clothing against the super-pale skin. You know, stereotypical vampire-wannabe."

I can't help but make the connection that the girl before me has many of these same features. "Where can I find him?"

"He has an apartment not far from here."

"You said everyone in town knows everyone. Did Emma know the other young women who died?"

Kaitlin shrugs. "Not well. She mentioned partying a few times with Chandler. But Chandler was a cheerleader. They weren't friends or anything."

I note the possible tie to Chandler Jones, the second victim. I thank Kaitlin and write my cell number on the back of one of my cards. "Call if you can think of anything—any bit of conversation that comes back to you about Tristan. Even if you don't think it's important."

Kaitlin turns the card over in her hand. "Lucy?"

"I go by Luce." I wind the scarf around my head.

My truck's engine eventually turns over, slow and sludge-like, but catching, thank God. While the car warms up, my cop gut pulls at me. I remember the damage to the victims' vaginas. The precise incisions to replicate some sort of flower or the brutal removal of the flesh. The posing of the bodies. Our killer is an artist of sorts. It seems an odd coincidence that Emma was interested in photography—a visual art. Coincidences and crimes, I've learned from experience, rarely go together.

When I was in the academy, I studied with a professor who claimed all serial killers were artists at heart. The difference between a celebrated artist and a vilified serial killer, this professor said, is that at some point in their young lives the creative vision turns dark. We value art that speaks of humanity, but a serial killer values art that speaks of consumption and death. Instead of the examination of life, serial killers examine what it means to inflict unnecessary pain. I think of Rowan, who paints and sculpts for a living. Like other artists, she's generally in need of supplies. Wilson's would provide supplies and the full knowledge of Emma and her schedule.

Before I pull the gear into drive, there's a tap on my window. Ice patterns splinter and I can't make out the dark shadow on the other side of the glass. The window's frozen closed. When I kick the door open with the sole of my boot, it's Kaitlin shivering in her thin clothing, all elbows wrapped tight around her skinny waist.

"I remembered something else. Emma teased Tristan and said he only knew about blood from vampire movies. He argued with her. I think he said something about putting makeup on dead people."

Something clicks inside me. I bounce my gloved thumb against the steering wheel. *The funeral home. The dead.* The pieces fit. Emma Parks had been with one of the Willow's Ridge police department's prime suspects in the three murders: Nicholas Sambino, aka Tristan.

CHAPTER FOUR

I sink into a deep armchair inside Captain Davis's office and wait. Everything is in its place—from the files neatly lined in the inbox to the police procedure manuals inside the bookcase arranged from tallest spine to the shortest. Even his coat and scarf are hung square and smooth on a hanger on the back of the door. This is Davis's way of controlling the chaos. His office is as neat and organized as an Ikea model room, while the biggest case of his career mushrooms around him.

I expected an office like this from Davis. His appearance borders on immaculate with every hair in place. While I noticed that he has the body of a runner, I am surprised by all the running medals and celebratory photographs of him and teammates at finish lines. It makes sense that Davis is an endurance runner; he has the patience and the intensity of someone used to pushing himself to be nothing but the best. There is one element missing from Davis's office that I didn't expect: no family photos. I'd taken Davis as a family man, or at least a father who was very proud of his children and their accomplishments. Yet the office is completely devoid of any photographs of children or scribbled drawings of unidentifiable objects that only parents can love. The untanned circle around his ring finger tells me the split is fresh, and judging by the impersonal flavor of his office, he's not too happy about it.

I reach for my iPhone and check for messages. Nothing from Rowan. I turn to my next-favorite activity on the cell phone, flipping through my pictures: Rowan and the kids, Toto and Daisy, our two Labs; Rowan and her latest painting that's so obscure I only recognize the amazing spread of color; Rowan with her explosion of natural curls, lounging on the beach in Maui in her old T-shirt that says *I'm not a dyke but my girlfriend is!*; and a multitude of Maui beach shots.

This morning, Rowan and I fought over my involvement with this case. I tried to hide the details from her, particularly the fact that the serial case was located in Willow's Ridge. She'd overheard the location during my phone conversation with Sanders. After her initial burst of anger and my defensiveness, we sat together on the corner of the bed, the dogs wrapped around us like enormous commas.

"Why didn't you tell me?"

I reached over and took Rowan's hand in mine. Her skin was smooth and warm—so safe.

Rowan closed her eyes. "I can't go through this again, Luce. You know that."

I squeezed her hand in mine. Even though the words weren't spoken aloud, we both thought about my recent bout with depression, a crippling darkness that settled in and left me close to catatonic at moments. "It's different this time, Ro."

She shook her head, but her voice trembled. "We won't make it."

Her words stunned me to silence, but I didn't let go of her hand. The dogs panted with affection around us.

"If I want to keep my job, and you know I do, I don't have a choice. I just took two weeks off for the Maui trip and they worked three cases without me." When this declaration of missed cases doesn't work, I switch tactics. "This is a serial, Ro! You of all people know how long I've waited to work one."

Rowan eventually softened next to me.

"It'll be okay. You'll see."

We sat together, uncomfortably hand in hand for a while, neither of us saying aloud what we were both thinking, that the Willow's Ridge case could be the end of us. I never like to admit it, but I sometimes struggle without Rowan near. We haven't been apart for more than a day or two for over a year. She met me halfway for a quick kiss before she went downstairs to start the coffee. I put my hand to my lips. I pressed my fingertips there as if to hold in Rowan's kiss—to memorize it—to never let it go.

Nothing will make Rowan like my job. The dangers of what could happen terrify her. Most days when I'm headed out of our home in Dublin and she's loading up her art supplies, she says, "Remind me again why I fell in love with an agent."

I can't help but to crack jokes in those moments. "Maybe the uniform? Don't tell me it was the gun?"

I put the iPhone back in my pocket and touch my Christmas gift, a silver ring, just to make sure it's still there. The warm silver band is a reminder that the whole trip to Maui with Rowan really did happen. Rowan designed the ring for me, a thick band with continuous etchings of swirls and waves. She even embedded a spray of small diamonds in the eye of the ring, ones that she picked out from a diamond dealer in Columbus. Inside the band she engraved the infinity symbol. Rowan nearly burst in the attempt to keep her plan and ring hidden. She can't keep a secret to save her life. Still, the plan went off with only one hitch. On one knee in the sands of a Maui beach, she presented the ring on the last day of the year while the island's signature New Year's Eve firecrackers crackled around us, painting the sky and sea brilliant yellows, greens, and reds.

I love Rowan. But something always holds me back, something I can't quite explain. I term it my personal Berlin Wall, a sort of block I can't get past. Everyone holds something back from a lover, no matter how many years they've been together, right? Don't most people keep that get-out-of-jail-free card tucked inside their back pocket, just in case?

Sometimes, though, in the quiet predawn hours, in bed with Rowan asleep beside me, I find the courage to be honest with myself, to pull a few stones down from that wall one at a time. No matter how tragically slow the process, the wall *is* diminishing. There is hope for me, Rowan says. She places all her trust in that, but I can't shut off the constant deluge of what-ifs. That faint doubt in the back of my mind stokes my conscience. What if Rowan leaves me? Finds someone new? What if she gets hurt or deathly ill? *What if, what if, what if.*

Rowan surprised me by popping the question with the ring. Even though we'd been together over two years and living together for a year, I never saw the question coming. Call me stupid. The ring, the humid island, the fireworks raining down around us. The question hung in the air between us like a word balloon from some kind of cartoon. I looked down at the ring on my hand, the silver against the berry-brown tan from the Hawaiian sun, and said, "I need to think it over."

Rowan turned away, looked out over the water. "That's a no."

"It's not a no and it's not a yes." I didn't want to hurt her; I only wanted to love Rowan and keep everything the same. It was Rowan, though, who finally conceded that my silence and lack of eye contact meant it might not be the right time. We should only do it if we were both 100 percent sure.

Rowan is sensitive, fragile, with an artist's temperament to match her career as a painter. My hesitation to accept the proposal was like a jackhammer to her shivering heart. Still, no matter how hard I try, my Berlin Wall holds steadfast even with its chips and breaks, and there is no way to maneuver around or over it. I twist the band round and round on my ring finger and wonder when I'll be okay with the commitment of marriage. No matter how many scenarios I sift through, I just cannot see myself ever getting to that place. If I could, it would be with Rowan.

Captain Davis closes the glass door behind him and takes a seat on the other side of his desk. His lithe movements are whisper quiet, his demeanor calm and controlled. There is an element of exhaustion in his movements, though, the pull of sleep along the corners of his eyes. "What do you think, Hansen? What sort of profile are we working with here?"

"Our guy's an artist, of sorts." I pull the case files from my satchel and place them on the desk. "If you look at the way the bodies are laid out, the intricate cutting, it's as if we're looking at a visual art piece. He could have used another medium like a painting or a sculpture, but instead he's using the canvas of the human body." The crime-scene photographs are spread out before us like a deck of cards at a poker game. "I've seen many crime scenes that have many layers to them, but these killings are blatant in their artistry. He's our Picasso."

"Picasso." Davis rolls the name around on his tongue. "I like it."

"We're looking for someone whose job involves some sort of artistry. The appearance of a space is vital to our guy. He might work in design or the remodeling of homes. He could be a woodworker or even work in an art-supply store. Whatever his job, it will be one where appearance is absolutely vital to the success of his business." A woman dressed in a business suit waves through the large glass windows of Davis's office. With her heavy makeup and big hair, it's clear she must be a television reporter.

"They're here already for the press conference," Davis says as someone from the front desk collects the reporter. "Can't keep the media away from this one."

I ignore the media comment and continue with the profile. "But when it comes to making art, he is an amateur—maybe someone who paints landscapes as a hobby or someone who works on his sculpture late at night when he cannot sleep."

"Why amateur?"

I push some of the crime-scene photographs across the desk. Davis leans in closer. "In these photos from the Hannerting case, there is disturbance around the body." I point to the victim's left shoulder. "Notice the slight abrasion to the shoulder blade? She was pulled or pushed to a very specific location."

Davis picks up the medical examiner's photo and examines it. "Mitchell guessed that scrape to be from the struggle with her attacker."

I shake my head. "If there'd been a struggle, even with the victim drugged, we'd see more scrapes and bruises. It looks to me like he placed her on the ground and realized he was off on the exact placement. He pulled her to the location where she was found."

Davis holds the photo close to his face and leans toward the window for additional light. Tiny wrinkles of concern gather in the corners of his mouth and the space between his eyebrows.

"The precise placement indicates that this killer has a vision that he is replicating," I continue. "I'm not sure how much experience you have with artists, but many talk about finding their voice in work, whether it's writing or painting or photography, or whatever. We are witnesses to this killer as he perfects that voice."

Once Davis puts down the Hannerting photo, I hand him a crime-scene photo of Jones. "The killer is much more precise with Jones. He's either displayed the body correctly the first time or manipulated it in a way to hide his efforts. We don't see the same amount of disturbance around the body," I say. "And as he gets more skilled with his art…"

Davis finishes the sentence for me. "He's becoming faster and shortens the time between his kills."

"Exactly," I say. "From what I can tell, he makes mistakes with each kill. He learns as he goes. He's got a taste for it now, though. He won't stop until someone stops him."

Davis leans back in his chair and crosses an ankle over his knee. "What are the other mistakes?"

I draw a diagram for Davis on a piece of police station letterhead. Three columns—Hannerting, Jones, Parks. Under Hannerting I write: *Dragged body to exact location.* Under Parks I write: *Didn't kill her, either misread her body signs or interrupted.* I draw a large circle over the center of the page which includes Jones.

"This is the only one that went off without a hitch." I tap the end of the pen to Jones's section. "He got cocky after this kill. He didn't take nearly the precautions he should have with the Parks murder because of it."

"So he's after perfection?"

"That and recognition. He wouldn't leave his work so close to trails and roads if he didn't want us to appreciate his art," I say.

Davis takes a moment to digest my profile. Then he asks, "What do you make of the crosses?"

I shrug. "It could be a number of things. Perhaps the victims were chosen with some sort of religious idea in mind, or as Mitchell said, he might consider himself to be very religious and was offering each girl a prayer after he committed the crimes. But…" I scratch my head and think of how best to say it.

"Go on."

"It could be that these girls were some sort of sacrifice for a God, Goddess, or whatever."

"Shit, Hansen. Don't tell me these are satanic offerings."

"I don't think so. Why leave a cross if the bodies are a sacrifice for the devil?"

Davis groans and scrubs his face with his wide palms.

"I know," I agree. "We have to keep that information out of the media."

"The crosses?"

I nod. "And the details of the genital destruction. It will only cause panic. Once word gets out that we have an active serial killer in the area, we won't be able to stop the media. Every outlet will send their own correspondents and reporters. You'll need to instruct your team as to what can be discussed with media and what cannot." I thumb back at the hallway through Davis's window. "Little Miss Ready to Interview is exactly the early bird that we need to watch. If any of these details break, the killer will change his MO."

"And we will have no way to test a suspect's knowledge of the crime scenes."

"Exactly. We also need to try and keep Parks's possible homosexuality out of the press as long as possible."

The rest of Picasso's profile is a bit formulaic, but one I'm willing to bet money on. He is a local man and knows the area very well. I'd guess his age to be between twenty-five and forty-five. He is white and blends into his surroundings, maneuvering inside this community without causing any suspicion. Like the BTK killer in Kansas, this guy is an active member of his neighborhood, his family, his church. No one knows about this side of him—there's a dark, nonsocial side, like a Jekyll and Hyde.

"The BTK guy coaxed the media," Davis adds. "This guy has been silent."

"He's kept his ego in check so far. We've caught him early in his career, but he'll make a big mistake. I'm guessing he'll be tripped up by his OCD. He can't leave a body before doing whatever it is he does with the cuts and the crosses. He has a method and a plan—he cannot deviate from that without causing himself severe psychological distress."

If there is one thing I know about serial killers, especially guys like BTK, it's that they have serious anger issues and narcissistic tendencies. The entire world revolves around them. If we can manipulate the press release to poke him, we might spur him on to make another crucial mistake very soon.

Davis tips back in his chair, arms folded out in a stretch like butterfly wings. His biceps are thin but well-muscled. He examines me on the other side of the table. "I've hired on a detective to help the team. I had to pull his ass out of retirement—he's one of our greats in this area."

The rattle of knuckles against the glass door fills the room and in steps a grayhair, someone who's spent years on the beat and weathered it all. A pin on the lapel of his sport coat reads *Proud to be an American* under a waving flag.

"Ainsley," I say, not sure exactly how to react. Sudden flashes from the past filter through my mind.

Detective Cole Ainsley reaches to shake my hand. "Good to see you again, darlin'. I bet you made your daddy proud with that big, fancy badge."

Ainsley was a friend of my father's and worked a number of cases with him over the years. I haven't seen Ainsley since my dad's funeral. I feel like I'm standing on ground that has suddenly shifted beneath my feet and its unsteadiness might not hold. Detective Ainsley looms above me at a little over six feet with a shock of thick white hair and a wooly mustache and eyebrows to match. He has that upside-down-triangle body shape with the broad, beefy shoulders and the whittled-down waist. "They're getting my badge ready in human resources," Ainsley says. "I need to check in with them and then I'll report back for orders."

Davis and I watch him go. "Ainsley's been up my ass about the connection between these latest murders and the Tucker case." Davis looks out the window, his eyes hooded against the light. "He's a good cop, Hansen. Most of the guys around here think he's cracked because he's been in here screaming about Tucker." Davis's gaze comes back to me. "I tell the guys to be grateful. Ainsley's not half as cracked as the psychics that have been through here."

I laugh with him. Davis has a playfulness about him, an aura of humor that probably comes through much clearer under different circumstances.

"This might surprise you, Agent, but there have been no credible psychic leads yet."

It is simply impossible to have a case this big without the psychics crawling out of the woodwork. We'd been warned extensively about most psychics' need for attention in the academy. It's not that I don't believe messages from beyond exist; just, in my experience, the so-called psychics who have come forward to help have not had the most honorable of intentions or accurate results.

"You see no connection to the Tucker case at this point?" Davis asks.

"It's a long shot," I concede. "A killer like the one we're dealing with has a need to kill in order to survive. He's making a statement with these crimes. How would he have been able to stop for all those years? Also, Tucker was not mutilated or given any drug. She died from a beating. It's a different pattern." I dump another packet of sugar into my sludge-like coffee to kill the awful taste. I need something to hold in my hand, something to ground me after seeing Ainsley. "As far as I'm concerned, the only connections with Tucker are location and gender. Maybe our killer moved away after Tucker and moved back a year or so ago, but that's a shot in the dark."

"I'm partnering you with Ainsley." Davis tries a pen on a pad of paper, scribbling for a line of ink. He tosses it aside for another. "Let's get going on that press statement."

❖

All around me toilets flush and reporters freshen up before the press conference. I've locked myself inside a stall to stop the tremble in my hands and the shiver that pulses through me, which rattles my teeth. I suddenly hear my father's voice: "It's all in the breath." Eyes closed, I try to forget Ainsley, and I listen only for the steadying of my choppy breath. *Focus.* Equal lengths of inhalation and exhalation.

My father had no doubt that chaos could be controlled. He also didn't have his memory to contend with, a past like a minefield. I never know what will stir the memory—a spoken word in just the right pitch, a touch in the same location and with the same amount of pressure. But my father knew one thing for sure: my past made me into the woman I am today and those experiences have made me a much stronger agent.

The water slowly begins to recede. With each exhalation, my ears unplug and I slowly rise to the surface.

Breathe in.

Breathe out.

Breathe in.

By the time Captain Davis takes the podium to deliver a statement about Emma Parks, a healthy pack of media representatives has descended on Willow's Ridge and fills the small conference room with cameras and microphones. Reporters set their voice recorders. I stand in the back of the pressroom, my badge hidden while I pose as a reporter. I scribble notes on a pad of paper and observe everyone around me. It's been known for a killer to pose as a reporter at a press conference about his own crimes. Crazier antics have been done by murderers so desperate to interject themselves into the investigation. It always amazes me how so many serial killers are fascinated with the law enforcement teams who work to solve their crimes. Hiding in plain sight is a skill Picasso has already mastered.

Davis looks nervous and stiff in his dark suit and tie. The harsh lights wash out his skin tone to the color of ash. Still, he manages to hold his voice steady and deliver the statement in only three minutes. After detailing the victims' names and ages, Davis gives some information about what each girl was doing at the time she went missing. "We are looking into the possibility that there may be a serial killer working within the Willow's Ridge area."

A hush falls on the room after Davis uses the magic words: *serial killer*. Only the clicks of cameras fill the room. After a few moments, Davis explains that the most recent victim, Emma Parks, was able to give a statement before succumbing to her wounds, and her statements have been a significant help to investigators.

It was my idea to insinuate that we'd gotten information from Parks before she died. I hoped it would enrage Picasso.

"Make no mistake"—Davis leans in to the cameras just as I'd instructed—"we *will* find you." He pauses for dramatic effect.

Davis's words are slow and measured, just like we'd practiced. The room is silent except for the continued click of camera screens. Davis immediately thanks the press and leaves without answering any questions.

I'm certain the killer is watching the statement.

CHAPTER FIVE

Ridgeway Inn is the only hotel in Willow's Ridge, and from the looks of the room, it hasn't been used since the leaf-peeping tourists came through last September. I drop my bag on the hotel bed and half expect dust particles to scatter in a gray poof from the flannel quilt. The bed frame squeaks a tired whine of protest. The old box-style television and the burnt-orange shag carpet are a real sight, and I'm willing to bet there's no exercise equipment to speak of in the hotel. Certainly no pool for my daily workouts.

I splash cold water on my face in the bathroom and glance up at the mirror above the sink. Beyond my reflection is probably the biggest bathtub I've ever seen. A double-wide of white, shimmery porcelain that's a stark contrast to the dark '70s decor. And there is no shower. Who takes baths anymore anyway? Especially in a dingy hotel that looks like a time warp that only Austin Powers could truly appreciate.

Leaning against the oversized bathroom counter, I twist the hotel towel up in my hands and think of Ainsley. I hadn't expected him. Hell, I hadn't expected Marci to be brought into the case. The last thing I want is for my past to be broadcast on the news, the past I've worked so hard to keep a secret.

I snap a picture of the tub and text it to Rowan: *Wish u were here.*

A severe cold has settled in for the night. Outside the hotel window, the snow and ice glow a bluish silver under the streetlights. I'd forgotten how dark it gets in such a small town at night. The quiet would have matched the darkness if it weren't for all the ruckus from the arriving press. It's amazing what happens once the label *serial killer* is used. Americans can't get enough of these killers. It's been a long day and we still have an interview to conduct. I usually thrive on the fast-and-furious pace of a murder investigation. Not tonight.

Downstairs, I find Ainsley in the hotel lobby leaning against the front desk in an attempt to get closer to the manager. My dad always said Ainsley was quite the ladies' man, a master flirt who smooth talked many women he worked with over the years. "He can get any woman to give up her secrets," my dad said. I wonder what his wife thinks of his tactics and why she has stuck around so long.

"Ready?"

"Ah, Hansen. Meet Alison, the owner of this fine establishment. Her daddy and I used to play hoops together in high school. She's sworn to keep your affiliation a secret from all these media goons," he says, in a voice only Alison and I can hear. "Right, Alison?"

She nods, her thick blond ponytail bouncing, and gives me a quick smile. "Don't worry."

"She's proof that the apple doesn't fall too far from the tree," Ainsley says. Standing next to him, I'm nearly choked with the excess of his aftershave. He's recently spritzed up.

"Have you sold out your rooms for the night?" I ask.

"Tonight and for the next week. We haven't seen the likes of this sort of business since the centennial anniversary of the limestone quarry." Alison gives me a nervous smile. "We're sending people out to Caldton, the town next to us, to find rooms."

Ainsley hands Alison his card. "I know you got Miss Special Agent staying with you"—he thumbs over at me—"but if any of these reporters get out of hand, give me a call."

Alison holds the card a few seconds as though it's valuable before she slips it into her back pocket.

Ainsley hands me a cup of steaming coffee. Grateful for the caffeine, I wrap both hands around the piping Styrofoam. "Where did you get this?"

"The perks of knowing the owners."

I take a sip. "Well done."

We make our way for the entrance through the lobby filled with camera crews and reporters.

"If we could just do our blessed jobs without the media breathing down our necks," Ainsley says.

The glass doors slide open. "We go back a long time, Ainsley, but for the record, I don't answer to darling or Miss Special Agent."

"No?"

His boyish grin's infectious. Despite my best efforts, I grin back. "No."

He chuckles and nudges me with his elbow. "Got it, sweetheart."

Ainsley drives a slow winter-weather crawl through the main portion of town toward Eldridge Funeral Home on the edge of town. The bright streetlights reflect off the lenses of his glasses. A mass collection of key chains bounces against his knee. Ainsley has the standard law-enforcement Swiss Army knife, which clinks against a plastic picture frame. A young girl smiles in a school portrait on one side, while the back features a photo of the girl with Ainsley.

"How old is your granddaughter? She's a cutie."

Ainsley gives me a startled look, then realizes I'm referring to the picture on the key chain. A smile spreads across his perfectly white teeth. "Sophie. She's in kindergarten out at Willow's Ridge Elementary."

"She looks sweet. Must be nice to have her living so close to you."

Ainsley nods. After a second he adds, "She's actually my niece's daughter. Sophie calls me gran-Cole." He chuckles and there's a twinkle in his eye. "My wife's gran-Nancy. Do you have any children, Luce?"

"Can't claim any. Sometimes I wish I could."

Ainsley nods beside me. "Being a parent can be the most beautiful gift but it can be a quiet curse sometimes. I keep thinking about how these families are handling the murders of these girls. Christ, I can't imagine."

In the glare from the streetlights, I examine Ainsley's profile. It's hard not to be drawn to him. He's stubbornly gruff, no doubt about that, but he has a nice sense of humor. He may not be the best communicator I've worked with, but it's clear that his passion outweighs most of that. And he's always been known for his incredible police work. While Davis didn't tell me he believes Marci's case is linked to the present murders, the fact that he hired Ainsley does. If, and that is a very faint if, this is a serial case that began with Marci's murder, Davis hopes the presence of Ainsley might throw the suspect, let him think we know more than we actually do.

"It must have been something terrible to find your friend like that, Luce. You and Marci were both so young. I know you cared for her."

I nod and look out the passenger window.

"I want you to know I never gave up on her case. I always kept her school picture under the glass top of my desk to remind me."

"Thank you," I say. A heartbeat passes. "It changed my life, finding Marci like that."

Ainsley nods. "I know that the Marci Tucker case is connected. Davis tells me you have your doubts."

Ice collects around the edge of the windshield. "Twenty-plus years is a long time to go without killing for one of these guys. And the quarry. Could there be a more perfect place to hide a body on this planet? I'm not convinced we can count location as a tie."

Ainsley shrugs. "I give you that, Luce. That's exactly why I know our guy has at least one partner."

"Ainsley—"

He cuts me off with the slice of his hand through the air between us. That's the other thing about Ainsley: he has a temper that tends to get him into trouble with his coworkers and suspects. "Nobody wants to say what's really going on here, Hansen. No one wants to say aloud that we have a hate crime on our hands. All of these kids were dabbling in places they didn't belong, correct?"

I look at him hard. Ainsley's white hair shimmers silver under the streetlights. I understand why Davis hired him out of retirement. Marci Tucker is the case Ainsley hasn't been able to let go of. We all have one of those cases, one that cuts too close to home, that wrenches our heartstrings and never lets us go. We resolve we will crack that crime before we retire. We *will* see justice prevail. This is Ainsley's too-close-to-home case. Even in his retirement, he can't forget.

It's also suddenly clear that Director Sanders put me on this case for exactly the same reason. Marci Tucker, in essence, has always been my case, too. I see Ainsley with a new appreciation. Based on our past, our symmetry, we are a perfect partnership. If we do it right, combine our need for answers, we'll make an unstoppable team.

The theory of at least one partner working with the killer is not improbable. It also, conveniently, clears up the age issue that knocks Nick (aka Tristan) Sambino out of the running for killing Marci. He very well could be carrying on the murders for someone else. Ainsley had been very outspoken with his work on the Tucker case, giving radio and television interviews, talks at the local schools, and questioning community members at length. If Sambino was involved in that murder, he'd recognize Ainsley and realize that we're onto the fact that this case spans many years. Still, it's a real stretch.

"Ainsley, there's no evidence of more than one killer."

"Hell, Luce, there's not much evidence of anything." His fingers drum on the steering wheel. "It's all so clean. Whoever committed these murders planned them out well in advance and must have had help. A spontaneous crime doesn't go down so clean." He adds as an afterthought, "And this Sambino kid is a real piece of work."

"Is Sambino a homosexual?"

Ainsley's thick eyebrows knit together while he contemplates the question, and then he shrugs. "It wouldn't surprise me. It's so cool to be gay now."

Pregnant pause.

"I'm not one for the equal rights of gays," he says, as if suddenly remembering who's sitting in the car. "Marriage and all that."

"I didn't expect you were, Ainsley." I bite my bottom lip to not add *like most older male cops I know.*

"Why do you ask?"

"Emma Parks was apparently friendly with Sambino. What did these two have in common? From what I've heard, Sambino is about as different from Parks as you can get. Yet they apparently saw each other in gay clubs. That connection might make her trust him."

"She probably thought Sambino was a lost soul who needed some understanding." Ainsley's words drip with sarcasm. "He's one of those young people doing everything he can possibly do to make himself different."

"Unique and independent," I say. "That's what they call it now."

"How's this for unique? Sambino says he's a vampire back from the dead. We have a statement from his last employer at Walmart who said they let Sambino go for bringing in what looked like a canister of blood. I guess he let it sit in the work fridge like it was Pepsi or whatever and drank it with his lunch."

"How Halloween-y of him."

Ainsley's rug of a mustache bristles when he giggles. He's playful now and flutters his eyelashes at me over his shoulder. "I vant to drink your blood." He peels back his lips and we both laugh. It's been a long day.

"I swear if my Sophie ever comes home and says she's a vampire, I'm shipping her off to Transylvania." The jokes between us are like a release valve for some of my stress and all the tightness that was there at our first meeting.

"When I talked to Kaitlin from the camera store today, she said Sambino had been in there bragging about his holy vampirism. He told Parks he was also risen from the dead."

"Wait till you see his vampire teeth." Ainsley taps the brakes for a red light and we skid on the icy black road. The back end fishtails a bit to the right, but nothing he can't handle.

A comfortable quiet settles between us for a few moments. When the long light turns green, Ainsley asks if I've seen Marci's family since the murder.

I shake my head. The truth is she never would have been there if it wasn't for me. I'd been late to meet Marci in our secret place inside the quarry, a limestone cave she called Stonehenge, her hiding place from the world. I reach in my left pocket and my fist closes over the chunk of limestone I always carry with me.

Banded limestone. That's what Marci called the paper-thin, layered rock from the quarry that summer. She placed the stone in the center of my palm and folded my fist inside her warm hands. *Not a gratitude rock*, she'd said, *but a Marci rock. Carry it in your pocket and think of me.* With her hands wrapped around mine, it was as though I could feel the beat of her heart through her fingertips against my skin. I imagined my own pulse a match with hers—a constant thrum of us.

My Marci rock. Now I hold that Ohio limestone and trace each layer line along the sides with the edge of my thumbnail as if it contains the answers. I've worked hard to bury our past over the years, to keep it entombed so tight that not an ounce of daylight could shine through. Marci always said that people are like limestone: just when you think you can't stand another minute of pressure and pain, you do. Softness, she said, is the key to limestone formation. It is the acidic layers that permit the elements to shape the rock as it will: a stream of water that peels away the grains that hold it together, the wind that whips patterns into its skin, the ice that drips into the open pores and explodes the rock into scattered chunks only to begin the process all over again. It is the ultrathin layers that keep limestone in a state of constant flux, morphing itself into something completely new, while holding traces of its surroundings and whole histories gathered over time.

It is the holes in the limestone that get me thinking, the bubbles of air stuck inside the layers that ultimately leave the rock weak. What exactly do those bubbles of air hold? Sound? A sliver of an hour from that long-ago summer? I used to imagine cracking that rock open like an egg to see what secrets might spill out. Could the rocks in the limestone quarry contain sliced images of what really happened to Marci? Then my rational thinking would set in, followed with fear. Always that bone-rattling fear.

Ainsley clears his throat. "You didn't kill her, Luce." He reaches over and squeezes my knee to let me know he's there, always has been. His dignity strikes me like a blow to the stomach, then melts my heart. His face reminds me of a sweet grandfather with a massive collection of crusty edges. "We all have our pasts. That's what pulls us to this job. For what it's worth, I bet Marci would be thankful you're on this case. She might just lead us somewhere."

My eyebrows furrow not because I'm mad, but because I'm trying to understand. Is Mr. Conservative with his collection of Republican bumper stickers really talking to me about Marci's ghost?

"All right, look. I'm not one for all this psychic mumbo jumbo, but I got a relative into this sort of thing." He points to Sophie's photo. "Her mama. Anyway, when she describes it, I picture that scene in the first *Star Wars* movie when that little round robot flashes that greenish image of Princess Leia. You know what I'm talking about?" He puts on his female voice and imitates Princess Leia's distress call.

"Nice voice," I tease. "The robot is R2-D2. You mean that hologram?"

"The hologram. My niece always says murder victims have this sort of ability and call out to people to solve their case. She always told me Marci had a hold on me with that same sort of hologram. I bet she's got one on you, too."

The floating image of Princess Leia begging for help fills my mind. Her words flicker and fade as though it's a terrific struggle to get the message for help across. A quick flash of goose bumps rise up my arms. "I never took you for a spiritual type, Ainsley."

"If by spiritual you mean God-fearing, I most certainly am. But that psychic stuff is about as crazy as calling yourself a vampire."

Not every cop believes in the power of the dead the way I do. Then again, not every cop has a ghost of a dad who helps her with current cases as if he's still very much alive. Call me superstitious or blame it on all those '80s slasher films I watched as a kid. Even now, though, I still wonder if Marci's spirit is trapped inside that limestone cave, caught between two worlds, and unsure of how to get out. The year following Marci's death I used to lie awake at night, staring at the ceiling, and wonder if it could be something else. Something much worse. What if Marci haunts Stonehenge and guards it, if her ghost is patiently waiting for the return of the one who should have saved her but didn't? What if the promise of vengeance against me has kept her grounded to this world? Those were the fears of a sixteen-year-old girl.

When it comes right down to brass tacks, though, it is the truth that I fear most of all. Just like forensic evidence, our own personal histories, I know, are like those bones and prints not buried deep enough in the layers of rock. Something always surfaces—the poke of a skull through the weathered soil, the point of a femur that the dog uncovers for himself, the droplet of blood wedged away inside a hidden doorjamb. I'm not ready, and maybe never will be, for my secrets from Willow's Ridge to be revealed. Do I really have the courage to dig and brush away at the makeshift grave until all the answers are unearthed and finally washed clean?

"I guess every cop has a case that gets under his skin and refuses to let go. I was so naïve then. I'd never seen anything like the Tucker case. Hell, none of us had." Ainsley shakes his head and grunts at the grisly memory.

My eyes burn, sudden and fast. Instantly I remember. It's the grunt that gives Ainsley away. I look over at his profile against the car window and see an Ainsley twentysomething years ago, his hair a solid black and his body leaner and stronger. Handsome. He gave me a small teddy bear in the police station.

"You're too big for this, I know," Ainsley said to me. "But there are times we're never too big for a teddy bear."

I still have that bear. Even then, I heard his voice as a granddaughter would. Ainsley and I share a bloody history.

"How old are you now? Midthirties?" He waits for my nod. "You'll understand this better when you get on in years, I suspect. There are sections of our lives, chapters, I guess, that need closure in order for you to move on. I can't let go, Luce. I made a promise to her parents. Hell, I made a promise to *you*, and to Marci, that we'd find who committed that murder and bring him to justice. I can't turn my back now."

I take a deep breath. I blink back tears, bite my bottom lip. This is not the place for a crying jag. Ainsley ignores my emotions bubbling beside him and drives. He gives me the space I need. Finally, I say, "All I'm asking is that you don't work so hard to make all the pieces fit. Deal?"

"Anything else?"

I nod. "And that you keep your temper under control. No hothead outbursts."

Ainsley considers me beside him for a few seconds and then grunts his agreement. "You're a hard sell, Hansen. Just like your father."

Once we turn into the Eldridge Funeral Home driveway, I realize with a quick flush of panic that I've been here before.

Marci.

I hadn't even considered that we've been driving to the same funeral home where Marci's services had been held. My breath catches in my throat and my heart rockets into high speed. I half hope for Marci's hologram to appear on the dash telling me all will be okay.

Breathe, I remind myself. *Just breathe.*

The Eldridge Funeral Home is a mammoth house from the turn of the century. Over the years, the owners have reconstructed its back lawn into a parking area. The building is well lit with only three cars in the lot—no funeral tonight. Davis beat us here and he is parked near the green awning that covers the front entrance, blanched by hot days of sun and worn by wet, windy weather. Headlights turned off, his car rumbles in the cold, spitting out clouds of white exhaust.

Although Davis and another detective questioned Sambino at the funeral home twice in the last few days, we now have enough to bring him in for formal questioning at the station. Kaitlin placed Sambino with Emma Parks near the time of her attack. He may very well be the last person to have seen her alive. Ainsley wanted to have Sambino brought into the station for questioning from the start, have uniforms pick him up, but I argued that I needed to see Sambino in his natural surroundings. From what we've learned, Sambino worked mostly nights, which makes his place of employment a sort of second home to him. He will see our presence as an intrusion in his space. A trip to the station would only give him extra time to plan a statement and to steel himself against our questions. And we don't want to arrest him before we have enough for the DA to charge him. We need more than vampire makeup and being the last one to see her.

"Well," Ainsley grunts while the car tires beneath us crash through the lot, rutted and pitted with snow and ice, "here goes nothing."

CHAPTER SIX

While we wait in the funeral home foyer, a phone rings behind closed doors in a nearby office. The caller doesn't hang up. Davis, Ainsley, and I act as though we don't notice its shrill cry in the stillness. I try not to think about what could very well be Mrs. or Mr. Parks calling to set up funeral services for Emma. I've never been comfortable with funerals, something you'd think I would've warmed up to by now given my choice of occupation.

Most people don't understand what I mean when I try to explain that there is a difference between death and funerals. Death, in all its nakedness, has a peace that comes with it that allows me to look directly into its raw, bloodless face. Funeral homes cover death with bright eye shadow, too pink blush and lipstick sprinkled with Bible verses, and scratchy, frilly clothes. Maybe it's the calming music that plays a little too loud or the much-too-kind way the staff speaks. Why is it that every funeral home I've been in has those fake fountains with the falling water that's meant to calm everyone's nerves but never does?

"Generations of Eldridges have lived here since what seems like the beginning of Willow's Ridge," Davis says. "Just give him a moment. He'll be down."

"The owner lives upstairs?" The remnants of snow melt from my boots on the welcome mat and the heat from the wood fireplace begins to penetrate my layers of clothing.

"Chad, his wife, and two young girls. I suspect they're teenagers by now. The Eldridges are known as a family-oriented business, and so many people around these parts love that."

Davis, Ainsley, and I are surrounded by a lavish home in high sheen: antique sofas and large arrangements of colorful flowers line the doorway. A polished oak staircase winds up to a second level. On the edge of each alternating step, a basket of red and gold poinsettias leftover from the holiday season are still in full bloom. A solid wood grandfather clock ticks nearby and startles us all when it chimes the half hour.

"The Parks girl will have her funeral here," Ainsley says. "They told Doc Mitchell when the body was released."

Davis runs his fingertips over his short hair. "The Jones funeral had lines out the door. I suspect this one will, too."

I picture the swarm of people who must have come to pay their respects to the local girls. There had been more visitors at Marci's funeral than the funeral home could hold as well. Davis, Ainsley, and I, and other plainclothes law enforcement officers, will have to filter through the crowds during the service and at the burial. It is such a violation for the killer to attend the funeral of his victim, but so many of them do in one way or another. It is like he's killing her all over again.

"Disgusts me no end to think that Sambino prepared those girls' bodies for burial," Davis says.

"It's not enough that son of a bitch took their lives, but he had to gloat and relive it all in their deaths." Ainsley hisses, "You know that fucknut was jacking off the whole time!"

"Ainsley." Davis hushes and gives his head a hard shake.

Chad Eldridge opens the upstairs door and descends the stairs adjusting his tie. He's so thin that his collarbone and shoulders hold his button-up white shirt like a hanger. "Frank! I wasn't expecting you. Everything okay?" He holds out his hand to Davis.

"Sorry to bother you at this hour, Chad. I hate to disturb you and the kids, but this can't wait until morning." Davis turns to me. "This is Special Agent Luce Hansen from the Ohio Bureau of Criminal Investigation, and you remember Detective Cole Ainsley."

He nods hello to Ainsley and shakes my hand. Chad Eldridge's nails are all filed perfectly with a clear polish and he wears a thick gold pinkie ring. It's not just his nails; Eldridge is impeccably groomed. It's not hard for me to imagine him at a mirror combing his blond hair over and over until all the comb grooves are in line. His suit pants look tailored to fit him perfectly while his cuffed shirt has been recently ironed. I look down at my frumpy self. I'm so layered up, I look about ten pounds heavier than I actually am. My black pants and boots are worn, nothing like the polished, tasseled leather loafers Eldridge wears.

"Chad and I run half-marathons together," Davis tells me. "Correction—most days, I run far behind him."

Eldridge gives an easy laugh. "Don't let this man fool you. He's as quick as the Road Runner, I tell you."

I watch as Davis shifts from small talk to business. He has a gentle way of dealing with people. I have yet to see anyone not warm up to him in seconds. "We have some follow-up questions for Nick Sambino. Is he working tonight?"

"Downstairs. We got the girl's body this evening."

Ainsley says, without preamble, "We have a few questions to ask you, too."

Davis adds, "Again, we're sorry to intrude," to soften Ainsley's words.

Eldridge holds up his hands to halt Davis. "I understand. I want these crimes solved, too. Funerals are my livelihood, but I don't want the business because of a murderer."

I follow the others down a wide, long hallway toward a conference room. Davis walks in front of me and I picture his arrow-like shoulders cutting through the air as he runs.

On my left is a coffin and urn salesroom. Colorful track lighting shows off the mahogany and oak caskets that glisten along the wall. Different satin linings are displayed for a build-your-own casket. Other large viewing rooms follow.

It's impossible for me to place which room had been Marci's for her funeral. I stop for a moment outside of one with my hand stuffed deep in my pocket clutching my Marci rock. A tightness settles deep inside my chest and a shiver rolls along the skin of my entire body.

Before that July, I'd only been to one funeral, and I wasn't so sure that even counted. It was for Mrs. Henderson, who lived down the street from my dad and me, the older woman I saw only a few times a year when I needed to sell something to raise money for sports at school. Marci was different—she was the first person who died that I loved.

The day before the funeral, I went back to Stonehenge. With each footfall I whispered a prayer that this was all just a bad dream and that Marci would be waiting inside the small cave for me. I could almost hear her contagious laugh spilling out from the entrance to Stonehenge: *My God, you are slow. And you run track at school? What do they call you? Turtle Hansen?*

I couldn't make myself move any faster. It took me three times as long as it usually did that day to navigate through the thick elms and sugar maples pocked within the limestone. When I finally rounded the boulder that led to Stonehenge, yellow crime-scene tape greeted me and the mark of Marci's blood was darkened almost black against the light-colored stone. I knelt to touch the stain, letting my fingertips graze over what was left of Marci, and a sudden swell of emotion burst somewhere deep inside me—a tidal wave that almost knocked me over. I felt the water swirl above my head, as I drowned in the cocoon of watery silence. Couldn't I stay here? Why couldn't I take refuge inside this safety with Marci?

It was the first time I ever thought of suicide as a viable option. I found myself outside of Stonehenge peering over the rocky ledge and into the watery quarry below. If I jumped, would it be high enough to kill me? I learned that summer that nothing is heavier than the invisible cloak of guilt, nothing more tenacious than the slimy coat of shame. I looked over the edge again. If I angled myself just right, I could hit my head on one of the jutting rocks on the way down. That would kill me. Mesmerized by the prospect of my own death, I gazed down into the crack of the earth.

The voice spoke softly at first, a gentle nudge that grew in its persistence. I looked around me. Where did the words come from? No one was there. *Get out. Get out of here now!* At first I didn't obey. I walked back into the center of the cave wondering if I'd finally lost my mind. Could it have been Marci? Maybe her ghost? I'd certainly come back here in the hopes that I would find her. It wasn't completely outlandish to consider that she might speak to me. Was she really so angry as to tell me to go? Then I remembered what my dad always told me: *Trust the voice inside you. Follow your gut.*

Suddenly my breath came quick and jagged and rushed. I grabbed as many limestone chunks from the entrance to Stonehenge as I could fill my pockets with and raced back through the rocky canopy the way I'd come. Behind me, someone was there—eyes on me, a hot breath not far behind. The heat of its exhalations told me this was real, even when my mind insisted that it wasn't. I ran faster than I ever have, my feet tumbling over one another until I finally burst out of the limestone quarry and into the safety of my dad's truck. Locking the doors and starting the engine, I scanned the entire area, but there was no one there. No one at all.

Many police and emergency workers attended Marci's funeral. The cops stood out so much they might as well have worn their uniforms. I'd been around enough of my dad's police friends to recognize their wide stance, their watchful gaze that took every movement in like some sort of human recorder.

"Don't be afraid," my dad said from the chair beside me. "They're here to protect us. To watch over everyone and keep us safe."

It was only then I realized it wasn't only my dad and me who didn't know what happened to Marci. The police had no idea who'd done it either. Worse, they thought the killer could be among us, a mourner, a family member, a friend of Marci's. Doubt consumed me and I took in every adult in the room with the same question: Did you kill Marci? Did the man in the plaid tie smash in my girlfriend's head and watch her bleed to death? Did the guy with the ponytail see me on his way out of Stonehenge that day and choose not to kill me? I wanted to know. I *needed* to know why someone decided to let me live and to kill Marci. Why couldn't it have been the other way around?

After the prayers, we filtered past the coffin to say good-bye. I inched up toward Marci, my sweating palms barely able to hold on to the rocks. The heavy, polished casket was open and lined with a silky powder pink. Marci's blond hair, freshly shampooed, fanned out over the satin pillow like a whispering spray of corn silk.

Still, it wasn't Marci. It was her body, yes, so small inside the pillowed bed with her hands clasped over her chest clutching a dark, heavy crucifix. Both Irish and Catholic, her family followed many of the traditions. She wore a frilly white dress that reminded me more of a wedding gown with lace crawling up her pale neck and slipping down her arms and wrists. This wasn't *my* Marci. I felt only the endless pull to touch her, to lean my head down against her fragile shoulder and tell her for the millionth time how I wished it had been me and not her.

I emptied my pockets and dropped each stone along the inside of the casket—*these are Luce stones*. I imagined that those rocks sent Marci—wherever she was—memories of us, of Stonehenge. Maybe those bubbles of rock really did hold our images, snippets of our laughter and words inside that rocky canopy, the way her skin felt under my fingertips, the way her breath felt against my neck.

When they lowered Marci into the earth, I stood as still and rigid as I possibly could. If I moved even one centimeter I feared that I would shatter apart like glass and the anguished scream stuck inside me would pour out of the cracks. That scream would never end. I held my breath, closed my eyes, and imagined the moist, cool earth covering me beside my Marci, smothering us whole.

❖

Inside the funeral home's conference room, shuttered away from the viewing and funeral rooms, I take a seat at the table, across from Ainsley and Davis. A fireplace crackles and pops with burning wood and I fight off the sleepiness that inches up around me. With the heat and dimmed spotlights that surround the room, I'm ready to call it a night. Everything in the room has a soft edge to it, a shadowed ambience. A large-screen television is turned off and only reflects our faces and movements against its shadowy black screen. This is not the time for an attack of drowsiness. These are the moments when you have to take everything in as an investigator; you never know what will become important.

"I wish I could say I'm surprised to see you, Frank." Eldridge looks at the captain. "I knew I would see you again soon."

Eldridge looks away from the captain a moment, somewhere out over our heads. His dark eyes weaken into a look of sadness behind the lenses of his glasses, as if he cannot deny the truth any longer. "I always chalked up his looks and crazy notions to his art, you know?" His gaze then comes back to focus on Davis. "It's been really tense around here."

Davis clears his throat. "We're looking at every possible angle we can get here, Chad. I have to ask, I mean, I'd hate to think…donations for the services and burials of the victims?"

"Donations?"

"Anyone who has given a substantial chunk of money to help the families with costs, whether they gave anonymously or not," Davis says. "Guilt for his actions can drive a killer to donate, or sometimes it's a sort of pride at what he's done."

Eldridge's manscaped eyebrows knit together as he filters through his memory. "I'll check the records, but I don't remember any significant donations. We collected money at the Jones funeral for a scholarship fund in her name."

"How long has Sambino worked for you?" I ask. I imagine Chad Eldridge is an exceptional record keeper, probably with a rigid personal schedule that would earn him the title of Mr. Organization.

"Going on nine years now. He's the best embalmer and makeup artist we've ever had."

"Has he discussed anything with you about the murders or the questions from our last visit?" Davis asks.

"No, but I only see him for a few minutes when he comes in for his shift. We're the proverbial ships that pass in the night. I'm leaving at that point, so I give him directions about what needs to be accomplished that night and head upstairs to my family."

Eldridge's response doesn't ring true. The cops question his employee about three or four homicides and he doesn't even ask Sambino about it?

"Do you ever come back down during the night?" Ainsley's fingertips sweep over his moustache.

"Rarely. If I need to go somewhere, we have a private entrance, separate from the funeral parlor." Eldridge crosses his arms over his chest. "Sometimes we get calls in the middle of the night to pick up more than one body, and then I'm needed. But most nights are very quiet and Nick takes care of anything that might come up."

My mind settles on Eldridge's last statement. Sambino works alone. I don't remember seeing this information in the notes from the last interview. "So it is possible that Nick could be gone during his shift and you wouldn't know it?"

"Possible," Eldridge concedes with a shrug. "But he always gets everything done and that would be difficult on many nights if he was somewhere else. He's meticulous in his work and takes hours to get the makeup a perfect color, the clothes a match against the coffin fabric." Eldridge touches the tips of his thumb and forefinger in the air to indicate the precision of Sambino's job. "Besides"—he flips his hand through the air as though he's pushing away the thought—"I can see his truck through the upstairs window. I've never seen him leave or noticed the truck gone."

Davis asks, "Was Sambino working last night?"

"Yes," Eldridge says. "I had no reason to come downstairs." Eldridge leans forward and whispers conspiratorially. "Look, Frank, I know Nick's got his problems. I just can't wrap my head around the idea he could've done any of this."

"He might not have." Davis gives Eldridge's shoulder a quick, reassuring squeeze, a touch that reminds me of the way Ainsley squeezed my knee in the car not so long ago.

Eldridge turns for a heavy wood door that leads downstairs to the preparation areas. I stop him before he escapes down the staircase.

"You said that you've never noticed his truck gone during his shift. He doesn't pick up bodies in the truck, does he?"

"No, a hearse."

"Where's that hearse generally parked?"

A few seconds pass and most of the color drains from Chad Eldridge's face. "The garage." His words come out strangled.

The garage, I learn, is out of view from the Eldridge's bedroom, kitchen, and family room. "Does Nick have access to those keys at all times?"

"He's been issued a key to the hearse and one to our business entrance." Eldridge drops his head into the heels of his hands. "I'm sorry," he says. "I've never thought to check the mileage. I've never had a reason *not* to trust Nick."

❖

Nick Sambino steps into the conference room, his flabby body filling the frame until he decides to kick the door closed with a thick-soled boot, most likely steel-toed. The slam of the door carries in the quiet home. "Detectives"—he pulls out a chair closest to him—"to what do I owe the pleasure of your company?"

Holy hell. This pudgy, greasy postadolescent cannot be who everyone has gotten so excited about. Sambino is nothing like I expected. His pouch of a belly tells me he's spent most of his days and nights smoking pot and gorging afterward. A black hoodie has a few nights' worth of dinner dribbled down the front and his dark jeans are much too tight. Nick Sambino is definitely no Tom Cruise or Brad Pitt from *Interview with a Vampire*. And he's certainly no Edward Cullen.

Sambino's gaze settles on me and he pulls his lips back into a sneer of a grin meant only to reveal his pointy white incisors. He's clearly pleased with himself and these gigantic teeth. I swallow a laugh. Ainsley has filled me in on the latest fashion craze of the wannabe vampire world, fangs made from acrylic. These veneers are permanently attached to the incisors by a dentist for quite a hefty fee. In order to attach this new fashion statement, the dentist has to drill away all the enamel from the incisors, leaving behind only stumps that contain the tooth's nerve. The acrylic fang then fits over the root and is buried into the gum for a more natural look. Sambino's fangs, though, are a blinding Hollywood white next to the cigarette-brown teeth that surround them.

"We have a few more questions," Davis says. "This is Special Agent Luce Hansen. And Detective Ainsley."

Sambino shifts his gaze to Ainsley. Black eyeliner runs at the corner of his left eye into a white powder so thick on his face it looks like paste. He leans forward, his elbows spread wide on the table. "I figured you'd be back." He glares at Davis. "For the record, it wasn't me."

A muscle in Sambino's left cheek twitches near his mouth, an intermittent pull at the corner of his lip. A nervous tic. He sees me watching the movement and licks his black-painted lips over and over again in an attempt to hide it. He only draws my attention to the tiny cuts that line his bottom lip where the fangs naturally fall, a sign that Mr. Sambino is not the seasoned vampire he claims to be. In fact, he is still learning to use those fangs.

"How well did you know Emma Parks?" I ask.

Sambino lets a lock of dyed-black hair spill over his pale face, covering one eye completely. He stares down at the table and pops his knuckles one at a time. His hands are completely disproportionate to the rest of his chunky frame. Wide with long, green-bean fingers, his hands aren't the bear paws I expect. They're also paws that aren't scraped or bruised in any way. The other piece that doesn't fit is Sambino's high level of agitation. Our killer, from what I know of him, is very secure and certain in his movements and thought processes.

"Sambino," Ainsley demands in his guttural voice. "Talk."

"I already told you. I don't know nothing." Suddenly Sambino pushes back hard in his chair, scrapes the screaming legs over the wood floor. He kicks one worn steel-toed boot at a time up on the table and settles his glare on me.

"Feet down, son," Ainsley growls.

"I'm not your son." There is the slightest nervous tremor of his lips.

"I'm warning you. Don't push me. Feet on the ground now."

This is it: Sambino's last stand. It's his last attempt to show some sort of control in a situation where he has none. So when he doesn't move, Ainsley smacks his ankles with a fisted hand until Sambino winces and drops his feet to the floor.

Even though Sambino doesn't make a move to defy him, Ainsley is worked up. "You'll need a new dye job before we send you to prison," he says, pointing to Sambino's light brown roots. "Those boys will be lined up to take a turn with you." Ainsley works hard for a rise out of Sambino. "All that makeup. God, they'll love a good bang with you!"

Davis puts a hand on Ainsley's arm, directing him to say no more. "That is, unless you talk to us tonight."

Sambino drums his painted black nails on the table. The motion is too quick, though, not lackadaisical, the way he wants us to see him.

"Mr. Sambino, or is it Tristan?" Davis says. "Your silence tells me you know Emma Parks."

A suspect's body tells the truth so much more than any words out of his mouth. We all watch for any movement that signals a weakness. If we can catch Sambino in a significant lie tonight, it will be enough for the judge to sign a search warrant for his property.

"Am I under arrest?" Sambino finally says.

"That depends," Davis says.

"On what?"

"You," I say. "Answer the question."

Sambino sighs dramatically. "Emma liked tattoos. She wanted to see my latest one."

"Let's see it."

He glances at me. "The tat?"

I nod.

He places his pale wrist on the table for me, palm up. About two inches in length, the black symbol is so new that redness puffs his skin out around the edges. "What does it mean?"

He eyes me, gauging my sincerity. Finally, he says, "Oh, so you're the good cop. It's a symbol."

"Of?" I ask.

"The ankh."

I shrug and turn to Davis. "It looks a hell of a lot like a cross to me."

"An ugly cross," Ainsley says.

"It *is* a cross." Sambino pulls his wrist away and covers the looping cross with the edge of his sleeve. "Egyptian, to be specific. It gives protection and eternal life."

"Hmm," I say, "I thought it was vampirism that did that."

Sambino smirks at me.

"What did Emma think of the tat?"

"She liked it."

"She liked it so much she agreed to get into your vehicle and go back to your place?"

Sambino shakes his head.

"Let me help your memory." Davis lays out a photograph from Emma's senior year in high school. Eventually Sambino pulls at the photo's edge and slides it in front of him.

"Where were you last night around eight?" Davis asks.

"Not sure." Sambino continues to tap his fingernails against the table. "It's been a long twenty-four hours." He yawns for impact, then chuckles. "*The First 48*. You guys ever watch that show?"

"Who else was in your apartment last night besides Emma?"

When Sambino says nothing, Davis relies on the gory crime-scene photograph of Emma, bloodied and frostbitten, for shock value.

It's the ever so slight pull-back from Sambino that tells me he's never seen Parks like this before, a muted version of surprise when he sees her genitals splayed open. The horror before him has weakened his resolve; he'll talk with some gentle prodding. Before I have time to formulate my plan in action, Ainsley slams his open palm on the wooden table. The noise ricochets throughout the room like a gunshot and Sambino jumps.

Ainsley is up and uses his size to push much too hard into Sambino's right shoulder. "I'm tired of playing with you. Hear me? Where were you?"

"Here! I clocked in at nine, like always."

Quick as a flash, Ainsley slaps Sambino across the face with an open palm. Sambino draws back, his eyes darting for a way out of the room when Davis pulls rank.

"Detective! Outside." He stands and waits for Ainsley to leave. "Now."

Ainsley leaves after kicking the table and the door shut behind him, his anger lingering in the room long after he's left. Davis rejoins me at the table. Unfortunately, Ainsley's boorish behavior has left me nowhere else to go. I have to use the information I have. "We know you brought Emma back to your place to meet a woman you both encountered at a club in Columbus."

There's a quick flicker of panic in his eyes.

"Here's what I think. You tricked Emma into thinking the woman was in your apartment. You brought her home and once you had her inside, you killed her."

"No! I was at work."

I shrug. "You clocked in at nine. You picked up Emma at eight. She was dead before you got here. Then you went back a few hours later to take her to the quarry and do your fancy knife work."

"No!"

"Yes. You have a boss who sleeps while you work. You have a job where no one else is present. You have a work vehicle available to you at all hours. Nick, you could have easily left for a few hours and your boss would never know. The same way you did with Vivian and Chandler."

"No." Sambino unhitches a thick lock of dyed-black hair from behind his other ear, letting it all fall across his pale face to mask both his eyes as though behind a curtain. "Check my time card."

"You and I both know how unreliable time cards are."

"I didn't do anything to Emma. Or Chandler. Or Vivian."

"Tell me this," Davis says. "Why should we believe you?"

"Because I didn't have anything to do with these crimes. Nothing!"

"Then how about you let us look around your apartment?"

"Not without a warrant and a lawyer." Sambino stands up, his face flushed from Ainsley's hard slap.

I shake my head but say nothing. Ainsley's strike ended any chance of Sambino's cooperation. Davis can look forward to a happy lawsuit from Sambino, and if we do build a case against him, it can be used in court.

"Think about it, Mr. Sambino. Think *real* hard," Davis says. "Confessions are always so much better for everyone involved."

Sambino stands in the doorway leading to the basement, his hand still on the doorknob, unsure of whether or not to leave. He looks much smaller than when he came in, hunched and deflated. He cannot hide the subtle shudder of fear in his shoulders. We've rattled him or, more specifically, Ainsley has. Our killer wouldn't fall so easily to a cop's bravado and piss-poor interview antics.

❖

Davis and I find Ainsley in the parking lot, a hulking shadow leaning on his car. The red glow of a cigarette lights up his face. "That little fucker is guilty," he grumbles at us.

Sambino may be the best lead so far, but my gut tells me he's not a fit. It isn't his age or even Ainsley's push to include Marci's murder, but Sambino's image. His get-up is a Halloween costume, a ploy to scare others and most likely keep people away from him. He doesn't strike me as the murdering type. Angry? Yes. Attention whore? Yes, but nothing more. If we stripped Sambino of his black clothing and makeup and fangs, he'd be nothing more than a cowering little boy who'd been bullied throughout his school years. He's been emotionally hurt, so much so that he decided to develop an alter-ego of Tristan.

"Whatever that was in there is not going to help us nail him," Davis says.

Ainsley scoffs, "That little shit won't say anything."

"That's not the point, Ainsley, and you know it. One more move like that and you're off the case. No questions asked."

We huddle around the car while Ainsley sulks and smokes.

I ignore him. Nothing irritates me more than a bully cop. "We don't have enough for a search warrant."

Davis nods.

I hug myself against the cold. The air surrounding the lot's bright lights looks like crystals. "Sambino now knows that someone told us about his connection to Emma that night and that he drove her. Let's see what a long night of simmering on that information does for him." I look at Davis. "If Sambino hasn't already, he'll be in the hearse cleaning it tonight."

Davis says, "Eldridge owns that hearse. If we can get his permission to search it, we don't need a warrant." Davis rubs his eyes. It's been a long night. "But we just assaulted his employee, and he might not be in a generous mood. Let's call it a night. I'll put an officer on the hearse until the morning."

Sambino's anxiety and refusal to talk tell me he knows something. Seeing a cop car out in his work parking lot all night will put the pressure on and turn up the heat.

CHAPTER SEVEN

Ainsley and I drive what would be Emma's route from the photography store to Sambino's apartment on the way back to my hotel. Questions plague us and I choose to focus on these rather than confronting Ainsley about his brutish behavior with Sambino. That will be for another time. For now I cannot stop thinking about this: What if Nick Sambino *didn't* drive Emma Parks home from his apartment in the hearse? We have no proof of that. No one actually saw her. It could have been any vehicle that sidled up to her as she walked away from the photography store.

My mind runs wild with the possibilities. It's late, I'm tired, and that makes me prone to imaginings. Tonight, I can see it—Parks, lost in her thoughts, as her steps crunched down the frozen leaves and snow on the sidewalk. She was excited to meet the hottie, a vampire wannabe. Even though she was mystified over her feelings for this other girl, Parks swooned over the way hottie might use those new fangs to trace the outlines of the veins in her neck, steal quick, playful bites to her skin. She had only told her best friends about her feelings for other women. She struggled with herself about whether or not she should just go home. She didn't even hear the vehicle roll up beside her.

The school photographs in Parks's file tell me she was a good girl. Her grades tell me she was a thinker, not the type to get inside a car with a stranger. But what if that stranger was a beautiful woman who she recognized as the hottie from the club in Columbus? Could I be looking at a version of the classic story of good girl attracted to bad girl? I've seen so many scenarios of this trope played out over the course of my short career. There really is an undeniable force that pulls these opposites together. Any question of danger and cautionary tales go out the window. Warnings are forgotten and the good girl falls hard.

I'm certain of two things. One, Emma Parks knew the driver who pulled up beside her. Two, it wasn't Sambino. I keep these thoughts to myself. Ainsley has already demonstrated his loose tongue. Mix that with the high anxiety inside any questioning room, and any sort of edge we might gain could be lost.

❖

My ritual for setting up my hotel room work space: push the old, brick-heavy desk away from the hotel wall; turn that wall into a makeshift whiteboard—a murder board—and post everything I have about the case with pushpins (once I leave, the hotel will hate me and send the bill to Sanders); examine the spread from as many angles as possible, including sleep.

My dad taught me how to make a murder board. We always had two set up in the basement of our house, tucked away in the far corner where my father worked on his cases until the early morning hours. The constant was filled with information on a serial killer my dad had been tracking most of his career. The other board held his most recent cases. Every crime-scene photograph, tip, and bit of gathered information found its way into the column titled either *Victim* or *Suspect*. I was never allowed to touch the murder boards. When my father was at work, though, I'd sneak into his corner and slip off the white sheets he used to cover them, taking in the crimes that perplexed my father. I was fascinated by the way the murder board grew, how each piece of information had a vital place in the solving of the crime. He never kept his murder board at the station, he said, because he wanted full control over it. He didn't want someone to be able to take something down or add to it without his knowledge. Many times, the ones in our house were full of photocopies and the originals were on a board at the station.

Like my dad, I need to see the evidence spread out before me and have control of it. Maybe it's a superstition, but I swear it works on my subconscious. So now, I slowly build my murder board, pinning up bloody photos and police reports in three deliberate sections: Vivian Hannerting, Chandler Jones, and Emma Parks. I leave Marci's case file on the desk chair with only the report peeking out along the edges of the worn folder. With the lampshade removed from the large desk light, the crime-scene spread is illuminated with ghoulish flair.

Once the rearrangement is done, I sit on top of the cleared desk, cross-legged, in worn boxers and an old Ani DiFranco T-shirt. I had a bath as soon as I returned to the hotel and my hair has dried around my shoulders. I've left my boots on because I'm terrified to touch my bare feet to the carpet. I do not want to solve the mystery of what could be growing inside that nest of fibers.

Up on the wall, the three victims' similarities are clear—age, location, gender, race. I scribble *lesbian* on a Post-it Note and tack it into Parks's column—this is the wild card. It has been nagging at me all evening. There has been no mention of a serious boyfriend or husband for Hannerting or Jones. In fact, Hannerting had been a student sharing a rental house with another woman. And then there'd been that staunch denial of homosexuality from Kaitlin at the photography store. Is it possible all these young women were lesbians, or at the very least, girl-curious?

When I was sixteen years old, my father and I drove every Saturday afternoon to Willow's Ridge. Once he was certain I had the hang of it, I drove myself. I'd been driving my dad's truck for years before I got my license that spring—one of the perks of being the police chief's daughter in a small town. It was quite a weekly trek, three-hour round-trip commutes from Chesterton. My father called it church, a time for fellowship and growth with Christ. The rest of the world referred to it as One True Path, a strong ex-gay ministry built on the belief that a person can pray the gay away and heal from homosexual addiction. Historically, Willow's Ridge has been associated with ex-gay ministries because one of the largest groups in the Midwest was based there. Many people, like me, drove great distances to attend the weekly meetings. Could hate crimes against homosexuals in this area be seen as some sort of homage to this group? Although Willow's Ridge and the surrounding communities are very small, it has always been an area where creative people live. Art stores line Main Street and the artists all live with nature to inspire them. A higher percentage of LGBTQ people live in Willow's Ridge than in surrounding small towns.

Suddenly, Dad is here, his large body spilled into the hotel's lime-green velvet armchair. "Lucy-girl, trust your gut."

I drop my head into my hands. "Christ, Dad. I need to get some sleep."

"Sleep when the case is over. It's too early to rule anything out." He points to a photo of the backseat lined with food for delivery.

"Jones?"

He nods. "Who was she delivering food for?"

"Her church." I scour every line of the Chandler Jones's file. She had been delivering to the shut-ins of her church when she disappeared. A noble deed. Finally I find it, and the name of the church shoots a bolt of adrenaline to my heart: Heartsong Southern Baptist.

"I've heard that name. Heartsong was directly linked to One True Path, right?"

He grins at me over the laptop.

A simple Google search finds it. One True Path is listed as one of the primary ministries at Heartsong Southern Baptist.

"If all of the victims have had same-sex relationships, then Ainsley's right. Marci Tucker's murder *is* related."

My father agrees. He observes me closely over his steepled fingertips. "Can you connect this church with all the victims?" His eyes trail me as I pace back and forth, my brow furrowed with thought.

"Well, Marci, certainly." I stop suddenly and face him. "Dad, come on. One True Path is an ex-gay ministry, not a cult designed to go out and kill people who go against their teachings."

"You used a key word there: designed. Anyway, who said the entire group?"

A swell of defensiveness bubbles up inside me. I'd been a part of this group for a short time with Marci.

"Hate can drive people to do unimaginable things," my dad says. "I'm just saying, don't rule anything out."

I stop a second, struck by this thought. If it was relatively easy for me to find this connection, then why hadn't Ainsley? After all, Tucker had been his case. He knew it inside out. Why wouldn't he connect the sexuality element and find the church?

My cell phone rings its tinny jingle in the near-silent hotel. With a start, I realize it's well after one a.m. I was supposed to have called Rowan no later than eleven. I watch the phone light up with the call, then turn back to the murder board. My father has already vanished from the armchair.

"Ro, this is a bad time."

She does what I hate the most: nags me. Finally, I blame not calling on a run and bath.

"Run?" she asks. "When was the last time you ran?"

"There's no pool here." I groan.

"I didn't hear from you. I was worried."

"Everything's fine, love."

"I need to know for sure when you're coming home. My mom's invited us to Sunday dinner and needs an answer."

"God, Rowan!" She knows how much I hate these dinners with her mom. Mention of her always brings out a fiery hot reaction from me. "Can't you tell her I'm working and don't know when I'll be back in town?"

"I thought this case would take two days. Three, tops."

I look up at the makeshift murder board. "Things have gotten more complicated."

"What do I tell my mom? Yes or no?"

I feel my frustration ratcheting up. "Christ, Rowan, she's your mom. Can't she be flexible? If we're there then we're there."

"She needs to know, Luce. You can't leave people hanging."

I take a deep breath. "Let's not do this, okay? Not now."

Rowan doesn't say anything for a moment. For a second I think she might hang up on me, but then she also pulls in a deep breath. "The kids miss you."

I imagine the dogs sidled up to Rowan in bed, their warm bodies smashed together in a blur that makes it difficult to see where one body ends and the next begins.

"Talk," Rowan demands, and I hear their friendly howls and playful barks.

When we'd first moved to Dublin, Rowan talked me into adopting a puppy. I worried that my older cat, Hadley, might feel slighted by a new pet, particularly a slobbery young pooch who demanded all the attention. Dogs are a layer of safety, though, and with my job, I finally relented to a friendly, but big, dog. Two days later, Rowan saw a sign at the local farmers' market advertising a neighbor's litter of Lab mixes. For reasons I can't even begin to explain, in the midst of all Rowan's coos and pleas, we came home with two puppies: Toto and Daisy. The battle with Hadley was on; he had the Labs' ears pinned back in seconds. The dogs, unfortunately, are nothing more than oversized lap kitties; it's my Hadley who's the guard dog.

Looking at the stiff hotel bed, I suddenly want to be home more than anything with Rowan and to feel the soft, warm fur of my pets. I want to sleep against the comfort of their warm spines.

The whisper of our morning argument filters through the phone connection. "How's it *really* going out there in Willow's Ridge?"

I rub my tired eyes. "We've got a strong lead."

"Come on, Luce. You know what I mean."

The heater below the window whines as it constantly blows—just not always warm air. "I really haven't let myself think about it."

The *it* hangs in the space between us, both of us hyperaware that my past is never far.

"Hmm. Does Willow's Ridge make you think of your dad?"

Rowan has this way of calling my BS every time. A smile crosses my lips. Of all the women I've known in my life, Rowan knows me best and still loves me. That's a rare feat. "I'm glad he's not alive to see this. God, I miss him, but he'd want to drive up here and get together with the Jamesons again. That's all I need, a One True Path reunion."

Even after all these years, I still cringe at the thought of Pastor Charles Jameson. He'd been my biggest nightmare as a teenager. My dad found the Bible-touting Baptist and his One True Path group when he learned that I had a crush on one of my best girlfriends in high school and assumed the two of us were doing more on our sleepovers than talking about boys. If only Dad had known that I spent long hours throughout high school *wishing* my best friend wanted more than to talk about boys. I prayed night after night just to feel her touch, to kiss her lips.

My dad had certainly been wrong about the activities with my best friend, but he knew me well enough to be dead-on in his assessment of my feelings for other girls. Years after Marci's death, we never spoke of my relationship with her, though there was an unspoken understanding of what went on between Marci and me. When I eventually brought home another woman for him to meet, he handled it with a grace I hadn't expected. We'd made peace long before his death after he'd finally given up his attempts to change me.

Even though the police station was my dad's family and, by way of that, mine, we were the only blood we had. His parents were gone, he'd been an only child, and my mother packed up and left me crying on his hip when I was only two. She said she was leaving for a life in front of the camera in California and we never heard from her since. Dad always said it was me that kept him alive after he watched my mother's red taillights wink out down the road that day. Then he'd looked into my watery baby-brown eyes and said, "Blood takes care of blood." He'd repeated that phrase to me my whole life, but it wasn't until after he was gone that I realized he continued to say it as a reminder to himself. He simply wouldn't endure risking my red taillights slowly vanishing the same way his wife's had so many years ago, no matter what sort of sin I might commit.

I groan and remember my promise to Rowan from this morning: no secrets. "There's a theory milling about that Marci's death could be connected to these recent ones." I wait but Rowan doesn't respond. "It's far-fetched, but I can't rule it out."

Rowan's sigh is deep and loud. "Don't, Luce."

"Don't what?"

"You know what. Get so entangled in this case you can't get yourself out."

It's the frustration that curls Rowan's words through the speaker of the phone. It's the anger at Marci, a girl she's never met, that gets my back up. "I'm doing my job, Ro."

"Fine. Do the job." Her voice has gotten louder. "That's not what I'm talking about and you know it. It's the mind-fucking I can't take. The torture you put yourself through and me in the process. I meant what I said, Luce. I'll leave."

I'd sworn off Marci's case months ago after a particularly intense mind-fucking, as Rowan put it. Years had passed since her death and I decided to reexamine her crime scene while working on a murder case in the Columbus area—I thought I could handle it. A nineteen-year-old woman in a Columbus suburb was killed by repeated rock strikes to her head while jogging along a wooded trail. I couldn't help but to make comparisons between this athlete's death and Marci's. In some strange way, their cases melded together for me until all the details and clues churned into one. Just like Marci's case, the case in Columbus wore on for months and eventually all the suspects' alibis cleared. I wouldn't let the case go cold, though. The memories of Marci's murder sent me into high gear; I would not give up on the nineteen-year-old's case. I let no tip go and my hours at work began to skyrocket.

In the end, it was the constant comparison to Marci's case that drove me crazy. I'd convinced myself that if I could only solve this murder, if I could only put her killer away for good, then it would solve Marci's case as well. When we finally caught the young woman's killer, no one but Rowan could figure out why I wasn't celebrating. I'd gone into a depression so deep I couldn't work, eat, or sleep for days, but only stare out glassy-eyed at the TV from the couch, only a shell of me.

For three months, Rowan waited. She watched as I added more stones to my Berlin Wall, folding into myself like a work of origami.

Only I didn't emerge a folded eagle or crane or bear. I simply never emerged. I started sleeping on the sofa and found multiple reasons to work late. It wasn't until she packed up and threatened to leave me that I was able to reach up from that tar-like abyss I'd fallen into and grab hold of her extended hand.

I'm suddenly so tired. "I have no choice, Rowan. Besides, you aren't here. You don't have to hear about it."

"I'm *never* with you, am I? Even when I'm sitting beside you." Rowan gives out a hard sound, almost a cough. "I never signed on to compete for you with a ghost."

"Rowan!"

The phone cuts off on Rowan's end. I punch the pillow beside me over and over again until a scream lodges somewhere deep inside me. No matter how hard I try, sometimes nothing comes out right. I don't call back. Instead, I lie down between the scratchy sheets with no warm spine to rest against. The bed is rock hard and I try not to think about how much I miss Rowan's curled body inside my arms. The television roars with late-night reruns that my eyes don't take in. The images flash across the dank room turning everything an eerie television blue, the same color as Princess Leia in her flickering hologram. Only this time it's not Princess Leia I see and hear but Marci Tucker: *Help me, Lucinda Ann Hansen...*

The girl heaved for the relief of a deep breath but received none. She bit and scratched and kicked at the dark shadow's chokehold until she fell under the veil of unconsciousness. The man with the slim hips gripped the girl under her shoulders and pulled her back into the thick woods, away from the entrance to the quarry, far from safety. Her bare feet scraped over the rocky ground and underbrush, leaving only a thin trail of crimson behind.

The dark shadow might have been slight, but he was strong. He tossed her lifeless body over his shoulder as if the girl weighed nothing more than a sack of potatoes. Her thin arms draped down behind him with long fingertips reaching for something, anything.

Inside the cave she had escaped from, he propped her against the stone wall next to the camera. Her chest rose and fell with scattered, uneven breaths. A phlegmy moan escaped her purple lips from somewhere halfway between consciousness and unconsciousness. He stood over her a moment, his gaze taking in the girl before him. The crotch of his pants rose with his arousal. Slowly, he knelt and unzipped her jean shorts, then ripped her thin shirt collar down to expose the girl's chest. He fiddled with the exact placement of the shirt's collar, exposing one breast fully, then covering the second. He fumbled with attempts to keep the flaps of her shorts open. A guttural groan came from the dark shadow as he worked, his crotch now a full tent of desire.

A call from somewhere in the wood. "Marci!"

The dark shadow sucked in his breath as the female's voice grew closer. "It's your fault for running, bitch," he seethed at the girl. With one swift and frightful movement, he backhanded her across the right cheek and the distinct crack of her bone filled the cave.

Fast now, he gathered his camera and tore apart the tripod. Then he turned back to the girl. The large rock came down on the crown of her head again and again and again. The voice's rustle wasn't far from the cave. The girl was dead. He grabbed his bag and scanned the cave for safety. There was only one place to go—the same place the girl had tried to go for safety. The back section of the cave.

The dark shadow crept on hands and knees into the hidden back corner just as the voice broke through the entrance of the cave.

"Marci!"

❖

I wake gasping for breath, fighting the hotel bed for solid ground. The dream. It's just the dream again. My T-shirt's wet with night sweats and I make my way to the bathroom. The cold water spreads over my face and neck while my breath begins to settle into a rhythm and my heartbeat slows back to normal. I watch myself in the bathroom mirror drink a tall glass of water. My face is eggshell white, and dark circles have appeared under my eyes. I'm beginning to look as haggard as Davis. Gripping the sides of the bathroom counter, I wait for my hands to stop trembling. "You are safe," I whisper to the reflection in the mirror.

Safe. Hadn't that been what Marci said about Stonehenge? Our safe place? We'd never really been safe, though, always teetering on the edge of something very dangerous where we both failed to see the warnings.

May 1989. State Route 55. Green with scattered sunlight exploded everywhere through thick boughs that canopied the highway. *Like driving down a part in long hair*, Marci'd said. I rode shotgun in her convertible, the top down with the wind blowing her near-white blond hair into a halo around her face. I flipped through the radio stations until I found anything Def Leppard, and she threw her head back with a scream that taunted the sky: *Just try and rain on us!* We had the pattern set by then, both of us converging in Willow's Ridge quarry an hour before the One True Path meetings every week. L&M time. Cigarettes and peppermint candies. Her laugh and my off-key singing. Her confident touch and my hesitation.

"Ready? she said, pitching the car up the hilly road until it crested, and as always I lost my stomach, the drop so quick like a beast of a roller coaster. I looked over at her smiling face, all white teeth and glistening navy eyes and thought, *This is how I will remember Marci— happy and so free.*

It had recently rained and she took the curve too close. We spun around while the tires squealed against the pavement, the wheel turned round and round in her hands but caught on nothing, and we both screamed, thinking about the wooded ravine not more than a quarter of a mile away from the berm. Instead of the ravine, though, the car spun wildly into a shallow ditch alongside the road. Together we pushed and fought the car from the ditch, a vicious battle with wet mud that made us late for the meeting.

Pastor Jameson met us at the door when we finally arrived, eyeing our muddy clothes and battle-worn gym shoes. He was a short, sturdy man with a powerful voice. But it was the glare he gave us both through glasses that only magnified his eyes into steel blue marbles, the look of sheer horror that made me want to slink away from the group in shame.

"Girls"—the pastor glowered at us underneath heavy brows— "you've disrespected the group with your tardiness." He demanded that we pray for forgiveness. Forgiveness for what exactly, the entire group understood, without our infractions spoken aloud. Marci and I both understood what was coming. The pastor never just demanded prayer for forgiveness; a punishment always followed.

"Leviticus 20:13," he bellowed at us all. "*If a man also lie with mankind, as he lieth with a woman, both of them have committed an abomination: they shall surely be put to death; their blood shall be upon them.*" The pastor's face burned red and he leaned toward us. "Do you think you are any different because you're female?"

Marci and I shook our heads in rapid unison.

"Hell awaits if you do not change. In case you forget how important it is that I save your lives, you each must handwrite the entire chapter of Leviticus five times." He snorted in disgust through his flared nostrils.

The real damage done that day wasn't to our clothes or the group or the car. The real damage was that the secret of Marci and me slipped away from us and out like tendrils of smoke under a closed door.

Later, on the phone, Marci and I laughed about the car wreck, the near brush with disaster, and the sheer miracle that the old convertible's engine turned over. We complained horribly about the pastor and Leviticus. We carried on about the injustice of the One True Path organization, the place our parents made us go in order to change us.

What I didn't tell Marci during that phone call was that the spinning and the loss of control of the car that day had given me an enormous thrill. In my sixteen years of life that car ride had only been matched with the recklessness I felt when Marci kissed me, or the breakneck careen I felt when she reached for me, pulling my body so close to hers. I could hardly admit, even to myself, that I felt a few jolts of exhilaration that the pastor *did* know about Marci and me and that he couldn't do anything about it, even with all his preaching and prayers and punishments. He simply couldn't stop us. All those love stories I'd heard throughout my life, all the prince-saves-princess stories, the Romeos and Juliets of my English classes—I understood now the force of love. The sheer determination of it. I couldn't deny that whatever this was, it was real. In some skewed version of our world, I recognized that this gave us power over the pastor. In that intoxicated state, I didn't think about what the pastor had taught us about power until after Marci died: power eventually punishes unless it's deemed righteous by the Lord.

CHAPTER EIGHT

Thursday, January 10

The Rise and Shine café straddles Main Street with its tiny parking lot overflowing with vehicles. The siding, peeling off in long egg-yolk-colored strips, gives the squat building a tired look. Shoddy at best. Inside the breakfast place is loud and bustles with every table filled and a gaggle of people waiting to be seated. I find Ainsley and Davis in a booth at the back of the restaurant, well lubricated with multiple cups of coffee.

"There's the sleepyhead," Ainsley says when I slide into the booth beside Davis. I wave the waitress down for a coffee—very black and very strong.

I apologize and unwrap myself from my puffy coat but leave on my Russian hat. The Rise and Shine is only a few blocks from the hotel, but even by car, Willow's Ridge is blindingly cold. My thick gray pants feel frozen from the frigid air, sandpaper against my winter-dry skin. I press my fingertips to my cheeks to stop their burning. Even though I've lotioned up my face, it's beginning to chap.

"This place might not look like much," Davis says to me, "but the food is out of this world." He's wearing an electric-blue silk shirt with no tie and his clothing hangs from his thin frame.

Men and women in scrubs and medical office uniforms surround us. Their white, thick-soled shoes squeak against the exhausted brown tile. Men in suits line the bar and read the morning paper, while mounted televisions in the corners are set to Fox News.

"Our boy is as cool as can be this morning," Davis informs me. "The hearse has been under officer surveillance since we left last night.

No action from Sambino until he left the funeral home at seven a.m. for his apartment. He's been there ever since."

"I'd love to rattle those fangs right out of his head." Ainsley stuffs a tremendous bite of runny eggs into his mouth.

"What about permission to search the hearse?" I ask.

"Waiting for normal business hours to make the request."

We all know the hearse will be clean without so much as a fingerprint left behind. Sambino may not be the smartest suspect I've worked with, but he has to know what could come down the road for him. I am surprised, though, that we haven't already heard from an attorney this morning, someone Sambino plucked from a quick Google search. The fact that he remains without legal counsel impresses me to some degree. Either he is a man who has done nothing wrong or he is a man with a death wish.

Sambino, I'm certain, knows something. His anxiety and the messages from his body give him away—the half-chewed lips, the roll of his temples as he grinds his teeth, the way he picks at his black nail polish, the bounce of his knee during questioning. Sambino's body also tells me that he's been threatened to keep quiet. We need to figure out who has issued this threat and why.

While we eat runny eggs and bacon that drips with delicious grease, Davis details the assignments for the day. His eyes are bloodshot from lack of sleep and the pressure mounting on him. He's never faced a serial murder before, and the nation's eyes are on Willow's Ridge at the moment. It's Davis's face that everyone recognizes on the evening news. Fair or not, he'll be the one who either rises to hero status with the capture of the killer or falls to the point of losing his job if more victims are taken. Davis must understand the implications of either outcome on his career.

Davis explains that in the past two days we've gotten close to eighty tips on the case. The website and tip line have been singing with all the increased media presence.

Ainsley, in usual fashion, talks over Davis to me. "We got something at a grave."

"What?" I almost choke on a bite of food. Graveside activity can be worth a hundred phone-call tips. Since serial killers are driven by fantasy, we hoped he'd eventually visit the victims to relive his conquests. Techies had set up infrared-sensored recording equipment at all the graves, including Marci's.

Ainsley nods and dumps a blast of black pepper onto his remaining eggs. "Forty-two minutes long. A visitor after midnight."

"Which grave?" I ask.

"The Jones girl. I'm willing to bet money it wasn't grieving relatives at that hour, but it could be a rabbit eating the girl's funeral flowers. IT is getting the recording set up for us now."

I look to Davis, whose shrug says, *We'll see.* After he wipes his mouth and hands, he gives Ainsley and me a computer-generated log from the tip line. Phone numbers and who they are registered to are reported along with timestamp and date of call. Even hang-ups are registered.

"My officers have tips to check out within their patrol zones today. That leaves the three of us with the top ten most credible calls."

Nine times out of ten, tips on these lines don't take us anywhere. The revenge calls take the longest to weed through and waste so much of our time. It never ceases to amaze me how many people will call in tips on the neighbor who hoards and doesn't mow his grass, or the college kid who parties in his pool all hours of the night, or the ex who exhibited road rage long ago. We're after that 1 percent, the rare tip that will give us a tiny piece that will lead us to the next.

Davis adds more sugar to his coffee as I explain that there's a chance all of the victims were linked in a way we hadn't considered, that all may have been lesbians. "I think we need to consider the Tucker case as related."

Ainsley's I-told-you-so grin explodes across the table from me. "I like this girl!"

Davis ignores Ainsley. "Hate crimes?"

I hold back the piece about the One True Path ministries. I need more evidence. "We need to check in on some of the local groups like PFLAG and any support groups at the local high school."

Ainsley grumbles, "We don't have things like that in Willow's Ridge."

"All towns have things *like that*." My sarcastic response comes out stronger than I mean it to.

"She's right, Ainsley. Even if there's the slightest chance this could be related to sexual orientation, we need to warn these groups." Davis turns to me. "Why don't you start at the high school and talk to a few faculty members? Meet with some of the kids. Take Ainsley with you."

I groan on the inside.

"Almost forgot." Davis bites the strip of bacon between his teeth like a cigarette and pulls out an ID card from his pocket. "Here's a temporary ID that will get you into the station anytime." He hands the card over with a parking pass for the police lot. "Sanders called. He's held up in Columbus with another case. He'll be here within forty-eight hours."

"Keys?" Ainsley says. "I guess you're a keeper."

I'm in no mood to joke or to try to figure Ainsley out this early in the morning. I might have slept an hour since I last saw these guys. My head feels foggy. Arguments with Rowan always knock me off-kilter; she's my balance and my safety that I never quite recognize until she's no longer there. A swing of my elbow and the water glass tumbles down to the tile and shatters at my foot. Quiet settles for a few seconds around us. My body is tired, stiff, clunky, and I drop to my knees to collect the detritus in the palm of my hand.

A waiter who introduces himself as Martin greets Ainsley and Davis and kneels beside me. "Careful. These glasses throw shards everywhere." He hands me a cloth napkin while I fumble with apologies, and together we collect as many of the glass fragments as we can find. He asks about the case. Like everyone else, he's been following it.

"Ow!" My finger shoots up to my mouth and I suck the weak line of blood. A sliver of glass has lodged deep beneath my fingertip.

"I told them to get rid of these cheap glasses." Martin takes my hand and squeezes my injured finger, holding my hand almost up to his eyes in order to see. All that emerges from my fingertip is a quick bloom of blood. "Let me get you a bandage." I sit next to Ainsley and watch Martin walk off, his blond hair all one length below his ears.

"You gonna live?" Ainsley says but doesn't wait for my reply.

Davis hands me a fresh napkin and grabs the bill from the corner of the table on his way out to the cash register. "Finish up, you two. Check in regularly."

"Partner," Ainsley finally says, "do you recognize that waiter?"

"Who, Martin?" I suck my fingertip. "Should I?"

"It's Martin Tucker. Marci's older brother."

Martin? I hadn't thought of him since the funeral. Marci always talked about him, but he was a few years older than us, off at college and far away from Willow's Ridge, out of his parents' reach. We'd met only briefly at the funeral, a parting handshake to say I was sorry. I couldn't remember three-fourths of the people I spoke to that day, all those empty condolences swimming about while Marci eavesdropped from the heavy casket at the foot of the room. But I remember Martin and his glare that said, *You killed my sister!* He held on to my hand a moment too long and a lot too hard while his eyes, so bloodshot from all his tears, drilled into me. I'd felt as though I was shrinking before him—smaller and smaller—until I was able to finally scuttle away to the safety of my father's side.

Martin walks toward me, weaving between tables, and now that I know who he is, I take in every curve, every movement. The hidden shadows of Marci hide in his face. Martin looks up, his eyes catch mine, and it's like a knee to the stomach. Martin has almost the same shade of navy eyes as his sister.

"I forgot he worked here," Ainsley says, almost an afterthought. We both watch as Martin gets stopped by a table near ours for a coffee refill. I realize, with a start, I've been holding my breath.

"Marci's family has had a hard time of it. Especially the parents." Ainsley pauses a moment, but when I don't respond, he continues. "They've passed on now, but Martin's married with a little girl. He's tried to keep his sister's case open. He gets one of the reporters from the *Tribune* to do an anniversary story on her death. Every year, Willow's Ridge gets a reminder that we still have a killer on the loose."

I am familiar with those articles, but they never show a current picture of Martin. My heartbeat quickens and I don't take my eyes off his back. What if he recognizes me? Has he only grown to blame me more over the years?

"We haven't had any new suspects until these recent murders. Our number one suspect back then was Marci's father. We could never get anything on him, and he never slipped up—not once. I used to be convinced it was him. Not anymore." Ainsley finishes his last bite of eggs and throws his napkin next to his plate.

I struggle to regulate my breathing: in and hold for two counts, release and hold for two counts. Marci's father had always been a mystery to me, and to Marci as well. She never connected with her dad and his rock-hard exterior. He'd been a factory worker at a car plant and spent his hours outside of the job racing boats. Sometimes it seemed like Marci would have done just about anything to get her dad to notice she was even alive.

Martin hands me a bandage. "You okay?"

My breath catches. Is he looking at me a little more closely this time? "Sorry about the glass."

Inside the car, my breath settles back into its rhythm as I wind the Band-Aid around my fingertip, stopping the trickle of blood. My hands have a slight tremor to them. Questions return and I can't help but wonder why Ainsley would bring me to a public place where one of Marci's close family members works. Ainsley couldn't have possibly forgotten Martin works here. Was he hoping to get some sort of rise out of me?

The sliver of glass moves under my skin; even though I can't see it, I can feel it. I pick at the wound, determined to win, over the sliver's stubborn refusal.

❖

I push through the heavy glass doors of the hotel on my way back from meeting with the president of the local PFLAG chapter. He printed me a list—all of four brave teenage members. There is no formal high school group for LGBTQ kids in Willow's Ridge and a local nondenominational church allows the group to meet, free of charge. With such a lack of social support, it's no wonder some of the LGBTQ youth and adults in this area turn to the One True Path ministries for help. Others find another option: they find one another and disappear into the quarry the way Marci and I did.

I rush past the reporters who mill around the entrance of the hotel, where there is a coffee machine. They've got nothing but time on their hands. I've only got a minute to run upstairs and change my shirt from this morning's spill before I join Davis and Ainsley to look into tips. Orange juice on a white blouse is difficult to hide. One reporter asks the hotel manager, Alison, if she knows the home addresses of local cops. She looks at me with relief when I enter, happy for the interruption.

"Someone here to see you." Alison points to the lounge. "She's not a reporter."

There, in the corner chair, sits Rowan with her backpack and easel beside her. Neither one of us moves, each only watching the other, the wounds of last night's argument still fresh. Panic rises in my throat, a thick bloom of acid along my tongue. Would the argument really have brought her to Willow's Ridge without warning?

"Is everything okay? Is it the dogs? The house?" Rowan shakes her head, the mass of curls tumbling around her shoulders. I reach out for her arm but my hands find only the shell of her heavy coat instead.

Once inside my hotel room, Rowan drops her backpack and easel by the door and crosses her arms over her chest. Her cheeks are still pink with cold, her lips glossed and shiny. When she doesn't speak, my frustration explodes.

"Come on, Rowan! I'm working." I turn away from her and try to close my bursting suitcase that spills out sweatshirts, flannel lounge pants, balled-up socks.

"This can't go on," Rowan finally says. "I can't take it. My heart can't take it." She rests her hand on my arm and turns me so we stand face-to-face. She waits stone quiet until I lift my eyes to meet hers. "You're asking too much of me, Luce. I love you, but I cannot compete with your past."

I yank away from her grip. "You show up here in the middle of the biggest case of my career. For what? A fight?" I toss the clothes I've been folding onto the floor in the corner.

True to form, Rowan does not argue. She only sits on the corner of the bed while I throw clothes into my suitcase and the used towels into the bathroom. My weak temper tantrum. When I finally turn around, quiet tears stream down her cheeks. She looks as though she's been swallowed inside her winter gear, her tall frame engulfed in padding. In the harsh light, her cheeks appear sunken with no traces of the Hawaii sun and a deep groove has settled between her eyes. It takes me a moment to realize Rowan isn't watching me, but taking in the crime-scene photos I've tacked up above the desk with all the information we have on each suspect.

I slowly sit down on the edge of the bed beside Rowan. I've tried to shield her from crime-scene photos of my cases before, but it's too late. There is no way to take back what she's seeing. Closing my open palms together between my knees as though I'm praying, I look out at the gruesome collection of a serial case with her. She's focused on the autopsy photographs and those of the genital mutilation.

"My God, Luce." Tears stream down her cheeks. "What kind of animal would do this to another person?"

Rowan's question sounds so innocent, her words so heartfelt. When she turns to look at me, I see in her eyes that she finally understands what's at stake, what my job actually entails. There's a shift, like a breath of fresh air in the dingy hotel room, a breath that pulls us closer. I reach for her hand and wind my fingers through hers.

After a few minutes, Rowan stands and walks closer to the photographs and clues. "I'm here to stay." Her hand lands on Marci's case folder. She opens it, then takes out each crime-scene photo one at a time.

"These pictures…it's Marci?"

A quick flash of anger burns the back of my throat. I take the file and pictures out of her hand. "This is my work," I say, shoving the thick, worn file into my bag. "You shouldn't see this stuff." Before I can stop myself, I toss the bag against the far wall.

"I'm sorry."

"Why would you choose now to make a stand?" When she doesn't answer, I can't stop myself from adding, "It's about Hawaii, isn't it?"

Rowan turns her back to me and her shoulders shake. Holy hell! The flood of guilt washes over me. Why is there always this constant battle within me, to love her or push her away? Torn, I wrap my arms around her waist from behind and drop my chin into the basket between her neck and shoulder. After some time, when I'm certain she will listen, I say, "I tried, Ro. I tried to look at Marci's photos last night, but I couldn't get past the first one."

"Marci didn't deserve to die, Luce." She leans back into my chest. "You didn't either."

"I'm trying to make it all right." My voice comes out garbled against her skin.

Rowan turns, hugging me long and hard. "Let me in, that's all I'm asking."

We hold each other this way for a few minutes, both of us saying a wordless *sorry*.

"What about your art show?" I ask. "It's only a few weeks away. How will you work here?"

She pulls away and faces me. "I talked to Tony yesterday about postponing the show for a month or so. He's willing to wait. I brought my sketching tools." Rowan slips out of her coat. "Don't worry. I left the dogs in good hands. Dan's staying at the house."

The clock on the nightstand catches my attention. I need to get back to the station.

"Luce, promise. Settle these ghosts once and for all."

I turn away from her to collect my bag.

"For us, Luce," Rowan pleads. "To save us."

When I finally nod, Rowan leans in and we seal the deal with a kiss. I'm certainly relieved she is here, but not nearly as confident as Rowan. Do I really have the strength I'll need to help solve the recent murders and face Marci's?

CHAPTER NINE

Next to Ainsley's, my desk looks absurdly vacant with only an old laptop and a slim folder of the tips I've been assigned. We've been given the only available office in the building, which happens to be nothing more than an oversized storage closet. We're not even located on the same floor as the rest of the team, but at the edge of a cluster of offices that hold the mayor and city trustees. It seems those offices are rarely used more than a few days a week. Ainsley and I should generally have the floor to ourselves.

Ainsley's spread is really quite impressive. I'm not sure where all that paperwork has come from, but he's managed to cover every inch of his desk. Wrappers from beef jerky sticks litter the desk and around the trash can. He's also a terrible shot.

I scrunch my nose in disgust. "How can you eat those things?"

"What? These?" He bites off a chunk of a stick and reaches out to share it with me. "It's a staple, Hansen. You don't know what you're missing." He shrugs when I don't take it and continues eating. His annoying voice booms along the empty corridor with each call he makes to talk to tipsters.

Chad Eldridge gave Davis permission to search the hearse but requested that we hold off until after he used it for work this afternoon. We all realized we should have requested a warrant. Evidence or no evidence.

I scroll through the surveillance from the cemetery one more time. The techie determined that the recorder was tripped when an animal of some kind ran over Chandler Jones's grave. The camera malfunctioned and didn't stop recording for forty-two minutes. I've spent the last five hours going through all the recordings again and again. There was no animal. The camera didn't even catch the edge of a squirrel's tail or the ear of a rabbit. Nothing. Somehow the angle of the camera had been pushed to the left and the lens did not rotate the way it was programmed to work. Instead, it held steady in one obscure angle that gave us virtually no information. According to Ainsley, these are all chance mistakes. Too many, if you ask me, but it doesn't answer the main question. If a person had been at the grave, why didn't the camera record at least some glimmer of a human form? After all, a grave site isn't *that* big.

"Forget it," Ainsley says. "Probably a chipmunk. We got tons of those things around here."

"Is a chipmunk smart enough to turn the camera lens and lock it in place to keep out of range?" I scroll back the recording and set the timer to run even slower, frame by frame. Beside me, Ainsley rolls his eyes in a most exaggerated way and resumes his calls.

The ten tipsters haven't panned out, so Davis asked us to start calling other names from the tip lines until he had something else for us to do. It's been a very long afternoon and I'm nearly mind numb. Still, I can't get this morning's breakfast and so-called chance meeting with Marci's brother out of my mind. Was it some sort of test, bringing me face-to-face with a person from my past? I'd felt so comfortable with Ainsley only last night, talking about Marci. I'd even chalked up his bullheaded behavior while questioning Sambino to his moody personality. I don't want to believe he'd purposely try to throw me off. What did he have to gain from that? It doesn't make sense.

"Ainsley—I got something."

He rolls over on his chair and joins me. I back up the frames and play numbers thirty-two and thirty-three.

"What am I looking at?"

I play them again. "See the grass here in this frame?" I point to the corner where the blades are winter yellow, only centimeters from death. There is no movement. I flip to the next. "There! See the bend?" I roll it again.

"It's the animal." Ainsley rolls his chair even closer to get a better look at the screen.

"Maybe. Or it's the edge of a shoe. What if the person knew the camera was there and shifted the lens away? That movement would start the recording."

"Okay, so where is this person?" Ainsley dares me.

As we both can see, nothing else on the screen moves.

"The techie went out there this morning and said he saw nothing disturbed. The photographs he took show no footprints," Ainsley says.

I pull up a local weather report. "According to this, Willow's Ridge got almost an inch of snow between two thirty and four thirty this morning. Someone could have been there at midnight and the snow would hide the footprints."

"An inch?" Ainsley scoffs. "We'd still be able to see the footprints under that."

"Not with the frozen ground."

Ainsley's desk phone rings. He grunts into it, then hangs up.

"Who left the flowers?"

"What?" Ainsley turns to me, rubbing his bloodshot eyes.

"Who left the flowers that you say the chipmunk was going for?"

I can tell by the way he drops his head to his chest I'm getting nowhere. He takes a deep breath. "Looks like we got something going in our favor. Evidence from the Tucker case is headed to the lab for DNA testing."

"Hasn't the evidence been tested?"

Ainsley stands and gives his arms a good stretch over his head. "The tests we did back then didn't give us anything, but the technology keeps improving. It costs an arm and a leg though"—he smacks my shoulder with this pathetic attempt at a joke—"and with no new breaks in the case there was no justification for the expense."

I follow Ainsley to the stairwell. He talks to me over his shoulder as we descend. "This link with the Tucker case is giving us the juice we need." He's excited that his theory is gaining traction and he explains that Davis will meet us down in the evidence room. He wants us to get the samples over to the lab and wait to follow up with the tipsters until first thing in the morning.

Thank God. No more tipsters.

"I really want to know who brought those flowers," I say to Ainsley's back.

"What fucking flowers?"

"The grave!"

It's almost eight p.m. and it feels like we've gotten nowhere today. I hate the dog days of an investigation where we simply wait: wait for the killer to make a move, to snatch another girl. My stomach growls and thoughts surface of a late dinner with Rowan. Collection of cloth swatches shouldn't take long. That's exactly how I tell myself to think about the job ahead of me: not Marci's personal items left at the crime scene, but a victim's items that need to be tested. No emotion. This is just like any other case I deal with on a daily basis.

Pull Marci out of it.

Due to cutbacks all over the state of Ohio, the Willow's Ridge police station houses evidence for the three surrounding counties, which share CSIs, medical examiners, a morgue, and the storage of evidence. The basement feels like a vast land unto itself. The lack of windows underground leave the basement dark and near silent, the air tinged with the sour scent of mold.

The officer in charge signs us in and Davis, Ainsley, and I snake between the multiple rows lit with buzzy tubes of overhead lighting. Tall metal shelves flank us, stacked high with banker's boxes, each sealed and labeled in black marker with the victim's last name and the date of the crime. The boxes are supposed to be filed by date, but we're cops, not professional organizers. Sometimes it takes days to locate the exact box needed. The enormous volume of cold case evidence can be maddening. I stop for a second and look up. Towers of stacked legal boxes rise all the way to the ceiling. My breath catches when the truth smacks me in the face: *each and every box represents a life.* Some of these boxes are lives that were taken, others who were raped, beaten, or kidnapped. Every single box stands for people whose lives have been unfairly disrupted through an act of undeserved violence.

After a few misread dates and an hour with the three of us searching, Ainsley calls out from the far back corner, "Got it!" The Tucker box is on an upper tier shelved between the inaccurate dates of May 1997 and January 1976. The officer in charge climbs up a rig and brings the box down, then sets it on a table at the front of the room, in plain sight of his desk.

The edges of the cardboard have settled together over time and it takes a stronger tug than Ainsley expects to remove the lid. Davis and I glove up. No one speaks. We peer over the edges. I let Ainsley dig through the sealed bags holding artifacts of Marci's belongings, every object that he excavates is something she'd worn or had in her pockets that day. He lifts out a bag with a faded yellow T-shirt, one of her favorites, the one with the iron-on Mork and Mindy, now cracked and blanched. The aged cotton tee has deteriorated in places, the color faded from its original canary yellow to a weak, bleachy pastel. Was this really the shirt Marci had been wearing when I found her? All this time I've remembered finding her in the short-sleeved button-up, the blue and purple faded plaid that she had worn the first day I met her. Perhaps she'd been wearing the T-shirt under it. If that's the case, where's the button-up plaid?

Ainsley's fingers dig into the plastic crinkle of evidence bags, and one by one he unearths Marci's bloodstained jean shorts, two plastic flip-flops well-worn into dark, curved *C*s, and her blue-striped cotton panties rolled in a tight ball, as if the box was a laundry hamper rather than a forgotten resting place.

"There should be one more shirt," I tell him and tug at the edge of the box. It rattles on the metal table with only a few items left.

Ainsley opens up the log. "Only shirt listed is the *Mork and Mindy* tee."

I step back and cross my arms. It's possible I only *wanted* to remember her in that shirt. It had been my favorite on her—the one that heightened the navy in her eyes so much. It had been the shirt she'd worn on our first date. At least, I called it a date.

I sat on a parking stump painted bright yellow outside Michael's Mini-Mart, in the back of the lot. It was one of the very first sunny days of spring and I stretched my legs out long to feel the warmth through my jeans. It was the first time my dad let me take the truck alone to Willow's Ridge and I spun the keys round and round on my finger as I waited. A few cars passed by and one pulled into the lot, but it was an older man who pushed inside the store. My racing heart settled.

I was early, at least fifteen minutes, but I had this horrible fear that Marci wasn't going to show up. It had been her idea to meet an hour before our One True Path group. She mentioned in that breezy way of hers that she had some books from the program to lend me. So it wasn't technically a date. Not even close. But no one else from the group had been invited. When I thought of being alone with Marci my heart skipped a few beats and everything inside me got warm. Most likely Marci meant nothing by the invitation, I cautioned myself. Even then I had already learned it was dangerous to get my hopes up.

I slid out of my jean jacket and let the sun hit my winter-white arms. I thought about Marci and that college girl from the soccer team. Her mother had told the pastor that something was going on between them. She'd been forced to quit soccer and join One True Path. Sure, Marci said she no longer saw the soccer girl, but that could have been a lie to appease the pastor. Every time I thought of the college soccer girl, I got an acidic and bitter burn on the back of my tongue. I couldn't let myself read too much into this meeting with Marci or allow myself to overthink her intentions. Sometimes lending a book really was just about lending a book.

When Marci finally pulled into the space beside my truck in that navy blue Grand Am her brother was fixing up for her, a car that matched her eyes, my breath caught and the world spun before me. She stepped out, one long and lean leg after another. Her blond hair was pulled back in a ponytail, still damp from the shower. Her worn Def Leppard T-shirt was cinched at the waist with her favorite plaid long-sleeved button-up, the arms tied in a knot. She looked down at me on the parking stump and smiled. "Hey."

I nodded because I couldn't trust my voice. My heartbeat roared in my ears as she stepped closer.

"Want to get something?"

Inside the Mini-Mart we loaded up with forty-four-ounce Mountain Dew fountain drinks and Marci grabbed a bag of those little round peppermint candies.

"Where you been keeping yourself, sweetheart?" The cashier, Doug, an older guy with a greasy, thinning ponytail took in Marci beside me. He did nothing to hide his admiring gaze as it eased over her strong body and up to her face. Since I'd been around Marci, I realized everyone noticed her attractiveness. I dug change out of my pocket and wondered if she ever got tired of men looking at her like that.

Marci didn't skip a beat. She gave him that easy grin of hers. "Hey, Doug."

He rang me up but kept his eyes on Marci until it was her turn. He wore a pendant on his blue work vest that said: *Thank me! I'm a Vietnam Vet.*

She slipped a ten dollar bill across the counter. "Marlboro Reds, please." Leaning into the counter, she bent over so she could look up at him with those irresistible navy eyes. I watched Doug melt under her gaze. He didn't even question her age.

"You're my man!" she told Doug as we pushed out the door and she left him the change.

Marci smiled at me as the door swung shut behind us. "I'm a regular," she explained. "Gotta have my smokes."

We sat side by side on the parking stump and I watched her unwrap the cellophane from the cigarette pack and pull a smoke out. Marci's fingers were short like mine, but her nails had those tall, white half-moons that I always wished I had. She lit the cigarette and took a deep pull.

"How did you get caught?" A trail of smoke spilled from her mouth. She handed me the cigarette. When I closed my lips around the butt, I thought about her lips that were just there and how it was kind of like a very distant kiss. Just thinking the word *kiss* around Marci made my insides turn to jelly.

"My journal. You?"

"The college girl from soccer." Marci shrugged. "Everyone talks."

I took another long drag from the cigarette before I handed it back. I hated this soccer girl and I didn't even know her name. "Do you still see her?"

She shook her head. I could tell by the way she looked out at the main road that talking about the girl still hurt. After a moment, she came back to me. "What about you? You have a girlfriend?" She handed me the near-gone cigarette, and this time our fingers brushed. It was like one of those huge, color-filled fireworks went off in my heart, the trails of burning smoke sinking low into my belly.

"Nope."

"Nope for now or nope you never did?"

At first I didn't know what to say. I couldn't believe Marci asked me so directly about my experience with another girl. No one other than the pastor ever had. I was sitting beside a girl I liked a whole lot and who I was pretty sure wasn't a virgin, given the whole college soccer girl thing. I wanted to look cool, not like the novice I was. But somehow lying to someone you hold hands with in a prayer circle once a week seemed so pathetic. I looked down at my worn Chuck Taylors and ground the cigarette out with the ball of my foot. "Nope. I never did."

I waited for Marci to laugh or say something snide because sometimes she could be that way. I waited for her to say, *How pathetic! They got you before you ever even got a chance to commit this sin.* But she didn't. We were quiet beside one another for a long time, watching the occasional car pull into the lot. She lit another cigarette.

"The pastor's full of shit," she finally said. There was something about the way she spoke that made her seem so much older than me.

There was never a lilt of doubt in her words, never an intonation of questioning. Even her movements were full of confidence.

"Why do you go to the meetings?" I already knew the answer, but I wanted to hear her say it.

"My mom." A stream of smoke sailed out through her front teeth. "She's afraid I'll go to hell."

I thought of my dad then, the intervention and the way he'd had tears in his eyes most of the meeting. I didn't want to disappoint my parent either.

"Loving another girl isn't bad," Marci said.

"No? They all say it is."

"How can love be wrong?" Marci looked at me with those huge eyes of hers practically seeing right through me, and a chill scattered along my spine when I recognized that I probably already loved her.

Marci threw back her head and sang out.

I laughed. I never expected Beatles lyrics from her.

She smacked her open hand against her thigh and sang again, then handed me the cigarette. "John Lennon never said that love had to be with somebody of the opposite sex."

My dad had always seen John Lennon as some sort of sage. I wondered what he'd think of this conversation. When I looked up, Marci's eyes were on me again and her face was no more than a few inches from mine.

"You've got a great smile," she said.

Neither of us moved a muscle. I didn't dare to breathe. Marci was so close to me. So very close…

Suddenly she stood up and headed for her car. The whistled Beatles song trailed after her. I finally took a breath. She reached into her car and pulled out two books for me: *The Truth—Leviticus*, and *Healing Your Sexuality with God.*

"Enjoy," she said with dripping sarcasm. "I had to get those things out of my bedroom." She reached down and opened the bag of peppermints. "We got a few minutes before we have to be at the pastor's." She handed me a wrapped candy.

I took one last pull on the cigarette and ground it out. The candy tasted cool against my warm, smoky tongue.

Marci kicked out a long leg and put her hands on her hips. She looked like she hadn't a care in the world. "Want to meet here again before next week's meeting?"

I shrugged and did my best to look nonchalant as well. Inside, though, everything was jumping up and down. She wanted to see me again! "Sure."

I watched her climb back into the car that her brother would soon turn into a convertible for her, and a little soccer ball dangled from the rearview mirror.

"It's our secret," she said out the car window. "Give me a few minutes' head start."

I nodded. When she pulled away, I thought, *This is May and I have all summer with Marci.* Those warm months stretched out before me and I imagined lazy days with Marci, those eyes never far from me. In that moment, everything seemed so freaking hope filled. As she drove off I couldn't help but sing that John Lennon lyric. I was convinced as I tossed those books in the bed of the truck, all I really did need was love. Marci's love.

In the evidence room, we gather around the silver table and Ainsley lifts the panties from a sealed bag with the end of a pen. Small sections have already been cut out of the fabric, particularly in the blood-soaked area, pencil-eraser-sized circles missing from the decayed fabric.

"Here." I point out a bloody section along the waistband. The UNSUB would have had to grip the cloth here in order to pull them down.

Beside me, Davis twists off the sealed cap of the glass test tube and hands me the bottom. With Ainsley documenting every step with both photographs and voice recording, Davis cuts a swatch, collects the bloody cloth with a pair of tweezers, and drops the sample into the vial. I seal it quickly and sign the seal.

"Let's take a few more," Davis says. "It's a long shot, and we may as well go all in." What he doesn't say is this is the last time anyone will test this evidence, so there's nothing to lose.

Ainsley talks to me as he and Davis work. "The limestone cave area where Marci's body was found? It's become a local legend. It's rumored that her ghost still lurks down inside the caves of the ravine. Kids from all over try to hike down the ravine at night, and most do it on some sort of dare from other kids. Dumb-asses always end up scaring the shit out of themselves." He chuckles and looks over at me. "Halloween week is when the real fun gets started. Davis can tell you—we always get at least two phone calls about the ghost in the quarry."

"Let that ghost haunt you and you only," Davis says, elbowing Ainsley. "I want nothing to do with those things."

"Try the waistband of the shorts," I say. While Ainsley packages away the panties, I reach into the box for the cutoffs. I pull out two bags: one with the shorts and another with a simple gold necklace with a tiny Celtic cross pendant. Marci's necklace.

I hold the bag up to the overhead light to get a better look at the small cross Marci never took off. The chain is broken, most likely in the struggle she had with her attacker. Both halves of the chain, though, are in the bag. My gloved fingers push away the edges of the chain to better reveal the cross that's still shiny. Suddenly that familiar sensation of water rising over my head begins, the bubbles of oxygen escaping through my nostrils as I sink farther and farther toward the ocean's floor and slip back into a memory.

We surrounded Pastor Jameson, all of us sitting cross-legged on the warm grass, while he stood in the center of our circle. In order to avoid his beady eyes, we picked at our fingernails, carefully shredded blades of grass, or tied our shoelaces in knot after knot—we'd do anything not to meet those accusatory eyes with our own. Our avoidance might have been comical to an outsider, but the terror we felt of this man who slicked his hair to the side as if it were oiled was all too real.

"Marci." The pastor walked over to our section of the circle. His enormous shadow hovered over the two of us. "Let's hear what you've got so far."

All around us, the other group members let out an audible collective gasp of relief. The edges of Marci's notebook curled with the moisture in the air. Her hair that was usually straight and came to just below her shoulders was now lying in waves from the humidity. Our weeklong One True Path retreat was held at Camp Jesus in the Hills beside Lake Erie. For the first time in five days, the sun had finally decided to join us.

One True Path retreats were never about fun. They were all about purging ourselves of the homosexual demon that festered inside us all and paying homage to the ex-gay movement. They were about studying the word of God to gain his true meaning through meditation. They were about finding salvation through heterosexuality. Never once did we consider what others did during retreats, fun stuff like swimming, boating, and songs around campfires.

It was the end of the retreat and we were all faced with the duty of writing *the letter*. This was the culminating activity that we'd all heard so much about and dreaded. According to the pastor, homosexuality was not our fault, but something caused by our early childhood experiences and upbringing. We'd been infected with the sin. We'd become damaged goods somewhere along the line and it was not our God-given nature to feel this way. Therefore, each of us was required to write and deliver a letter that laid the blame on the person who was most responsible for raising us. For Marci, this was her mother.

From the corner of my eye, I watched Marci's hand shoot up to her neck, to grasp hold of the silver Celtic cross on the chain she never removed. Her mother had given it to her when she joined the chorus at church. Marci hadn't wanted to sing in the choir, but she wanted to make her mother happy. The church was her mother's life—endless hours of church duties like Bible study, food preparation and delivery to the sick, and organizing the chorus. The cross represented a door for Marci to enter her mother's world, a door that Marci wasn't willing to close.

Around us, the sweet odor of sunscreen filled the air while birds cawed and squawked as they flew around the water. Marci was beside me, all knees and summer-tanned skin. No one spoke. I folded down the edges of the letter to my father. I wanted to hide the letter, ashamed I'd even written down the words, let alone thought those blame-filled words. Would he understand I'd been pressured to do it? Would he still love me? I sat and stewed quietly. One thing I knew for certain was that my turn to read what I had written would come soon enough. No one was ever spared in the pastor's retreats.

"Marci, read it."

"I don't see how this will help, Pastor. My mom…it isn't her fault."

The pastor's hand shot up. Enough. "We've been through this. You must determine what went wrong in the past in order to heal. For you it was your smother-mother." He stopped just as his voice reached a crescendo. With a deep breath, he softened as much as he was capable of and turned back to Marci. He looked down on her and the sunlight behind him was so bright she had to shield her eyes with her hand to look up at him. He looked as though a halo shone from his head.

"You're doing her a favor, Marci! Your mother doesn't realize what she's done wrong. She needs to know that her smothering behavior caused your sexual deviancy. Read. Now."

Marci took a deep breath. Her hand never left her neck, holding tight to that small cross like it might actually save her.

❖

The empty glass vial slips from my fingers and smashes against the steel table and I break through the water's surface. For the second time today, I'm scrambling on my knees to pick up shards of glass.

Ainsley stomps his foot and ignores my apologies. "Fuck, Hansen!"

Davis says nothing but readies a new glass tube. This time, he holds it himself. I gather the glass into the palm of my gloved hand as they work, but I wonder why Ainsley and Davis didn't get the DNA samples themselves. Why bring me along, given that I had a close relationship with the victim? Maybe Davis isn't completely aware of all I've gone through with Marci Tucker, but Ainsley certainly is. Could this be an attempt to show me up, some sort of test, in the same way taking me to a restaurant where Marci's brother works had been? I freeze and look up at Detective Cole Ainsley. He's calmed down and works diligently to get the sample into the tube. His wide shoulders are solid and determined. He keeps his large hand on the side of the evidence box as if to signal to me and Davis that this is really *his* case.

Ainsley's trying to get rid of me.

❖

My car feels like a freezer after so many hours parked in the police lot. The heater is set to blow on high but only gives out a blast of cold air. I've picked away circles of ice from the windshield and passenger-side window with my sad excuse for an ice scraper. The blade has seen better days, its edges broken and beaten, but I'm able to chip away enough ice to get me safely back to the hotel. Back to Rowan.

A tow truck pulls into the lot for the scheduled hearse pickup in the morning. As it reverses, beeps pierce the quiet night. The ice and snow twinkle in the truck's red-taillight glow. I let the car sit and warm up, ignoring the plumes of white smoke that spill from the exhaust while I let the truck do its thing.

I work at the shard of glass still lodged beneath my skin from the broken glass at breakfast. It seems like it happened a year ago, not only this morning. I squeeze the skin into a ball of swollen red until I can finally see the tip. And then the tiny shard of glass shoots out, the pressure of the squeeze releasing it, leaving behind a rush of fresh red blood.

❖

Steam from my bath covers the bathroom mirror. Rowan sits on the bathroom counter, her legs dangling as she kicks her feet back and forth and watches me pull a brush through my tangled wet mess of hair.

"What I wouldn't give for a shower," I groan.

Rowan's been lost in thought, contemplating my theory that all the victims were lesbians. We're both treading lightly; discussing my work is new ground for us both.

"Why only lesbians? Why not gay men?"

I pick at the huge knot of hair at the base of my skull. "He's targeting a very specific community. I'm sure he believes he has a good reason for it."

"But if it truly is a hate crime, wouldn't it be all gay people?"

"I doubt he's thinking that way, Ro."

The flick of her eyebrow asks me why.

"That thinking is way too rational. These crimes are all about power and domination." I toss the brush into the sink. The knot refuses to let go.

"Come here before you rip out all your hair." Rowan waves me to her and with my back turned, I step back between her parted knees. Soon her fingers are in my wet hair gently picking apart the knot. Rowan's hands have always been my fascination. Such strong hands. Such capable hands—her instruments of creation.

Rowan kicks her socked feet out one at a time and the innocent movement reminds me how much I want to keep her safe. Crime is my world, not hers. I want to keep her far away from that darkness.

Rowan has questions, she always has, about my involvement with One True Path. Ex-gay ministries are a completely foreign concept to someone like her, who has always accepted herself as she is. Rowan respects my space, though; she hasn't asked personal questions, only listened to the bits of my past I've dealt out to her piecemeal.

"If you feel this strongly about the connection, Luce, you're going to have to tell the captain."

She's got the knot out and pulls the brush through my hair. "Why are you holding back this theory about the organization?"

I recognize the ridiculousness of it, but strangely, somewhere inside I need to protect this group of people. I want so much for my instincts to be wrong. I'm still connected to One True Path in so many ways.

"It's complicated."

Her hand squeezes my right shoulder and slides down toward my elbow. She whispers into my ear, "There's nothing for you to be ashamed of."

She's right, of course. Somewhere in the very core of me I am ashamed I ever took part in such a group. That shame, most days, feels like I've betrayed my own family. To tell the captain and Ainsley would mean I'd have to reveal those dirty secrets about myself.

Rowan closes her knees in around me and I smell her, that heady combination of Downy fabric softener and clean skin. Turning to face her, I settle into the bowl of her arms. Her wild eyes, green with specks of gold, see through me. Rowan's so close, so very close, that my Berlin Wall quakes with her intensity. Somehow this woman still loves me. Suddenly my throat tightens and I feel as though I might cry.

Rowan knows best what to do—those strong and gentle hands that touch so deep. She reaches out, cups my face, and strokes my cheeks and lips until the teary feeling passes and her mouth softly closes on mine. Wrapping her legs around my waist, I carry her to the bed. I'm hungry for her, suddenly starving, and the ache for her inside me is damn near unbearable.

CHAPTER TEN

Friday, January 11

The team meets in the Willow's Ridge crime-scene processing area. Clad in protective goggles and gloves, we watch the analysts in action. The hearse's back gate yawns wide and the front seats have been lifted out from the car's frame. The carpet has been extracted from the bed of the hearse and is spread out over a large metal table. Even the doors lie on the cement with their locks and handles removed. The crime-scene guys are running different tests on the hearse and its parts: a stain that might be blood, trace that might be drugs. Nothing is overlooked.

When the team arrived at the Eldridge Funeral Home with a warrant to seize the hearse hours earlier, there'd been no drama from Mr. Sambino. He'd merely met Captain Davis and the officers at the back door, alerted Chad Eldridge the police had arrived, and watched all the action as though it were a movie. Eldridge, however, had been much more vocal. He argued that he needed the hearse for his business and that the police had next to no evidence.

I don't blame Eldridge for demanding a warrant. His business will suffer because of the suspicion placed on Sambino. As a business owner, he's in a difficult spot. Sambino has a lot of responsibility and can not easily be replaced. But if he keeps Sambino as an employee, families will go elsewhere for funeral services.

All around us, drills screech as they take apart the hearse. The passenger-side door lies on the cement not far from me and I kneel down as an officer swabs the innermost corners of the hinge. Spilling blood is like pouring a pitcher of sugar water—the sticky liquid seeps into the slightest of cracks and even a pinprick-sized drop leaves just enough behind for testing.

The lead analyst reports to Davis, Ainsley, and me. "It's been thoroughly vacuumed and the outside washed with a cleaning agent that has a bleach base. There's also a thick residue of cleaner over the dash, the steering wheel, and the doors." He rubs his recently buzzed hair. "Tell you one thing, sure is a thorough cleaning job."

"A fool's errand," Davis says with the shake of his head. "Run all the tests just to make sure there's nothing, but then close the hearse up and return it to Eldridge."

Ainsley kicks at a screwdriver that's been dropped near him, cussing Sambino. With all the commotion, I don't think he notices when one of the crime-scene analysts approaches me with a small evidence bag. It looks like a gum wrapper inside.

"Not sure if this will help, Agent." She hands me the bag. "We found this stuck to a current auto insurance card inside the glove compartment." In black ink, someone had scrawled: *Dr Weaver 9 Richards*. "There's a thumbprint on the back of it that's a match for Sambino," she says. Davis took elimination prints from Sambino and Eldridge when they collected the vehicle.

Earlier, Davis confirmed with the morgue that it had been Sambino who picked up Chandler Jones's and Emma Parks's bodies, not Eldridge. In fact, no one in the morgue witnessed anyone else with Sambino. There's no telling how recently the gum wrapper was left in the hearse. Yesterday? Two weeks? Two months? Based on date, the insurance card has most likely been in the glove compartment for four months. Judging from the meticulous cleaning job someone gave the hearse and the absence of any other miscellaneous crap, I'm holding something I'm not meant to see.

Thank God for mistakes.

❖

It turns out Dr. Eli Weaver isn't nearly as hard to locate as I thought he would be. Sambino has left me all the information I need. After a few computer searches, I learn that Dr. Weaver is a tenured professor of religious studies at Sandon University, a small, private Catholic institution on the outskirts of Columbus. I've been sent alone to meet with Dr. Weaver at his office in Richards Hall to find out why Sambino would have his information scrawled on the back of a gum wrapper inside his work vehicle.

Columbus is just over an hour's drive from Willow's Ridge, and I soon merge onto the crowded belt that surrounds the city. Davis stayed at the station to review some case reports, and Ainsley was sent on his own hunt to track down four different leads from the tip lines. The truth of the matter is no one really believes that this interview with Weaver will lead to anything. After all, it's entirely possible that Sambino might have considered enrolling at Sandon University. It's odd: none of the information I'd read on Sambino suggests to me that he'd be interested in a college degree, much less one in religious studies. He barely graduated from Willow's Ridge High and had only done a few classes online for a mortuary science certification that he never completed. So my curiosity has gotten the best of me. Why would Sambino, aka Vampire Man Tristan, visit a religion professor at a Catholic university?

My cell rings and I hit speaker so I can talk and drive.

"Do you know it's almost six o'clock?" Rowan asks.

The sound of Rowan's voice reminds me of last night and my body warms instantly. "That explains this heavy traffic."

"You promised me dinner tonight."

I grunt as a pickup truck nearly swipes my front end as it slides into my lane. "I've got an interview in Columbus. We'll still get dinner. Just not at six thirty."

She doesn't have to say it—I can hear what she's thinking in the silence: *Here we go again.*

Rowan may not be a BCI profiler, but she certainly knows my behavioral patterns. We got close last night, closer than we've ever been, and when things like that happen, I run. I make myself scarce for a few days to build protection back up.

"Ro?"

"I'm here. I'll see you when you get back."

"This won't take long. Eight at the latest. I promise."

From the moment I met Rowan, I understood that she loved differently from the way I do. She has absolutely no fear. Rowan loves her lovers, family, and friends with a wide-open heart. Nothing is guarded. Her love is flat-out fierce.

Rowan was the photographer hired by the bureau to do our portraits and the monthly newsletter. When I signed on with BCI, I was scheduled for a sitting within the first months of duty. I sulked my way into her studio in full agency garb. I'd rather pull my toenails out with tweezers than sit for professional photographs.

It was her hair that caught my attention right away, that swarming nest of curls that spilled all around her, the golden-hued spirals that lined her face. She moved all around me with her black camera, all this hair on a tall body angling around the room. She bounced around with a smile that I couldn't resist. When she primped at my hair and adjusted my coat, sheer electricity shot through my every blood vessel. There's simply no other way to say it. When she handed me her card on the way out, her number was scrawled on the back: *Call soon.*

I thought long and hard about those sparks later that evening during my three-mile swim. I thought about how her emerald green eyes showed no fear and how her light touch warmed everything in me. And that was through clothes! Skin on skin? That could be an addictive intoxication.

I stopped midlap to catch my breath against the side wall. It had been so long since I'd let someone in. Still, I knew I'd call her within a day. Letting the water rise over my head, I sank down in the swimming pool, the coolness taming the burn of my cheeks at the thought of Rowan. *Yes,* I thought within the safety of that water, *I'll definitely call her.* And when my thoughts raced ahead to imaginings of us together months down the road, I chastised myself within that water. *Don't,* I cautioned. *Don't set yourself up for more hurt.*

It's been over a year since Rowan and I didn't share weekends together or work a couple of hours on one of our endless house projects. It's been over a year since we didn't rock-paper-scissors it over whose turn it was to let the dogs out at midnight or put off a grocery run another day—we could make do one more day, couldn't we?

I miss all that. I miss what I had with Rowan. Why does talk of commitment and ceremonies have to change anything?

❖

Coincidence. Random elements. Chaos theory. Rowan would say it's karma, that wheel of life coming back around to bite you in the ass one more time. Call it what you will, but the connections this case had with my past can't be denied.

When I was eleven, my father decided it was time for us to start going to church. I'd been to a few services with my grandmother before she passed on, but never with my father. Once my mother left us, it was all my dad could do to work every day and take care of me. He stumbled through cooking mac and cheese, bathing me, and getting me to school on time. I realize now he'd been overwhelmed with grief and duty.

We'd attended a new church for about a month when one Sunday after service my dad turned to me at a stoplight on the way home. He looked funny in a suit with a tie without his uniform. Even his black duty boots were left beside the front door, and he slipped in and out of his new black loafers all through the church service. "Does it make you feel better to think that everything happens for a reason? That there's a God taking care of us?"

I looked over at him then, my father who had never been anything but a hero to me. I smelled his potent aftershave, evergreen and way too strong. It was his eyes that told me how hard he'd been trying. He questioned why my mother left, why she left *him*—even then my instincts were strongly honed. I could sense his confusion, his anger, and I felt some of those same feelings. I convinced myself that I was fine without my mother as long as my dad was there for me. "It makes it sound like we're just in a game or something," I said. "I want to be in control of what happens to me."

"We're not, hon. Sometimes we're just not."

"You're doing a good job, Dad." I looked out the windshield as I said it. Sometimes it's just too much to look people dead on. "We don't need her."

Tears rolled down his cheeks, though in the silence I couldn't tell if they were from relief or grief or some sort of mixture of both. I stared out the window with steely resolve. *We don't need her.*

I wait beside Dr. Eli Weaver's office door thinking of those words I shared with my father. Not long after that, we abandoned the church idea for some time until my father began to feel guilty over my lack of religious training all over again. The next church we attended was the one that directed us to Pastor Jameson. If I'd had any control, we never would have stepped foot inside that church.

Here I am once again, face-to-face with the universe showing me I'm not in control. Never in a million years could I have possibly guessed that this professor and scholar specializes in the study of ex-gay ministries and conversion therapy. But Google says it, so it must be true.

Dr. Eli Weaver opens the office door and steps out. He has to duck his head not to knock the door frame. "Agent Hansen"—he reaches his racquet-sized hand to shake mine—"I'm so sorry to keep you waiting. Come in, come in."

I like Weaver instantly. He has a spring in his gait for such a tall man, probably close to six and a half feet, and a comforting office painted in different shades of blue. Crosses of all different variations hang on any available bit of wall space. The entire double windowsill is filled with flowering plants of all shapes and sizes. Weaver has pinned up an overgrown vine that wraps along the wall and over a large abstract painting that features the colors of the LGBTQ freedom flag. Soft classical music lulls in the background.

Weaver has a gentle way about him and he handles me with a quiet ease. He offers an oversized chair that curls around me and he moves behind his desk in one loping step.

"Do you mind if I record our conversation?" I ask. "The police captain wants to hear it."

Weaver drops into his high-backed chair and nods. He weaves his fingers together and puts his open palms behind his head. His shoulder span's immense, at least twice mine. His shirt sleeves, though, ride up his forearms, dreadfully short. It must be just as annoying to never have sleeves long enough as it is for me to never find sleeves that are short enough. "Anything I can do to help, Agent Hansen. I don't know anyone who could be involved in a homicide."

"Please, call me Luce." I set the recorder on the edge of the desk between us. "Your secretary was able to look back at your schedule for the past school year, and at student records. There's no current or past student under the name Nick Sambino." I reach into my pocket and place a photocopy of Sambino's gum wrapper on the desk. Weaver leans forward and investigates the writing. "Why would he have your office information if he's not a student?"

Weaver taps his long fingers next to the paper. "Everyone I meet with here is either a current or potential student in religious studies here at Sandon. There hasn't been anyone I've met who doesn't fall into those categories."

I pull the file from my satchel. Sambino could have been here for information on the program. *Why?* It's so far-fetched that he would want to attend this conservative Catholic university given his fascination with vampires and dead bodies. "Do you recognize anyone in these photographs?"

Weaver takes the photograph of Sambino from me and looks at it closely. "I do remember this guy. But his name's not Sambino."

Weaver turns to his computer and does a quick calendar search. "Here it is. From September. He said he had a religious studies undergraduate degree from another university but was looking to get an MA and possibly a PhD." Weaver's fingers jump all over the keyboard. "Here's the name: James Smith."

Finished with his undergrad degree? "Did this James Smith tell you he was from Willow's Ridge?" Outside the office window, the arena lights flicker and flash as a basketball game is under way.

"I can't recall." Weaver leans back a second, then pitches forward. His whole face opens wide. "Wait a minute. Is this part of those murders in Willow's Ridge? Oh my *God*."

"There are confidentiality issues, so I can't discuss the details." I put on my professional voice. "But Nick Sambino—the person you know as James Smith—is a person of interest. Why did he tell you he needed to meet face-to-face? I'm assuming the program information is on the university's website."

With a deep breath, Weaver rubbed his shaven head that gleamed like a cue ball. "He wanted to hear about our grad assistant teaching program. He said that money was an issue for him, and he was only looking into colleges that offered this type of program—we offer full tuition remission plus a stipend." Weaver spins a gold band around his ring finger; he cannot be much older than me.

"It was an odd meeting. I felt uncomfortable but he said that he wanted to work in the ministry, so I continued the meeting."

"Uncomfortable how?"

Weaver shrugs. "He wanted to know about my life outside of work. That almost never happens."

"With potential students?"

"My sexuality throws most students off around here."

I can't help but smile at this comment. An out religion professor at a conservative, Catholic institution is certainly not what I expected either.

"I remember this guy because he works as an embalmer in a funeral home. He said he wanted the degree so he'd be able to officiate at funerals."

Sambino? A funeral director and in the ministry? It simply does not add up. But Sambino must have known about Weaver's particular line of work before he stepped foot in this office. He already knew more than I do about Weaver. What connection could this gentle giant possibly have with the case?

"Anything else?"

"He showed me a drawing of a tattoo he wanted. An ankh," Dr. Weaver says. "That's a cross that many vampire historians attribute to eternal life. He found some papers I wrote on cross studies in graduate school and wanted to talk about what he thought the rituals were for them. It threw me."

"Rituals?"

Weaver shrugs. "Well, that's just it. The only ritual I know of is the belief that the bearer of an ankh will have eternal life. He seemed disappointed."

Dr. Weaver stands and pulls a book about world crosses from his vast bookshelf. He flips to a page that shows variations on the ankh symbol, the Egyptian cross. The text claims that many practitioners of vampirism honor the ankh as something that will feed them when human blood is not available for consumption. The tie to the Christian crosses left with the murder victims does not slip past me.

"I was surprised when this young man wanted to talk about crosses." He tags the page so he can make a copy of it for me. "Generally my appointments only wish to talk about what classes they must take for a degree or what I've found in my studies of ex-gay ministries and conversion therapy. Crosses are a fascination of mine, but one I haven't really written much about since graduate school."

"Did Sambino ask anything about ex-gay ministries or conversion therapy?"

Weaver points out two framed photographs on the corner of his desk, one of Weaver and another man, the other of the two men with two young children. "My family," he says, nodding at the pictures. "That's Michael, my partner going on five years now. We adopted both of our children. Sam is one and Charlie is nearly four."

"Beautiful family."

"Thanks. We met through One True Path and Sambino seemed angry about that. Finally I told him I had another meeting to attend. I wasn't comfortable sharing any more about myself."

It isn't uncommon for partners to meet in ex-gay ministries, though I didn't know many who generally admitted to such. Here it is—that chaos theory slapping me once more in the face.

Weaver leans back in his chair and crosses one leg over the other. "Sometimes I get strong reactions from people when I discuss my topic of research. I'm one of the ex-gay ministry's strongest opponents."

I've been quiet for too long, scribbling away on my pad. "I know about ex-gay ministries," I say, explaining my silence. "I'm a survivor as well."

Eli Weaver's wide shoulders reach high above the back of his chair. "I'm glad you made it out. I don't mean to bring back any bad memories for you." His eyes are soft and genuine as they examine me. "How long were you a member?"

"Only one summer," I say. "And that was more than enough."

Weaver chuckles. "Were you a member of a group here in Ohio?"

"The Willow's Ridge group, actually."

"Ah, Pastor Jameson! He's still going strong out there. He refuses to let me interview him." Weaver holds up his hand. "It will interest you to know that Sambino said he'd been to some of the One True Path meetings in Willow's Ridge."

Here's another piece of the puzzle slipping into place, a cornerstone that ties back to One True Path.

"He gave me the sense that he still attends from time to time," Weaver says. "He claimed something that I know only too well. Many of the men at these meetings are so repressed that any other man they get close to is someone they could easily develop a crush on. One-night stands are not unusual. You know as well as I do that those meetings portray homosexuality as an addiction. So if you fall off the wagon one night, you climb back on the next day. He said he enjoyed being the one who helped men fall off the wagon."

"He didn't say he zealously believes in the organization's ideals or teachings?"

"Not at all," Dr. Weaver says. "Quite the contrary."

"But Sambino seemed angry about you meeting your partner at a meeting."

Weaver nods. "I think that had more to do with our commitment rather than where we met."

"Meaning?"

Weaver shrugs. "He gave me the impression of a young man who likes to spend one night with a guy, not a lifetime."

"You said you also specialize in the study of conversion or reparative therapy. Did Sambino ask at all about this?"

"He asked me to explain to him how the process works. I'm guessing you know from your time with Jameson that these types of therapy can be tragically damaging. Jameson is one of the strongest proponents of this therapy in the state of Ohio. He pushes members into relearning gender and sexual roles. From what I understand, he has a conversion therapist who comes to the meetings and works solely with the group."

My stomach rolls over. I've never been to a conversion therapist, but members of my group had. I knew how severe their training could be, including electric-shock therapy, self-mutilation for same sex sexual thoughts, and the strong encouragement of 1950s-era gender roles. Just like ex-gay ministries, the practices of reparative or conversion therapists have been denounced by all medical fields. Still their businesses survive. Nothing breeds fear like deep-seated shame.

Our killer could very well be a victim of ex-gay ministries and/or conversion therapy. Ainsley's probably right: there could be two working together. One of them could be Sambino. I know from my own experience how angry and ashamed these treatments can make a person. For some, angry enough to kill.

Weaver opens a document on his computer. "I'm going to print you a copy of my latest publication. Sambino asked me a few questions about the numbers of members in these ex-gay organizations, and unfortunately, the numbers are increasing. I detail their ties to reparative therapy in the article."

"How did the ankh tie in with his questions about ex-gay ministries?"

"I'm not so sure it did," Dr. Weaver says, rubbing his brow. "The way I saw it, he came to find out about the Egyptian cross and wanted to chat about the ex-gay world once he found out what my studies were in. He never enrolled in any of our classes."

Weaver hands me the pages, then holds my hand a few seconds too long. "I know you're consumed with this case, and God knows we need someone as smart and capable as you to solve it, but once you're done, I'd love to share my story with you about my own time in the ex-gay ministries." His smile is warm and wide, and a beautiful set of straight white teeth shine at me. "We can swap tales about our root causes."

I laugh with him at the absurdity of our pasts. "God, I haven't thought about my root in years. I think I might've blocked that word from my vocabulary." The ex-gay organizations claim all homosexuals have a root cause of their sexuality issues. Everything, they say, can be traced back to the root. It's healing the root, they claim, that heals homosexuality. Hence why they believe it is so vital to blame everything on your caretakers.

"The sharing of our stories heals us, you know, keeps us strong. We all need to support one another."

"I'd like that," I say, sliding into my coat and leather gloves.

While I wait for the elevator, I skim through Dr. Weaver's extensive paper. It's thick with statistics and details of the dangers associated with ex-gay ministries and conversion therapy. But it's not the numbers that stand out to me. It's a Bible verse that catches my attention. A verse from Mark 4:22 that resonates somewhere deep inside me, like the final stillness of a musical tuning fork after it's been struck:

For there is nothing hidden, except that it should be made known; neither was anything made secret, but that it should come to light.

CHAPTER ELEVEN

Rowan greets me at the hotel door, her hands and fingers blackened with charcoal from sketching, her hair a mass of unruly curls. Sheaves of newsprint are scattered about the room. She's found inspiration in the snowy scene outside our hotel window—leafless branches with mounds of snow precariously balanced along the thin, fragile lines of them, a timeless wooded scene lit with parking lot lights.

Rowan groans when I dump the stuff from the car in the corner of the hotel room, realizing that I've brought along the case folders. I ignore her protests and hug Rowan tight, not willing to let go. It's my way of apologizing since it's almost ten p.m. After a moment, I hear her stomach growl. Then she giggles, and it's so unexpected that I dissolve in a raging peal of belly laughs that leave my eyes tearing. God, I'm *so* tired.

"You promised me pizza and a beer!" Rowan explains through laughter. "Look how late it is."

I kiss her forehead. "I did, didn't I? I think everything's closed up around here by eight. This isn't the kind of town that has anything open twenty-four-seven. Delivery pizza?"

Rowan steps into the bathroom to scrub her hands and arms clean. She lifts the oversized sweatshirt over her head and stands in a bright blue bra with her hip bones pressed against the bathroom sink. Her natural curls tumble below her shoulder blades. When her hair is wet and brushed straight, it falls to her waist. Rowan's hair, I like to say, has a presence all its own. Not only is it sleek and shiny as a seal's back, but it's the color that most people notice right away. Not black, definitely not brown, but instead some sort of palette mixture of burnt sienna, gold, and earthen tones. I love it when Rowan wears her hair in a fat, messy bun held together with pencils and long paintbrush handles. I like to joke that it's the mass of hair that holds her slight body down in a wind gust. Rowan's body has a remarkable grace to it, a flow of movement that reminds me more of a dancer than a painter.

Rowan looks out at me through her reflection in the mirror while she finger-brushes her hair into a ponytail. "I figured you'd be late," she says. Her words state a fact not an accusation. "Pizza's on its way. I called in the order as soon as your car pulled up. Check the fridge."

Jammed inside the hotel's minifridge is a six-pack of cheap beer, the only brand the never-closing Michael's Mini-Mart carries. Rowan knows me so well. Sometimes I wonder if I would ever be able to survive in this world without Rowan.

The cable music channel on the television spills out something called adult alternative. This genre is a complete mystery to me. When did I stumble into this age and music category? It absolutely floors me when I hear songs I rocked out to as a teenager played on the easy-listening channels, in elevators and doctors' offices. Rowan likes this channel, though. She argues that we are the alternative to adult.

Since I'm using the desk for the case, Rowan and I sit cross-legged on the floor, with the mostly eaten pizza between us and the disturbingly ugly hotel comforter under us. The frantic pattern is enough to give me a migraine. Rowan calls this setup a middle-of-the-night hotel picnic.

I crack open my fourth can of beer. "I can't pretend that Marci and everything else didn't happen."

Rowan closes her eyes, takes a deep breath. "I'm not asking you to forget. I'm asking you to let Marci go."

"Isn't letting go the same as forgetting?"

"Luce." Rowan's voice trails off like an exhausted sigh. "What are you so afraid of? What do you think will happen if you let her go?"

At rare times in my life, I've imagined saying good-bye to Marci. Then the guilt comes rushing back, smothering me like a tsunami. "Don't I deserve to carry her with me? To not forget? *Someone* needs to remember what happened to Marci."

Rowan moves closer until her knees line up with the bends of mine. She takes both my hands in hers. "What if it'd been you that died that day? Would you insist Marci punish herself and never move on from your death?"

I wouldn't wish these feelings or memories on anyone, most of all, Marci. Down the hall, the elevator buzzes and the shower kicks on in the room adjacent to ours. R.E.M. sings on the television about the end of the world as we know it.

Rowan's hands knead mine. "Tell me what you're thinking."

"It was her necklace that upset me most."

"Marci's?"

I nod. "They need to run more DNA tests. Everything from her crime scene is in the evidence room." A shiver passes through me. "No one ever thinks they'll end up a box there, you know? Especially a sixteen-year-old small-town girl." Rowan squeezes my hands, urges me to continue. "I tried to focus on my job, but I could see her wearing that necklace, the sunlight glinting off it around her neck. I could see her like she'd been then, her hair in a ponytail, her cutoff jean shorts. I wanted to grab those clothes from Ainsley and bury my face in them to see if her smell was still there. She had this Marci smell, you know? Fruity shampoo and cigarettes. And peppermint. She was always chewing on those hard candies." My eyes mist over and the tears blur my beer can. I take another long gulp and a memory assaults me.

Marci tore along the path through the quarry with me hot on her heels. We'd made a game of it, which of us could get to this secret place first. The problem was I had no idea where we were going. It was a built-in win for her, something I was positive she hadn't accidentally overlooked.

"Hurry!" she called out over her shoulder. "It's perfect!"

It had been one of the first warm days of summer and my pale legs showed the sunless winter. I charged after Marci while branches slapped against my bare arms and legs and she giggled because I didn't know where to move to get away from them. We were full of play and I realized as I chased after her that this was the first time I'd seen Marci drop all her guards. In the quarry, Marci was nothing but herself.

Marci burst onto a rocky ledge, me right behind her. I stopped myself just in time not to slip over the ledge. A rocky drop-off filtered down to a running stream. Marci took hold of my hand and led me along the skinny path until we turned into the mouth of a cave.

"Welcome to Stonehenge."

The cave was tall and wide enough that we both could stand, and the temperature had dropped a few degrees inside the stone cavern. Marci held on to my hand and I let her. "How did you find this place?"

She shrugged. "I've played in this quarry forever. There are a lot of these old caves around and I've been in them all. This one's my favorite."

I looked around at the layered walls and uneven floor beneath my feet. Stonehenge looked like any other small cave I'd ever seen, but there was a beautiful steady stream of light filtering through its opening. "Favorite? Why?"

Marci gave me a smile that said she was only waiting for me to ask. She pulled my hand and led me deeper into the cave, so deep I thought we were going to walk right into a stone wall until she made a sharp turn to the left and crouched to slip into an opening. I followed on my knees as though I were passing under a rock bridge. A whole other secret section opened up where we both could stand and move around. Just enough light seeped in that I could see the outline of her in front of me. She turned on a small flashlight that she must have kept hidden in the cave. And that small beam of light showed me a work of art I never even imagined could be possible. The ceiling was high and the walls were pocked, the markings like books of all different lengths on a bookshelf. But it was the colors that got me most, the pink hues of the stony earth, the mauve layers of rock, the silver threads mixed throughout.

"This is Stonehenge," Marci whispered.

"How often do you come here?"

"Whenever I need to be alone. I've never shown anyone before."

I couldn't help but smile. I wanted to be special to Marci. Her hands reached for mine and pushed me gently back against the stone wall. Before I knew it, her mouth was on mine and I was sandwiched between the warmth of her body and the cold of the stone at my back. I hesitated. "No one can find out."

"We're hidden inside the earth," she whispered. "No one will know." Marci made a sound then, barely audible, like a small groan. She made the sound that my body cried out. That groan broke the thin membrane between us until we were all lips and tongues, all hands, all skin on skin. All those hours of sitting beside one another in meetings being told we couldn't have one another came rushing out in an explosion that screamed *Yes we can!* Marci dropped the flashlight, its beam of light rolling away from us along the floor, and I wanted to tell Marci that she was so right, that Stonehenge really was sheer perfection.

❖

A few seconds of silence pass between Rowan and me. "They shouldn't have asked you to collect evidence from Marci's clothes," Rowan whispers.

We sit together with the music, and the cheap comforter scratching against our legs. She lines up the empty cans of beer inside the pizza box lid and waits for me to say something more. When I don't, she says, "I have an idea that might help me understand." Rowan's cautious with her words. "Look at Marci's file with me. Explain what happened." Rowan squeezes my hands tight inside hers. "Take me through that afternoon."

❖

Inside the quarry it was always summertime. That day the rays of sunlight seeped through the leaves and landed on my skin in slanted spreads of buttery warmth. Pine needles scattered beneath my sun-browned sandaled feet as I followed the call of birds that guided me on the climb and through the thickets of greenery. It was on the crest of a ridge—the one spot, where I could see most of the rocky ravine below, that caught my breath and held it hostage every time. God's View. It truly felt that way, like a sudden gasp, really, of pure hope at what lies below—Marci. My Marci. Everything's so green and aching with life that I had to squint a moment; it was all so bright and alive, it hurt somewhere deep inside my chest.

I was on hold: suspended between here and there, afloat on that crested ridge for a few heartbeats, my hands and feet aquiver, my lips trembling with the urgency of what would come, a dizzying shower of anticipation. Then, just as suddenly as I crested that ridge, the threshold broke and it all crashed down with my footfalls, the sound of my breath ragged with excitement, the swish and snap of branches, the unsteadiness of my feet on the forest floor, the needles' slick backs threatening to toss me down to my hands and knees with each footfall.

Marci was there, waiting for me like always, hidden away inside the mouth of Stonehenge. I dropped to my bony knees beside her and paused a second to catch my breath from the run down the rocky embankment. She was leaning up against a large rock, her knees bent in an upside-down V as if she'd fallen asleep shading herself. Marci had the fine blond hair of corn silk, streaked with dark hints of gold. Even her eyelashes flittered gold in the direct sunlight, only to show off the spatter of freckles across her nose, under the navy sea of her eyes.

"Marci." I leaned in to her.

She didn't move.

"Come on," I said. "Stop playing."

Somewhere outside of the cave a tree branch snapped. A quick scuffle of underbrush.

I nudged Marci with my elbow to see if she heard the sound, too. That's when her head rolled back and I noticed that her hair wasn't right, tangled and strewn across her brow, clumped with thick maroon, the back of her head sticky and cold in my hand. Marci's shirt was ripped at the collar, her jean shorts unzipped and yawning wide in the heat of the summer sun.

"No," I said. "No!" But when I touched her cool skin, called her name, and began to shake her, my own heart galloped at breakneck speed. Something was terribly wrong and all I could think was that Marci needed help fast. I thought of my dad and how he always said not to move a person with a head injury and call 911. I bolted through the forest the same way I came in, branches scratching and snapping off as I raced past. My chest heaved with oxygen, blood thrumming in my ears, when the toe of my sandal caught the corner of a large stone and it rocketed me into—

Outside our hotel door, two children holler and chase one another down the hotel hallway for the ice machine. An adult follows behind, shushing them, but it doesn't work. I'm dizzy with exhaustion and drop onto the bed, thumbs to eyelids, rolling my burning eyes. The children squeal over the whir and clatter of the ancient ice machine.

"Who lets their kids stay up this late?" Rowan goes to the door and glares while she puts out the *Do not disturb* sign on the handle. She stands over me. "Luce, please," Rowan pleads. "Tell me."

"No." My voice is mumbled and groggy against the pillow. Rowan's scared; I can hear that waver of doubt in her words. She's afraid I'll end up exactly as I did with the case in Columbus: unable to sleep or eat and slumped on the couch in some sort of catatonic stupor for weeks.

I can't go on with the past tonight. Not with the water rising, gurgling over my ears and nose. The water holds me and I'm weightless under its surface. Thousands of miles below the water's skin, this is where I'm safe.

Rowan eventually gives up on me and collects Marci's file from the floor. She moves to the desk. Pages shuffle as she clears Marci's case away so we don't have to look at its reminder another second. I'm too tired to ask Rowan to stop. Instead I listen to the swish of reports and photographs sliding into the file and water burbling around me. In the hall, the children continue to chase one another and use the long hallway as a track, the poor adult lagging behind in an attempt to tame them with a shrill voice in the quiet hotel, as though her words could make any difference.

CHAPTER TWELVE

Saturday, January 12

The main conference room of the police station has been turned into a case study with five large whiteboards chock-full of information. It's an overgrown version of the murder board from my hotel room. This layout, though, has an entire section reserved for information on Sambino. Next to his photo from the DMV someone drew a set of pointy fangs with bloody teardrops raining from them. Next to the fangs the artist scrawled: *Forget Team Edward or Jacob, I'm Team Sambino!*

Davis listens again to the recording of my interview with Dr. Eli Weaver. I've already edited out the portion of our discussion about my personal involvement with ex-gay ministries because I don't want that information entered into any kind of case log. Instead, I verbally came clean with Davis and Ainsley—the crib-notes version and as brief an explanation as I could possibly get away with. An uncomfortable silence settled once I finished, and I am grateful to have Weaver's voice filling the room now. Davis rewinds the recording once again, listens, and then rewinds it some more.

This morning I received word that my assignment to the Willow's Ridge case has been extended for three more days. As I got ready for work, Rowan packed up and left for home. She said she couldn't stay three more days after all. The dogs needed her, she explained, and she wanted to get back to painting for her upcoming show. Neither of us mentioned the night before and my stubborn refusal to tell her more, but as I put on my shoulder holster and badge, I wondered if Rowan's departure was a sign she'd had it, that my Berlin Wall had finally proved too much for her. I can't blame Rowan. My wall is as fierce and protective as Rowan's love and I can't imagine it ever coming down.

Now, though, my chest tightens, sharp and painful, at the thought of Rowan leaving me for good.

Davis shuts off the recording. "This group is local to Willow's Ridge?"

"A branch of it. One True Path is a global ex-gay organization."

"Ex-gay?" Davis rubs at his furrowed brow. "What the hell does that mean?"

Ainsley chuckles beside me. Conservatism wafts off him like the smell of shit in a nursing home.

"Ex-gay. Meaning a person was once a practicing homosexual and is no longer," I say. "The One True Path organization preaches that homosexuality is not something people are born with but a learned behavior that happens because of a childhood trauma. They promise with their training and God, a person can heal from homosexuality."

"Hansen." Davis looks out at me through his steepled fingertips. Beside me, Ainsley scoffs. "Don't tell me we're going to piss off the church in this investigation. Please."

I pull out my notes from the interview with Weaver and the paper he gave me. I can't help but chuckle. "Weaver claims everyone and their brothers have denounced the ex-gay ministries."

Davis shakes his head at me. "Come again?"

"This is not really a church thing," I explain. "Look, all the major religions, the American Psychological Association, and lots of other medical affiliations have said that these groups are harmful and have no merit. Many different denominations of the church have as well."

"And you're also telling me we have our own branch of this ex-gay thing here in Willow's Ridge. Some of the churchgoing folks in this community must support it or it wouldn't be here." Davis leans back in his seat and crosses his hands behind his head. "Why don't more people know about this One True Path thing here in Willow's Ridge?"

"They meet in the pastor's basement. It's not like the group is out waving signs to raise money with a carwash or candy-bar drive," I say. "It's hidden."

"Like a cult?" Davis groans. "Hell, this case keeps getting bigger and bigger, a snowball rolling downhill. And we got nothing."

"We got Sambino," Ainsley says.

Davis turns to Ainsley. "What's the connection between Sambino and this religious group?"

"I bet he's gay." Ainsley looks directly at me, his eyes trained to take in my reaction. "I know the Tucker girl was supposed to be at one of those religious meetings at the time of her murder."

"Let's not piss off the church in our efforts to get Picasso, okay?" Davis drops his head into his hands, rubbing above his ears. "The entire state is watching us. It's a hell of a lot bigger than that now—we got the BCI sitting here and media from across the nation." Davis's cheeks are pink, but the rest of his face has lost color. He looks as though he hasn't slept in a week. "We can't afford any screwups. Do you know what the press called the city of Boulder during the Ramsey case? A task *farce*." Davis drums his fingertips on the table as he speaks. "We cannot be task farce number two."

I bite back a snicker.

"I say we lean even harder on Sambino," Ainsley says. "Lean until he breaks."

"It's not Sambino."

"Come on, Hansen!" Ainsley stands up and steps toward me. "Are you really going to sit there and tell me it's not Sambino after your interview with Weaver? Even you acknowledge the obvious tie between the crosses left with the bodies and Sambino's whole fascination with the…whatever the hell it is." Ainsley's hands wave in front of my face, sketching the shape of the ankh. "Why the fuck else would everything point to him?"

I shake my head and ignore his drama. "He's not our killer. Yes, the tie with the crosses is significant, and I'm guessing that Sambino does know something that could help us. We're up against some sort of hate crime. Tell me this, Ainsley. What's Sambino's motive to kill young lesbians?"

"Hell, he hates lesbians." Ainsley nears a yell. "Maybe his mom was one. Or his first lover turned out to be a dyke. Come on, Hansen. You know how it goes with these guys!"

"It's not him, Ainsley." I whisper these words. Still, Ainsley storms off, slamming the door behind him so hard the glass partition rattles. Davis and I sit in silence for a few moments while Ainsley's emotional eruption still vibrates within the room.

"He's volatile," Davis finally says, as if this alone explains Ainsley's disrespect. "But he's one of the best cops I know. We need him." Davis waits a few beats as though he's searching for the right words to say. "Hansen, you've been through a lot on this trip down memory lane. I'll interview the Jamesons about these ex-gay meetings."

"They don't know you." I lean forward, my fist against the conference table to prove my point. "He'll feed you a bunch of lies and half-truths about the organization. I've been in this world, remember? I'll call his bullshit."

Davis stands up and looks out the office window. The snow has started to fall again, light and airy flakes floating in the blistering cold. "It's too risky," he says. "You have an emotional connection."

"I can control it, Davis! I know I can."

He turns to me. His look is long and hard. "We both know I could dismiss you from the case right now for cause and call in for a replacement. You're a good agent, Hansen. Don't make me regret my decision."

I'm not willing to give up so easily. "Jameson will not talk to outsiders."

"You *are* an outsider. A failure of the program! What makes you think he'll speak to you?"

I put my hands up and flutter my fingers in the quote sign. "God's masterpieces are always in progress." I go to Davis's side at the large window. "He believes that there will always be a chance to save me and that I can decide to quit the homosexual addiction and find the heterosexual way with God. As long as I'm in Jameson's presence, he'll believe that God will change my heart. I've heard him say it a million times. I've watched many members leave and come back."

Davis takes a deep breath that says I'm wearing him down. "What's your plan?"

"That I've come back to Willow's Ridge to get straight and I cannot do it without his help. My gut's screaming that these meetings are key, Davis. I have to become one of them again."

"What about your job? And the murders?" Davis says. "Won't he question whether you're only there to get information?"

"Not if I play the part. Not if I say the right things."

"Dammit, Hansen"—Davis shakes his head—"there's no way we're going to solve this case without pissing off the church." A smirk crosses his lips, though, and the edges of his eyes soften.

He's in.

❖

I'd learned a lot about Charles Jameson's ministry in Willow's Ridge over the years, and I'd heard some of the stories from the pastor himself at meetings. His church wasn't always affiliated with the One True Path Global Ministries. At first it had only been a small meeting among friends to worship God. Charles always had the gift to lead and it eventually brought him to the art of preaching. He'd spent his entire life in the pews of the Evangelical church, he liked to point out, and who says you need a degree to speak the word of the Lord? He liked to remind anyone who would listen that Jesus did not have any sort of higher degree other than the hard knocks of life. Charles, too, believed that he was well acquainted with life's hard knocks.

The group met three nights a week, and Charles would preach for hours on the damnation that surrounded us all, peppered with Bible study that would make the most conservative of Christians seem liberal. His wife, Mildred, sat faithfully nearby to shout her amens, and his only child, Chaz, learned to sit still and not cry during the services that could last upward of three long hours. Both Mildred and Charles took to spreading the Lord's word and news of their church door-to-door. Sometimes Chaz went on these recruitment ventures, and the success of the fledgling church became a family endeavor.

In the early 1980s, Charles Jameson began his branch of the One True Path ministry for many of the same reasons other ex-gay ministries cropped up across the United States. Parents all over the nation faced a dilemma they never expected: little Johnny or precious Mary came out of the closet. Under the guise of a sleepover with a church friend, Chaz Jameson was caught kissing another young man. Under intense interrogation, Chaz admitted to his parents that he might be gay. Pastor Jameson couldn't stand to hear another word. *Homosexual?* His Chaz? An abomination of the Lord? It simply couldn't be. He and his wife had raised Chaz to fear the almighty Lord. Now Chaz sprinted into the wide-open arms of the devil.

Afflicted with distress over his son's condition, the pastor withdrew into a locked bedroom for three solid nights and days of fervent prayer. *Lord, what to do? Why my son?* Mildred and Chaz waited and prayed on the other side of that closed bedroom door for God's message to come to Charles. They didn't eat or sleep. Their fervent prayers became louder and louder and louder.

Finally it happened. Angels delivered. The idea of a Willow's Ridge One True Path ministry came to Charles, he claimed, in a vivid and life-changing vision. God's command was to build the small group of men and women of all ages who had strayed into homosexuality. Jameson would help those the Lord led to him find the one true path to

God. Hadn't this sort of thing been what the pastor had been preaching about for years? The devil in their midst? The one in sheep's clothing who had been slinking around his house for so long? The pastor declared war with that devil. He would save his son from the fiery pit of hell.

In those early years, Jameson built his ministry around fundamentalist Baptist teachings. He also adopted the model of heterosexuality boot camps or prayer retreats, which had sprouted up across the country. Every member of his group was required to attend three retreat weekends and one boot camp a year at Camp Jesus in the Hills. Jameson preached that a homosexual could be rewired into God's vision—heterosexuality. With enough prayer and devotion, Pastor Jameson promised that God could turn anyone straight. *Pray the gay away* might have been coined for the Jamesons, but it wasn't only prayer that the Jamesons used. There were conversion therapy sessions where the participants were trained to feel revulsion toward same-sex images and to desire the appropriate genitalia. The Jamesons would not permit their son to be gay. Many other parents across the country felt the same way, including my own father.

I learned later that it wasn't so much that my dad would not allow me to be gay, as the guilty conscience he carried over raising his daughter without a mother. When he learned about my tendencies, as he called my attraction to other girls, he immediately blamed himself. My dad was a chiseled hunk of a man who fit all the gender stereotypes. He once told me that it was his fault I didn't know how a woman was supposed to act. Soon a string of women appeared: wives of cops, a few daughters, ladies from a local church. These visits were staged, even the ones from Nora, a woman I could tell my dad was sweet on, who gave me a weekly cooking lesson. Nora was fun for a while, and I loved that we felt like a family, but her relationship with my dad didn't last long.

By the time my dad heard of Jameson, he'd gained quite a reputation as a healer and my father desperately wanted me to be healed. Talking to a pastor who dealt with these issues seemed logical to my dad. With the power of God, the righteousness of God, Jameson could turn the sinner back to heterosexuality, and, therefore back to God. This was exactly what my father hoped would happen for me. In his mind, what could possibly be damaging about sending your kid to a religious counseling group?

It was in this savior, Pastor Jameson, that my father placed all his hope. My dad wanted nothing more than for his daughter to be healthy, normal, and straight. So I made the trek for support and fellowship, always under the guise of a weekly visit with a made-up cousin. Everyone, including me, believed all the prayer and education was working. We all heartily believed in my miraculous change. We all believed, until I met Marci.

❖

The Jamesons' canary-yellow ranch-style home on Acorn Lane looks smaller than I remember, the shutters now worn to a muddy brown. Everything else is the same, though: window boxes frozen but waiting to be planted in the spring, a manicured yard with a house address box that glows in the dark, and one enormous maple tree that engulfs the front yard. I'm willing to bet money that a fat welcome mat still rests outside the front door. Although the near-sheer curtains are drawn, shadows move around in the cramped but warm kitchen.

I suddenly rage with a desire to stomp up and bang the butt of my pistol on the front door. I want to show the Jamesons my new ring from Rowan with the infinity engraving. I want to tell them that despite their teachings, I *have* found love. I *have* found salvation. With another woman.

Or have I? I question how much longer Rowan will stay if I can't break down my Berlin Wall. Am I really happy? I shift gears into park and pop each of my knuckles, like firecrackers inside the silent, cold car. My mind races with what it will be like to face the Jamesons after Marci's death. One look in the rearview mirror reminds me that I did insist on this meeting. Captain Davis and one of the technical officers are in the unmarked van not far down the neighborhood street, gearing up the recording equipment, while Ainsley has gone to follow up on the graveyard recordings.

Mildred Jameson steps out the front door for the newspaper on the stoop. Although she looks smaller and her hair has grayed to a near white, she hasn't lost her slim, dainty figure. Mildred, I remember, was quite a few years younger than her husband and their relationship was scandalous at one time in their religious community. I doubt many had my scandal with Marci trumped—two star-crossed lovers using the support group that was supposed to make us all straight as a way to see one another, to touch and sneak off to steal kisses and sock away moments of passion that would only fuel our desire until our next meeting. We'd made a farce of their meetings, Marci and I, and a public spectacle of One True Path after Marci's death.

No, I figure shutting off the car, the Jamesons won't be happy to see me. As far as they're concerned, I've already pitched a tent with Marci in Lucifer's neighborhood. If the Jamesons truly believed what they preached, however, Lucifer could always be denied with the organization's help.

My hands tremor as I adjust the tiny camera and microphone. Everything is embedded inside a miniature Christian cross pin that's been attached to my scarf. Somewhere on the other end Davis waits for me to do something. When I finally gather the courage to open the car door, the good Mildred Jameson looks up with the paper in hand. Her eyes squint as she strips away the years from me.

"Lucinda!" she calls out. "You've finally come home."

CHAPTER THIRTEEN

I hold the steaming cup of tea between my palms balanced on my knee, thawing out my winter-chapped hands. I sit across from the Jamesons. We're hardly three feet apart, and with nothing between us but our feet, Charles and Mildred have managed to take from me all of the natural barricades. The what-ifs barrage my mind. What if they realize I'm not being truthful? What if I blow the case because I lose control of the interview? What if I get kicked off the case?

Breathe, I remind myself. *Just breathe.*

A tall wood-heavy grandfather clock tick-tocks so loud it's almost deafening in our silence. The living room's completely composed of worn tans and taupe. Years of sun and foot traffic have blanched the brown carpet a dirty khaki. From where I sit, I can see the door that leads to the basement and that locked basement door I remember so well.

My first One True Path meeting. We stood in a circle and the two guys on each side of me took my hands in theirs.

"Don't worry, you'll be safe tonight," Chaz said. "This is how we begin each meeting after opening prayer."

I'd expected the prayer, but what was going on here? What did he mean by safe? Somewhere at the top of the basement staircase the door slammed closed. Soon after, I heard the soft click and firm switch of the lock.

Pastor Jameson stood in the center of our circle. "What is said in the circle stays in the circle and with the Almighty. Agreed?"

I nodded along with everyone else, the movements short and quick. I felt anxious, on the edge of something huge, something dangerous.

"Okay, then. Simon, let's start with you. What do you have to confess this week?"

Simon stood across the circle from me. His head dropped to his chest when his name was called. He said nothing.

"Simon? What sins are weighing on your heart?" The pastor stood directly in front of Simon.

"Nothing has happened this week, sir."

"Simon, please. Let's show Lucinda exactly how this is done."

Silence filled the basement. I only heard my harsh, ragged breaths in the circle of eight people. Finally, Simon spoke. "Well, there is a guy at school."

"Yes," the pastor said. "Confess now."

"I notice him a lot. He's in my algebra class and always dresses in button-down shirts."

"And you've thought of him, right? In *that* way?"

Simon nodded.

"Even our thoughts and desires of homosexual sex are sins. They must be confessed so God can forgive us. Simon, tell us now. What did you fantasize about with this boy?"

"Pastor!" Simon's voice cracked as he pleaded. We all waited in silence until the quiet grew so heavy it was nearly unbearable.

Simon's resolve broke and he choked out a painful sob. "His hair, okay? It's his dark thick hair that I think about. I wonder what it would be like to touch it, to put my fingers in it. I wonder if another boy ever touched his hair like that." Simon choked back a sob. "And I wonder where else on his body he has hair. Pastor Jameson," he pleaded through his tears, "I wouldn't do anything. I've changed."

"Have you?" The pastor turned and faced all of us one at a time. Quickly I looked away, afraid for his beady stare to catch hold of mine. "What do you think, group? Has Simon changed?"

One by one, we each whispered our admittance that Simon had not changed. He watched each one of us fall from his side that day, his eyes following each of us until no one in the circle was standing up for him. Simon's eyes shone bright with tears of utter abandonment.

"Homosexuality is a disease," the pastor said. "Remember that you are weak against it without the Lord to take on this battle for you. Pray to Him in these moments of weakness. Simon, be honest with us and with God. Touching this boy's hair is not all you thought about. Speak."

Tears ran down Simon's cheeks now. "I swear, that's it."

"Simon, tell us how you imagined his penis in your hands. Tell us how you imagined that penis in your mouth!" The pastor yelled and spittle flew from his lips. "Tell us, Simon. Tell God!"

Simon choked and slobbered with sobs and snot. Beside me, Chaz silently cried. I wondered how many others in the circle were also crying. When I looked down at my own hands, I saw I was shaking and my teeth chattered despite the stuffy warmth of the pastor's basement.

I looked around at everyone's face in the circle. I thought about my dad and the shock victims he helped. Everyone but the pastor had that haunted, displaced look of trauma victims. I wanted out. I wanted to beat down that locked door at the top of the staircase. No matter how much my gut screamed for me to go, I stayed. I stood still.

Now, Mildred smiles at me. "You've let your hair grow."

"Yeah," I say, my hand immediately shooting up to finger-brush its length out below my shoulders.

"I like it so much better than the buzz cut you always had." Is her smile strained or am I imagining it? "The longer hair is so much more feminine on you."

My swallow of tea nearly chokes me. There are those pesky conservative gender roles again that these two can't seem to get past. Some things never change. My own smile is forced, nothing more than my lips pulled back to show my teeth. "How's Chaz?"

The pastor's clothing has the same worn look as the living room: a collared button-down shirt now yellowish rather than the original white, polyester gray pants that ride up his calf, and leather loafers so worn the creases across the top have cracked. He clears his throat. "He's doing well. He's now part of our One True Path outreach that goes into high schools all over Ohio and provides help for teens suffering from homosexuality. We need to get them while they're young."

"You haven't seen our newest little angel." Mildred walks across the room to get the framed photographs beside a well-worn Bible that's been in that exact location since I'd been coming to meetings at this house. "We just don't know what we'd do without our Sophie and our latest addition, Lauren."

The photographs depict what appears to be the all-American family: a handsome, athletic father (with a little less hair than I remember), a subdued mother, and two smiling, happy-looking little girls. It's the mother I focus on. I know this woman. It takes me a few seconds to place her. She'd been an active member of the One True Path meetings when I was there. Maureen! If Chaz had to marry a woman, why not a lesbian? At least they could reach an understanding that they would be roommates and not lovers.

"Beautiful girls. How old?"

Mildred beams. "Sophie is almost ten and Lauren is…how old?"

"Five, I think." The pastor notices my questioning look. "Both girls were adopted. They just got Lauren a few months ago."

Adoption. The family makes perfect sense to me now.

In the pastor's arsenal of proof that his ministry is the real deal, Chaz became their shining star. Like some sort of circus sideshow, he was touted as evidence that homosexuals can become straight. Through Jameson's prayers, the One True Path meetings, and interventions with conversion therapists and other men of the cloth, Chaz was supposedly healed. He became the ultimate image of the organization: heterosexuality through the worship of God.

Chaz and I had a special connection, a link neither of us could put into words. It wasn't only that we were a week apart in age, but something stronger, something that allowed us to sit in silence together and not be uncomfortable. He suffered tremendously, like the rest of us. Chaz had always been anxiously quiet and the pressure-filled interventions and weeks away from home at heterosexual boot camps terrified him. He wanted nothing more than to please his parents. I remember once, maybe at my third or fourth meeting, Chaz told me that as only children we had the weight of our families placed on our shoulders. My weight, though, wasn't nearly as heavy as Chaz's.

Once, at a retreat when Chaz and I found ourselves alone for a few minutes, I asked him what the conversion sessions were like.

"You really want to know?" He stared down at his hands, the nails bitten to the quick. "You asked for it." In the next few minutes of Chaz's narrative, I'm certain my jaw hit the table multiple times. First, the doctor would talk with Chaz to assess how many homosexual urges he'd had over the past week. Chaz was expected to keep a journal and write down every possible thought that could be linked to same-sex attraction. Then they would move on to the aversion portion of the therapy. Chaz was hooked up to a small apparatus that produced a strong electrical shock. In the beginning, it was only placed on his hands, but when it seemed this method wasn't working, the doctors hooked the machine up to Chaz's penis. Chaz would look at gay porn and with each sexy picture a shock would be delivered to his hand and penis. Sometimes, Chaz told me, the machine would leave burns on his skin that later scarred. Then heterosexual porn was shown to Chaz and no shocks were delivered. The machine was removed and he was given a cooling ointment to heal the wounds. Other times, Chaz was given a drug that made him vomit while he looked at gay porn.

Chaz and I both cried as he detailed these hellish weekly sessions until he could say no more and wound up sobbing in my arms.

Mildred clears her throat to get my attention. "You might not have heard. Chaz married Maureen almost ten years ago." She can't help but grin from ear to ear.

"She's a good girl," the pastor says. "We're lucky to have her as part of the family."

I think about the way both Chaz and I became so deft at sneaking past our parents to visit our lovers. Certainly his marriage is nothing more than a façade with a man or two waiting in the shadows. He can't have changed that much since we last saw each other.

"I hope you'll get the chance to say hello to them yourself before you leave Willow's Ridge," Pastor Jameson says. "I'm happy to see you've finally made it back to us. I've been praying for you, Lucinda. All of us have. It's taken some time, but somehow, some way, we all make our journey back to the arms of God."

"Yes, Pastor, I suppose that's true."

"Confess to us, Luce. Have you engaged in homosexual activity since we last met?"

My left hip feels the persistent pressure of Rowan's ring, lodged within my pants pocket. The hard silver is a comfort. In her own way, Rowan is with me and gives me strength. "I have, sir. I've also realized the error of my ways."

"That's good," Jameson says. "I want to remind you of Proverbs 3:5. *Trust in the Lord with all thine heart.*" He leaned forward, pointing his finger at me. "Let's not misread this second part, Lucinda. *And lean not unto thine own understanding.*" Over the years, deep lines have sunk around Pastor Jameson's mouth and a fold of skin hangs under his chin. It looks as though Jameson's face has fallen, that the skin has merely given out. "You hear me, Luce? Don't trust your stinkin' thinkin' on this one! Only trust Him." Jameson points toward the ceiling.

He still has the piercing dark eyes that I remember, a look that can drill out a confession from the hardest of criminals. His eyeglass lenses have become thicker, only magnifying those daunting eyes, but the frames are large and rimless now. He still has a short spread of gray hair, maybe a bit thinner than I remember, but not much, and fuller cheeks that are always flushed. Age has a way of always shocking me; it sneaks up when I'm not looking, as though we all stay the same, our looks frozen in time. While I hope that has been the case for me, it hasn't for the man before me.

"Just when it seems despair will swallow us whole, Lucinda, God provides. He gives us a solution. Let's not forget the next verse: *In all thy ways acknowledge Him, and He shall direct thy paths.*"

Although Jameson's face has aged significantly, his body certainly hasn't. He's always been tall, over six foot, and he's lost none of his muscle mass. He may be in his late sixties, but the pastor's been lifting and working out. From the looks of him, every day.

"Amen," I say. "Like you always said, Pastor, there aren't any mistakes with God at your side."

"He's brought you here for a reason."

"Hallelujah!" In her joy, Mildred reaches for my hand. "We no longer meet in our basement. We have a space out on Simmons Road."

"If you remember," Jameson says, "I'm an accountant by trade. Chaz and I went into business together once he graduated. We are a growing business and growing ministry. So many calls and visitors. We needed a bigger meeting area." He pauses to give me a smile. "God sure has blessed us."

Or Satan has. I almost laugh out loud at my own knee-jerk reaction. I chew the inside of my lip to stop the grin. I've always hated how he can give any response with that canned smile. When I was younger, I imagined him sending people to hell with that same blank smile.

"We have about thirty members now," Mildred continues. "Since you left us, we've added a licensed therapist who donates his time."

"Wow, thirty members," I say, shifting in my seat. There had only been about nine or ten of us when I attended.

"You're one who could benefit from therapy with Dr. Goldson."

"Conversion therapy, I assume?" I set my cup on the floor. "Certainly you must be aware that there's been a lot of controversy over those practices."

"I hope that I am correct, Lucinda, in my assumption that you are now ready to receive the Lord's help in changing your ways." Jameson glowers at me over his lenses, the same aggressive look he uses to scare all newcomers into admissions of guilt.

Lucinda. The name my father always called me. For a quick

moment, tears burn the corners of my eyes at the thought of Dad. I wonder what he would have thought of me sitting before Pastor Jameson again. Hopeful of me changing? Horrified? Both? Blinking the wetness away, I don't answer for a few moments, sipping my tea to give me a reason to stall. My gut screams out that I'll lose Jameson if I only confront him as law enforcement. *Put your feelings aside. Do your job.*

"I am one hundred percent committed to making the change at this point in my life," I say. "I was only sixteen back then. I just needed some time to find my way back."

"It certainly wasn't *all* your fault," Mildred says. "Your father didn't help matters any by pulling you out of the group as soon as Marci died."

My stomach clenches at the mention of my father. "He lost hope after that," I say. "Maybe I did, too."

"I heard about your father's passing," Jameson says. "I'm so sorry. Take comfort in the knowledge that he'd celebrate the fact that you've come back to us."

My father, the burly man who came to the rescue and kept people safe. Would he now see this so-called pastor in front of me as a sort of fellow rescuer? I don't think so, but as I sit here in this room with the Jamesons and relive history, my focus has altered and blurred. It's like looking through a kaleidoscope and attempting to recognize the shifting shapes.

"We still meet on Sunday, Tuesday, and Thursday nights, so we'll see you tomorrow." Mildred stands. "Let me get you directions to the new place."

It's time. I have to tell them. Most likely they've already seen my name in the newspaper or on newscasts associated with the biggest case Willow's Ridge has ever seen. If I don't disclose my affiliation, it could jeopardize any future criminal cases against the organization. "Actually, my visit is for two reasons."

I pull my ID from the satchel at my feet, hoping my honesty will gain their confidence. Jameson reaches across the space between us to take the badge from my hand.

"I am one of the investigators working on the recent murders here in Willow's Ridge." I spread my knees wide and lean forward, my elbows resting on my knees, ready for anything. "Pastor, I'm trusting Him now." I point to the ceiling. "God has a plan for me. I will be at the meeting tomorrow night and I'm excited to change. These murders, though," I say, "affect us all. Any information you could provide would be invaluable." I end my words with my own fake, sweet smile.

The pastor runs his fingertips over the ridges and valleys of my badge as though he's reading braille. His shallow breath tells me that he's known my position all along. "I'm happy to see you've grown so much professionally, Lucinda, but no one can nourish their soul without also fearing the heavenly father." He hands back the badge. His cold, chapped fingers brush against mine like dead fallen leaves that collect under barren trees in October.

I've disappointed him. For a moment I'm back in my sixteen-year-old body, back to cowering before the pastor spewing his threats of hell and the devil. The waterline rises first to my chin, then my nose. The distinct odor of chlorine fills the room. The pastor's eyes are still locked on mine. Underneath his glare, I'm torn. While there is a part of me that wants to curse him, hit him, and scream out the anger and pain he's caused me, there's also the part that nags, *What if he's right? What if there is a vengeful God who will roast me over a pit of fire for eternity? Maybe my father would be happy I'm back.* As quickly as these thoughts fill my head, a feeling of horror washes over me. I thought I was past all these questions. I thought I'd moved on. Haven't I?

In order to break the staring contest with the pastor, I twist in the chair and my left hand catches the edge of the side table. Its sharp, quick gouge yanks me back to the plan and to the words Davis left me with as I was getting wired: *Follow the evidence, not your emotions.*

"God's masterpieces are always in progress. Isn't that what you both always told us?" I watch Jameson's expression, the eyes not softening, but the mouth curving slightly at the corners in a suppressed smile.

"Lucinda"—Mildred sets her teacup down and crosses one ankle over the other—"what would ever make you think One True Path has anything to do with these horrible crimes?"

"We have information that some of our suspects and victims might have been members at one time or another."

When neither the pastor nor his wife reacts, I name names, taking liberties with my hunches. "Vivian Hannerting." There's no response from either Jameson.

"Nick Sambino." There's a quick flicker of recognition in the pastor's eyes. Mildred looks to her husband to see how to respond.

"Chandler Jones." His eyes are hooded while he looks to the floor. Her knee begins to ever so slightly bounce up and down.

"Emma Parks." The pastor shifts in his seat.

Jameson finally speaks. "As you know, Lucinda, everything said here is confidential." He's almost whispering. "I am clergy and I take everyone's confessions to the grave. Even yours."

"The clergy-penitent privilege, even if it does apply, doesn't extend to the mere fact of attendance at your meetings, Pastor."

Mildred suddenly moans, her silvery hair shining with a purplish hue in the overhead lights. "These murders are just awful. We've been praying night and day for those victims' families." She softly nudges her husband with her elbow. "Tell her, Charles." She turns back to me. "We all want these murders stopped."

I've never had much of an opinion about Mildred. *Nice* would be a word I would use for her, completely nondescript. She's one of those people so plain you forget what she looks like unless she's facing you. I always saw her as the flit of a wife who took care of drinks and snacks while asserting a loud amen to the pastor's prayers. I realize now that she's been subservient to her husband in the roles of the cook, the maid, and the voice of agreement no matter what. Her suggestion to confirm or deny membership in the group catches me by surprise. She's found her voice. It's weak, but it's now evident.

Surprise registers in Pastor Jameson's eyes as well. He's caught off guard and in that fluster, he complies. "Parks attended a retreat we had last summer at Camp Jesus in the Hills. She was not a regular participant after that."

"How long was she a member?"

"Two months? Three?"

So Parks had been the rebel. She'd been the one who didn't believe the rhetoric. I try to catch Jameson's gaze with my own. He refuses, only staring at the arm of the chair. "Jones was a current member. She had been linked to the ministry through her Baptist church."

Mildred says, "We thought that fellow from the funeral home might be wrapped up in witchcraft from the way he looked." She shakes her head. "But we take everyone in. If only he'd held on a bit longer in our program. My willingness to let him go so easily might be one of my biggest regrets."

Mildred's sentiment regarding Sambino is exactly what most of the community believes: he looks like a devil worshipper; therefore he's committed all the murders at Willow's Ridge. If I'm to thank God for anything in this colossal mess of a case, it's that the community isn't trying Nick Sambino, or he'd be sentenced and hanged without any evidence.

"We've investigated Mr. Sambino, yes. We're also looking into other leads. Because these could be hate crimes against homosexual women, we believe that the killer may be conflicted over his own sexuality. He may seek out groups like yours for support. Do you have any newcomers or people that leave and then return to the group over and over again?"

Jameson's eyebrows knit together. His round face reddens. "It's the nature of sin. Sometimes it takes people years to realize our group is the only way to salvation." His beady eyes drill into my own, his comment clearly meant for me.

I ignore his accusatory gaze. "We're looking for someone who's really struggling. He would have left and returned to the group a few different times since you first met him. Sometimes he would be fanatical in his beliefs and other times doubting the group's message."

"We've had a few new ones in the last six months or so. But those people either joined and found God with us or left and didn't return." The pastor smooths down his paper-thin comb-over with the palm of his hand. "Some of our members travel quite a distance to get to the weekly meetings. We've had a few who were driving in from Indianapolis. Most of the calls we get from out-of-state people, though, never follow through and join us."

"Maybe someone who's been completely compliant with the program without offering any resistance?"

"Lucinda." Jameson puts on his stern preacher's voice. "Any sexual activity, even thoughts of it, outside the bonds of marriage is a sin. But homosexual sex…" He shakes his head at me. "I shouldn't have to remind you how evil that is. Anyone who's compliant with the program is smart. Resistance only adds to relapse, as you well know."

The dam breaks. Anger rises up my chest and throat, burns my cheeks with rage. I feel the skin of my neck burst with the red rash that always accompanies it. God, I want nothing more than to shove this man's rhetoric up his tight homophobic white ass. But he has me over a barrel. If I want the information, I need to hold my temper.

Charles Jameson shakes his fist as he speaks. "Any amount of sin, even only doing it a few times, is enough to turn God away. So, yes, to answer your question, we have *many* members who are very conflicted over their feelings. That's why we pray and hold confessions. I'm in the business of saving souls, not killing them."

I seethe in silence, struggling to keep my anger in check. I imagine Davis listening in with a rant of curses at my emotional reactions. What a pathetic joke life has thrown at me. I'm reminded of a line I heard a few weeks ago: Want to hear God laugh? Tell him all your dreams.

Perhaps I've been wrong to think I could harness my anger toward these people for the sake of the case. The weight of my past may simply be too much. I hate to admit when I'm wrong, but maybe it's time for me to throw in the towel. Director Sanders could turn the case over to another agent, one more qualified than me, and I'd have to take whatever retribution comes my way—desk duty for a month or so, or worse, filing all the cold cases. Then there is that strong, persistent voice I hear inside me, though, the hard silver of Rowan's ring: *Give it one more shot. For Marci.*

I take a deep breath and return to the line of questioning. "What about a volunteer? Some sort of supporter?" I ask. "Do you have anyone who's not a member of the ministry but volunteers time or money?"

"Cole." Mildred speaks up before her husband can stop her. "Cole Ainsley. He volunteers many hours to us. God bless him."

I almost choke on my now-cold tea with a fit of coughs. *Ainsley?* "The detective from the Willow's Ridge force?" Mildred agrees, but Jameson is silent, his face a blank. "How long has he worked with One True Path?"

Mildred shrugs. "The last seven or eight years, I guess. Really, Lucinda, Cole has been a huge blessing to us, such a help." She turns to her husband. "Sometimes I don't know how we would survive without him."

Interesting that Cole Ainsley has not told me about his involvement with the organization, particularly since the group had been the topic of our conversation with Davis. Is this the reason Ainsley is off on another lead instead of with Davis listening in? "How so?"

"He screens all of the phone messages and e-mails we receive. Sometimes people are not honest in them, and we get the occasional hate message. Yes," the pastor grudgingly says, "we too are sometimes the victims! We need to reach those who are aching, and the Internet is the method of communication for this generation."

Mildred adds, obviously excited, "We even have a Facebook page."

"Yes." Charles barks out a laugh, hard and long and much too loud. He catches himself, then brings us back to the topic. "Cole sifts through all these messages and contacts people who are legitimately seeking membership in our community," Charles says. "Many times, he meets with them to explain how we work and does an initial interview."

"He gets those names and numbers before you do?" I'm so far on the edge of my seat I almost fall out of my chair. "Ainsley actually meets the potential member *before* you? Alone?"

Mildred nods. "You'd never imagine how much work it takes to prepare the meetings and keep our own business going. Cole's great on the telephone and meeting these people who are so conflicted and seeking change. He's a real people person."

My own initial reaction to Detective Ainsley was similar until I caught the moody side of him. There were times when I thought of him as a surrogate father figure. Loving and kind. Even protective. Any newcomer to One True Path, with all the nervous energy that goes along with it, would be drawn to that same type of personality.

"Do you keep a record of the people Ainsley has worked with?" At first it confused me that neither the pastor nor Mildred reacted to Vivian Hannerting's name. It's entirely possible, though, that he and his wife never met her. Perhaps Vivian called the organization seeking help, then Ainsley met with her without their knowledge and eventually killed her. Is this why Ainsley has been thwarting my efforts, making every attempt to throw me off my game? Could *he* be involved in the crimes?

CHAPTER FOURTEEN

E ven though I remind myself to brace for the cold air, the initial blast of icy wind shocks me, like one hundred bee stings to exposed skin. My bomber hat isn't much of a match for the frigid weather. Eventually, as I make my way deeper into the frozen Willow's Ridge foliage, the pain of the wind chill subsides into numbness, anesthetizing my gut full of hot, raging anger.

I left the Jamesons' home after planning to attend their group meeting tomorrow evening, only to find Davis radioing me in the unmarked car to head immediately back to the station. I assumed it was about the connection Ainsley had to One True Path.

A technician pulls the wires free from my chest and tape rips away from my body. I rub the raw skin and wait for the technician to close the door behind him. "How are we going to handle this information about Ainsley?" I ask.

"Ainsley?"

"He had access to these women before they came to the group."

Davis shook his head. "Didn't you hear what they said? Sambino attended for a time. If I recall, Mildred Jameson said—What? It was a mistake that they let him go so easily? It's not Ainsley."

"Why keep it a secret when we started to look at them? Why not tell us and offer to talk to the Jamesons himself?"

"He told me in private he's been working with the group." Davis dismisses the theory with a flippant wave of the hand. He sits with a hip down on his desk, one leg swinging, the other anchoring him. "The profile's right, don't you see? We got Sambino."

"Except Sambino isn't an artist. He embalms dead people. How do you explain the artistic element to these scenes?"

Davis shrugs. "Eldridge called Sambino an artist with his makeup, remember? He also hung around a photo shop. Maybe he dabbles in the arts. His interest in attending college to study religion explains the crosses found with the bodies. He might have killed these women because they were gay."

My mind reels. I run my fingers through my hair and rub the back of my neck. I try to take a deep breath. Why is Davis unwilling to at least look into Ainsley? "We should hold off on Sambino until we have something more."

Davis stands up. "You're too close to this case, Hansen. You only see the trees, not the forest." I recognize the warning in his voice. Davis stares at me long and hard. "Back off Ainsley. Whatever kind of pissing contest the two of you have going, end it. Now." He points at me as though I'm being scolded. "Or I'll call Director Sanders and request your replacement."

"Yes, sir."

"We move on Sambino."

❖

At first, I'm not sure I've taken the right path to Stonehenge, the forest and snow occluding what I'd known by heart so many years ago. It's been so long, and the trees and snow meld together into a fuzziness that doesn't help. I push on, just a little farther, my boot steps stomping down snow and frozen leaves with the occasional snaps of branches. Just as I'm about to give up, I see the boulder, a hunk of rock shaped like an arrow, the place known as the Staircase. Sheets of limestone had settled in a stair-step fashion down part of the ravine. It was the most photographed location in the limestone quarry. Circling around the point of the boulder, I head down along the path, catching myself with the occasional slip on the frozen earth until I reach the point that takes my breath away every time: God's View.

It's a mystery how Marci found Stonehenge. What lies below God's View seems to be only a maze of trees and rock, not a refuge for a teenage girl. Between the forest and the steady downward slope, I focus intently on my footing. Marci, I knew, had been visiting Stonehenge long before we met. She needed to get away from her parents' watch; she said they never let up, eyeing her every move. Marci had come to Stonehenge to write in her journal, to think about her life and future, and then left those thoughts tucked away behind a stone in the back of the cave. It was the only place her parents didn't know to look. She'd shown me the journal a few times, even a page with a scribbled *I heart Luce* surrounded by squiggles of color and hearts and our initials: *M.T. + L.H.* The police eventually found the journal after Marci died, its pages edged with moisture, ink, and earthen stains.

The path turns from hardened earth to limestone outside of Stonehenge, and I hold on to anything I can grab to steady myself. Stonehenge is only one of the many pocket-sized caves that climb above the ravine. Some caves run deeper and a few are long enough for minor caving expeditions. Stonehenge, though, has a small opening that gets larger the farther in you go. Its depth is a surprise. Most people don't delve deep enough to find what Marci had, a curve to the left at the back of the cave, making a space large enough for a few people to sit within the natural light that carries in from the opening. It's in this hidden back space of the cave that Marci and I fumbled through our love.

Stonehenge, the real monument in England, was built with an inner circle of rocks and an outer circle. *I'm a fan of circles*, Marci told me, *the never-ending symbol.* She even had a circular pattern of loops designed for a tattoo to enclose her wrist, which she planned to get when she turned eighteen. This cave reminded her of the sacred site she'd studied in school. She spent her summers exploring all the caves that pocked the walls of the ravine and found this one that was set apart from the others. For Marci, in many ways, her Stonehenge did become sacred—a place of quiet and reflection, a place for us to explore one another. Above all, Stonehenge became Marci's secret-keeper, so much that it even contained the mystery of her death.

Inside Stonehenge, I feel that same jolt of excitement in my stomach that I felt so many times when meeting Marci. Because I've heard so much about the softness of limestone, I expected the space to look different, to have changed with the years of weathering and erosion. The only difference I detect is the feeling that no one's been inside the hidden back chamber of the cave in quite some time. Cobwebs line the darker corners and I consider something I never did at age sixteen: bats. Thankfully, nothing flies out other than a pocket of warmer air. I've forgotten that the cave is a sort of refuge from the winter cold and the summer heat, the rocks equalizing the temperature. I sit down with my legs crossed in the back corner where I always sat with Marci.

I've been unsure what might erupt for me inside Stonehenge. This case has me feeling like a cauldron of different emotions that churn inside me. Stepping into this place of Marci, or over the place where I found her body, it's almost like asking for it. But my heart wouldn't ease until I went. To my surprise, I only feel a calming comfort and a sense of safety. It's like I've been holding my breath all this time, until this confrontation finally happened. Now I can breathe easy. Marci's presence beside me becomes palpable, reminiscing with me over the past.

Remember when we kissed for the first time, wads of bubblegum in our mouths that got in the way?

Remember when we would drive in the convertible with the top down, music blaring? I loved those times, singing to the radio at the top of our lungs. What was that song you loved so much? Some old Bon Jovi song?

Remember when we couldn't wait to get into the hidden safety of Stonehenge, almost on fire to touch each other?

Remember when the pastor pointed out we were getting awfully close and we needed to find opposite-gender folk for our socialization?

Remember how we couldn't keep our hands off one another, always tapping and tugging and tackling each other into a wrestled softness?

Suddenly, I realize with a start, I'm laughing and talking out loud, carrying on a lively conversation with only myself.

"Marci," I call out, my voice an echo against the stone. "Marci." That's when the tears come—silent rivers that feel like they might never end.

"I'm so sorry." Then in the next breath, "It should have been me."

The matter of timing, specifically my own, that hot August day, was something I couldn't forgive myself for. I'd been late meeting Marci at Stonehenge, as usual. This particular time, though, I was very late, at least forty minutes. I blamed it on the drive from Chesterton and the argument I'd had with my father about taking the car alone to Chesterton. He finally relented as long as I called him as soon as I arrived.

One True Path was to hold a four-hour revival that night, and I had been harassing my dad for permission to attend for days. This wasn't just my chance to see Marci, which always drove my desire to attend these meetings, but we were also meeting with two other groups from Ohio, all affiliated with the One True Path organization. Everyone would be under the age of twenty-five. I'd learned that while there were some sincerely trying to change in the program, there were many others like Marci and me who were only attending out of a duty to someone else and looking for others who felt the same way. Twisted, yes, but a way nonetheless to meet other young gays and lesbians.

There'd been a traffic jam on Interstate 70 that day, a car that had crossed the median and crashed head-on into a semi at full speed. I'd gotten to the mess at the tail end of the cleanup, the crews sweeping splintered glass and twisted metal from the roadways, and the car scrunched like a closed accordion on the shoulder of the road. Traffic was a slow crawl through the bottleneck, putting me even farther behind to meet Marci at Stonehenge. I'd been so excited that we would have almost two whole hours together before the meeting began.

"That was a long time ago," I say and reach over to the edge of the cave, where the wall and the floor of limestone meet. Rock fragments scatter the floor and I pick out a stone, a little larger than a quarter, pink around the edges with distinct white striations. I hold the cool rock in my gloved hands at my heart, close my eyes, and offer up a promise.

"With your help, I'll solve your murder, Marci. You are not forgotten."

After a few minutes, I tuck the stone inside my pocket, right next to my Marci rock. The weight of the stones is surprisingly light. There's a distinct shift in the fast-approaching night air, a slight settling, much like a gentle exhale.

❖

Davis made it clear that he didn't believe Ainsley had anything to do with the crimes, but that doesn't mean I'm not going to watch him extra-close. From the backseat, I'm angled so I can see Ainsley's every move. Davis's cruiser speeds through town, knocking Ainsley and me from side to side while the heater blasts on high. A bitter cold has set in with the darkness, a bone-crushing blister of wind. While I'd been MIA at Stonehenge, Davis used my interview with the Jamesons to obtain an arrest warrant for Sambino as well as a search warrant for his home and vehicle.

Inside the cruiser, no one speaks, but the excitement is palpable. Everyone gears up before an arrest in their own way. I pull into myself and tap into some sort of strength that's buried deep within. You can't predict how a suspect will react to the cuffs. Ainsley shows more anxiety than usual, wiping the lenses of his glasses with a handkerchief over and over while his left knee bounces up and down. Davis talks endlessly about how this arrest will be good for the case, as if he's trying to convince himself. Finally, we pull into the funeral home lot and block the employee door with the cruiser. Behind us, two more cruisers arrive.

Sambino's truck is parked in the lot next to the hearse. He would have clocked in for his shift just over an hour ago. Everything is quiet and still in the neighborhood, with only the barking of a lone dog in a nearby yard.

"Ready?" Davis calls out to us, then pushes through the funeral home door. A loud buzz sings our presence. This time, we don't wait for Chad Eldridge to make his way down the stairs from his living quarters. We snake through the building and descend the back staircase with pistols drawn.

The large work area for embalming and cleaning bodies stretches across the basement. There are the blinding lights against white floor tiles and walls, as well as the glaring shine of silver work tables. Formaldehyde burns the inside of my nostrils and the tip of my tongue the same way it does in the morgue. There, next to the table beside the large basin sink, is Nick Sambino dressed in scrubs and a paper gown that covers him from head to toe. He leans over the head of a body that's naked and stretched out on the work table. I don't need to see her face to recognize Emma Parks. It's the scrawl of the Y incision on her chest that I recognize, the paleness of her young skin. Sambino looks up wearing splashguard glasses that magnify his dark eyes to egg size. He's hard at work on Emma Parks's eyes, filling the sinking places around them with tiny shots of embalming fluid while the glue to keep the lids closed dries. Plastic surgery for the dead.

Sambino blinks his buggy eyes at us, a needle in hand. He's not wearing gloves. He's bothered to cover his entire body with protective material, but no latex gloves. Odd.

"Nicholas Sambino!" Ainsley's words belt across the basement, his trigger finger cocked and ready. "It's my pleasure to place you under arrest."

Just like that, we have Sambino. He doesn't argue; he doesn't protest. In the middle of Davis reading Sambino his rights, Eldridge emerges through the doorway. Although his hair is perfectly combed to the side, his cabled green sweater is too big and the tails of a white button-down hang below the end of the sweater. He rights his glasses and sidesteps Ainsley and me for Davis.

"You're arresting him?"

"Damn straight," Ainsley says. Together we push Sambino from behind up the staircase toward the employee exit.

"Do you have to arrest him here?" Eldridge says, his voice lilting up to a whine. "The media! We have services in the morning. The body isn't ready!" Eldridge's panic spikes.

"I have a warrant, Chad," Davis says. He stands on the outside doorstep and talks with Eldridge while their warm breath blows plumes of smoke into the night air.

Ainsley opens the back door of a cruiser and smacks Sambino's head against the hood of the car. "Oops, watch your head." Two patrol officers snicker until it's time for them to take Sambino back for booking. Davis, Ainsley, and I will join the other detectives and the crime-scene team to search Sambino's home. A tow will arrive at the funeral home within the hour to take Sambino's personal vehicle.

"Don't worry, Sambino. I'll mail you a skirt!" Ainsley calls out, the swirling emergency lights of the car flooding his amused face in blue, his white mustache an edge to a toothy smirk.

❖

Somehow the department managed to keep Sambino's impending arrest quiet, a rarity with so many members of the media swarming throughout this small town. We've managed to get to his apartment before the camera crews have arrived, with only a few collected gawkers from the complex. Soon the crowd will grow, with media bringing the bright lights of cameras and reporters calling out for comments. All law enforcement officers have been advised to answer no comment to all questions. The details of the victims' manner of death and sexuality are the stuff of sensational tabloid sales.

The apartment complex is older and quite small, only thirty units or so. The double-storied buildings look untended with a broken lamppost outside the main entrance and a lot of peeling paint. Sambino's building holds eight apartments, four upstairs and four down. Through the car window, I scan the location for anyone who looks out of place.

"Do you have someone to take photographs of the crowd?" I lean up between Davis and Ainsley from the backseat. In front, Ainsley is keyed up from the arrest and the excitement of the search. His face is flushed and he's leaning forward with his breath shallow and fast.

Despite my plea to hold off on the arrest of Sambino, I'm ramped up as well.

A criminal will sometimes return to the scene, posing as media or even just an interested onlooker. It's a sick game psychopaths like to play, insinuating themselves into the investigation.

"I have two plainclothes officers en route who will pose as a reporter and photographer from the *Columbus Dispatch*," Davis says.

A low murmur surrounds us as more officers arrive on the scene. Crime-scene tape ropes off the building and an officer stations himself to check IDs. Davis flips on the overhead car light and scribbles out the time log.

Davis mumbles while he writes. "Sambino should kiss our feet for locking him up. Once word of his arrest gets out, folks just might lynch him."

"It would save us the time and money," Ainsley adds.

Through the frosted window, I watch an older woman in a robe use her dog as a reason to walk past Sambino's building. She joins a group of apartment dwellers gathering on the corner to gossip about all they do not know about Nick Sambino. I rub my eyes. It's been a long day and it's about to get even longer.

Ainsley tips his head back to needle me. His moody energy fills the car. "You still convinced it's not Sambino?"

"Sambino is just a showman and narcissist," I respond. "He's a Johnny Depp wannabe. If there's any conflict in him, Detective, it's how to wear his hair each day."

"He's our man."

"He knows something, Ainsley. I'll give you that."

"Enough," Davis says, tossing the metal clipboard on the car's dash. He reaches for the door. "Let's do this."

CHAPTER FIFTEEN

Picture this: A Hollywood vampire lair complete with realistic-looking plastic skulls used as cereal bowls and ashtrays, a long black cape thrown over the edge of the bathroom door like a robe, and the walls covered with posters of some of pop culture's best-known vampires: Angel, Brad Pitt and Tom Cruise's characters from *Interview with the Vampire,* Dracula, and yes, even Edward Cullen. Instead of a bed, a large, plush coffin sits in the middle of the bedroom. Remnants of black hair dye stain the kitchen sink and counters. A half-eaten box of Count Chocula cereal spills its contents across the counter. To top it off, all the lights have been replaced with black lights, bathing Sambino's apartment in an eerie purplish glow. I feel like I'm on the movie set of some sort of B slasher movie on a shoestring budget.

"Vampire stereotyping at its finest," I say and stick my head into the tiny bathroom. Big surprise—he's hung a black shower curtain. A damp heap of dark towels lies in the corner near the toilet.

The black lights make the search difficult, painting shadows everywhere. Two officers work in the kitchen, removing all the contents from the cupboards and refrigerator. Another officer works in the family room, ripping the back off the worn sofa.

"Anything yet?" Davis asks.

"Nothing but a lot of stale food and dirty laundry," an officer says. "This guy's a slob."

"Take apart everything in the bedroom, bath, and that coffin," I direct. "He will keep mementos, souvenirs of some kind from the victims. He'll cherish these keepsakes and keep them in a location where he feel safe enough to relive the crimes."

The apartment stinks. The concoction of curdled milk and rotten bananas reeks. Fruit flies have gathered in the kitchen around the bananas. I pull the collar of my thick sweater up over my nose and mouth and walk through the kitchen to the bedroom. The makeshift filter doesn't help much and I'm back to trusty open-mouth breathing. When I pass through the door frame once again, an officer flips on the wall switch and the bedroom in engulfed in the now-familiar thick purple glow. On the far wall, scrawled letters gleam a yellow-green.

The brilliant mass of neon letters is indecipherable; it's a language I'm not familiar with. Latin, maybe? While a detective runs searches on his laptop to translate the message, I help Davis and Ainsley dismantle the inside of the coffin, peeling away the red velvety lining from the dark and oiled wood.

"Nice coffin," Davis says. "Expensive. Can you imagine sleeping in this thing? With the lid shut?"

"Or having sex?" Ainsley quips.

"Eww!" He gets a rise out of all of us with that one.

"He must have gotten a discount on the coffin for being such a good employee at the funeral home." As Ainsley rips a large section away, a book falls out. He holds it up. "Just what we need, guys, *The Vampire's Complete Handbook*." He reads from the well-worn cover. "How to psychically tap into energy fields for ultimate feeding." From inside the back flap, two unused condoms tumble to the floor. "At least we know our guy is practicing safe sex."

"I like a woman who bites." A slur of sex jokes follow the investigator's comment. I can't help but to laugh with them. This is by far the oddest crime scene I've ever investigated.

Another item falls loose from the lining. A small statuette, no more than five inches in height, fills the palm of my hand. Beneath a demon-like figure, I recognize one word. "Incubus," I say and trace the carved letters with my fingertips. "Hey, Ainsley, look up *incubus* in that book, would you? I've heard that name before."

"Got it," Ainsley calls out after a few minutes. "A being that seduces young women while they sleep and drinks their blood. Attached to vampire lore and sometimes considered to be the lord of the night."

"Huh." The face of the incubus looks up at me from my fist. "He sees himself as some sort of lord."

"I've got a few of those phrases from the wall in here, translated." Ainsley holds the book out for all of us to see. "They come from a section on what pure blood will do for vampires. Blood promises longevity and vitality."

"Longevity in jail," a detective calls out. A few of the guys chuckle.

"Pure blood," I say. "How is that defined?"

"Virgin blood's pure, apparently."

My thoughts turn to Marci. She'd been a virgin—at least with men. I'm willing to put money down that Vivian, Chandler, and Emma were also gold-star lesbians. Could this be the tie to the young lesbian community we've been looking for?

I join Davis, who has been working in the small space of the bathroom.

"It's hard to tell what anything is with this damn lighting," Davis says. He slides a gloved hand along the baseboard and around the toilet. A pile of makeup cases cover the area around the sink. I pick up a container with dark purple eye shadow in a gloved hand and hold it under the flashlight. Most of the shadow has been used.

"Find any women's clothing? High heels?" I ask.

"No," a detective says from the bedroom closet. "Just makeup and a curling iron."

I shine the high-beam flashlight along the base of the tub. The yellowed caulking doesn't look new. Davis lifts the lid off the toilet tank.

"Anything?" Ainsley says, sticking his head into the bathroom and stepping inside.

That's when I see it—the jagged edges along the short wall, the corners of the carpet not tucked in as carefully as they could be that pop up even higher under Ainsley's weight.

"Take up the carpet," I direct. "See how it's one complete piece in the bath and bedroom? There's a new piece of carpet that starts over here, at the beginning of the hallway."

Two officers comply and roll back the aging vomit-green carpet to reveal a worn pad and a thick layer of concrete slab beneath that. Cracks splinter through the slab like a spider's web. Particles of dust and dirt fly everywhere.

"Piss-poor foundation," Ainsley says. "This place will probably cave in in the next few years."

"Got something." The crew crowds around me as I lift the edge of the carpet in the hall to show the side of what appears to be a dark package made from some sort of silk. Gently, I position it in my gloved palm. The silky fabric envelope is a deep navy blue and reminds me of the popular cloth wallets and bags I've seen women carry in Asian films or on Travel Channel shows.

I unclasp the back of the envelope, a small shiny button, and let the contents fall into Davis's open gloved palm beside me. A stack of photographs emerges, each featuring a naked Nick Sambino with a nude female corpse. In most of the pictures, Sambino stands near the corpse's head, a hand on the shoulder in some sort of twisted caress while his veneer fangs flamboyantly drip blood from the corners of his mouth. Beside the bodies, on the steel table of the funeral home, sit Sambino's piled tubes of fresh blood.

The photographs are professional quality, the paper a thick stock. A fanged Sambino poses for the camera in each photo, complete with long acrylic fingernails painted black. I thumb through the rest of the stack. Twelve nearly identical photos—only the victim on the steel gurney changes.

"He's draining their blood," Davis says.

"That's what they do when they embalm a body," Ainsley says. "Not this way, obviously, but they start by draining all the blood and then replacing it with an embalming fluid."

"No one would've even noticed." I hold the beam of my flashlight on a photo. "He filled them back up with the fluid and kept the blood."

"But it's not fresh," Davis says. "It's not live blood."

"It's still blood," I say. "He's a copycat, remember? It's good enough to fool all these young women that are so taken with him."

"Sambino's smarter than I gave him credit for," Ainsley says. "But where is the blood? He couldn't have kept it at the funeral home. Chad would've caught him." He directs a detective to dismantle the old refrigerator.

"He drinks it." I think of the rumor that we'd heard about why Sambino had been fired from Walmart, with the blood in his lunch. Obviously a rumor based on truth.

I fan the photographs out on the coffee table, each photo more disturbing than the last. Davis kneels next to me. "The funeral home basement is our kill scene," I say. "He's bleeding them out there and then someone is transporting them to the quarry for placement."

Davis nods. "This answers why we found no blood at the crime scenes."

"Someone?" Ainsley says. "Come on, Hansen. Give it up. We got Sambino."

I ignore him, looking for something more. When I flip through the pile to photograph number twelve, I push it across the wood table toward Davis. "Look."

Although the last picture shows Sambino in his usual getup and pose, this particular shot features another figure hidden between the corpse's thighs on the steel table. Only gloved hands are visible around the dead woman's hips, pulling her closer, clearly wanting something much more than just dead blood.

"Christ." Davis can't say aloud what we're seeing. Someone other than Sambino appears to be performing oral sex on a dead woman who must be in her late seventies. The naked body shows numerous abrasions and long open incisions.

"Meet Picasso," I say. "The camera must have been set on a timer. It took the photo before he could completely get himself out of the frame. See?" Sambino's body's blurred with movement. "Sambino isn't posed yet."

"Sambino has some other guy to help, at least with this part." Ainsley leans in for a closer look.

I shake my head. "Sambino *is* the other guy, not Picasso. Look at the destruction to this particular body. It's far worse than the others."

"Like he's been practicing. Fuck," Davis says. "He's completely out of the picture except for the bends of his wrists and gloved hands. This could be anyone."

We all know he's right. If Sambino can drive the hearse without Eldridge even knowing he's gone during the night for hours on end, then Sambino can certainly sneak anyone inside the funeral home.

"Picasso's nothing like Sambino," I say. "Not an ounce of showman in him. He knew a photo would eventually be taken. He's gone to great lengths to be out of all the pictures."

Davis gives the last photograph to the techs to see if they can pull any extras from it.

"Here's Sambino's secret," I say. "He can lead us to Picasso. We need him, Davis."

"On what charges?" Ainsley asks. "It's not like we have photos of him killing our girls."

"It's a felony—desecration of a corpse," I say and fan the photos out in my hand like a deck of cards. "We got multiple felonies here, boys."

Davis steps away to make a call downtown. Twelve new charges to hold Mr. Sambino.

"One night in a cold cell with a few guys ready for Mr. Fairy Teeth and Sambino will be screaming the answers," Ainsley chuckles.

But I'm not so sure. Sambino's been threatened by our mystery Picasso. Those threats to remain silent can go a very long way.

While Ainsley gets evidence bags, I study the photographs again, this time scanning the counters and floor of each for any personal belongings. There, in photograph number seven, on the corner of a counter, lies a pair of eyeglasses, folded neatly. They would have been invisible if not for the reflection of the camera flash on one of the lenses.

"Rimless," I whisper and trace my gloved fingertips over the glasses.

"Pull up the carpet in the entire place," Davis calls out. "Let's get Luminol in the kitchen, bed, and bath."

Techs spray the bottoms of the bedroom walls, around the tub and toilet, the sink drain, and over light fixtures. They also spray heavily the area where the photographs have been found.

"Showtime," one tech calls out after a few minutes. He kills the lights and everyone turns off their flashlights. A trail of smear glows and leads to the sink while other occasional droplets shimmer in the darkness. An eerie blue design surrounds us.

"He's a sloppy feeder," I say, pointing out that the kitchen is only glowing around the sink area. "We need to match this blood to victims." I walk back to the far corner of the family room.

"Keep searching," Davis calls out. "We need DNA profiling and the entire place tested for prints."

The air pressure around me shifts, the floor tilts much the same way the cave did the day I found Marci—these are my instincts kicking into high alert. Detectives swarm around me and flashlights sweep across my body yet I am standing still. Their voices dim to only the pulse of my blood rushing inside my ears. My skin prickles and the hairs stand up. I know with every fiber of my being that our Picasso's much too smart to leave pictures hidden under some outdated, puke-green carpet. He'd never draw attention to himself with the high drama antics of role-playing a vampire and drinking blood from corpses.

From the corner of my eye, Ainsley swirls the thick brush inside the canister of print powder and then sweeps it across the front door handle and lock. He sneezes. Then again.

"Damn powder," Ainsley grumbles under his breath. He pulls the glasses off his face and digs his fingertips into his reddened eyes. "Gets me sneezing every time." Ainsley gives a long, harsh snort and sets the rimless frames on the wood beam that serves as a mantel.

"Davis." I wait for him to appear by my side. "See this?" I point to the glasses in the photograph so as not to alert Ainsley. "Now look over there." I point to Ainsley's glasses on the mantel.

Suddenly Davis has a firm grip on my elbow. "I need to see you. Now."

Outside Sambino's apartment, I follow Davis until we're a few feet away from the officers at the front door. Davis turns to face me and crosses his arms over his chest. "I see what you're doing."

"You've lost me, Davis."

"And we're losing time, Agent. I need you focused on Sambino, not Ainsley."

I tuck my hair behind my ear and avoid eye contact with him. "There's something there, Davis. I feel it."

"Luce, there's nothing there." Davis's definitive words match his glare. "We don't have time for this now. I'll pick you up at the hotel tomorrow morning at seven."

Davis turns and is almost back at the apartment door before I can ask, "Wait. Why?"

"Tomorrow. Seven a.m."

CHAPTER SIXTEEN

What's my standard answer when everything in my life seems to fall apart? When all I really need is blessed sleep, but it's mountains away, beyond the violent churn of my thoughts?

Wine. Boxed wine, actually, since it's the only kind the never-closing Michaels's Mini-Mart keeps in stock. I left the familiar store with a brown bag full of the cheap red stuff and Hot Pockets—a dinner of true champions. In thick, fleecy sleep clothes complete with a spattering of dark hairs from the dogs, I plant myself in front of the television for old reruns of *CSI* (it's my guilty pleasure) with little plastic hotel cups full of wine and semidefrosted cheesy ham Hot Pockets.

Three and a half episodes and an empty wine box later, I've got a magnificent buzz on. Even drunk, my mind continues to work the crime scenes, to twist them into every possible angle, searching for evidence that might have been missed. Sometime after midnight, I finally understand I can't avoid it any longer. I sit cross-legged in a T-shirt and boxers, perched on top of the desk before the murder board, while the soles of my boots bite against the bare skin of my legs. The pinch feels good, real, somehow, a reminder that I am here in this hotel room and not in the limestone quarry during the summer of 1989. Finally, I open the case file I've avoided since my arrival in Willow's Ridge: Tucker, Marci Ann. DOD: 7/27/89. Case # 7124285.

"Pull back," I whisper to myself and close my eyes. I call up the words of advice from so many of the instructors at the academy: Think of yourself as a doctor. You have no emotional attachment to the body that is before you. If there is no attachment, you can examine everything without judgment or feeling. The body before you is simply a vehicle to the truth.

I'd practiced this level of detachment throughout my career, though I don't always succeed. Tonight liquid courage aids in my quest for the truth.

Marci's high school picture tumbles out of the side sleeve and her blond hair shimmers in the desk light. My fingertips trace her smile full of metal braces and I can feel the softness of her warm lips, still fresh with laughter. All at once it's as if Marci's right beside me; I smell *her*—fruity shampoo and Downy on her cotton clothes. I take in the distinct aroma of peppermint from her candies, laced with cigarette smoke. Marci's palpable beside me and the tears I've been holding in for days erupt.

Hair so blood filled, I'd never guess she'd been a white-blonde.

Sobs heave through my core and there is nothing for me to grab but the edges of the wooden desk. The earth has shifted below and I can't trust my balance or my own strength. I head to the water's edge, the place I always run to in my mind when the emotions are too overwhelming. The water's different tonight, though. I find myself at the surf's berm, the sea a frothy churn tumbling around my legs as I walk out past the break of waves. The water rises, slipping over my mouth and nose, soaking my hair that floats around me in tendrils. Oxygen bubbles flit up and away as they have a million times before. But something different happens this time. Something new. I'm desperate to reach the surface for a breath. Lungs burning, I spread my arms and kick for the ocean's top, but it's so far away, hardly any light filters down into the depths. What's happening? I've never needed breath before in this safe, watery world, and in my panicked fight for oxygen, salty water seeps into my nose and mouth.

Above, a familiar hand reaches deep beneath the surface for mine. Through the thick sheen, Marci's shifting figure pulls me up. The choppy movement of the water obscures her face. She's saying something to me, words I can't make out underneath the rush of water, until finally she hoists me through the water's surface. Sputtering and gulping for air, I look around, but there's no one else. I'm floating in the center of a sea alone. The flow of my breath, haggard and harried at first, finally settles into an anxious rhythm.

Something about this waking nightmare is too real; she was here. Marci has been here all along, and that knowledge gives me the strength to wipe away the tears, to keep going.

Breathe, Luce. Just breathe.

I flip to the police report. Marci Tucker's file begins by listing the primary detective on the case, who I'm surprised to find is not Ainsley.

He's listed as secondary. Detective Mark Smith led the investigation and typed up the notes. Apparently the station hadn't shifted over to computers yet and the paper is filled with those little white typo-correction squares. Near the bottom of the page he let the errors go—must have gotten tired.

On Thursday, July 27, 1989, at 3:27 p.m., dispatch took a 911 call from me, Lucinda Hansen, aged sixteen. My call to 911 from the pay phone outside Michael's Mini-Mart was quick and panicked with short phrases that my friend needed help and was very hurt, maybe even dying. I detailed the amount of blood for the operator and told her Marci had been bleeding from the back of her head. I told the operator I was supposed to have met my friend at 3 p.m. but was late, and I gave the directions to the cave inside the quarry. Smith noted that I refused to remain on the line and told the operator I was going back to be with my friend to wait for help.

Police and EMS workers arrived in the quarry parking lot at 4:02 p.m. Marci was pronounced dead at the scene at 4:16 p.m. The cave was declared a crime scene and more detectives were called in to photograph the body and investigate the area for clues.

Officers found me along the rocky edge of the quarry soaked and unconscious. I have to read this bit of information again and again. How did I get into the water and so far from Marci's body? No explanation is given and I cannot remember what happened once I returned to Stonehenge. I was immediately transported to the Willow's Ridge hospital, where doctors found me in good health except for a few minor cuts and scrapes, though I couldn't remember how I'd gotten into the quarry's water. Police bagged my wet clothing and notified my father that I had found Marci's body. Once he arrived at the Willow's Ridge hospital, police questioned him, but he was quickly dismissed as a suspect with so many witnesses at the police station.

All of the blood tested at the scene was found to be O positive—Marci's blood type, but also the most common. Nothing else was found on Marci or at the crime scene. Investigators collected a rock near Marci's body, a heavy stone about the size of a softball. The rock had one rough edge to it, a jagged ridge that most likely was used to hit Marci's skull. Traces of clotted blood with a few blond hairs caught in it were linked back to Marci.

Investigators continued to search the quarry for weeks after Marci's death, combing through the lush vegetation of summer, but found nothing. No one claimed to have seen or heard anything. The last known person to see and talk to Marci was Doug, the clerk from Michael's Mini-Mart. Marci stopped in at 2:41 p.m. and purchased a forty-four-ounce fountain drink of Mountain Dew and a pack of peppermint candies. Doug told the detectives that this was her usual purchase and that she paid with a ten-dollar bill. She'd left the change for him, as usual. Doug seems to have conveniently left out that her usual included a pack of Marlboro Reds. He would have been fired for selling cigarettes to a minor. He reported she acted the same as she did any other day: happy and without any sort of agitation.

Detective Smith quickly cleared Doug on the basis of the mini-mart's surveillance video that clearly showed him behind the counter at the time of the crime.

Detective Smith also led my interview in the hospital emergency room after my father arrived. He described me as very fearful and clinging to the teddy bear that Detective Ainsley had given me. He documented that I answered all his questions with streaming tears and appeared weak, shell-shocked, and much too innocent to be involved. I chuckle at the *too innocent* comment. I'm not so sure the Jamesons would agree.

Marci's parents didn't believe I was innocent either. Most parents of murdered children have their suspicions about who might have killed their child. Most times, it is the person they believe was the last to see their child alive. Marci's mother was quoted in the file as blaming me: *That Hansen girl is stronger than she looks.* Her father remained silent on the matter. Marci's mother claimed that although as parents they had led their daughter to the word of the Lord, they couldn't force her to drink. Detective Smith's notes insinuated that Marci's mother believed her daughter's death was retribution for disobeying the word of God.

Marci's father had been a strong suspect early on in the case, mostly due to his silence and refusal to take a lie detector test. He'd been questioned at length because he frequently butted heads with his only daughter over issues like her insistence on playing soccer or her determination to be with the female assistant coach, that left everyone questioning the nature of their relationship, but he had a strong alibi. He'd been on his second-shift job as a hospital janitor when the murder took place. Due to his distant and aloof nature, though, many people in Willow's Ridge never quite believed that he was completely innocent of the crime.

Marci's older brother, Martin, had also been interviewed by Smith. Martin was arrested for a DUI only two weeks before the murder of his sister. Martin said he had been working at Bing's Service Garage in Willow's Ridge on car repairs at the time of Marci's murder; his alibi had been checked and cleared. An addendum had been added to the notes that Martin had required hospitalization at Willow's Ridge General Hospital for a suicide attempt on August 12, 1989. The assigned psychiatrist reported to police that Martin's attempt could be attributed to the grief over losing his only sister, with whom he had been close.

Cole Ainsley questioned Marci's soccer coach and the assistant—soccer girl. Both of their alibis cleared. They were together at a soccer coaching clinic in Indianapolis for the week. The assistant told police that Marci had been quite happy in the weeks before her death. She claimed that Marci had been preoccupied with a new relationship and the rumor on the team was that Marci had a new girlfriend. I was named as the girlfriend in question through the interview with Marci's parents and in Marci's personal journal that had been found at the scene of the crime. Smith concluded after reading portions of the journal that Marci and I were more than friends and that Marci's secret affair probably meant that she was also keeping many other secrets from those who loved her.

I know better; everything Marci cared about went into those journal pages. Writing was the way she processed her feelings and planned for her future. If Marci had another secret besides me, it would have been inside those pages.

Where was the journal? When Ainsley and Davis pulled Marci's items from the evidence box for DNA testing, there was no personal journal. Even though Marci's case is cold, it remains open, and nothing from the crime scene should be missing from the box of evidence. Clearly, Detective Smith had the journal at one time. That information could be critical to the case, but I also know how evidence tends to go missing in police stations: items get misplaced, lost, and discarded. Any person in law enforcement or the legal community had access to these files and boxes of evidence. Anyone could have taken the journal.

Smith's notes certainly highlight different suspects, but I'm not surprised to see that he felt strongly about Pastor Jameson's involvement at one point. Smith questioned both Charles and Mildred because Marci and I were supposed to arrive at the meeting that day, scheduled for five p.m. Smith had to have known the group was ex-gay, but he left this information out of the report. Instead he described Marci as *an active weekly participant in Jameson's religious organization.* Still, something about Charles Jameson struck Smith as odd. He noted that for a pastor, a man of God, Jameson was surprisingly cold and apathetic about the violent death of the young girl that was part of his ministry. When questioned, Jameson only said: *Our God is a vengeful God.* The team requested a polygraph test from Jameson but he refused, citing religious reasons. Both Charles and Mildred Jameson had been preparing for the weekly meeting that was to include other teens from the Ohio region at the time of the murder. Many people had arrived early for the meeting and had seen them both. Smith and his team eventually ended up back where it all began: with a murdered teenager in one of the caverns of Willow's Ridge limestone quarry and no strong suspects.

I spread the crime-scene photos out on top of the wooden desk and that day comes rushing back so clearly, I feel like I could touch each picture and fall back in time to Thursday, July 27, 1989.

"It is work," I remind myself, "nothing else." The batting down of emotions finally wins out, or possibly my sheer emotional exhaustion. For one of the very first times ever, I'm able to focus on Marci's case without the baggage that generally comes with it.

One photo strikes me most from the handful of shots, the one I can't take my eyes from. Marci's body looks so small, so *fragile*, draped across the rocky wall and floor of the cave. With her head and back propped up against the cave's wall, her full weight leaned against the side of a large rock. Marci's arms were spread wide and out to the sides, while her thin, bare legs rested together in a V, knees clamped together. I look at this photo for a very long time, from different angles and in varying levels of light. Something rings familiar about the photo, something more than the memory of finding Marci in this very position.

Four autopsy photos are included in the file along with the postmortem report. Autopsy findings state that Marci died from head trauma to the base of the skull, most likely from repeated blows to the back of her head from the rock found at the crime scene. Photos show the back of Marci's head where her hair was shaved to reveal the wounds and the jagged lines etched like a fault line after an earthquake. The report notes a fresh welt on her right cheekbone, cause unknown, and heavy skin damage across her neck. The ME concluded that came from the intense pressure of a forearm choking off Marci's air supply until she passed out. No semen had been found in or on Marci. However, because she was found with her cutoffs partially pulled down, investigators determined the murder might be a sexual assault gone wrong or the act of an UNSUB trying to make it look like sexual assault, to throw off police.

I sit back and stretch my neck to each side and catch my breath. My thoughts turn to Marci's brother, Martin. I completely understand his desire to kill himself after Marci died; I felt it, too. After Marci's funeral, my father took me to see the psychiatrist that worked with Chesterton's police, fire, and EMS units. Night terrors plagued me and a new fear overtook me: I was suddenly terrified for my father to go to work. I had never felt that before, but with Marci's death, I worried he too would leave me. The psychiatrist strongly advised against my return to the One True Path meetings. I never went back to Willow's Ridge or the Jamesons' basement. My past with One True Path faded into the distant fold of my memory. Everything in my life eventually got better, except for the night terrors.

What helped me most in those early months after the murder wasn't really the psychiatrist. Detective Roy Tyson of the Chesterton police department was one of my father's best friends, and with my father's permission, he took me on a ride-along. Tyson believed the activity would keep me busy and ease my worry that they would never find Marci's killer. To everyone's surprise, even my own, I wanted to learn about the job I had lived with my entire life. But not from my dad—it had to be someone else who showed me the ropes at that point. I spent the fall and winter months at Tyson's side, and eventually I understood that Marci's murder hadn't been forgotten. The police were simply waiting for more information. Every weekend I tagged along with Roy on run-of-the-mill small-town cases and learned the basics of investigation and interrogation. Something else happened during my time with Roy—somewhere along the line I decided I wanted to be a cop. Not just a beat cop, but a detective. I wanted to be the one who solved cases and brought answers to families like Marci's. I wanted to be the one who fought against all odds and helped justice to win out. When I walked for my high school diploma, I knew exactly what career path I would follow.

The hush of two a.m. settles around me. I've been at the file for hours, yet I cannot stop myself from flipping back to that photograph of Marci propped against the cavern wall. That image of Marci was sealed into my mind so long ago. Under the desk lamp, I turn the photo round and round. Crime-scene reports state that there was no indication that the cavern walls had been used as a weapon. The ME determined that the killer held the rock that had been slammed into her head and she was choked from behind and was standing at the time of the attack. Those actions would have caused Marci's body to fall forward. Yet there was no blood on the cavern walls and very little on the cavern floor to match her injuries. Smith and Ainsley concluded that Marci's body hadn't been posed, but a person with a head injury does not fall into a seated position with her knees pulled into her chest.

Marci's killer had manipulated her body after death, just like whoever committed the new murders. Unlike the most recent cases, though, he didn't leave a cross of any kind on Marci's body. I look back over the crime-scene photos and focus on one that depicts Marci from the breasts up. There it is, as plain as day. Her shirt had been pulled open at the neck to reveal the Irish cross Marci always wore. He didn't need to supply one for this murder; the victim already wore it.

The killer's attack strikes me as an incredibly passive way to kill someone. Choking and beating someone from behind would prevent him from seeing her face. Most serial killers enjoyed watching their victims die. Ted Bundy talked at length about how much pleasure it gave him to see the light of life slowly give out in a victim's eyes much the way a candle flame dissipates without oxygen. Additionally, he made a grave error: he didn't consider that someone might be coming to meet her. Not very well planned, as he seems to be now. All of this evidence leads me to believe that Marci was an early kill, if not his first; she had been Picasso's training wheels.

Maybe it was the strength the killer needed to choke Marci, or the force it would have taken to bash her head open. Either way, Smith dismissed me as a suspect after my first interview. He was confident that I was just as surprised as everyone else that someone would want Marci dead. Then I saw the handwritten addition to the bottom of one of the last pages in the file, only a scribbled-in afterthought: *Ainsley wonders re: Lucinda Hansen's involvement in the murder. Led killer to victim?*

I hardly remember being questioned by Smith or Ainsley at the time of Marci's death. I try to replay all the conversations I've had with Ainsley since I arrived in Willow's Ridge for this case. It's late and my mind begins to spin with conspiracy theories. Was it really only the universe bringing me back to the case of my past, as Rowan says, or are there human elements involved? No matter what, the inescapable conclusion remains: *I* may be Ainsley's main suspect for Marci's murder despite the fact that there is absolutely no evidence to support that theory.

And because Ainsley believes all the crimes are connected, *I* may be his number one suspect for *all* the Willow's Ridge murders.

❖

"*Marci!*"

The dark-haired girl's racing feet pounded along the ridge over what served as a path while sweat dripped from her brow in the hot summer sun. When she rounded the corner into the entrance of Stonehenge, her flushed face spoke of pure panic. She stood above the girl still slumped against the cavern wall.

The dark-haired girl dropped to her friend's side and froze with the thick, warm liquid seeping around her bony knees. She looked as though she could sit there forever lost in this trance, but the noise from the back corner of the cave alerted her. The dark-haired girl's eyes flashed into the cave—but it had only been a scrape of something against the limestone floor.

She reached for her friend. "Help is on the way," the dark-haired girl told her. "Please don't go!" With shaking hands, she reached out to her dead friend to check for a pulse and a breath once again, but found none. "They'll be here soon," she repeated and her eyes flooded. "Don't leave me," she begged.

Then another noise. Something hard and metallic. The dark-haired girl's senses sharpened to high alert and the tiny hairs on her arms and neck rose. She looked past her friend's dead body into the depths of Stonehenge. She strained to hear any other noises. Goose bumps rose over the rest of her body. Slowly, she stood and took a step toward the back corner of the cave. Then another step. That's when she saw him—a stranger huddled in the darkness of the back corner. At first, neither one moved, each only watching the other for a reaction. It was he who lunged for her, knocking his head on the bridge of the cavern ceiling. The dark-haired girl spun, jumped over her dead friend, and sprinted out of the cave toward the trail she'd just come from.

The dark shadow bolted out of the cave after her. She looked over her shoulder to find that he was within fifteen steps of her and gaining. She'd made this run twice already and her legs quivered under the pressure to run faster. Quickly she turned to her left and shot through the heavy forest. Her sudden change of course threw the dark shadow off for a moment, and he had to slow down to make a turn toward where she had gone. Thick trees and heavy vines bit at the dark-haired girl's bare legs and arms, swiping against skin, leaving the screams of welts. Still she pushed on, tucked her chin into her chest, and barreled one frantic foot over the other. The change of course had gained her a few steps, but the dark shadow wasn't far behind. The jagged breath and the pounding of his feet grew closer.

I wake, sweaty and shivering. Gasping for air, I'm unable to take in a full breath and tears seep from the corners of my eyes. I half walk, half crawl to the bathroom and throw handfuls of cold water over my face. Ever so slowly the cold water brings me back to now.

My reflection in the mirror shows the horror of what my memory has blocked. I'm pale and wide-eyed with fear. All this time I thought I'd been dreaming of Marci's attack. But *I* saw the silhouette of the killer; he chased me, too. Somehow I outran him. Somehow I survived after interrupting his kill and stopped him from setting the ritual with Marci. My hands tremble and a tsunami of fear breaks over me. The killer *knows* me. He tried to kill me, too.

"Fuck!" I slam my fists against the bathroom wall. My mind races, caught in an endless loop that goes from Ainsley to the killer and back to Ainsley.

There is still a half carton of wine in the fridge. I line up three hotel cups and fill them to their plastic rims, enough wine to stop these shakes and ease my nerves. When the hotel cups are empty and my belly burns with the cheap alcohol, I fill them again and start all over.

CHAPTER SEVENTEEN

Sunday, January 13

Davis slams the gas, and the cruiser belches and hurls us over the last big clump of snowdrift. At the top of the winding single-lane road, Davis throws the car in park. The town of Willow's Ridge lies below, where chimneys steam out white, puffy trails from their fireplaces and furnaces against the early morning light. My head pounds with thoughts of last night's drinking binge, the empty cartons beside me this morning when my alarm went off. Everything looks foggy and my body feels much too slow to be anywhere but in bed.

Davis pushes open his door. "Follow me."

"Davis!" I protest.

"Follow me, Agent."

Davis and I weave between rows in the Willow's Ridge Cemetery, among gravestones of all shapes and sizes. As I trail behind him, my boots look like those of a child within the imprints of his. Even in the icy folds of snow, Davis is quick and light on his feet with long, loping strides. He leads me up another snowy hill and behind more rows of gravestones. From this vantage point, the highest spot of the surrounding area, I'm able to see how large the cemetery actually is. Markers dot the rolling hills below and new graves have begun to spread out past each base. Some of the gravestones are nothing more than small slabs, and time has weathered the engravings away. Others are large monuments, a mausoleum for an extended family. A section of veterans' graves features flags and medals.

Davis finally stops at the foot of a grave, and I step up beside him to see the large marker featuring a cherub in full wings. The stone as tall as my waist reads:

BELOVED SON,
REST IN THE COMFORT OF GOD WITH PEACE YOUR CONSTANT COMPANION.
TIMOTHY MICHAEL AINSLEY
1976–1999

Black fattened crows caw and squirrels sprint for the shelter of large trees. Up here, under the blankets of snow, everything seems peaceful.

"Ainsley's only child. He always called Tim a miracle baby because he and his wife conceived late in life. They never expected to have a child. Tim's death nearly devastated Cole." Davis looks up a moment, takes in a deep breath. "Tim committed suicide. Cole was on duty when we got the call. We had to physically restrain him from entering his own house until we were able to process the scene." Davis shudders at the bitter cold air that whips through the trees. "Cole's wife came home from the grocery and found their son hanging from a banister."

I can't speak. A knot of something I can't quite explain has lodged deep within my throat.

"Tim came out when he was around sixteen and was active with One True Path. Once Cole began volunteering his time to the group, Tim withdrew. His suicide note said that he couldn't get the homosexuality out of him and he couldn't stand to look at his father's disappointed eyes any longer. The poor kid."

I swallow the knot. "So you did know about the Jamesons and the One True Path meetings."

Davis's body stiffens, his muscles bracing as if waiting for impact. "Cole Ainsley's not perfect, Hansen. He's been through a lot. One True Path is a mission that is near and dear to his heart. He saw it as a beacon of hope for his son and for his family." Davis's words defend his decision not to let on that he'd known about the Jamesons. He did it to protect Ainsley and his family's past.

"It didn't work, though." I can't stop the words before they spill out. "Those meetings only added to this kid's guilt and shame over something he couldn't even control. One True Path shamed Tim to death."

"Maybe. Maybe not." Davis struggles. He starts and stops a few times before he finally finds the words he's searching for. "There are two sides to this, Hansen. Cole says that the months his son spent with One True Path were the first time he'd seen his son happy since childhood. Tim felt connected at those meetings. There, around everyone else who struggled, Tim found hope."

The longer I look, the more it appears that the cherub inside Tim Ainsley's gravestone grins and winks at me as though we share a long-lost secret. Maybe we do. One True Path is a club where we all suffered tremendously in order to be ourselves. The silence settles between me and Davis and this might very well be a first: I don't have a response. This time, in this moment, I am listening.

"I'm not asking you to be Ainsley's best friend, only his partner for the remainder of this case. He wants this thing solved as much as you do. It's that determined drive to solve these crimes that makes you the perfect partners."

I'm not so sure I agree with *perfect partners*. Still, the captain's quiet resolve beside me is profound. Before we leave to return to the station, I kneel at the side of the headstone of Timothy Ainsley. With gloved hands I brush away the snow that has collected on its sharp ledge. I wipe my fingertips along the deep grooves of the snowy, engraving letters. It's the cherub I save for last, finally sweeping clean his wings, readying them for flight and the pursuit of peace.

❖

The team watches Sambino through the enormous one-way mirror outside the interview room. A wall-mounted camera records all of Sambino's movements and sounds while he waits. Beside me, at the table, Dr. Eli Weaver helps formulate questions. His enormous length drapes over his chair, his limbs spread out: legs the length of trees veer out beneath the table, capped with brown loafers. His pink button-up shirt shows off the remnants of a holiday tan, while faded jeans keep him somewhat casual. Davis has requested Weaver's help with the case, based on his expertise with ex-gay ministries and his previous encounter with Sambino at the university. Weaver had been waiting at the station since eight a.m. when I arrived at ten, but he greeted me with a warm hug and one of the biggest smiles I'd seen in days. Weaver's one of those people you can't help but to grin back at, someone who's happy despite the hardships he has faced in life, someone who's content with what he's got. I could learn a lot from spending time with Weaver.

I spent the last two hours retracing Ainsley's investigation into Marci's soccer coach and the assistant. They now lived together in an old farmhouse outside Chillicothe. The coach, Leslie Hamilton, had debilitating arthritis and couldn't move through the house without a walker. In her early sixties, she appeared to be much older as she hunched in a La-Z-Boy watching daytime court TV shows. No way would this woman have the strength or speed to kill our victims in the quarry. It was the assistant coach that I was most interested in, though. I wanted to see the woman Marci had been so crushed out on, the woman I'd been so very jealous of. While she was a good fifteen years younger than her partner, time hadn't been kind to her health either. Melissa had grown into an obese woman who lost her breath escorting me from the front door to a sitting room. Melissa explained as she hobbled along that her knees had gone bad and she was in need of a knee replacement. Clearly she couldn't have committed the murders either.

Then there was Doug, the final person to see Marci at the mini-mart. The police station still had the video that served as his alibi at the time of the crime. There on the old VHS tape I found final images of Marci as she pushed into the mini-mart and purchased her usual with a big grin on her face. I reached out for the pictures of her, the hologram lost in time, and my fingertips traced her outline against the monitor screen. *My Marci.* Her cutoffs hiked up over her thighs and I saw what I'd known all along. She was wearing her favorite plaid button-up. Somewhere between the mini-mart and the evidence box, the shirt had gone missing. My heart ached to see her movements so clearly: the way her shoulders lifted as she giggled, the way her long hair swiped along her back as she walked, the assuredness of her stride, and the strength of her steps that had drawn me in so quickly from the first time I saw her. *My Marci.*

Inside the interrogation room, Ainsley, Davis, Weaver, and I watch as Sambino tips his chair back and forth on two legs. He stares directly at the camera mounted in the top corner of the room and does his best to look confident. He knows the questioning is coming, he just doesn't know when. Sambino has surprised us all by not yet requesting an attorney. Ainsley said it was Sambino's attempt to show his willingness to work with us. He's hoping for a way out. I'm not so sure. Everything about Sambino seems like a dress rehearsal for a play. He isn't able to be who he really is. I notice, though, that his orange county jumper is ruffled and he looks like he's gotten next to no sleep. The jail-issued outfit makes him look so much younger than he did in his black vampire garb. His stringy dark hair hangs over his face, now so pale under the overhead lights without any of his thick Goth makeup.

"Ready?" Ainsley asks.

A techie hands Ainsley and me tiny earpieces smaller than the size of a pencil eraser. The techie helps me to insert them into my ear canal so that Davis and Weaver will be able to feed us questions and comments during the interview.

"Assume you're on the right track unless I cut in," Davis directs. "Ainsley, no wild rides. Got it?"

Ainsley grunts his approval, but he's already revved up. The anxious energy wafts off him in long, hot waves. He's determined to bring Sambino down.

The interview room's not much bigger than a closet, and I sit across the table from Sambino. Detective Ainsley stands, his large frame leaning against the wall, steps from Sambino's back, a hand on his hip near the badge clipped to his belt, the other near his pistol. Our physicality will continue to close in on Sambino throughout the interview, more of our not-so-pleasant police pressure cooker.

"I trust that the jail accommodations suited you last night, Mr. Sambino." I place the file folder on the table between us. Sambino drops all four chair legs down and he examines me through strands of greasy hair. There is something different about his eyes, though, a hint of uncertainty around the edges. Perhaps the night in lockup has done him some good. "Before we begin, Detective Ainsley has some small business matters to take care of."

Ainsley steps in and leans over Sambino without actually touching him. He holds out a pen to point where Sambino should sign to waive his right to an attorney before we begin.

Sambino takes the pen but doesn't sign. "Why should I talk to you?"

I shrug. "To clear your name."

"I don't know anything about these murders."

"Sign it," Ainsley says and nudges Sambino's shoulder a bit too hard with his hip. "Then we talk."

At first it looks like Sambino's going to hold his mug. A moment passes before he glares up at Ainsley, takes in his size, then turns away. He scribbles his name on the line. As soon as Sambino finishes, Ainsley takes the pen and paper from him and steps back toward the wall, clearly to grant me the lead. Maybe some of Davis's orders have finally sunk in. Ainsley is Ainsley, though. The fire to solve this case lies just below his controlled movements.

"We have an awful lot of circumstantial evidence against you."

Sambino shakes his head. "Just because I knew Emma doesn't mean I killed her or anybody else."

"You might be right about that. How about you explain these to me?" I open the case file and spread out four pictures that show Sambino with the female corpses. "Did you kill these women, Nick?"

"No! They were brought into the funeral home dead. I took their blood, but it would have come out and washed down our hazards drain anyway. It's not even like stealing."

"And you needed this blood for...?"

Sambino spreads his lips apart wide and points to his veneer fangs. "I'm a vampire, remember?"

The showing of the fangs breaks Ainsley's resolve. His eyes spark and his tongue unleashes. "Let me get this straight. You expect us to believe that you *needed* this blood? Because you're a vampire? Vampires are supposed to drink the blood from a live vein, dumb-ass." Ainsley hisses the word *dumb-ass* with a low growl.

"Not all vampires attack their victims that way." Sambino rolls his eyes as though Ainsley and I are the dumbest humans on earth. "What do you think I did with it? I mixed it with vodka every night."

"Ahh," I say to Ainsley. "It was only a nightcap."

Ainsley plays along. "A morning cap, Detective. A bloody vodka after the night shift. Why didn't I ever think of that when I was working traffic?"

"Blood is blood," Sambino says. "I'm not worried about freshness." With his arms crossed over his pudgy chest it's clear that Ainsley's questioning of vampire authenticity has perturbed Sambino.

"Where did you store the blood, anyway?" Ainsley says.

Sambino doesn't answer.

I fan out the eleven photographs like playing cards, and place one on the table at a time, careful to keep photo number twelve to myself. I want to save the one that has caught the ghostly glimpse of Picasso. With each new photo Sambino sinks farther into his seat. Unable to look at the dead women, he picks at the chipped black polish on his thumbnails.

"Eleven women," I say. "That's an enormous amount of blood."

Sambino grins and licks his lips as if he can still taste the blood on his tongue. Suddenly the switch flips inside Ainsley and he's all fists and yells and spittle in some sort of Hail Mary move destined to fail. It's not that he accuses Sambino of the crimes so much as the threats of what will come to him—rape and beatings as other inmates become vampires against Sambino.

"Detective!" I try to stop Ainsley. "I got it." Our radio earpieces are blowing up with demands that Ainsley step down. For a moment Ainsley and I have our own standoff until I finally hear the crackle of Davis in both our ears telling Ainsley to get the hell out of the room.

Once the door slams behind Ainsley, Sambino takes in a deep breath. "I knew you were the good cop."

"You can repay me by explaining this one." I position the final photograph, photo twelve. "Who is this in the photo with you?"

Sambino closes his eyes. His knee bounces up and down so violently it shakes his whole body.

After a minute, I continue. "The glasses on the corner of the table. Whose are they?" When he doesn't answer, I say, "He was there with you every time you took blood from the bodies, wasn't he?"

Sambino says softly, "No one was there but me."

"Whoever this is seems to be enjoying himself inside each dead woman's crotch."

"I told you. No one was there but me."

"You and your amazing four arms, huh?" I pound my finger against his blurred image on the photograph, but Sambino isn't budging. I lean back in the chair and rub my eyes. "We're circling back to photography, Nick. That's where we began, talking about Wilson's Photography shop and Emma." Sambino doesn't say anything. For now, anyway, he's shut down and confirmed all my suspicions that he must be terrified of Picasso and what Picasso could do to him.

"Let him steep a bit." Davis's voice crackles through my earpiece. I wait a moment after the instruction, looking hard at Sambino who can't bring his eyes up to mine. I then slowly collect all the photos except for the last and let it lie in the center of the table.

An hour later, Sambino still sits in the same chair as Weaver enters the interview room alone with a quick duck of his head. His size spills into the tiny interrogation room filling so much more than Ainsley and I did together.

"I'm sorry to meet again under such circumstances," Weaver says, always so cordial. He shakes Sambino's hand. "I've brought some reading material for you."

Sambino takes the Bible from him and turns the plain paperback book over inside his hands. He lets his fingertips trace over the gold lettering.

"I wanted to bring you an ankh replica, but the jail won't allow it."

Sambino puts the book down next to the photograph. "Why are you here?"

Weaver spreads his long, matchstick legs out beside the table. His loafers look like a size twenty-five at the ends of his skinny legs. "The detectives found out about our meeting at the university and thought I might be able to help."

"You're a professor, not a cop."

Weaver nods. "That's exactly what I told them. But you're in a tight spot. I want to be of help to you, Nick." Weaver holds his voice only a level or two above a whisper. Sambino has leaned into the table in order to hear, and we all are taken with the liquid calm of his tone. "Tell me about the One True Path meetings."

I can't get close enough to the monitors. Weaver's off the grid of questions we worked on for him.

"What the fuck?" Ainsley smacks the table.

I shush him.

"What are you talking about?"

Weaver sighs. "Unfortunately we both know far too much about those meetings."

Sambino drops his gaze back toward the table. He doesn't deny it. Weaver has gotten to the heart of something that Ainsley wouldn't let me get to in two days.

"You researched me before our talk at the university, Nick, or you never would have known I wrote my dissertation on the different types of crosses." Weaver's voice has a gentle drawl to it, as though he grew up in the South and it's a lingering accent that hasn't let go. "You also knew that my area of expertise is ex-gay ministries, though you never really asked me much about it during your visit. Talk of the ankh and other crosses was a ruse—I'm sure of it now. What did you *really* want to talk to me about that day, Nick? Did something happen to you in those meetings?"

"It wasn't a ruse," Sambino whispers.

Weaver sits in silence with Sambino, allowing space and time for words to follow. When Sambino doesn't use it, Weaver finally does. "I know a whole lot about these types of groups, Nick. Not just from my studies, but I got pulled into it years ago. Just like you."

"You told me, remember? About how you met your man."

Weaver nods. "I did meet him through those meetings, Nick. We also went through hell and back in order to accept ourselves."

Sambino swallows hard and his Adam's apple slightly quivers.

"Four years, Nick. Four years before I finally found the courage to leave."

Sambino's fingertips graze the cover of the Bible. Although he's sunk far into his seat, you can tell he's listening close to Weaver's words.

"I never would have found the courage to leave without Dave. He's the one, really, who insisted we end the charade. I was scared out of my mind."

Ever so slightly, Sambino nods.

"I was so afraid that I failed God, that all these teachings from the organization were true and that I'd be cast away from God forever. I struggled with this terror that I wouldn't be able to survive without the group. In a way they'd become closer to me than my own family. We were all in that mess together. I loved them all, even the leaders in a very bizarre way. You understand?"

"Yeah."

"Love can give us the strength of Samson," Weaver says. "Who did you find the courage to leave with, Nick?"

On the other side of the one-way mirror, Davis and I lean forward in our chairs, anxious to see where this exchange will go. Weaver's taken the personal angle with Sambino and I would have chastised myself for not doing more of it if I weren't so enthralled with the questioning. Beside me, Ainsley has settled back in his chair, his bearlike frame quiet and stone still.

"What other possible reason could there be to leave the family, other than true love?" Weaver asks. "It's common, you know. So many of us find our partners there."

"It wasn't love."

"No?"

"At least not on his part."

Weaver nods his understanding. I can't help but think as I watch him that he'd make a great therapist, someone I'd like to talk to. "Ahh. I see. Unrequited love. You fell hard for a man conflicted over his sexuality. I've been there."

Sambino chuckles. "Not like this."

Weaver hedges his bets. "Is he the other person in the photograph?"

When Sambino doesn't answer, Weaver presses him. "Did you get yourself into something you couldn't get out of? Like I said, love gives us the strength of Samson, but it can also be a debilitating fear. No one wants to lose love, Nick."

Sambino chuckles. "I've already lost him."

"Tell me how that happened."

Sambino goes on lockdown, with not so much as a peep or a look up from his new Bible. Weaver sits in silence with him, prodding him at times, but Sambino won't budge. Everything about his body language tells me Sambino's answer is yes.

"He's been threatened," I tell Davis. "Picasso's got him scared silent."

After some time, Davis hooks his chin at the clock. "We've held Sambino in the tank since midnight. We can't keep him much longer. Defense lawyers will claim he's been coerced and deprived if we don't get him some food and water. We'll hold him on the new charges and resume questioning tonight."

"We got nothing!" Ainsley storms. In his rage of frustration, he can't see what Weaver's gotten for us—the verification that Sambino met Picasso through the meetings and that One True Path is the heart of this whole investigation. Weaver's taken a blurry photograph and completely pulled everything into focus.

"I should have known," Ainsley grumbles. He knocks a metal clipboard to the ground. "The fucking queer's a wussy."

Ainsley's words take a sharp stab at my gut, but I choose to ignore it. If this morning's outing with Davis proved anything else to me other than Ainsley's innocence, it's that we all have our hang-ups about sexuality.

❖

The afternoon hours crawl by as I follow up on the tip line. All dead ends. The frustration eats at me. Everything moves in slow motion. Time stands still. This is the part of investigative work I hate most—the waiting. My thoughts continually turn back to Rowan. She hasn't answered any of my texts since she left yesterday morning. Fear wraps around my gut and squeezes when I think about my attempts to tell her how I found Marci. My Berlin Wall came down only a fraction, just enough to let Rowan inside for a few seconds. Then those tenacious bricks piled right back up. Although Rowan never said it aloud, her frustration when she left Willow's Ridge had been palpable. I don't know how much longer she will wait for me. Is it fair for me to even ask that of her? I want Rowan to be happy and, at some point, we will both have to admit that it might not be with me.

"Heads up, Hansen," Davis calls out of his open office door. Because of the friction between Ainsley and me, Davis reassigned me to an empty patrol desk outside his office. Concentrating in this large room full of working officers and ringing phones is next to impossible.

Davis points a long arm out toward the front of the bullpen. "You have a visitor."

Rowan makes her way through the officers, and although she's buried within a peacock-green scarf and a long woolen coat, her eyes are determined. She holds my gaze once she reaches the foot of the desk. "I need to see you, Luce."

At first I don't move. She has never come to my work before. Irritation burns in my throat. How could she come to the station to see me when she knows how rough the case is going? I don't need the interruption or the other detectives speculating about my relationship with her.

"Luce, it's important."

Davis offers us his office, and once inside, I close the door behind Rowan. Her eyes meet mine for a fleeting moment, tired and darkened underneath as if she hasn't slept at all since we last saw each other. Rowan reaches for my hand.

"What are you doing here?"

Rowan digs into her bag and pulls out papers. "Take a look at this."

She spreads an array of photocopied images on Davis's desk. The desk lamp leaves most of the interior room in shadow, and I squint at its brightness. Marci's crime-scene photographs spread across the desk like fortune-telling cards.

"How did you get these?" I demand. Rowan must have made copies of the originals when I shut down on her. "Do you understand how much trouble I could be in for this?"

"Listen to me, okay? Flip on that overhead light." She has taken on a demanding tone I rarely hear from her. "*Listen.*"

I knock on the overhead lights with a smack to the light switch. I turn slowly back to her, my fists planted on hips. The faster Rowan says what she wants, the faster I can get the photocopies back and destroy them.

Rowan unwinds her scarf. "I recognized something about these photographs, but I just couldn't place it."

She points to the one crime-scene photograph I spent so long examining last night, the one with Marci's arms outstretched and her knees bent together in a V. "What do you notice about the way her body is positioned here?"

I let out a dramatic sigh. "I don't want to analyze the artistic merits of these crime-scene photos with you."

"I know you recognized it. I saw it in your face."

She's right, of course. I did recognize something. The photograph *is* startling with the odd position of Marci's body.

"What strikes you?"

"Her arms stretched wide over that rock behind her."

"That's what caught my attention, too. Look at this." Rowan pulls out a print from her bag of an old painting: a portrait of Jesus nailed to the cross, his chin resting on his chest, his knees closed and bent, his feet bleeding with the wounds. "Picture Marci up on a cross, not sitting down."

"My God," I whisper as my mind places one image over the other.

"That's not all." She places a photograph on the table of an older man with a thick white beard and bushy gray eyebrows. "Meet Hans Klosenova. He died in 1967. His photography was never really recognized in the States except to those in the art business. He won all kinds of European awards for composition and shadow."

Rowan hands me another print done mostly in black and white with just a hint of green across the edges of leaves. In the wooded scene, a woman rests with her back against a large rock, but her skirt's open and pulled down to expose her crotch. The model's legs are stretched out in front of her, bent at the knee in a V, while her arms are out to the sides draped along the rocks. Her head has fallen forward and to the side with long hair scattered across her brow and face.

Rowan holds up Marci's crime-scene photograph. "Imagine a black and white."

I cannot deny the striking resemblance. Marci rests against a rock in the same position, even her hair falling across the brow in the same way.

"Look at this." Rowan points to the top left edge of the Klosenova photograph, almost like an afterthought, the model's sandals lying with the toe of the left shoe crossed over the toe of the right. Marci's flip-flops were found positioned in the exact same way at a similar distance from her body.

"My God." I pull the photo closer to analyze it. "In the case files it says she must have slipped off her shoes when she got to Stonehenge. I thought they were too neat, not kicked off in her usual way. The killer positioned them."

Rowan nods. "Klosenova's work wasn't mass marketed, Luce. You need to be looking for an artist, an art dealer, a collector. Someone who specializes in photography."

She spreads out photocopies of the crime-scene photographs of Chandler Jones and places them beside another one of Klosenova's photos. "It's snowy in Chandler's photo and not in Klosenova's, but take a look at the body. Look at the positioning of the head."

Klosenova's features a young woman, again in a wooded scene. This photo shows the model sitting up, her back against a large tree trunk, her legs stretched out in front of her. Her head rests forward, chin to chest, long brown hair tumbling over to hide her face, her hands resting palm up away from her sides. The glint of a golden cross lay in the model's lap. Chandler's positioned in the exact same way, cross and all.

"God," I whisper. Rowan's found the pattern I've been searching for. "What about Hannerting?"

Rowan positions Hannerting's crime-scene photograph with the young woman lying flat on her back—much like someone would in a casket with the cross inside the folds of her fingers across her breast. Klosenova's photograph looks the same including the angle of the branches above the body.

"And that's not all," Rowan says, her face flushed with the excitement of the find. "Klosenova's collection is called *Crossed*. It has seven photographs to it. Seven, the magic number that God works with so much in the Bible. Klosenova was a deeply religious man, almost to the point of fault with some of his work."

"Crossed?"

"Don't you see it?" Rowan traces with her fingertip the lines of each victim's body, the spread of the models' arms in each picture. "Each one is positioned like Jesus." She points back to the painting of Jesus. "A cross."

"You said there are seven photos in the collection?" Bile burns the back of my throat.

"Yeah, and here's the thing. This is what initially threw me. Marci is the replica of the first photo in the collection, but it jumps. Vivian Hannerting and Chandler Jones are numbers three and four. Emma Parks is a replica of number five."

My heart skips a few beats. "He didn't stop, did he? Somewhere out there is victim number two. That's why it's been so long between Marci's murder and the recent killings."

"It looks that way," Rowan says. "But why would he leave Willow's Ridge only to come back?"

"One True Path." I've never been so certain of a motive in my life. "Even if we find that missing number-two victim, it still leaves two photographs to replicate. He's on a roll now and he must be planning numbers six and seven." I look at all the pictures spread before me and everything becomes crystal clear. "We've caught Picasso in the middle of his religious masterpiece."

CHAPTER EIGHTEEN

Nothing more than a storefront church, the One True Path ministry sits in a strip mall outside of town near the highway exchange. The building is a new addition since I was last in Willow's Ridge and features all the makings of Midwest America: Walmart, the Dollar Store, Great Clips, and a local pizza place called Jake's. Only two cars sit in the lot outside Jake's, including one that has driven up onto the sidewalk with its blinkers going and the delivery sign nearly falling off the roof.

Through the oval of ice I've scraped off the outer windshield, I maneuver into a spot outside the One True Path entrance and scan the area. This can't be the correct address, I tell myself. The Pastor Jameson I know would never have wanted his ministry paired with the quick stops of America's Midwest. Perhaps he didn't have a choice in the matter. My Internet research found that the national organization fully backs Jameson's group and provides substantial funding. They pay the rent and demand the ministry be in a high-traffic location within the community.

One True Path has a simple square sign in the window, one of those cheap black felt boards with the punch-out white letters to announce its business name and hours of operation. There is nothing that signals a ministry's inside; rather, the space looks like the window front for some sort of travel agency. Two large posters hang from the front windows: *You Could Be Here*. A bright white light shines underneath these bold words surrounded by flowing waterfalls and the fresh bloom of flowers. One True Path's version of heaven.

"I guess this is it," I say louder than I need to, the mike taped firmly to the skin along my sports bra. I adjust my sweater for the hundredth time just to make sure the mike is in a good spot. I imagine Davis and

Ainsley sitting with the other end of the transmitter hearing only the rustle of clothes as I untuck the T-shirt under my sweater from my jeans again. Despite the frigid temperature inside the car, my palms sweat against the frozen steering wheel and my heartbeat races, quick as a rabbit's. I let a deep breath go that clouds in the cold and then speak into the mike. "I hope you guys are there," I whisper. "I'm nervous as hell."

Davis and Ainsley have parked the van full of listening and recording equipment a few streets over in a McDonald's lot. It's not that Davis expects anything dangerous to go down, but we are all hopeful for new leads. There is silent pressure from the team to find the key to the case, and fast, in the form of a boulder weight between my ribs.

"I'm going in." Near breathless, I kick open the car door. Although it's just shy of seven p.m., the darkness of the winter sky makes it feel like midnight.

Inside, a bell chimes as the glass door slowly closes behind me. The smack of warm air and fresh paint assault me. The business office walls have been painted stark white and appear sticky in places. The entire place is carpeted in gray and a white welcome desk stands in the entryway with a sign that reads: *One True Path Bookstore*. I browse the shelves, which hold Bibles and pamphlets with titles like "You Don't Have to Sin Any Longer" and "Homosexuality Is the Devil's Playground." A large selection of self-help books are also on sale, so many more than when I'd been a part of the organization. Smiling young men with content women at their sides cover the jackets of books.

"One True Path is still selling a dream," I whisper, brushing my fingertips along the slippery covers of the glossy hardbound books. When I came to the organization with my father, he bought into this dream and purchased a handful of books that would sit at the side of his bed for years. Books that promised change was possible for his only daughter, books that provided hope that God had not forsaken us. After he died and I moved out all of his belongings, I found the books just where they had always been, at the side of his bed. I could see the farce of those covers, the smiles practiced to mere perfection. I wondered if my dad ever noticed the strain of those cover models' smiles. Regardless, the ancient bedroom carpet still held the imprint of that book pile, a hopeful memory not so easily erased.

My father drove me home after my first meeting with One True Path, the new books strewn across the backseat. "It's all going to be okay," my father said. His voice came out light and filled with relief.

"Something tells me this is just what I've been praying for." He smiled and his warm hand patted my knee in reassurance.

"God will not forsake us, Lucy-girl," he said, shifting his eyes back to the road. "He's been with us all along even though sometimes it hasn't felt like it."

My father got his confidence back, found his will to fight, now that there was Pastor Jameson to lead us to redemption. I wanted to tell my father that I wished I could be as confident in the pastor as he was, but I didn't speak. Looking out the side window at the world rushing by, I thought about the new girl I'd just met, the one with deep-sea-blue eyes I wanted to know better, corn-silk hair I desperately wanted to touch, and soccer-strong legs I wanted wrapped around me. Marci was exactly what I'd been praying for God to bring me every night before I fell asleep shrouded in loneliness.

Standing in the lobby of the ministry, I recognize that the car ride with my father that night changed everything. Shame set in for me with the realization that my dad prayed for something so different than I did—the exact opposite. I had certainly felt shame before then over my feelings for girls, but in that sliver of time, the heaviness of it all settled deep within my bones. Secrets, I learned on that car ride home, would become my newfound way of life. Marci was my new secret. Even at the age of sixteen, I realized that in that moment I truly betrayed my father. He eventually forgave me, but something hard and painful still lodges deep within my chest, telling me I still haven't forgiven myself.

The overhead light panels are dim, casting the desk and a larger room in an eerie glow. A circle of folding chairs is set up in the center of the room, and a table is set with coffee and what look like very stale cookies. The only sound within the building other than my quick, shallow breaths is the boom box that plays a recorded gospel show. The Evangelical minister hollers for the salvation of all his listeners. *I call on the Lord for mercy for every single listener out there. Only He holds the power to forgive us our sins. One thing I know for sure is that He is a merciful Lord when the seeker is pure of heart.*

I check my watch again, only a few minutes early. "Hello?" I call. "Pastor, are you here?"

It's the smell of him that alerts me to his presence first, that sweet mixture of Old Spice and lemon drops that I came to know and rely on during my time in the One True Path ministry. Chaz Jameson is standing behind me. I can't hold back from throwing my arms around the pastor's son in a huge hug. Even though I haven't let myself admit it, I have missed my old friend Chaz.

"Luce!" He hugs me back just as hard, his chest now so much fuller than it had been all those years ago. "It's so good to see you. Pop told me you were in town." He holds me out at arm's length, his eyes moist with our reunion. He's always been the emotional one. "I could hardly believe it when Mother told me."

Chaz was the pretty one in our group, the one whose lashes were long and dark and thick, the one who made the guys working so hard to leave the gay behind drool with want. He played basketball in high school and went on to play for Ohio State with a full scholarship. He only lasted his first year of college, then dropped out. He'd always been such a dichotomy to me—both pretty and masculine—someone so caught between the life he was meant to live and the life his father dictated, strong elements of femininity coupled with an over-exaggeration of masculinity to appease Pastor Jameson. It only compounded the issue that the pastor was his father.

Chaz has put on some weight since I last saw him, making him solid rather than rail skinny. His dark hair is thin, a bit of gray along the ears, and he's got new glasses, but he still is as handsome as ever. Maureen, the other girl in our group at the time, always said that if she had been straight, Chaz would be the man for her. Apparently, her wish became a reality.

"I've missed you so much," I say. After Marci's funeral, I never saw him again. His smell still has the same effect on me, though. I feel my breath become slower, fuller, and my hands relax into a steadiness. For me, Chaz equals calm. Besides Marci, he's the only other person in the group who signified safety for me. "You're a papa now, right?"

"The folks told you. They can't keep quiet about their two grandbabies." His smile nearly engulfs his face. "You know I married Maureen from our group. Cookouts on Saturdays and Girl Scouts on Wednesdays. Everything I've always wanted."

"Congrats," I say and try to hide my surprise at his happiness. Is this all smoke and mirrors, or could he really be happy? And what about Maureen's happiness? "I hope I'll be able to see her before I go. Where is everyone for the meeting?"

"Come," Chaz says. He reaches out and takes my hand, his fingers, warm and familiar, winding through my own. His touch catapults me into a memory I lost long ago.

The first time Chaz Jameson kissed me at Camp Jesus in the Hills, I didn't know what to do. His lips brushed against mine behind the mess hall after vespers at my first retreat with One True Path. We went behind the building to be alone, to talk about why I cried throughout the evening prayers. His lips hesitated briefly before they touched mine again, testing my permission, his arms wrapped tight around my waist.

I'd been upset, my face hot with tears, though I couldn't put into words—for Chaz or the group—what I felt. Emotions swirled inside me with this strange concoction of fear and anger and disappointment. I finally understood this minister really meant we would all go to hell unless we changed our same-sex desire, and fear filled me. Then there was the mind-numbing disappointment I felt as soon as I found out that Marci was not attending the retreat because of strep throat. The blanket of shame thickened when I realized she was the real reason I pushed my dad to let me go on the retreat. It had always been about Marci, not the pursuit of genuine change.

Our nightly ritual was set: Chaz and I met and made out behind the mess hall just after lights-out. Chaz and I didn't speak—we only touched. Each night our touches became braver, the rush a bit stronger. We both knew without saying aloud why we began touching one another, the exploration of it all such a strong pull. Everyone in the group, even our parents, hinted we would make a great couple. On that retreat I'd been saddled with such shame, such flat-out fear of disappointing everyone who loved me, I was willing to do anything to make others happy. Chaz felt the same. I'd done the one thing my father didn't want me to: fallen in love with Marci.

Both Chaz and I knew where all this touching would lead on the final night of our retreat, and almost as though it was an unspoken contract between us, I lay down on the picnic table and let him pull away my shirt and shorts. I never allowed Marci to leave my thoughts—it was her lips on my skin, always her fingerprints that lined my breasts. And I wasn't the only one fantasizing. There was something about the way Chaz rubbed my belly, a pause, maybe even a disappointment before he continued, that told me Chaz had his own vision in mind, probably the boy on his basketball team that he'd confessed so many times in meetings to have desires for. Chaz's shorts came off. There was surprising strength in his rail-thin body, and I imagined Marci's touch through his. My heart ached for her, my body pulsed for want of her touch.

Out of nowhere came a rustle from the woods around us, the sudden snap of branches. Chaz jumped up, standing only in his boxers while I rolled away from him, my hands over my breasts until I pulled my T-shirt over my head. It was quiet then, only the two of us breathing so heavily and waiting for the other to do something.

Neither of us had to say a word. Chaz and I got dressed at record speed. The rest of that night I lay awake in my bunk, staring at the ceiling, thinking that God must have stopped us for a reason. In my heart, I hoped that reason was Marci. My mind, however, told me I was only kidding myself.

The next morning, the unbearably heavy silence of the pastor engulfed me as I entered the small room behind Chaz, following him to the long bench. Chaz wouldn't look me in the eye and neither of us spoke. The pastor had a look of vengeance on his face. My heart sank. Someone had told on us. Chaz sat on one side of Maureen while I sat down on the other, sandwiching her.

"The very last night of our retreat!" the pastor called out, his hands thrown up over his head. "You couldn't hold back the devil just one more night! What kind of cowards are you?"

I shook with fear and anticipation beside Maureen and wondered if Chaz shook on her other side.

The pastor had been in a most dramatic mood that day—he even had the legendary photographs that I'd never seen but heard so much about. The pastor had a reputation for bringing out the horrific photos when he was most upset with the group. Pastor Jameson stood above me and handed me the three photographs. "Look at them, girlie!" His words spit from his mouth. "Take a good hard look at your future."

The breath caught deep in my chest when I looked down at the pictures in my hands, large postcard-sized photographs of three dead men. The top of the cards read: *Gay Cancer*. Along the bottom: *A Painful Death Is Just Punishment for Violation of the Laws of God.* The men lay naked on metal autopsy tables, their skin so pale it was translucent. Purple sores covered their faces and chests, like colonies of engorged leeches still pulling blood from their victims. I'd never seen men so bone-thin except in the movies my history teacher showed us about Nazi concentration camp victims. These men's bodies had wasted away into nothing but big eyeballs, teeth, and pointy shoulder and hip bones.

"Death will be your punishment, Lucinda." The pastor turned and pointed around the circle. "All of you! You may escape man's eye, but never God's." He ripped the photos from my hands and shoved them into Maureen's. Once my hands were empty, my body contorted with a violent sob.

The pastor went on about the gay cancer and AIDS and how it was only a step away from us, how it was coming for us, until everyone in that room readily admitted they had done something terribly wrong the night before. No matter the truth, this was about ending the wrath of the pastor. In the end, it wasn't Chaz and me that the pastor knew about, but two boys caught kissing in the bathroom sometime after two in the morning. Safety wrapped around me. Still, while each of the young men confessed, I heard Chaz nearly gag beside me, my own heart thump-thump-thumping.

Now that same pastor and his wife Mildred meet me at the door with tremendously overdramatized welcomes. Chaz leads me to the worn couch where I sit beside Maureen, and Chaz sandwiches her. *Just like our retreats.* We sit in a makeshift circle along with a man I've never met before.

Maureen awkwardly hugs me from the side and drops a quick kiss on my cheek. "I'm so glad you're back," she whispers.

"What's going on?" I ask Pastor Jameson. My mind begins to spin. Pure anxiety settles in, somewhere near the edge of full-blown panic. "I thought there was a meeting tonight."

In the silence, Maureen wraps her arm around my shoulders and gives me a squeeze. "We are having a meeting," she says with a sly grin. "A meeting to save your life."

My stomach lurches and feels as if it could drop out of my body. Sweat beads my skin. "Oh my God," I whisper, "not an intervention." I look to Chaz, but he avoids my eyes. "No!" I say to him and drop my forehead into my hands, the mike I've forgotten all about digs its wires into the sensitive skin of my chest.

"Let me introduce myself, since I am the only one you don't know here." The older man stands and steps toward me. "I'm Chuck Averies, the Ohio state representative for One True Path ministries." He holds out his hand. I don't take it. He's small and stout but has the presence of an aging rock star. His mop of gray curls hangs below his collar and wisps that he constantly brushes away fall into his eyes. "You've guessed right, darling. This is an intervention. And it's exciting!" He claps and his gold pinkie rings clang together. "You're looking at a whole new life ahead of you, walking in the path of Jesus. It's a good day for you! You've strayed, but this is the day that the Lord is calling you back to Him."

Around the room, expectant faces watch me. I've seen these expectant faces before.

"There's someone I want you to meet," my dad said, taking my hand and leading me into the living room of our home. He'd put together an intervention for me at the urging of our new minister. While I came in the door from school and dropped my book bag onto the tile entryway in a mad dash for a snack, they waited.

Pastor Jameson stood up, so tall and muscular back then, and pulled me into a tight hug. "We're family now," he said. "There's nothing we won't do to save family." He introduced me to his wife, Mildred.

"Save?" I sat down beside my dad on the couch we'd had my whole life. The minister from our new church gave me a smile full of pity.

Pastor Jameson sat across from me and leaned his elbows on his knees. "Listen, I know you're dealing with a lot right now. I've got a teenage son of my own, and the times sure have changed since your father and I were your age." He shot a conspiratorial grin to my dad. "These feelings you're having, well, they're just not right. We want to help you get back on track with God."

"Feelings?" I rubbed my hands together over and over. Sweat began to form on my brow and upper lip. The living room shrank around me. What exactly were these people here for? My mind spun over all my activities for the last month. I'd done nothing wrong. I felt the rise of anxiety bubbling in my chest.

Once again, Pastor Jameson looked to my father. "Lucinda," my father finally said, his voice cracking the silence. "I found the journal under your bed."

My breath caught in my throat. My father couldn't look at me—he just wrung his hands. I closed my eyes against the burst of panic tears, the gunshot of heartbeat inside me. All those words I had written down about other girls at school. My fantasies, my thoughts.

This was the moment my father betrayed me.

But things are different now. I'm no longer sixteen years old. I *can* say no. "I don't need an intervention," I say. "There has been some mistake." I reach into my back pocket for my badge.

Chuck, the liaison for One True Path, leans forward in his chair like he's ready to spring on me in his faded Levi's and polo shirt. "Lucinda, I know how you feel. Look at me." He waits in silence until I raise my eyes to his. "Darlin', I insist everyone look me in the eye. That includes you. Listen, I've been in your seat." Chuck pounds his open palm against his chest. A thick gold chain shimmers at the edges of his shirt. "I'm recovering from my own addiction to homosexuality. Today, by the grace of God, I've been free of my addiction for over twelve years. And let me tell you something about this side of the fence: life is *good*. It's nothing like when I was in the life. I suffered so much loneliness. I didn't know the meaning of hope. Look at me today. I never would have believed I would ever get to this place. I'm so strong now in my love of God and only want to help others like you, still struggling in the life."

Chuck points a finger at me while he examines me. His look has turned hard, accusatory. "So this really only comes down to one question, Lucinda. Are you or are you not living with another female in sexual sin?"

"It doesn't matter." Haven't I fought all these demons so that I don't need to deny my love for Rowan? "I'm here on the job."

"Oh, hold up there, sister. It does matter. It most certainly matters! Sharing a bed with another woman is the reason why you are here and why you need us." The stern tone of his voice softens. "I know your daddy has passed and he was the one who brought you to our ministry so long ago." Tears fill Chuck's eyes. "He might not be here in physical form, but I can feel him in this room just as sure as I can feel my left foot. We're all here to get you back on the right path."

The mention of my father feels like a sharp punch to my gut and it brings tears to my eyes. What would he do if he was here with me? Stand by my side or join in their rally against me? Suddenly, I'm not so sure. He loved me, this I know. But sometimes love has nothing to do with liking a person, even if it is your own daughter.

Mildred speaks softly. "Luce, you've been through this before. You know how it works. Let us help you! Just listen to what we have to say, then make your decision, whether or not you will do what needs to be done in order to leave your addiction behind."

"It's not an addiction," I insist. "I love her." My words come out sounding much more like a petulant teenager's than I'd hoped.

Chuck falls to his knees with his hands in prayer position. "Oh, Jesus, we got a sick one here. Help us help her!"

Pastor Jameson speaks. "This is not about blame, Lucinda.

Lord knows I don't blame you for these feelings and behaviors. It's our culture's fault. Sometimes I watch those sitcoms on TV with gay characters all full of laughter and fun, and I think, who wouldn't want to be gay? The media has a strong hold on us all, and here it is telling us all it's okay to be gay. Okay to be gay? Equal rights for gays and bisexuals, whatever that is, and now this transgender nonsense? *It's okay?* Lord have mercy on us all! The devil takes hold of our lives any way he can, Luce. Most of the time we never recognize him."

Career or no career at stake, I won't take this. Standing up, I feel the pull of Maureen's hand on my waist, holding me back. With a swell of anger, I slap her hand away and head for the door. I'm furious when Chuck Averies beats me there, theatrically throwing his body in front of it to block my exit. Rage tears through me.

"Oh, sister, I see that anger! I see that red in your eyes! I've felt it before." He spreads out an open palm in the air between us. His gold rings shimmer in the light. "Let me tell you something you don't already know. Anger is the first cousin of shame. Underneath all that rage what you got going on is the real deal—shame. Deep down inside, you know you've been doing wrong. Let's make that right today."

Mildred tips her head at the badge inside my hands. "Just give us a few minutes to read our letters." Mildred shakes the folded paper on her lap for emphasis. "Once you've listened, we can talk about your work."

"Luce, please." Chaz stands at my side, his hand wrapping around mine. I'm caught in a bad dream, some twisted space somewhere in between the present and the past. In this trance, I let Chaz lead me back to my seat. This time, he keeps hold of my hand and I don't pull away.

Maybe it's the shock that holds me there, or the thought my ghostly father might really be beside me, but I don't move. I know how intensely personal this process is to these people in the room. They need to go through this for themselves, to justify their beliefs and behavior. It's not really about me. As much as I hate to admit it, even to myself, I still care for Chaz, Maureen, and the Jamesons.

The pastor drops his head in prayer. "Oh, Lord, we pray for the courage to be truthful, and the willingness to live the life you have intended for us. Work inside our hearts, God, so that we may serve you."

Amens trickle through the group.

In our living room back then, the pastor described to me and my father the purpose of an intervention, and although I was only sixteen, I understood that this whole charade centered around something that I had done terribly wrong. Why else would these people of the church be collected in my living room to talk about my journal? The pastor insisted the purpose of the intervention was about surrounding the sinner with love and using that love to influence change.

Me, the sinner.

"You're a cop, correct?" Jameson waited for my father's nod. "Then you are familiar with this process. It is just like an intervention used on alcoholics and drug addicts. That's exactly what we are dealing with here—an addiction. Plain and simple."

Jameson leaned back in what was my favorite chair, a leather armchair big enough for me to curl into and read or watch television. It gave me a shiver to see this chunk of a man give a mini-sermon in my chair. "Back in the day, these sorts of activities were called exorcisms. People aren't so keen on that term anymore. It's the same thing—intervening to break this devilish spirit that's taken hold of your daughter. She's been possessed. Make no mistake, Devil, we won't back down until we have Lucinda back within the light of the Lord!"

The pastor went on to say that love was the most powerful force of change in our world, and that love that would lead me back to God. "Love, love, love!" the pastor called out. "It's our golden rule: love the sinner and hate the sin."

My father and the minister from our local church nodded and smiled as though this all made perfect sense. Love made sense to me, too. The problem, though, was that I felt no love. This sticky shame melded to me so tenaciously, I knew I'd feel it every day forward.

Now Chaz reaches over and rests his arm across my shoulders. He gives me a long squeeze.

"I've never stopped caring for you, Luce, even after all these years," Pastor Jameson says. "But you've got to know, somewhere deep in your heart, that this is wrong. Living with another woman as though she is your husband is plain wrong in the eyes of God."

"Make no mistake, little lady," Chuck Averies adds, "any sort of talk regarding the support of homosexuality is pure evil. I know it's popular to say as long as no one gets hurt, it's fine. But that's devil talk. Pure and simple."

A few more amens. Then Chuck directs Chaz to begin with his letter.

"Luce." Chaz drops his arm from my shoulder. I don't look at him while he speaks. "I'm here today because I love you and because I cannot watch you kill yourself any longer."

While Chaz speaks, my fingertips graze the ridges and lines of my badge, lying on my thigh. It's the glint of the silver ring on my hand that holds all of my attention, the ring from Rowan. I twist the warm ring round and round my finger, thinking only of the infinity sign engraved inside the metal, so snug against my skin.

"Since the day I met you, I've always known that you've been touched by the hand of God. Your smile and kindness have never wavered. Now, dear friend, it is our turn to repay that kindness to you. It's time for you to trust us."

I bunch my toes up inside my boots and will myself to remember the way the sand on the beach that night in Maui felt between my toes, the granules that stuck to the bottoms of my feet. It had been so humid that night and I felt wet, my hair chronically damp. When Rowan lay back on the sand to look at the night sky, I caught a glimpse of her profile shadowed next to the magnificent sunset. At that very second, everything came together for me: I'd never been happier or more satisfied in my adult life than the time I've been with Rowan. Watching her, I felt the swell of emotion clench inside my throat like an oversized fist. It held my voice in its grip—a grip I couldn't release to save my life. That's when Rowan popped the marriage question, the one I wasn't prepared to respond to, and my lack of an answer cut her so deep. It wasn't a complete surprise. I had thought about taking my relationship with Rowan to the next level. Nights when I couldn't sleep, I thought about what the next step would look like for us. Berlin wall or not, why hadn't I said yes?

"Luce," Chaz says. "I know you remember our times at the retreat that summer you joined our group."

His reference catches my attention. My body tenses. My breath shallows. He won't say anything about our time behind the mess hall. He wouldn't betray my trust.

Maureen's hand reaches in and swallows mine, surprising me with her warmth against my cool skin.

"You know what I'm referring to, Luce. Those nights at Camp Jesus in the Hills behind the mess hall. We kissed and became each other's training wheels for heterosexuality. Without your touch, your kiss, I never would have found my way to Maureen." Chaz stops reading to give Maureen a wink. "I wasn't the only one who felt something awaken in me during those nights. You felt it, too. You responded to my body. Heterosexuality is in you, too. I know it. Give it a chance to blossom."

Around me, everyone nods and Maureen even adds a hallelujah. *They all know.*

A roaring surge of nausea tears through me and smashes me against a rocky ledge. Why didn't I see it then? Maureen had a crush on Chaz. She was the one who followed us. It had been *her* who snapped those branches and caused Chaz and me to stop that last night at the retreat. Why didn't I put it together when the following day she was so distant, so elusive? I rip my hand away from Maureen's. The look on Chaz's pained face tells me all I need to know. It had been Maureen who threatened to tell the pastor if Chaz wouldn't confess our behavior. She'd been the one to tell our secret. The pastor had known all this time. He knew and didn't punish us in any way. That was his way of approving of our behavior. He simply turned away from it, hoping that his silence would encourage his son's heterosexuality.

I stand up fast, surprising everyone in the room. Chaz stops reading midsentence. I reach for my coat through the blur of my sharp tears. Maureen might have divulged our secret, but Chaz's betrayal leaves me breathless and stung, as though he's backhanded me hard across the face. I storm out as Chaz follows.

"Luce, please. If not for you, then me."

I turn back to him on the doorstep of the building. "I won't go through this again."

By the time I reach the car, my body shakes with something I can't quite name. My feelings swirl in a strange concoction. My breath now comes fast and shallow, on the verge of hyperventilation. I feel the heat of my pulse in my cheeks as hot, angry tears slip down them. From the glove compartment comes the chime of the emergency cell phone Davis gave me, the direct link to him that the station uses for drug busts and undercover operations.

"Yeah?" I try to hide the sound of my tears.

"Get over here, fast."

Chaz has been watching me from the sidewalk, most likely thinking I would change my mind. When I pull out of my parking spot, he charges toward the car, waving his arms at me to stop. I pull out on the main road and hit the gas, watching him slowly vanish in the rearview mirror until there is nothing left to see.

By the time I pull into the McDonald's parking lot, my breath has steadied. I line my car door up with the body door of an old box-style van from the '80s. It's such a dark maroon that it looks black in the darkness. Once inside the old junker, I throw my car keys against the wall of the van, tear off my clothes down to my bra, and rip the taped wires from my skin.

"You heard it all, right?" I slam the cables against the surveillance box sitting on the floor. "God damn it! I should have expected this. I knew they let me in way too easy."

My body releases waves of heat with pulsing anxiety. It's Davis's steady cool hand on my shoulder that halts my frantic movement. "You okay?" He gives my shoulder a gentle squeeze. Ainsley sits on the bench near the rear of the van, quietly collecting all the recording equipment.

I collapse onto the bench and run my fingers through my hair, tying and retying my ponytail, my knees bouncing a mile a minute. "All for nothing!"

The seats have been removed from the back of the van. Only one long wooden bench lines the left side, while all the equipment rests on a makeshift table. Davis sits down beside me. "We'll destroy the recording. I promise."

Ainsley takes the microphone equipment that I've thrown on the table and winds it up. "Interventions can be brutal," he says, still not looking at me. I pull my T-shirt back on, then the sweater.

"Luce, these people went to an awful lot of trouble to point out this problem in your life," Ainsley says. "Was the timing correct? No, but don't throw the baby out with the bathwater."

Both Davis and I look at him incredulously.

"I'm just saying that God has a way of working on His time, not ours. Maybe you should consider what these folks had to say. Take it to heart, you know?"

"Shut the fuck up, Ainsley." I drop my head into my hands, as if to rub away his words.

"I'm a volunteer with this group and I know they speak the truth. Don't let the fact that you had a bad experience with the One True Path organization derail your path to heaven."

"Bad experience?" I yell at him. "It was a whole lot worse than a bad experience." I stand up, my body swelling before him. "I suppose you believe Marci deserved to die that day, huh?" When Ainsley stands, I'm up in his face faster than he can blink. He takes a step back. "What about me, Ainsley? Should I have died that day, too?"

Davis attempts to pull us apart, the three of us clumped together like a ball of yarn in the tiny space of the van.

Once Ainsley says, "You said it, not me," there's no stopping my fists. They come at Ainsley, an onslaught of anger and pain that pound away at his chest, his belly, his shoulders. A scream erupts from deep within my own core.

Somehow Davis pries us apart and manages to push Ainsley out of the side door. He grabs the car keys from my unmarked vehicle and tosses them out to Ainsley, who's flushed bright red and still hollering about how I hit him. "Go home," Davis demands. "I'll get this equipment back to the station. Go on. *Now*."

Davis and I wait for Ainsley to pull off before he slams the door closed and I collapse onto the bench. It's like a dam breaks somewhere inside me, a fissure that I never knew existed that erupts into painful sobs. Davis stands there a few seconds watching me cry, telling me to take a deep breath, and clearly confused about what exactly to do. "How about some coffee?" he asks, settling on what all cops seem to love and understand. He steps out and heads for the McDonald's counter, leaving me alone to collect myself.

Its times like these, when the tears don't seem to have an ending and all the hidden wounds inside me make themselves known, that I worry I may shatter. It's not as if my body is weak or too badly worn, but it's more about the eruption that threatens to expel itself from my core. These emotions are so big and these memories are so powerful, nothing can stop them once they get started. When I was younger I used to explain to others that I couldn't cry or else I would never stop. It's like a volcano—it can't half erupt. Which is why I'm shocked when after twenty minutes or so I've managed to stop crying and get my breath back to some semblance of normal.

Eventually, Davis returns with two large piping-hot coffees and a bag of ice. He's spent too long inside the store in an attempt to give me some room. I appreciate that about him, this thoughtfulness. "For your swinging hand," he says.

"I'm sorry." I sip the strong black coffee.

Davis waves my apology off. "It's never fun when work and personal life mix. All I know is that I would never have been able to walk into that ministry if I was in your shoes. That took guts, Agent. Real guts."

We sit beside one another in the cold silence and sip coffee to warm up. The freezing ice wrap on my hand doesn't help. Davis offers a faint smile.

"My first job was on traffic outside of Cincinnati," Davis says. "I wanted nothing more than to make detective. My ex did everything she could to make sure that didn't happen." Headlights stream across his face. In the dim overhead light his skin looks ashen and worn.

"She a cop?" I wonder briefly if this is the woman who the missing wedding ring from Davis's finger belongs to.

"Worse. Dispatch."

"That is worse."

"That woman sent me on more wild-goose chases." He chuckles with me. "One time she sent me all the way across town for a possible gunshot at a nunnery at three a.m. Catholic or not, those ladies wanted to take my head off."

"I can see why you moved on to Willow's Ridge." This moment alone with Davis reminds me how much I appreciate his patience and easygoing personality. He's one of those distinct people who are generally quiet but always heard.

"We're a rare breed, us cops. So hard to get to know. We're prickly one minute and overflowing with generosity the next. I haven't met many cops who aren't moody as hell." He takes a drink of coffee. I notice for the first time that the cold makes his lips purple against his skin. "Ainsley means well, Hansen. He's just got some of the worst timing I've seen in my whole career."

My feelings for Ainsley are so jumbled, like a tangled knot in an electrical cord. I understand Ainsley's behavior, yes, but do I condone it? No way.

"We do have something, though."

I look up. "Sambino talked?"

"Not Sambino. The guys back at the station located a match for the second Klosenova photo. Confirmation came in thirty minutes ago."

"Who is she? Where?"

"Victim number two is Magda Rose Teru, found on March 22, 1999, in Carbon County, Wyoming. There was some delay about the reporting of the body because the men who found her had been illegally shooting deer in a preserve set up by the state. They were afraid they'd be arrested."

The police had faxed over a crime-scene photo of Magda Rose that shows her naked body propped up against a tree stump with a large cross whittled into the wood above her head.

"No victims to match Klosenova's numbers six and seven?"

"They're still searching, but nothing so far. We're flying in the lead investigator from the Teru case to help with our investigation. He'll be here in a few hours. He's landing in Columbus at the crack of dawn."

"In medias res." Davis looks at me like he's never heard the phrase before. "It means in the middle of something," I explain. "We've caught our guy in the middle of whatever the hell he's trying to do."

Davis crushes his empty coffee cup in his fist. "You realize what this means, Luce? Not only in medias or whatever you said, but we got a transnational case now."

I'd already thought of it. Separate states means that by law the FBI must be involved. Federal agents will be on the way to Willow's Ridge to take over the case. Soon I'll be excused and dispatched back to Columbus to await my next assignment.

I crush my own empty coffee cup. "I won't go until this ends for good."

Davis looks out the square side window at the cars scattered across the McDonald's parking lot. There's sadness in his eyes, but also sheer determination. He's not letting go either.

CHAPTER NINETEEN

White. Blinding white. That's the only way to describe the hotel bathroom. Everything's aglow—the tile floor, the enormous tub, the sink and counters. Rowan's attributed this overlighting issue to the three full-throttle wattage bulbs and has removed two of them. For once, I'm in the bathroom without squinting against the light's assault. The glow of the single bulb softly filters all around Rowan as she sits with her back to me on the edge of the tub in an oversized Indigo Girls T-shirt. The steaming water tumbles over her bare feet. She's uncapped a vial of lavender oil and dribbles a few drops into the mix of the water. The bathroom explodes with the smell of calm and my exhausted body immediately responds; my shoulders, which have been locked up near my ears most of the week, finally release. I sit on the bathroom counter, still in my standard black clothing from work, and listen to the water pound over itself in rushing swirls. I can't take my eyes off Rowan. The light shadows her slim neck and long hair into a beautiful portrait. Wild sienna-brown curls, growing fuller every second with the humidity of the bathroom, spill all around her back. I could sit here and take in the view for days.

"I was worried you might work through the night," Rowan says to me over her shoulder.

"I thought we would, but Davis sent us for a few hours of sleep. We can't do much until the detective from Wyoming gets here." I don't tell Rowan that I argued with Davis to stay and continue to run searches to match putative victims six and seven. He pointed to the dark circles under my eyes and insisted I get some rest. Although he worries about his team's health, I'm certain he's still at the station running those searches. He'll get no sleep tonight. These are the facts that the public never sees, the long, grueling hours, the endless searches police conduct that reveal nothing.

Rowan stands in the tub, the waterline just above her winter-pale knees. She shuts the water off and slowly slips out of the T-shirt. With a shy smile and the quick flush of her cheeks, she twists her nude body to the side. Generally the bolder of the two of us, Rowan's sudden display of modesty touches my heart. I guess this case has thrown both of us off kilter in one way or another.

"Hot! Hot, but good." She squats and pulls her knees into her chest, nearly hidden in the drifting steam. "Coming in?"

Kicking out of my pants, I let all clothing fall to the ground with a shiver. Even though the bathroom is warm and moist, the frigid night remains on my skin. I rub my palms up and down over my naked arms. The skin's dry and cracked in places, my body tired and weather worn and drained from this godforsaken case. Standing before Rowan without the safety of my clothes, I feel transparent, fully exposed. Tonight has stripped all my layers away. My emotions have run the gamut, and the past I've been outrunning since 1989 has finally caught up to me. I'm beaten raw.

The bathwater is so hot it shocks me at first, steals my breath. Everything within my body pulls tight and then gradually releases. I inch down into the water and settle myself between Rowan's widespread legs, my back flush against her chest and inside the wrap of her arms. The soapy water stings my chapped skin as it works its way into the raw crevices of me—a salve of sorts. My muscles soon release and welcome the comfort of bubbles.

"Relax now." Rowan drops her chin to the top of my head, her chest rhythmically rising and falling against my back with her deep breaths.

We rest this way, entangled in each other, for a long, silent spell until my entire body softens into this life raft of her. Balancing somewhere beautiful between wake and sleep, I understand that this is what Rowan ultimately is to me—a refuge. My sanctuary. Inside this spread of Rowan, this comfort of her, I feel safer than I have in months.

Eventually Rowan leans forward and reaches for a bathing sponge she found in the hotel's guest packet. She lets it get so wet it pours water from its holes, then rubs my back with the soapy sponge. She uses her hands to massage my shoulders, her fingertips reaching deep inside my stubborn, stiff muscles, using her strong yet soothing instruments that calm.

Rowan's hands are nothing remarkable to look at, really, just average sized with the nails neatly squared off. Most days there are remnants of paint and chalk under her nails. Once a week she uses a brush to dig all the colors out and wash them away. It's the *feel* of her hands that's so amazing, a tremendous strength that's so capable and reassuring—I'd put myself in the care of those hands anytime. Sometimes when she massages my shoulders after a long day, I think about those hands and how she uses them to communicate with the world through her art. Rowan's hands are the medium through which she puts out art and takes it in. She jokes that someday all her veins will puff out and rope around her knuckles and wrists like her mother's, but for now the pale skin's smooth and flawless. It's the touch, *her* touch, that turns me into Jell-O.

"The oils will help your dry skin," she explains and dunks the sponge over and over again, cascading the bathwater over my shoulders, my spine, my neck. Rowan and I have never taken a bath together, and while we've showered and lathered each other up many a time before, there is something much more sensual about Rowan's touch now. It's a version of tenderness I've not felt from her in quite some time. Or is it that I've never noticed? I don't always want to acknowledge the intensity of her feelings because it terrifies me that I can't, or won't, return them. Now, though, I feel as if I could melt inside her arms, release everything to her and the hollow hush of the water. We've found a safe spot, Rowan and I, in the midst of murder and hate and a town I wanted never to return to again. We've found our hideout, our own Stonehenge.

"You learned about the oils in India." Meant to be a question, the words come out much more like a statement. "Do you ever miss it?"

Rowan nods against my shoulder. "It's the smallest things that I miss the most."

Rowan spent two years studying yoga in an Indian ashram long before I met her. She'd steeped herself in meditation, yoga, and Hinduism in an attempt to find her own version of spirituality. She came away from that experience a Buddhist and refers to her time in India as recovery from her Catholic-school training. Her parents had been devout Catholics and Rowan was taught by nuns and priests until she went to college. Spirituality is a huge part of Rowan's life, but one she's never imposed on me. Sometimes I watch her through the cracked-open doorway deep within her morning meditation. The strangely beautiful guttural chants and the gentle long pulls of breath lift her chest, and I consider her practice with pure amazement and a stab of jealousy. I'd give anything to feel those quiet moments of solace and comfort.

"The bright colors. The smells. Even the clang of the morning bells, believe it or not. Sometimes when I first wake up after a long night's rest I hear the patter of bare feet against the stone-tiled floors and feel the vibrations of everyone's chants moving through every ounce of me. There is really nothing quite like it."

It's been a long time since I've listened to Rowan talk about India. While she's still an avid yogini and sometimes still dresses in the colorful saris, I shy away from all those painful-looking poses and odd sounds. Rowan claims the calm and deliberate movements help her creativity flow. Creativity flow or not, I have to admit the oil smells fantastic and my muscles agree.

"You do know oils aren't only used by people who practice yoga, right?" She nudges me with her shoulder. "I bet you didn't know there's a lavender farm right outside Willow's Ridge."

"What the hell's a lavender farm?"

Rowan bursts out in laughter. "A farm filled with lavender plants! Lilly's Lavender is so beautiful. It has this cute little shop that I went to today."

"Lilly's Lavender? You've got to be kidding me."

Rowan ignores my sarcasm. "You wouldn't believe this shop. She even has lavender mixed into paper products for stationery."

"You bought some"—I squeeze her knee inside my hand—"didn't you."

Rowan sheepishly admits she did buy the fully recycled paper. "And the oil we're bathing in."

I roll my eyes. "What about your show?" I ask. I am afraid to ask the more direct question: *What made you come back?*

Rowan squeezes the sponge over my left shoulder. "I talked the owner into giving me another month. One of the artists was able to move up to my slot. It all worked out."

"I'm sorry, Rowan."

"I'm here because I want to be."

"I'm glad for that, Ro." I feel her nod behind me. "Thanks. I definitely don't say that enough." I rub my open hand along the smooth line of her strong shin bone.

Rowan continues sponge-bathing me, spreading the water into all my hollows while I tell her about the murder that matches Klosenova's photograph number two. "He never stopped," I say. "He just moved away to Wyoming. For some reason, he made his way back to Willow's Ridge."

"There's no doubt it's your guy?"

"Nope. The posed body is a match. Davis wants you to come in with me in the morning and take a look at the crime-scene photos again. See if you recognize anything as out of place."

"I'd love to help."

I feel half-drunk on the lavender aroma mixed with the steam. Rowan lets more hot water in to heat up the cooling waters. The pounding of the water revs up my emotions again, tightens some of what the bath has loosened.

"Ugh." I drop my forehead against my bent knees. "We're too late to save them, Ro." My mind flashes to Marci's smile. "To save her."

Rowan tests the silence, then whispers, "If you'd been there with Marci, you'd be dead, too."

I'm not sure why this moment feels so right to talk. Maybe it's the emotional eruption I had earlier in the evening. Or maybe it's the steam or the lavender oil that opens me, but I feel like everything has shifted into place, as though I am a vault and the correct combination has been entered. Almost before I realize it, I'm telling Rowan details I've never told another.

"I was late that day, you know. There was an accident on the interstate. When I found her, she hadn't been dead long. There she was, hair a bloodied mess, her clothes half torn off her." I shake my head. "If only there hadn't been the accident."

"Then what? You were a kid, not a cop! The police would have found the two of you dead and hidden away inside that cave."

"Maybe I could have done something."

Rowan lets out a very tired and long sigh. "Marci knows, Luce. She knows. All she wants out there in the spirit world is for you to forgive yourself."

I close my eyes and shake my head. It's hard for me to believe that Marci has forgiven me. After all, she's the one who's dead and I'm the one enjoying a bath with my lover. Where's the fairness in that equation?

"Marci would never blame you for what happened. Look, I know you hate when I get all spiritual on you. I get it. But you have to understand that the mystics and my spiritual studies have made me who I am."

Rowan took two years of religion and philosophy classes while getting her art degree at the university. Her real studies in the spiritual world, though, were during the time she spent studying at the ashram. I've never seen someone who could fade into that prayerful place that Rowan sometimes goes while she twists her small body into some of the craziest positions that hurt me just to watch. I'm thankful that Rowan waited to get into all this until *after* I'd fallen in love with her. With my cop mentality, sometimes I wonder if I'd have gone out with her a second time if she'd slipped into cat or eagle pose while chanting in that haunting way that simultaneously calms and frightens me. My conversations with my dead father notwithstanding, some of Rowan's moves can be plain creepy.

"Finding Marci's killer and bringing him to justice will set her free. And you." Rowan takes a deep breath. I feel the air slip out of her over my right shoulder. "Set yourself free of the past, Luce."

Rowan continues to rub my back with soapy water, letting rivulets of warmth spill over my shoulders and down my chest. Silence lets her words sink in.

After some time, Rowan speaks again. "How was the meeting with One True Path?"

I groan. "It was an intervention. I should have realized they were up to something. It was way too easy to get the Jamesons' permission to attend the meetings."

"Like a drug and alcohol intervention?"

"Exactly. Only this was about my addiction to homosexuality. You have to admit that you are powerless over homosexuality before the group will agree to help you."

Rowan lets out an incredulous laugh behind me. "Holy shit. Are you serious?"

"As a heart attack. I've had two of those interventions now. Two too many," I say.

"You had an intervention with your dad?"

"I came home from school one day and Pastor Jameson and our own minister were sitting in our family room with my dad. It was so crazy because my dad had this finger food set out on the coffee table. I'd never seen my dad set out any kind of food except to throw a chip bag at a visitor. I knew something was really up when I saw those cold cuts and dip on the table. It made me really curious just how long he'd been planning this surprise event."

"How did you react?"

"Barely spoke a word," I say. "I didn't cry like you see people do on that show *Intervention*, but I felt wooden, stiff. Unable to speak. It was much later on that year that anger erupted."

"Is this how everyone gets into these groups? With an intervention? How does it work?"

"You really don't know?" I ask.

She shakes her head behind me. "How would I know? You never told me!"

"I didn't think you wanted to hear about this stuff."

Rowan tosses her hands up beside me while the water splashes. "You always get so upset. I don't want to bother you with the details."

There is so much of myself that I haven't shared with Rowan. All these feelings and thoughts I've kept bound up within me under the assumption that if I told Rowan about my past, I'd only hurt her or she would consider me insane. I kept this part of myself hidden, never talking about One True Path except to make fun or to joke about its craziness. Clearly, in my attempt to protect Rowan—and myself—from the past, I've pushed her further and further away.

I explain the organization's history to Rowan. "The national organization is really wealthy and makes its money by running these retreats and revivals. People from all over the world attend. They sell expensive tickets to seminars and self-help books about how to leave homosexual desire behind for good. It's a modern-day money-making machine."

"How Christian of them," Rowan chimes in.

"Exactly. The national organization provides funding and support for all the local groups to spread the message."

"That God can change your sexuality?"

"Homosexuality, they say, is an addiction caused by a traumatic event in your life. The idea is once you realize that root cause, then you can work with that in order to correct your sexual orientation."

Rowan slides out from behind me. "I need to see you," she says. She wraps her legs behind me and moves until we sit face-to-face. Wet ringlets cling to Rowan's cheeks as her eyes search mine for connection. "What is a root?"

In the ministry, so many of us were terrified of our own root causes. The pastor's insistence on identifying it only heightened that terror. Most of the time, we had no idea what he was referring to and let him guide the way. Anything just to get out from under the intensity of his gaze. "They believe that everyone is born straight. It's always an event in childhood that veers you off course into the land of homosexuality.

The big one is sexual molestation but there are others, like smother mothers and doting fathers."

"Smother mothers?" Rowan laughs incredulously.

"You heard right. It's like a doting father but a mother who will not allow her kid to grow and breathe without her constant guidance. The sexual feelings get transferred to her. Little boys become effeminate and little girls become dykes."

"Huh." Rowan's in deep thought. "What happens if you go through the therapy or whatever for the root cause and the sexuality urges don't change?"

"Great question!" I throw my hands up for emphasis. "One True Path's answer to that, because this does happen, obviously, is that you embark on the fantastic journey of conversion therapy—reparative therapy. Supposedly this therapy will uncover the real root cause that you have buried so deep inside you don't even know you have it. One True Path recommends it for all! They retrain you to be straight and teach you how to be with the opposite sex."

Rowan laughs again. "Teach? You mean how to have sex with a man if you're a woman?"

"Exactly. I've heard it's even crazier for guys who have to learn to get it up for women." We laugh together at that image, but then I sober. "One True Path still promotes this type of therapy even though psychologists and doctors have found just how damaging these groups are," I say.

"I know I'm laughing, but how awful," Rowan says. She drops the sponge and rubs her open palms up and down my arms, slowly, an attempt at comfort. "It must have been so crushing to hear that a part of you was a sin, especially as a teenager. Were there people in your group who really believed they were saved?"

"Healed, yes, based on the belief that God can heal the sick and broken. So they pray to be healed from the disease of homosexuality. The Jamesons' son claims to have been healed. He's now married to a woman who was in our group, and they've adopted two kids. There were also two men who were a bit older, in their forties, who claimed they were healed and only continued with the meetings to guide us fledglings."

It feels good to speak of what happened during this period of my life so seriously for once, to finally explain to Rowan why I sometimes behave the way I do.

"Sounds like those faith healing revivals they show on TV late at night."

I nod. "Sometimes it's not that far from it. My first visit with the group…" I'm not sure I can tell this part of the story.

Rowan squeezes my shoulder, then leans in to kiss me softly at the nape of my neck to urge me. "Go on."

"I had to first meet with the pastor and his wife alone and confess my lesbian experiences. Thank God I didn't have to do this in front of my dad. They wanted to know if my love with another woman had ever been consummated. So, there I was, trying to figure out exactly what they meant by the word consummated. I figured kissing did not mean consummated, and when I said no, the two of them broke out in a ruckus of thankful prayer. I could still be saved and healed into what God made me, a shining heterosexual, through the hands of Jesus." I mock their rhetoric.

With her head thrown back, Rowan laughs at my obnoxious reenactment of the Jamesons. It has been a long time since I felt this close to her. "I see it didn't change you." Rowan places her hands into the prayer position.

"Thank you, thank you, thank you."

She kisses my cheek again, gently. "That's the universe's way of telling you what you confessed wasn't a sin."

"Apparently Chaz still believes it is."

"You've never mentioned him. Were you close?" She nudges me when I don't answer. "Luce?"

"Yes." I've told Rowan this much, why not tell the entire story? "We were paired up together from my start with the group. The pastor had chosen me as a mate for Chaz. It just never worked out for the long term. Marci got in the way of all that."

"Are you serious?" There's no laughter this time. When I didn't respond, she says, "You are. Oh my God."

"It was sort of like an arranged marriage. My dad knew. Granted, he didn't believe we would be encouraged to practice sex with each other, but he knew." I tell her about the experimentation behind the mess hall. The words spill out of me in a quick flurry, like I've been waiting for forever to finally tell her.

"You've been through hell, baby. Thank goddess you made it back."

"I'm sorry, Rowan. I know you are"—I make the quote marks in the air with my fingers—"spiritual, with all the Buddhism and yoga. Does my lack of faith bother you?"

She leans in to me. "There's a big difference between religious and spiritual. I've told you before that my trust in the spirit, or God, if you want to use that term, has nothing to do with the church's teachings. I'd like to spend some time talking to the Jamesons about the spiritual realm, I tell you." Rowan sidles back behind me and holds me closer against her chest while her knees pull in to hold me tighter.

"And you know what? You've told me before that you have no faith. Go ahead—roll your eyes," Rowan says. "But the way I see it, you *do* have faith, you do believe in spirit or God or whatever, you're just so angry and hurt over what's happened. There is so much rage and pain over what you think God allowed in your life, but you're not even close to living without faith." She kisses my cheek. "Spirit is with us, Luce, whether we want it or not. The Jamesons' God is not the only one. Trust me."

Rowan holds me close long after the water turns cool. I memorize this comfort I take from her, this peace she gives me with her touch—wrap it up in my mind and save it for when I'll need it again. Inside that bathtub Rowan comes at my Berlin Wall from the side, sneaking in to quietly chisel away the bricks and stones, tearing down what stands between us before I even realize what has happened. She works diligently throughout the night, carving away a stone at a time.

When we finally emerge from the water, though, Rowan's no longer working alone. I'm there at her side, naked and somehow made new, with my own hammer and chisel in hand, pounding away at the rock and debris that has covered me for so long and kept me at such a distance from her. Rowan has given me a light at the end of the tunnel, and now that I see faint rays of that shimmering glow, there is no turning back.

CHAPTER TWENTY

Monday, January 14

It's six a.m. and the station reeks of burned coffee. Someone forgot to put the glass pots under the drips, leaving a gritty brown mess across the conference room floor. The carpet swishes with the weight of our steps as the entire team gathers around the conference table.

To a stranger to law enforcement, the room must look like a gruesome art collage exhibit: crime-scene photographs are projected onto the wall and multiple murder boards fill the room, each painstakingly loaded with every tip and every piece of information about the victims and suspects that we've been able to gather. It is Rowan's first time to see the innards of a serial, and the boards I make in hotels and at home pale in comparison. Rowan pores over each picture, every clue and detail. Davis sits beside me. Sergeant Rick Hodges from Wyoming faces us from across the table. His worn cowboy hat balances on his knee and his weather-tanned face is in desperate need of a good shave. The red-eye flight has made roadmaps of his bloodshot eyes, but he insists his mind's awake and ready to work.

Ainsley takes a swig of his coffee and watches Rowan's back at a murder board. "Artists." He shakes his head and then tries to catch my eyes. The sight of him there at the table stirs some of last night's biting anger. But then there was the bath with Rowan, and somehow I left much of that rage in the water that swirled down the drain. It's inevitable: Ainsley and I will have our conversation. Now, at this table with the case lanced open in front of us, isn't the time.

As soon as I awoke this morning, my hair still damp from the bath the night before, and while the thick darkness of early morning still covered everything, I ran searches on Ainsley. He's owned a home in

Willow's Ridge since 1974 and only changed addresses once. He's been employed by the Willow's Ridge police for thirty-five years. No other listed addresses or sources of income. With each additional search, my focus on Ainsley as the killer waned. Ainsley's challenging conduct toward me can be explained by his disapproval of my sexuality and his full approval of One True Path. He's also not too keen on working with a woman who outranks him. All of these observations added up to me closing the folder on Ainsley as our Picasso.

"Do you see something we missed?" Davis calls out to Rowan. He looks particularly subdued and gray this morning. He's wearing the same clothes he did yesterday, a clear indication that he worked through the night.

Rowan turns back to the table to face us, tentative at first. "He's definitely an artist." Her voice cracks. Intimidated by the badges in the room, she looks to me for support and I give her a quick wink. "My opinion is he's either a young artist, because he is still in the stages of copying the work of those he admires, or an older artist who has never gone beyond the stage of admiration and hasn't developed any ideas of his own. And if he's older, as he probably is, he's a frustrated man, angry, explosive. He hasn't found his voice yet."

"Why an older artist?" Hodges has a soft voice with a drawl that carries.

Rowan points at the crime-scene photo of Vivian Hannerting that has been paired with the Klosenova photo. Her confidence spikes—she's in her realm of the art world now. "If you look at this work, he's really quite good. The focus clearly captures the body and fades the surroundings. Even the exact foliage that was highlighted in Klosenova's is here. It takes a great artist to be able to replicate something at this high a level. It also takes a good deal of practice. A younger artist would most likely not have the experience with light and shadow work."

"Voice?" Davis asks.

"His artistic truth. The original statement or message we have inside us. It takes some artists longer than others to find it. Many never do." Rowan turns back to the murder boards. "I'm sure you're aware that other murderers have used death in their art. I once had an art professor who told us that serial killers are artists who use a different medium but are cut from the same mold."

"Our man's taken a wrong turn somewhere," Hodges adds.

While others in the room chuckle at Hodges comment, Rowan's not so amused. "Darkness and violence have always been a part of art," she says with a flare of the defensive. "We've all heard of the classic tortured artist. We're looking at the work of one."

Davis thanks Rowan then, clearly an attempt to thwart a theoretical discussion of art, and flips the slide projector to victim number two. He invites Rowan to stay and examine the crime-scene photographs with us. "Your insights are most helpful," Davis tells her. "Just remember that everything you see here is confidential. Understood?"

"Of course." Rowan takes a seat next to me.

Hodges takes his cue. "Miss Magda Rose Teru was found by a couple of deer hunters out in Carbon County in December 1999, in a touristy, yuppie-type village that attracts hunters and people visiting the parks farther along I-80," explains Hodges. "Teru lay spread out on a path just waiting for someone to come along and find her."

With the laser pointer, Hodges highlights in neon red an overgrowth of bushes around Teru's body in the photograph. "At first glance the scene looked like nothing had been manipulated. Our team later found evidence that some of the debris and shrubbery that surrounded the victim was carried in from other areas of the woods." Hodges circles clumps of vegetation surrounding the body. "The staged crime scene indicated a good deal of time had gone into the planning of it. We checked for fingerprints and DNA but found none."

Hodges clicks to the next photograph. It's a split screen of Klosenova's *Crossed* photograph paired with another photo of the crime scene. Identical. Klosenova's features a naked middle-aged woman with long dark hair, parted in the middle. Strands rain down across her eyes and face. Her mouth hangs slightly ajar with the tips of her lower teeth visible as she lies flat on the thick grass. Unlike the other victims, both Teru and Klosenova's model have their legs spread out in a long, wide V with their arms tucked against the body. The image of the cross has reversed itself. A crown of roped vines and thorns has been shoved into place around the victim's head. No one can deny the strong relationship between this image and the crucifixion. Twisted lines of blue veins road-mapped just under Teru's skin's surface. Around her body, a thick shrub functions as a sort of nest into which a space was carved out for her. Everything down to the placement of the leaves and the lighting matches the original Klosenova photograph.

"We couldn't identify her for almost a year," Hodges says. "A sketch artist came in and drew her from the neck up without the crown and with the hair out of her face. We had her picture in the paper and sent it out to all the police stations in the region. Eventually we sent the photos out nationally." Hodges passes around copies of the drawing. With all the dark hair out of her face, Teru's large eyes gaze out at me.

"We buried her in an unmarked grave. Jane Doe of Carbon County. One day, clear out of the blue, a man came to us from Alaska where he'd just gone to file a missing persons report for his sister. He saw the drawing of Teru hanging on a bulletin board in the police station." Hodges switches the screen to a smiling photograph of Teru next to an overdecorated Christmas tree.

"Random." Davis whistles.

"Or fate," Ainsley grumbles.

"Why did it take the brother so long to file?" I ask.

"She made a living as a prostitute since the age of nineteen. A wanderer her whole life. She started out as a runaway and in adulthood disappeared for weeks on end. The family rarely spoke to her except on Christmas, and the brother lived in northern Alaska while the rest of the family stayed in Anchorage. The family had no cause for worry until Christmas rolled around and Magda Rose was nowhere to be found. I guess it was her favorite holiday and she never missed it."

"Any idea why this woman was older than the rest?" I ask. "The others were no older than midtwenties. She's almost fifty."

"Convenience," Ainsley says. "The killer probably picked her up for a quickie and realized she had the same body type and hair as the original photograph."

I'm not convinced. Something had to have made this woman different than the others. With her dark hair strewn across her face, Teru did match the model in the Klosenova series, but the viewer cannot tell the age of the original model because of the covered face. He could have taken any woman with long dark hair and modeled her to match Klosenova's photo.

"Rowan, do you have any way to find out the age of the original model?" Davis asks.

"I can search the art databases and see what comes up. Klosenova wasn't very popular in his day, so not many scholars choose to write about him for papers and dissertations."

"Picasso has picked an obscure artist to emulate for a specific reason," I say. "He's sending us a message."

"Message or not, we need to get one step ahead of him." Davis sighs.

"I have an idea that might help." Rowan waits for Davis's approval before she flips the slides to the sixth and seventh photographs in the

Klosenova series and takes over the laser pointer like she's been doing these presentations her whole professional life. I hide a smile behind my fist. *That's my girl.*

She uses the red neon laser pointer to circle long columns of what looks like dead vine on both sides of the photograph. "Because he's so particular to match everything, locating a place that has this type of foliage will help you stay one step ahead."

She enlarges the slide of Klosenova's number six. The pointer circles the stone grave marker featured behind the model in the original photograph. She enlarges it even more and zooms in on the gravestone. Only the letters *SHE* are visible above the model's right shoulder.

There's an audible exhale in the room. We all missed the obvious clue. "If he's going to copy this exactly," Rowan says, "he'll need to find an engraved stone."

"I'll alert all the funeral homes in the state," Davis says.

"Our guy's sneaky," I add, making a note on my to-do list. "He could swipe a stone from an existing grave. Look how worn and old that stone appears."

Davis agrees. "Just in case he does try to purchase one, let's talk to Chad Eldridge. He would also be able to tell us where old graveyards are in the county. Get right on it after this meeting, Hansen and Ainsley."

I swallow down the urge to argue the pairing.

"Art critics have argued about the possible connection between photos six and seven." Rowan zooms in on the corner of the photograph, enlarging a tree stump. "Both photographs feature this stump and the very similar way the snow drapes across the surroundings. There is also the connection of light. In number six, the sun has gone down with daylight fading, possibly early evening, but in seven, night has fallen and he used special lenses to capture the image in the dark. Critics argue the photos were taken the same day in some sort of frenzy to finish the series."

"If he follows Klosenova's pattern, these last two murders could happen in rapid succession," I say. "Where were the original pictures taken?"

"A few different locations around the Kansas City area," Rowan says. "As far as I could find, none of his work was shot in Ohio or Wyoming. And he mainly worked in Northern California and Arizona."

"For some reason, your quarry speaks to the killer," Hodges says. "The change in location for the Teru murder must have been out of his control. Maybe a military posting or a job transfer."

Davis assigns tasks to each detective and urges Hodges to stay in Willow's Ridge and become part of our team for a few more days. Hodges agrees and we all feel the pressure of this mounting case, sense that we are so close to the edge and that everything will soon collapse around us. We hope to emerge from the wreckage with the killer in handcuffs.

Davis also thanks Rowan for her help with a genuine handshake and smile. "Hansen can drop you off at the hotel on the way to the funeral home."

"I'm glad I could help, Captain. Anytime."

It seems I'm the only one who is not all smiles. Signaling to Rowan I need a minute, I sidle alongside Davis. "I need to see you, sir. Privately."

With a nod of the head, he leads me into his office and closes the door. "I already know what you're going to say, Hansen."

"I'm still going to say it. I cannot run interviews today with Ainsley."

"It's one interview, Hansen. We'll see where it goes from there."

"Davis, I can't. Not after last night."

Davis sighs and sits on the corner of his desk. "You're too close to this whole thing to work alone in any sort of an interview. Everyone else has an assignment."

"Eldridge isn't a suspect." I can feel my jaw muscles working overtime in a clench that could take a finger off. I know what Davis is trying to do; he believes that if Ainsley and I are together today, we'll work it out in our own way.

"No, he's not, but you two need to give him a heads-up. Sambino is going to cause a shit storm for Eldridge's business. Fill him in on the charges. I'll meet with him later today." Davis leans toward me. "Look, the FBI will be here tonight. Let's show them we can solve this thing before they get here. None of us wants to lose this case."

His pleas soften my resolve. "I'm taking one for the team here, Davis."

He shoots me a quick wink. "You are stronger than you realize. And Ainsley is a good man despite his mouth."

I roll my eyes and push out of his office door.

CHAPTER TWENTY-ONE

Ainsley beat me to the Eldridge interview despite direct instructions to enter and run the interview *together*. Eldridge's daughter, a dainty, young teen with the body of an anorexic ballerina, meets me at the front door. With a swish of her waist-length dirty-blond hair, she directs me to the end of a long hallway and her father's library. As I watch the young girl depart, I'm reminded that I've never seen Eldridge's wife.

Rowan planned to go back to Dublin again once I dropped her off at the hotel. I want Rowan to stay—selfish on my part, certainly, but at least we're in a better place now than before. What would I do without Rowan in my life? She's been my anchor since we met, and now I see this as clear as my own hands.

Inside the library, Ainsley and Eldridge speak in hushed tones. I catch snippets of the conversation, veiled hints of words like *God*, r*espect*, and *not like us*. Words that smack of Ainsley's retelling of last evening's events. The forced smile on Eldridge's mouth tells me I've interrupted. Eldridge pushes a mug across the large oak desk to me. "Homemade hot chocolate from my wife."

I wrap my cold hands around the mug and lightly blow over the top of the dark liquid. "Does your wife help out with the funeral business?"

Eldridge gives me a broad smile and shakes his head. "This is my world." He points up to the ceiling. "Her world is upstairs with the kids."

"Happy wife, happy life," Ainsley chimes in and chuckles at Eldridge's agreement.

My eyebrows arch at Eldridge's stringent gender roles. He might just surpass Ainsley on the conservative scale, something I thought would be next to impossible to achieve. Eldridge, I notice once again, has a fastidious appearance. Not a hair out of place, not a spot of his clothing wrinkled. His navy suit looks custom-made, every detail fitted to his body perfectly. The cuffs of his white Oxford have hand-stitched *CAE*, and a heavy, large-faced Rolex rests on his left wrist. Eldridge's showy overcompensation suggests to me that he was probably the small kid in school everyone endlessly teased, the one who was nearly invisible unless he was the butt-end of a joke. Growing up in a funeral home couldn't have helped matters. Even though those early years are long gone for Eldridge, I imagine these memories are never too far from his mind.

The deep maroon and gold rug that covers the library floor looks like it cost more than all of my paychecks put together. Eldridge already has a fire roaring in his handsome office, and there are rows of shelved books along the walls. A mounted deer head hangs behind the desk along with a grandfather clock that's so polished, it shimmers. Despite the heat from the fireplace, there is the distinct icy chill of Ainsley beside me.

Even though there's flamboyance in Eldridge's tastes that have an element of femininity, there is also the purposeful display of masculinity that surrounds him, with the deer head and the deep colors of the room. Mr. Metrosexual. I feel frumpy once again in front of Eldridge, my worn black pants and button-up on another go-around for a case I hoped wouldn't hold me in Willow's Ridge for more than two days.

Chad Eldridge clears his throat. "The fire should help to shake the cold off."

"I wish my hotel room had one," I say. "It's darn near freezing at night."

Eldridge's gaze looks out beyond my right shoulder and through a large window. "When this cold spell finally breaks, we'll soon forget all about it."

"Forget?"

His focus comes back to me. "Isn't that how it seems? We're relieved of the cold and never consider it again until the next winter, the next time we drop to that same temperature again. It's what we do with everything that make us uncomfortable."

"I suppose you're right."

"Since we got Miss *B-C-I* here," Ainsley interrupts Eldridge, "I'll let her take the lead even though I know this case like the back of my hand." He chuckles the way he usually does when he digs a knife in deeper with his words.

Ainsley's presence sets my teeth on edge. I take a long sip of my hot chocolate. "Thank you, Mr. Ainsley." My voice is as sweet and calm as if I am a genteel woman out for afternoon tea. "As always, I appreciate your help."

The loud grandfather clock chimes the half hour and its sound echoes against the paneled oak walls.

"Where do customers purchase headstones?" I ask Eldridge. "Are they included as part of the services for a funeral?"

"Most buy the headstones through us," Eldridge says. "We order them from a company in Washington. Occasionally we get a family who has purchased a stone somewhere else that features something specific for the deceased. They ship the stones directly to the Willow's Ridge Cemetery."

"Is it possible to order a new headstone that appears weathered?"

"Sure." Eldridge nods. "We went through a fad about ten years ago where it was the big thing to do. People wanted stones to appear a century old. There's some kind of acid wash they can put on the stone. Then they chip away the edges." He drums his fingertips across the top of his desk. "Hand-crafted headstones are an art form," he tells us. "One that is dying. We have all these molds and machine-made headstones now. There's a distinct difference."

"Do you keep detailed records of which customer has bought which stone? Could you go back the last couple of years and search for any gravestones you've sold that had *SHE* anywhere near the top of the stone?"

"Of course." Eldridge leans back in his oversized leather chair. "I'll pull the records today. Forgive my questions," he says, his voice dimming a few octaves, taking on a conspiratorial tone. "Not that we can ever take him back on as an employee, but has Nick been cleared?"

I give Chad Eldridge my own forced smile. "Sambino's awaiting his court date." I explain the charges. "He's still a suspect in the murders, of course, but we're also looking at others."

Either Mr. Eldridge is a fantastic actor or he truly doesn't know about the photographs we found in Sambino's apartment. I've been worried about hints of necrophilia leaking from the department—it's the sort of detail that tends to pour out fast no matter how tight we try to keep things. People, law enforcement or not, can't keep their mouths shut about freaky stuff like this. Sambino's photos are the gritty details the sensationalist media would keep in the rotation for weeks, to pull in the ratings. I'm not ready to broach the subject of Sambino's photographs and activities with dead bodies just yet.

"Have your daughters ever reported any unusual behavior from Sambino?" I ask.

Eldridge shakes his head. "They have no contact with him. He clocks in when they're going to bed. I lock the connecting door from the downstairs when I go up for the night."

A faint rose tint blooms on Eldridge's handsome cheeks from the heat of the fire. From the side, it's hard to ignore Eldridge's chiseled jawline and the smoothness of his polished skin that hints of professional facials. "My wife is so worried, that she drives the kids to school and even walks them into the door of the building. The kids used to walk the three blocks on their own every day. Not now." His breath escapes him in slow exhalation. "It's hard for the kids to understand why we have to make the changes."

"How many do you have?"

Eldridge hands me a frame from the corner of the desk. "Two. Seven and fourteen."

My fingertips outline the little blondes lined up outside the funeral home.

"We need to ask a few more questions about Nick." Ainsley's tone tells me I'm moving too slow for his tastes. He's chomping at the bit to get to the photographs. "Has anyone been down in the prep rooms with him, other than your staff?"

"No." Eldridge laces his fingers across his trim belly. "What exactly is going on?"

"That's what we're trying to determine," I say. Damn Ainsley for jumping the gun and spooking interviewees before I can get anywhere with them.

One by one, Ainsley positions the pictures of Sambino with the naked corpses across the desktop. Thankfully he has the brains to withhold the final photo with the shadows of Picasso.

Eldridge's hands shoot up to his mouth to cover a loud gasp. He touches the corner of one picture with only the edge of a fingertip. "My God, that's Mrs. Woolensted." He averts his eyes as if it's disrespectful to look.

"I wish I didn't have to ask, Chad. These photos were found in

Sambino's apartment. Someone had to have been with him. He didn't take these pictures alone."

"He works alone at night," Eldridge protests. "It is possible he brought someone in the building, but I have never been aware of it." He drops his head into his hands. "My God!"

"Sambino's been charged with desecration of a corpse, and we want to make the charges stick," Ainsley says. "We have to find this photographer."

The color has drained from Eldridge's face, leaving him looking haggard and thin. His skin is so pale that I can see the tangles of blue veins above his left eye. "He's ruined my business." Tears swim in his eyes.

Ainsley collects the pictures and puts them back into the folder with finality. "It won't get out, Chad. You have my word."

"This will ruin me, Cole."

Ainsley continues to speak about the confidentiality of the photographs and asks Eldridge to speak with his staff. Perhaps the cleaning crew might have seen or heard rumors of a visitor after hours. Ainsley's questions are meant to distract Eldridge from what we all know will come—press coverage that kills the business. While the two men talk, I walk around the rich library and examine the intricate artwork and leather-bound books.

Snapshots showcase Eldridge's family at the beach, skiing, and huddled around Christmas trees. A large collection of CDs lines one shelf, all featuring the sermons of a Baptist minister that I recognize from my late-night television viewing habits. He's the one who built that colossal glass palace in Florida. Wasn't he recently indicted for tax fraud and stealing money from parishioners? I pull out one of the CDs. It's only then I realize that the beautiful hardback books that line the shelves are not real, but hollow spines with titles set in gold lettering.

I look over my shoulder again at Eldridge's ironed shirt and the initials sewn into the cuffs. This man is all about appearances and producing the image of his wealth to others. He's a narcissist, I realize, empty underneath that sparkly gleam of money. Narcissists are highly insecure and cannot handle any sort of criticism—one of the most brittle of personality disorders. Without professional help, Eldridge won't survive the collapse of his business. I make a mental note to find a referral for him from victim services. It's hard for me not to feel sorry for Eldridge. He simply hired the wrong man, and for that, he most likely will lose everything.

Brushed-gold-framed photography catches my eye. A series of three black and whites are perfectly mounted, each with a different close-up perspective of a lush, wooded area. It's a location I know well—God's View—the visual from the crest of the hill along the path to Stonehenge.

When Rowan and I first began dating, we visited many museums of art. I was willing to go anywhere as long as it was with her. Rowan insists that every work of art tells a story. At a photography exhibit she taught me how to read a photograph through the lines of composition and its distinct focal points. Now it's the borders of Eldridge's photos that I narrow in on. It's the hidden place, according to Rowan, where many artists choose to make the work their own. The edge of this photograph holds miniature suns in each of the four corners, a tiny, swirled circle with protruding rays that could easily be missed unless you're searching for it.

A signature. Rowan has her own, the *namaste* symbol that she embeds into each painting. She explained the signature as something every artist has, a mark that proves the work is original, the seal of the artist herself. It used to be the way ancient artists would distinguish their work from imposters'.

"These photographs." I interrupt Eldridge and Ainsley, who are chatting. "Who is the artist?"

"They're beautiful, aren't they? I couldn't take my eyes off them in the gallery." Eldridge stands beside me to view the photographs. His strong and expensive-smelling cologne engulfs me. "It's funny how many different ways you can look at the quarry and still keep it so engaging. It's a local woman, not much older than a girl, really."

"Kaitlin."

"You know her? I'm fascinated by her work."

"Kaitlin certainly is fascinating." With a collection of photographs that study the quarry over time, it's clear Kaitlin knows a whole lot more than she's told me.

❖

Outside, in the parking lot, Ainsley trails after me, and I hear him curse as he sinks into the ruts of the snow and ice. "Damn it, Hansen, slow down!" His pullover rubbers give him no traction.

"Get some real boots," I grumble. Who wears skinny little rubbers in this type of weather, anyway? I slump against my car and wait for Ainsley, my arms crossed over my chest. He slips and catches himself, then stumbles toward me. I don't move to help as he clutches the side of the car for dear life.

"This weather's for the birds," he mumbles as he gathers a foothold against the ice. "Should've let you take the interview."

I groan at his insincerity. "Davis told you to wait for me."

"Here we go. I knew you'd get your panties all in a wad. Look, I've known Chad for years."

"And so you two were just casually catching up about what? Your religious values?" I unlock my car door. "Did you tell him about the One True Path connection?"

"No, darlin'." Ainsley sarcastically digs another knife into the wound. "Your secret's safe with me."

"As if I can trust you." The words explode and I practically spit the consonants out into his face. "How do I know you didn't clue him in to what I would ask? The conversation wasn't recorded. We're supposed to be a team, Ainsley, a concept you've clearly forgotten."

Ainsley groans. "Miss All-High-and-Mighty. When you gonna get over last night?"

Un-fucking-believable. *Get over it?* "I've known some like you in my career—bulldozers who knock down everyone with their narrow-minded ideals." Turning from him, I open the car door.

Ainsley scoffs. His face is beet red against the cold afternoon. "Narrow-minded, huh? I've put up with you on my team, haven't I? You want to talk about professional behavior? Bringing your lover in on the case when she has no law-enforcement training like she's a teammate? Housing her on the taxpayers' dime?"

I slam the door of my car closed and don't bother to wait until Ainsley teeters over to grab hold of his own car. Gunning the engine, I rip his balance away from him.

To hell with Ainsley. I've got a killer to find.

CHAPTER TWENTY-TWO

Karma: the way I see it, everything comes down to second chances. Rowan tells me the concept is much more complicated than merely a do-over, but all I envision is the world's largest Ferris wheel of important moments that spins and spins. There is so much more at stake with a second chance; the problem is, I don't always recognize it as such until it's too late. This case has had more circling moments than I care to admit, and they just keep coming around and around.

Hamilton Street is next to empty while Ainsley maneuvers in the dark at a near crawl. The tires crackle over refrozen sections of ice as we search for unit 621-R. At 7:21 p.m. the entire town of Willow's Ridge has tucked themselves away behind locked doors. The eerie silence drafts the streets in ghoulish shadows around every corner.

After our argument at the Eldridge Funeral Home, Ainsley stayed away from the station most of the day. Target practice at the shooting range helps him clear his mind. He says it's the focus required of him for each shot, the enormous concentration on something outside himself, that does the trick. Ainsley finally returned to the station after dusk with something no one knew we'd been looking for: the address for Kaitlin's shared artist space.

"How did you get this?" I interviewed the same manager at the photography store only hours before Ainsley. Jasper Morgan put up a significant fuss over my request even though Kaitlin hadn't shown up for her shift. No one in the store had heard from her in over twenty-four hours.

"Everyone knows me, Hansen. Morgan just needed a little more time, a little more push from someone he trusted"—he winks—"and the bogus threat of a warrant."

Outsider. In such a small town, witnesses will be most comfortable with one of their own, not me. With all the emotion brewing over the last few days, I've made some amateur mistakes. I certainly rushed the interview with Morgan. I was angry with Ainsley, and my mounting frustration left the slow burn of acid in my gut. I let my emotions rule the interview and gave up far too easily when he offered the slightest resistance. And then there was the Eldridge interview. My biggest mistake on the case so far? Not trusting the judgment of my teammates, including Ainsley.

After my fumbling apology, Ainsley eventually nodded his acceptance. "I've got a big bite, Hansen." Then he smiled in the Cheshire cat sort of way. "Sometimes you just got to tell me to keep those jaws closed, even if you are a Democrat."

Learning about Ainsley's son's death changed everything. How would my own father have lived his life if I'd chosen to do what Tim did? My anger at Ainsley's bullheadedness and controlling ways has vanished. I can't help but smile at the old gray-hair, to notice the way his eyes crinkle with laugh lines when he teased me. He must have been one of those fathers who insisted on being a part of everything: the baseball team carpool driver, the Boy Scout father who took the troop camping and fishing, the one at every activity cheering Tim on from the sidelines. In other words, he's a whole lot like my own father and so many others in law enforcement—a good man, but not perfect. The fact that Ainsley hadn't shriveled with the death of his son, wilted away on some couch watching bad daytime TV, drinking his hours away or, worse, committing suicide himself, shows me he loved his son despite the suicide. That knowledge tells me more about Ainsley's devotion and loyalty than any medal of honor ever could. I'll never tell him about my trip with Davis to the graveyard. It's funny how sometimes you can see into the future, look forward to how you'll be able to keep secrets with such certainty.

"What's bothering you?"

"Hmm?" I've been working hard on what's left of my thumbnail, the metallic tinge of blood on my taste buds. "What isn't bothering me? Why, why, why."

Questions loop around my mind: Why did the killings restart in the last few years? What's so important about this time of year to the killer? Rowan has found no tie between the artist or the photos and lesbianism. Why this series? Out of the whole wide world, why these girls in Willow's Ridge, Ohio? My biggest question, though, has to do with Kaitlin. What is her connection to One True Path? She'd been quick to declare herself straight when we last talked. Could she be a member as well? These questions nag, pulling at the edges of my mind.

Ainsley shrugs and waits for the red light to turn green. "Do we ever know the why of most cases? It could be as simple as the killer studied Klosenova's photography series in high school and had a crush on the art teacher. Or maybe these photographs are what started his fascination with crosses. The reasons are so twisted with these guys that it does more harm than good to dwell on such things."

"I know what the general profile says. Opportunity is the element most important to the killer, along with a remote location. But you've spent all these years working on Marci's case. You connected the cases through the clues that everyone else dismissed. What's your theory?"

The light turns green and Ainsley gives the car some gas and considers the question. "Picasso is relieved."

The quick arch of my eyebrows asks Ainsley why.

"He knows we're close. He senses the end is near. Just this one final push to complete his destiny, to finish this series."

I'm not completely satisfied. There is the flipside of Ainsley's theory. Our killer is most likely intuitive in his own way, but how many times has law enforcement taken serial killers down when they least expected it? These guys believe they are untouchable. Untraceable. What I do know for sure is that seven murders will never be enough for Picasso. He has the taste for murder now, the need. He may have been apprehensive and unsure of himself when he killed Marci, but those fears have subsided and he believes he's on a mission that can only be stopped by God.

Ainsley rolls the car in front of 621-R, the rear of a secluded warehouse. The only address marker is scribbled in bright red spray paint across the heavy steel door.

"I still say we go straight to the horse's mouth," Ainsley says, falling back on his usual clichés. "Sambino's the one we need to be talking to, not this girl."

I throw my hands up in frustration. "We have no leverage against him! Besides, these two are connected deeper than we know. I feel it."

We both know Sambino won't talk to us. That's the whole point of tracking down Kaitlin. We've been over this a million times. If we can get something from her to confront him with, make him think we know something, we might be able to get Sambino to talk.

"Davis will be resistant to any sort of deal with this twit."

"That's why we have to get some information to make Sambino think we know more than we do. No deals."

Ainsley taps his leather-gloved fingertips along the edge of the steering wheel, his thoughts churning.

"I can get more out of her alone," I say.

Ainsley shakes his head. "She didn't tell you about this connection with Sambino."

"Is she a member of the One True Path group?"

"Not one that I interviewed. Why?"

"She's a lesbian, Ainsley. She's fighting her desire, but it's there."

"Hansen, come on. You saying I can't interview a"—I wait for the slur, but instead Ainsley puts his hands in the air and makes air quotes—"lesbian?"

Ainsley's got his back up again and I settle those feathers. "I'm saying she was willing to talk to me before, and I'm guessing that has a lot to do with my sexuality. Throw a man into this interview and everything will be stilted."

Ainsley ponders this, then ducks to look through the top of the windshield to a window on the second floor. A strong light filters through the beveled glass that makes it impossible to see inside. "Is this one of those gaydar things?"

"Gaydar?" A burst of quick laughter spills from me.

"Isn't that what you all call it?" Taking his glasses off, he chuckles and rubs his red eyes. We're both exhausted from stress and the long work hours.

"This Superman act is going to get your butt blistered with Davis."

"But I'm not solo." I unclip my cell phone from my belt and shake it at him. "If I'm not back in twenty minutes, bust down that door." I nudge him with my elbow. "Davis never needs to know."

"Famous last words." Ainsley dismisses me. Still, he's in.

❖

The thick, frozen steel of the warehouse door is hard as a rock against my fisted bang. I continue to pound until eventually I hear the clatter of heeled footsteps descending a metal staircase. There is no peephole, so when the door swings open, Kaitlin examines me with squinty eyes heavily made up with electric blue mascara. She wraps her skinny arms around herself to keep the chill away from her bird-thin sleeveless arms. She looks over my shoulder to make out who's in the car.

"Did you find the killer?"

"We've got a strong suspect."

"Who?"

"I've got more questions for you, Kaitlin. May I come in?"

Upstairs in the large wide-open studio, I follow her along tiled floors that remind me of the floors in school buildings. The ceiling is a mass of protruding, winding pipes that occasionally knock and ping. Kaitlin and the others have set up space heaters throughout the large room and covered the oversized casement windows with thick plastic to avoid losing heat. Surrounding me are art exhibits in different stages of development. Some of the walls hold pinned-up sketches and others display collections of prints. A clothesline runs from one corner of the room to a windowsill, hung with prints, and paint tubes litter the space under the windowsills. The smell of darkroom chemicals stings my eyes, while Kaitlin prattles on as if unaware of the smell. It reminds me of walking into someone's home that stinks of cat piss. The owner has smelled it so frequently she no longer recognizes the bitter stench.

Kaitlin chatters away, mindless talk that I take as a sign of a strong case of the nerves. The key is to find out why she's so anxious. She pops her knuckles as she paces and avoids eye contact with me. Instead of asking questions about what we've found and who we've arrested, she talks about this old building and how it's an abandoned factory that was leased out as studios and shops.

Either Kaitlin knows something has led me back to her and she's involved, or the fact that we are alone upsets her, further evidence of her struggle with her sexuality.

I lower my voice and remain as still as I can, tactics designed to help a nervous interviewee. "You've got a nice setup here. A lot of artists would kill for a space like this."

Rowan has always used a dedicated room in her home as a studio. The space to create, she explained when she first walked into the barn on our land in Dublin, was one of the most liberating moments of her life. The previous owners of our house had used the barn as a storage unit and hadn't given much attention to the building. Rowan cleaned it up and applied a fresh coat of bright purple. "Who says a barn has to be red, anyway?" she asked with her fists planted firmly on her hips.

While Kaitlin gathers paint-splattered stools from around a worn table, I take a closer look at a string of photographs hanging near me. The clothesline is filled with a number of shots taken in a wooded area. I immediately recognize the hilly landscape, the multilayered limestone, and the heavy tree line, winter-barren of leaves. She's taken both color and black-and-white shots of the caverns, the ravine, and most of all, God's View. There's even a multitude of photos from the famous Staircase—a location inside the quarry where the earth has created a layered, stair-step of limestone down a sloped hill. What strikes me most, though, isn't the location of the photos, but the weather conditions: snow and layers of ice gleam from the landscape.

"When was the last time you were in the quarry?"

Kaitlin sets the stools down with a thud that sends the steel floor beneath us vibrating. "These photos are part of a series that examines the landscape in changing seasons." There's the quick lilt of defensiveness in her voice. Of course, she's not selling out, she explains, only targeting the seasonal tourists who flood the area in the fall. "The new calendar unveils in September for the leaf-peepers."

She's hiding something. I sense it. "So there's no connection with the fact that these photographs are within feet of where the victims were found? What aren't you telling me?"

Kaitlin bites her bottom lip, her upper teeth pulling at the fleshy pink. "There's so much interest in the story…" Kaitlin tries to redeem herself.

Finally, I understand. Her calendar will feature each of the drop sites and the areas surrounding them. Which begs the question, is she certain there will be more deaths to fill the remaining months in the calendar? "But you're not selling out, Kaitlin. Right?"

She scoffs at my words. "Even the Parisian artists drew profile sketches for tourists along the river for quick cash. I've gotta eat, you know."

Kaitlin leads me to the far corner of the studio. "Art has always sold better if it has that element of violence. I'd be a fool not to use these sites."

I barely contain my groan. No matter what Kaitlin throws into this argument, I'm not buying it. Rowan and I have hashed out the argument of art for money's sake ad nauseam.

A framed, hanging portrait the size of a large poster confronts me and the breath catches in my throat. Soon the familiar rush of water rises around me, inching up past my shoulders.

"It's a project I've been working on for some time." Kaitlin's voice gargles through the thickness of water.

My fingertips reach out through the watery veil with a tremor. The Andy Warhol–like composition wheels brilliant colors and bold shapes. My index finger traces the tiny square photos, all of the same size and composition but in varying shades of color. Together, these small squares form an oversized portrait of Marci. Her navy eyes twinkle out at me. She's wearing the shirt I remember so well, the worn plaid in faded blues and greens.

Suddenly I hear Rowan's voice. *Karma*, she whispers to me. *Don't let this wheel circle round again.*

Like I said, I don't really understand all of Rowan's spiritual talk, but one thing I know for sure: karma can be a real bitch.

After my very first group meeting with One True Path, the Jamesons held a welcome party for me. Once I noticed Marci, I couldn't turn away. I watched her sip water, nibble on a rock-hard cookie, flip the spray of golden bangs from her brow while she smiled and laughed with the other members. From that point on, I became stealthy in my observations of Marci, stealing small glances at her from the corner of my eye, hanging on every word she said. She had the air of the bad girl, playful and headstrong, sporty and curious. By some stroke of major luck, or maybe the push of God's own hand, she sat next to me in the final group circle that first night. Cross-legged beside her, I watched Marci's bare tanned knee bounce along the folded edge of her jean shorts. For a fraction of a second our knees met and a pure shot of electric rocketed through my entire body until every one of my little hairs stood on end.

Pastor Jameson closed the meeting the way he always did—with confessions. Had anyone been moved during the meeting to confess? Had Jesus put upon any of our hearts the urge to purge the dark secrets we'd been holding on to? It was the moment in every meeting that had the power to make my heart stop and my palms drip with sweat. I'd go on to have nightmares of the pastor fixing his gaze on me, demanding that confession of me. On that first day, though, as the newbie, I was spared. I'd already learned that the pastor was a force to be reckoned with and when the Lord moved him to question someone, all promises were off. That day, though, that beady stare fixed directly next to me. Marci's nervousness was a boiled heat radiating at my side.

"Marci. I hear you've had quite a week."

"It's been okay." Marci leaned forward with her elbows on her knees as if she was ready to spar. I never imagined that anyone would have the courage to take on this man of God.

"That's not what your mother says." The pastor coughed in the silence that filled with tension. "Does that mean you haven't heard from the woman at the college?"

I watched Marci crack each knuckle. Strong hands.

"I ran into her."

The room erupted in whispers and movement. As if on cue, Mildred broke out in fervent prayer.

"You must confess, Marci. This is vital for your recovery and relationship with Jesus."

We all sat in a circle on the floor while the pastor stood in the middle. With the intense attention, Marci did something I never expected—she began to rock slowly back and forth and her eyes took on a distant glaze as if she was thinking of something that happened long ago.

"Marci," the pastor coaxed, "remember your mother. She'll be so disappointed to hear that you aren't recovering."

Marci groaned and threw up her hands. "We kissed, that's it! I only saw her because I wanted to tell her in person it was over. I at least owed her that."

"Owed her?" the pastor nearly hollered incredulously. His beady eyes could burn right through you.

"She's been a good friend."

"So said the sinners about one another in Gomorrah. She's tempting you, Marci."

The rest of us looked down at our hands, but Marci was defiant. Her rocking became quicker. She stared the pastor directly in the eye. Much later, after Marci's death, I realized it had been that fierce refusal to give in so easily to the pastor's ideals that caught hold of my heart that very first evening.

"I like her for who she is—all of her—not just for what she has between her legs."

"Marci, that's stinkin' thinkin'." The pastor stepped closer to her.

"Is it?" Marci didn't let up. "We're told to not be attracted to people only because of their looks, to not judge a book by its cover. Isn't that exactly what you're telling us to do? Only to be attracted to someone who has the right genitals? Isn't it what's inside a person that counts? That's what Jesus taught. To look for a person's soul and not what adorns their body."

At first, no one could believe she said it out loud. I'd be willing to bet that everyone around that circle had had those same questions at one point or another, but no one dared to agree with her. We sat in silence for some time and waited for the pastor's response while he prayed. Instead of speaking to Marci, though, he spoke to us all.

"Don't you all see? Marci freed herself from this woman. The devil is doing all he can to pull Marci back. Look." The pastor leaned in close and circled the group of us. "People who have the homosexual disorder lack healthy boundaries. This leads to gay relationships that are fraught with sexual and emotional addictions."

Fraught. It sounded to me like the pastor was reading aloud from some sort of medical dictionary or a textbook. On the other side of me, Chaz nodded. The others agreed.

My mind, though, was on Marci. My throat swelled with jealousy. A college girl? I could never compete with that. The pastor ranted on about how the devil was alive and well and we were all seeing his work in Marci. Conversion therapy, the pastor said, would cure Marci—that and a tremendous amount of prayer. Our eyes met and held a few seconds until Marci gave me a smile that told me she found this amusing. It nearly knocked me over to look Marci in the eyes; a frightful ball of intensity rose from my stomach and lodged itself in my throat. But I could take these secret glances in small amounts. These treasures. The tiny blond hairs on her forearms rested against summer-tanned skin. The way our touch sent both shiver and sweat throughout my body at the same time.

My heart nearly collapsed inside my chest when I imagined those arms, those hands around me, her lips on mine. Those lips moving down. And the room swam around me when it came time to join hands in closing prayer. When my palm pressed against hers, our fingers entwined. My palm that was sweating so much, I nearly lost my grip on hers.

"Lord, we pray for you to cleanse us, make us new again," the pastor called out. "Most of all, we pray to see your true light during these meetings, this gift of time from you." He turned in the circle to focus on Marci. "Please, Lord, we pray that you guide Marci into your light, loosen the grip that the devil has on her soul. He's taken her hostage, Lord, and she needs you now."

Marci's fingers closed tighter around mine. A shock of...something ran through me, like a shot of liquor firing through every vein. Like one thousand hands stroking me all at once.

Later that night, alone in my bed, I untucked these images of Marci I'd hoarded away. My body burned and my cheeks flushed with the memory of Marci's touch, and I called out to God.

Is this love? Is this a sign from you? Why are you letting me feel this way if it's so wrong?

In the heavy silence, I listened for an answer, for any sort of response.

"God, please." I resorted to presenting God with a bargain. "If you let Marci like me back, I'll never do wrong again. Just this once."

No answer dropped down from the heavenly gates. What did come was only more of the ache for Marci, the desperate want of her. Just to hear her soft breath. To smell her skin and hair. To feel those hands on me, over me, in me. My bedroom began to throb, pulsating around me until I could feel her against my skin, taste the heat of her lips on mine and feel the full weight of her body on top of me.

This, I reasoned with a shudder, *must* be love.

❖

Somewhere through the thick waters around me, I hear Kaitlin. "It's Marci Tucker. She was killed in 1989."

I imagine my feet touching the floor of the sea. I bend into it and push myself up, up, up through the surface of the water.

"I wanted to play with this technique I never really used before."

"Stippling. Only you've used photos instead of dots." I rub my tired eyes and try not to look at Marci's front teeth, squared and perfectly white. The likeness of this portrait is alarming—a photographic resurrection of sorts.

"Yeah, how'd you know that?"

It takes me a few seconds to collect my thoughts. I rub my throbbing temple. The mega-load headache's just around the corner. "Why are you so interested in her?"

Kaitlin's long hair's tied back in a bun, similar to the way Rowan keeps her hair as she works. I notice for the first time that Kaitlin has blond roots—near white—growing in against the black hair dye, and the image reminds me of Sambino's brown roots growing in. Doesn't anyone around here present themselves as they truly are? Kaitlin rubs her hands together with nervous energy, like she's trying to generate heat.

"Marci's a legend around here. A ghost story. When I was younger, my older brother used to dare me to go into those limestone caves to see if I could find Marci's ghost on Halloween night. It's the big thing to do around here, light candles inside the caves and do some silly séance that never works."

"Why did you do a collage of her?"

Kaitlin shrugs. "I felt for her, I guess." I say nothing, only watch as she picks at the remnants of dark polish on her nails, the bones of her fingers and hands as delicate as a bird's. "This will sound weird, but we had a sort of connection. Not that I talk to dead people or anything, but I understand her. I get what she was about. I mean, here she was, just this high-school girl who went to the caves to get away from this godforsaken town. She was the outcast. I can really relate to that. It's not easy being different in Willow's Ridge."

"I'm sure it's not."

"She had this artistry to her. In the school library I found old yearbooks. The one they printed the year Marci died had a sort of memorial for her and included some of the drawings she'd done. They were all these intricate, looping designs that only form a picture when you step back from them. Sort of like stippling, but with circles."

Circles and loops. I look down at my hands in my lap and, with my thumb, twist the silver ring from Rowan round and round my finger.

"My dad was a few years older than Marci. He told me she always was writing in this notebook, toting it around and making all these notes. I imagine her as a poet, really. The artist killed before her time."

A notebook. Marci's missing journal.

During one of our meetings, I sat on the edge of a stone and watched Marci draw circles with the end of a stick in the dirt outside the dusty cavern of Stonehenge.

"Scribbles," she said, "until you look closer. Then everything makes sense."

I thought about the real Stonehenge while I watched her draw that afternoon, how the English countryside held this place of great energy, a circle where all within was secure. It was a ring of safety, a giant hug for all who entered. Marci told me of how the real Stonehenge was thought to have healing and spiritual powers. The ancient people who frequented those magical stones came there to celebrate and to make offerings to a higher spirit. Was that how Marci saw her own

Stonehenge? A safe ring of rock that kept all the bad out, a place where she could be sheltered by the environment? I certainly did. It was the spot not only where I came to see Marci, but where I could come and lick my wounds from an insensitive world.

"Our energy never leaves the circle," Marci said. "You're here. I'm here. Even when our physical bodies are not. We'll always be a part of Stonehenge."

Marci, I realize, has become the boogeyman to Willow's Ridge. She's the monster story that parents warn their children with, the ultimate cautionary tale. *Me?* Marci would say. *The Willow's Ridge boogeyman?* And we'd collapse together in a peal of laughter. Kaitlin's correct about one thing, though. Marci's ghost is a palpable presence in this town, appearing when least expected.

"Do you really think the recent killings are linked to Marci's?"

"We're looking into it," I say and follow Kaitlin back to the table with the file from my satchel. "What I am sure of, Kaitlin, is that there is so much you are not telling me."

"What do you mean?" Kaitlin eyes the file between us. I wait for her to finally look up at me and then tell her with my eyes: *Cut the shit.*

I spread out the photographs of Sambino with the dead bodies, side by side, slow and methodical. Her body freezes into a rigid position that tells me she's surprised I have copies of them. We sit this way, both of us looking down at the pictures on the table in silence. When it's clear she isn't going to talk, I pick one up. "I bet the families would slap a lawsuit on anyone involved in these photos faster than the media hounds could get here." I pause. "It's the border of the photographs, Kaitlin, that caught my attention."

Kaitlin's face visibly reacts to the word *border*. Her eyes close to avoid any sort of contact with mine and her body visibly tenses.

"I know a painter who tells me that every artist has something called a signature. So when I saw this image"—I take the tip of my pen and point at the marking of the miniature sun—"I knew exactly what it was." I walk over to the portrait of Marci and tap at the tiny sun inside that border. "Your signature."

Kaitlin's like a deer frozen in the headlights, all eyes and tiny body focused on that small circle with outstretched lines in the border.

"I'm curious, Kaitlin. Why did you develop the pictures if you didn't take them?"

A few beats of tense silence pass between us as if she's trying to figure out if I'm joking or not. Finally, Kaitlin lets out a breath of relief. "How did you know I didn't take the photos?"

"It's obvious. The composition. The harsh lighting. It's not your work."

Kaitlin's teething her bottom lip again around the chunky, silver lip band. "Sambino paid me. He wanted black and whites with a classy look. His word. This is the best I could do with what I had to work with."

"How much?"

"I shouldn't have, I know." Kaitlin's voice takes on a tone I recognize from earlier in our conversation, defensive justification. "There's this art school in Chicago I really want to go to."

"How much, Kaitlin?"

"A thousand dollars in cash for about two hours of work. You've seen my crappy apartment. How could I turn something like that down?"

So Kaitlin had been there earlier, at the apartment, and chose not to open the door. I let this slide but tuck the information back inside my mind. "Who's the photographer?"

"I don't know."

"What did he threaten you with?" I recognize the same type of fear inside Kaitlin's eyes as I saw in Sambino's. Picasso has gotten to them both.

"Nick told me that he slept with this person." Her lower lip puffs out. "Nick said they're dangerous. Powerful. If I told, I'd be in danger."

"Danger of what kind?"

Kaitlin only shrugs.

"How do I know you're being honest with me now?"

"I swear." She grips at her chest as though the pleas cause her pain. Her arms are covered with goose bumps. Kaitlin's much too thin and small to have committed these crimes on her own; still, she could have been there.

"I had nothing to do with what happened to those dead people. I just needed the easy money."

"What gender is Sambino's lover?"

"A man, I think. When Nick tries to hide that he's been sleeping with a man, he's cagey about his pronouns."

"Is the photographer one of your partners from here?"

"Jen's a painter. Alex? No way. He can't stand the sight of a hangnail. Besides, his work is amazing."

She goes to a bookshelf and pulls down a hardback book for me. "Alex published this collection a few years back. Never in a million years would he settle for these terrible images. He doesn't need the money. This"—she taps her fingernail against one of the photos we'd found at Sambino's—"is not a photographer. It's a tourist shooter."

There is something about the way she speaks, the quiver that's left her voice and the direct eye contact. Kaitlin's finally telling me the truth. "A tourist shooter?"

"People who only take shots of family and their trips on vacation. Somebody who doesn't know how a camera works to save their life."

I flip through the book of photography. Magnetic colors fill images of trees and the town of Willow's Ridge until it's cranked up on color overload. The photography looks like a vision through a spinning kaleidoscope, all the colors mixing and curling into one another. Kaitlin's right; these photographs are fantastic. Any artist this good wouldn't be able to dumb his work down to match the amateurish pictures we'd found hidden at Sambino's.

"I'm not in trouble, am I?"

Kaitlin's lies about Sambino have pushed us back hours in the investigation. But mostly I'm angry at myself. How did I let this doe-eyed little creature trick me into ignoring her as a connection? Kaitlin had been the one to originally tie Sambino to the photography store, after all. Instead of recognizing that, I felt sorry for her and her struggles with her sexuality. "If you are willing to do something for us, I'll see about getting the charges dropped."

"Charges?"

"This is serious business. You've taken money and been a part of desecrating corpses, not to mention interfering with a state murder investigation."

Tears spring into her wide eyes and all I see is Kaitlin's frailness, her dainty features that look so weak. Despite what my head tells me, my heart softens. She looks so beautiful before me, so broken.

"I'll do my best to help you." I lean toward her and press my open hand on the top of the wooden table to emphasize my slow deliberate words. "But absolutely no more secrets between us or the deal is off. Agreed?"

She sniffs and wipes her cheek with the back of her hand. "I swear. No more secrets."

❖

I slip into the hotel bed with my hair still wet from the bath. I'm wrapped inside the Indigo Girls T-shirt that Rowan's left behind. The well-loved fabric smells of her. True to form, Rowan left a few of her items tossed around the hotel room when she left for Dublin. Most days, Rowan's habit of misplacing items annoys the heck out of me, but tonight it only makes me miss her more. In the dark, I call Rowan's cell despite the late hour—she turns her ringer off when she goes to bed. The voice mail picks up and saves my short message: *I miss you.*

I lie back and stare at the ceiling. Two FBI agents arrived this evening—a forensic psychologist and a team leader known as the tracker, a man who supposedly has tracked multiple serial killers over his years with the Bureau. So far, they haven't taken over the case, only added themselves to the team. Earlier, Sanders called to explain that he was giving me professional lead on the case and waiting to come to Willow's Ridge for a few days. "This is your chance," he said. "Show those sons of bitches what you got, Hansen." Thank God he doesn't know about the mistakes I've made; he wouldn't be giving me the benefit of representing our office.

Not more than ten minutes later, I surrender to that deep well of sleep my body has been craving for days. The case has revved down the steady pitch that's left my eardrums ringing with its siren call for the last week. There is nothing left to do until morning.

The gap between the shadow and the dark-haired girl narrowed. His rabbit-quick footsteps and lightness of stride proved he must have trained at some point in his life. The dark-haired girl pounded on until an exposed shaft of limestone caught her toe and tossed her forward. Catching herself before the fall, the shadow closed in. Only an arm's length away, his grunting breaths barked at her back. As quick as one footfall to another, she changed course and charged directly to her left, away from the path.

Darting between tree trunks as big as her body, the dark-haired girl tore through branches and gnarled vines that clawed at her summer-tanned skin and bit gashes that welted bright red. He trailed not far behind, slowed by the impact of a thick branch against a fleshy body part—a loud thwack that carried through the forest.

She broke through the foliage to the rocky ledge and her feet slipped forward with the sudden stop and the forward momentum of her body. Her toes tipped over the edge toward what lay below: the deep quarry and water, at least twenty feet down. The shallow edges glinted up at her. She balanced on that precipice, gazing down.

The dark shadow stopped a few steps behind her. He didn't reach for her. She inched closer to the edge. He didn't move.

Suddenly, the dark-haired girl flailed her arms and kicked off the ledge for the center of that pool. Her arms spun wildly as layers of limestone flashed around her. Dropping fast, she scissor-kicked her legs through the surface of the cool water, plunging into the swirled depths of sudden quiet. Bubbles of oxygen floated up as the water became a container of safety for the dark-haired girl, a body able to take on wild fear. She stopped fighting. She sank lower and lower, the weight of the water a pillowy cushion.

I wake, screaming at the top of my lungs. I reach for the lamp and it bangs to the floor. Rolling into a ball, I fold my legs in tight in the fetal position. *You're safe, you're safe, you're safe.* Huddled in the bed, my gaze falls on the murder board. The people that I love most are tied up with it: Marci with her murder, Rowan with her understanding of art, and my dad who saw me through the aftermath of finding Marci. My breath slowly settles into a gentle rhythm.

A question suddenly occurs to me. Did the shadow jump into the quarry after me? I go back through the end of the dream, replaying it in my mind. I never heard his body plunge in. I never saw his shadow underneath the water. I never understood why images of water come when panic hits me or why the water feels like an encasement of safety. How many times a week do I sink under the surface in my mind when things get to be too much? How many times a month do I hear those oxygen bubbles float past me when stress and emotions overwhelm? The water—how could I have missed it? It has always been about the water.

CHAPTER TWENTY-THREE

Tuesday, January 15

I've seen a lot of local jails in my career, but McCraken County has to be one of the most impressive facilities in Ohio. Much like the modern Willow's Ridge police station that comes complete with a fully loaded workout room and state-of-the-art electronic equipment, the jail also has exercise machines, movement-activated cameras that record prisoners' every move, and fancy electronic gates that work through staff fingerprints rather than codes.

The visitation room is built in a large circular open space with tables scattered throughout. Sunlight filters into the room through enormous skylights. Guards anchor themselves every thirty feet or so around the perimeter, an overkill show of force since only ten prisoners are allowed in the visitation area at a time. Still, I have to hand it to them, McCraken's never had a jailbreak or riot like some of the other rural county jails in Ohio. Ainsley, Davis, and I test equipment in an observation room on the second level that looks down over the visiting area. It reminds me of a basketball arena without the bleachers. When the prisoners or visitors look up, all they see are colorful ads for family services that line the top in an attempt to hide the one-way windows. Every prisoner knows the windows exist; it's like an urban legend that's passed down from one prisoner to the next.

Kaitlin has brushed her hair in a severe ponytail pulled so tight the corners of her eyes lift. With the heavy black paint around her eyes, she rings of a skinny Cleopatra. She twirls the end of the ponytail around her thin fingers with nervous agitation. The speakers spill out her quick, short breaths punctuated with the occasional pop of her knuckles. She has worn black jeans and a faded T-shirt just as Davis directed her to do. "Nothing special. Make it look like you came to visit out of desperation," he told her.

Kaitlin is Nick Sambino's first and only visitor since he's been incarcerated, other than his lawyer. Guards told him nothing more than his fiancée has come for visitation. Despite the fact he has no fiancée, he doesn't question it. His handcuffed wrists are bound in front of the ever-so-fashionable orange jumpsuit. The cameras around the room zoom in on Sambino's face, but what I see there isn't what I expect. Kaitlin's certainly not a surprise; Sambino's eyes show happiness at the first sight of Kaitlin and he bites back a silly grin as a guard leads him from the side entrance to Kaitlin's table.

"She better not fuck this up," Ainsley grumbles at the monitor.

It's true we've got a lot riding on this Hail Mary stunt: Kaitlin has to make Sambino think we have more on him than we really do. She has to get him to reveal clues about the identity of Picasso.

"Babe." Sambino slides into the bench seat and waits for the guard to walk away. The word babe sounds foreign and slow from his mouth. Sambino laces his fingers and puts his hands on top of the standard-issue metal prison table.

Kaitlin says nothing. Her eyes swim with tears for a few seconds as she reaches out to squeeze Sambino's bound hands.

"No touching!" a guard immediately calls to them.

"Damn, she's playing the role perfectly," Ainsley says.

"You doing okay?" she asks, moving her hand only inches away from his. "I put money in your commissary account." Kaitlin's rambling, and her nervousness shows in a voice that's strained and high-pitched. "Want some coffee from the machines?"

There is something about the way Sambino held on to Kaitlin's hands, something about the way his touch already knows the curve of Kaitlin's skin. Kaitlin's not playing a role, I'm suddenly certain of it—Sambino and Kaitlin are lovers. It all makes sense—another couple who found one another through One True Path. What holds Sambino and Kaitlin together is the fight against homosexuality—an inner struggle they each recognize in one another.

"Are you sure about the coffee? I'm sure it's not the greatest." Kaitlin prattles on about the quality of food Sambino must be eating and the cold temperatures outside. She's interrupted by a gaggle of small children who rush toward their incarcerated father, seated near Sambino and Kaitlin.

Sambino asks, "What are you doing here?"

Kaitlin lowers her voice to barely above a whisper and spreads her bony elbows wide on the table. "The cops think I took the photographs."

Sambino scans the room, taking note of each guard's position. "Kaitlin. Don't."

She groans and rolls her eyes in perfect exasperation at him. "No one can hear us."

Sambino looks up at the bank of one-way windows and then ducks his head to check beneath the surface of the table. He doesn't know that these wall cameras can zoom in on his nose hairs if we wanted to. He won't notice the tiny microphone attached to the edge of the table on Kaitlin's side as anything other than a black speck no bigger than a sharpened pencil tip.

Kaitlin settles her chin into her chest and looks up at Sambino with those big blue eyes of hers. "I cannot go to jail, Nicky. I won't make it." Soon tears spill onto her cheeks.

Davis marvels at Kaitlin's ability to cry so easily, but I see those tears as something much more. Kaitlin's and Sambino's fears are genuine. Both of them are into something way too deep and neither can see a way out.

Sambino reaches up and manages to wipe away a tear from Kaitlin's cheek before a guard hollers at him to keep his hands on the table. He abides but coos at Kaitlin until her tears diminish. "Don't worry. They're only fishing."

"That woman with the state police connected us through the photo shop," Kaitlin says, crying. "She's not fishing, Nick."

Nick's eyes scan the room.

"I didn't do anything!" Frustration spikes Kaitlin's words. "I'll tell them about Joseph."

Davis, Ainsley, and I perk up. Kaitlin is still holding out on us. So much for all her promises to keep no more secrets from me.

Sambino hushes Kaitlin once again. "Don't get excited and do something stupid," he whispers. "They got nothing or they would've arrested you."

"Why won't you give him up?"

Sambino says nothing, only sits back. His pallid skin shimmers in the overhead lights. Both of them look so young compared to everyone else in the visiting room.

"It'll go away," Sambino finally says. "They got a serial killer to catch, for Christ's sakes! They're not going to waste time on some sicko with a thing for old dead people. Go home, Kaitlin."

"Hello—the state cop thinks *you* are the serial killer."

"Go. Home. Kaitlin."

"She's an agent, like the FBI or something. Nobody fucks with them and wins."

Sambino leans into Kaitlin until his nose is only an inch or so from hers. "She'll get what she deserves." He stands and motions for the guard to take him back to his cell. "Go home."

Ainsley tosses his pen onto his pad of paper and runs his fingers through his white hair. Davis shuts off the recorder. "Any ideas, Hansen?"

Every single movement within my body stops. *She'll get what she deserves.* This morning, after waking up, I checked my cell phone. Nothing from Rowan. She hadn't yet answered my text from the night before, and I suspected that she'd already lost the new iPhone I gave her for Christmas. It was the only explanation as to why she would be out of contact with me. We never went this long without talking. Never.

Davis nudges me, and I turn to him with my stomach in a sudden painful knot. "They've got Rowan."

❖

Captain Davis swivels back and forth in his desk chair and clicks the end of a pen over and over. Ainsley is there, too, solid and still; only his eyes follow my pacing of the room. I've spent the last hour calling everyone and anyone who Rowan might have talked to: friends, the art gallery where she's scheduled to show her work. I even tried the neighbor we rarely see out on our isolated country road. Davis stopped me from driving home by dispatching a cruiser from the Dublin police department.

After Kaitlin's visit with Sambino, we arrived back at the station to find the two FBI field agents who have been dispatched to aid in our investigation doing little else than sipping coffee and reviewing the case file in the break room. We've all but ignored them with the current focus on Rowan and her location.

"What's taking that deputy so long?" I slam my fist against my thigh.

"Sambino said nothing about Rowan," Davis soothes. "You're reading too much into this."

I'm too nervous to argue—we arrested Kaitlin on multiple charges of desecration of a corpse, but it really was about the secrets she has kept from me.

"You said Rowan loses her phone a lot." Ainsley tries to help.

"She would have called from a landline by now." When was the last time I'd gone over twenty-four hours without at least a text from Rowan? At the beginning of our relationship, maybe, but not in the last several months. Something was wrong. Terribly wrong.

The radio crackles and the deputy's voice finally breaks through. "I'm in front of the house, Captain. Nothing looks out of place." I can hear his fist bang against the front door.

I lean over Davis's desk and grab the radio from Davis's hand. "Dogs barking?" My words are harsh and clipped.

"Negative."

Dan must still have the dogs at his place, another sign that Rowan's not been home since she left Willow's Ridge. "Walk around to the right side of the house," I direct. "See the two big windows that look into the kitchen? Anything on the table? Any lights on or the overhead fan?"

After a minute, he speaks. "No lights. No fan. Looks like there's a pile of mail sitting on the corner of the table."

Dan again. He's brought in our mail and Rowan hasn't been home to go through it.

"The next set of windows is the family room. Any bags?"

"Nothing."

"Go around back," I tell him. "There's a large shed. The studio key is under the window basket."

The deputy's quick, short breaths filter through the radio. "Kennels are empty." When he gets to the studio, he bangs on the door.

"Use the key!"

After a minute, I hear the soft click of the key turning the lock and the door opens. "No one here. There aren't any footprints in the snow around the shed."

"What's the temperature inside the shed?"

"The temperature?"

"Check the thermostat."

"Fifty-seven degrees."

I hold my head in my hands. If Rowan had gone home yesterday, she certainly would have been in her studio by now. Once inside, heat is always the first thing she adjusts. She hates to be cold.

Davis cuts the communication with the deputy in Dublin. He's already put out a BOLO in the state of Ohio and sent a photograph from the DMV to all officers in Ohio and, just to be safe, Indiana and Michigan, too. "There's no evidence anything has happened to her."

"There's no evidence something *hasn't* happened to her," I spit back at him.

"We need you, partner." Ainsley nudges me gently with his elbow. "The best thing you can do right now, Luce, is wait."

"Wait?"

Davis nods. "Give it time. Let everyone do their job while you do yours."

Deep down, I know Davis and Ainsley are right. I fight myself not to rush back to Dublin. Rowan, though, could be anywhere at this point. She may not be the toughest girl I know, but she's certainly smart and can figure her way out of most messes. Every cop in the region is looking for her. There is nothing left to do, not until we can make the next connection. I *need* to make that next connection. Both Ainsley and I take to the computer to filter through the email tips, officer notes, and recent tickets or arrests for anyone by the name of Joseph or Joe. Davis catches the new agents up on the case.

An hour passes and I'm getting nowhere fast. My mind reels with an endless looping of questions I have no answers to: Where's Rowan's SUV? Is it possible she had a terrible accident that no one has reported? There *is* a two-lane stretch off Interstate 75 on the way home. She could be stranded. With all the media and activity at the hotel, someone must have seen something if Rowan had been taken against her will. I open the most recent tip-line message and grin over the desktop screen at Ainsley on his way out to retrieve lunch for us. *See? I'm doing what you asked.* But I have other ideas. In my mind I'm stepping back in time, retracing Rowan's steps.

Rowan had been deep into her research of Hans Klosenova and his series *Crossed.* She used her contacts from the art world to find where each photograph had been taken and to locate any connections Klosenova might have had with lesbians or the gay community in general. Information on the artist had been sparse and scattered at best, though she found he had been a photographer for *National Graphic* magazine. Each of the seven images had been taken at assigned shoot locations. Rowan hadn't been able to find any record of his death, though given his lack of published work in the past twenty years, most everyone in the art world believed he'd passed. Could Rowan's sudden disappearance have to do with this research?

I see my father in my mind's eye. He takes a seat in Ainsley's empty chair, the gleam of his brass medals from the police force glinting against the overhead lights. "It's never easy, Lucy-girl." He gives me a lazy smile that calms me at once.

"Too much to ask, is it?"

My father's grin lights up his face, the edges of his mouth hidden beneath the thickness of his white mustache.

"God, Dad. If anything happens to her…"

He leans forward, balancing his elbows on his knees. "Your search is too narrow," he explains. "Remember how Rowan and Kaitlin use their signatures?"

"In the art work? The markings?"

He nods. "Images used to identify themselves in their art. Who says an artist has only one way of identifying himself?"

Rowan always said she loved to sign her name but also liked using the symbol, depending on her mood. Since her return from India, though, it's always been *namaste*.

"Like a pen name," I say. "Writers use different names for different types of work."

"Sure. A symbol. Even another name. Anything to keep his two worlds separate."

"His two worlds. The one that fits into societal norms and the other of art and killing." Another name. I immediately think of the name that Kaitlin and Sambino used: Joseph. Hadn't I heard Rowan use that name at some point with Klosenova?

I run a few preliminary searches through federal databases on Klosenova with the name James Joseph and it pops up under a national registry. "Dad, you're a genius."

He shrugs. "You don't keep me around for nothing."

James Joseph filed to have his middle name legally changed to Hans Klosenova for artistic purposes. He'd been using Klosenova for his work but hadn't been able to cash any of his paychecks. Legally changing his name solved the problem. He never resided in the state of Ohio. He owned a cherry-red 1951 Corvette. His wife, Alada Joseph, had her driver's license through the state of New York with an address listed in Rochester.

I search the federal criminal database for any sort of record. It's a long shot, but that's all I've got to go on right now.

I start with James Hans Klosenova Joseph and find nothing. Under the name James Joseph, however, I hit pay dirt when the computer screen loads a mug shot from February 18, 1959. Joseph has a shock of thick white hair protruding from his head in tufts. With squinted eyes, he looks as though he's holding back tears. With his bulbous lips, the photo reminds me of the famous picture of Einstein with his tongue sticking out of his mouth. Joseph's charge: first-degree murder of his wife, Alada.

Joseph was arrested on federal land in a national park in Wyoming. At the time of Joseph's arrest, he'd been in the process of positioning his dead wife's body in a field of high grasses along the edge of a forest. Photography equipment surrounded him. He was arrested before any pictures had been taken of Alada's naked and posed body.

The *Crossed* series was never intended to only have seven photographs. Joseph had stopped the series due to his incarceration. Alada marked a major turn in his work, the place where he moved from live models to a dead one. Joseph most likely had been an evolving serial killer himself. After all, what did we know about the girls who had modeled for the seven photos? Did they all survive the photo shoots to see the next day? They appear alive in the photographs, but they could have been drugged or unconscious. Joseph was arrested twenty-two miles from the spot where Magda Rose Teru's body was found.

Prison records state that Joseph died on March 12, 1967, in the Wyoming State Penitentiary in Rawlins. Reports show that Joseph was beaten to death by two other prisoners while the three cleaned the showers. Two assigned guards stood watch over the convicts but left when an emergency code was called. By the time they returned from the false alarm, Joseph had been battered with the ends of a mop and broom. The wooden handle of the broom had been shoved so hard into his chest, the end snapped off. Joseph died before he could be taken to the infirmary. The only other reference of interest is a note reporting Joseph's vicious temper.

"That's an inside job if I ever heard of one," my dad says. "Explains why Rowan couldn't find anything on him."

"I wonder who wanted him dead. Were the two inmates part of some prison gang or was it someone from the outside?"

Dad only shrugs. Whether the two prisoners carried out a job for someone else or not, Joseph didn't stand a chance of survival that day in those prison showers.

Rowan had said Klosenova—Joseph—made his money on assignment, shooting nature shots, something I imagine a serious art photographer might consider selling out. The lack of recognition had to have taken a toll on Klosenova's self-esteem as an artist. Did he take his frustration out on his wife?

I find only a handful of references to Klosenova and only two that discuss and contain images from the *Crossed* series. It is the last hit that interests me most, though—a blog that discusses Klosenova's final works and includes two shots that aren't part of the published series. Unless this is an art historian or family member, how did this blogger get these unpublished shots? Both photographs feature the now-familiar flat grassland in black and white.

Fotofan. There is something about the shape of the face, the spread of the cheekbones away from the nose in the blogger's thumbnail picture. The blogger is unmistakably Nick Sambino.

❖

Davis balances on his favorite spot, the corner of his desk, swinging his right foot out and back. His clothes have grown loose on his already thin frame over the last few days. A colleague of mine in the BCI calls this rapid weight loss during a case the murder diet. The stress, late hours, and a churning stomach melt the fat away. "This explains the location of the Teru murder, but not why he's chosen Willow's Ridge for the others."

"There has to be a strong familial connection here."

Davis looks down at me in the office chair. He'd interviewed Sambino only an hour before and blown Kaitlin's cover in order to find information about Rowan. Sambino refused to talk, only saying that he'd wanted to impress Kaitlin with his threats and had no knowledge of any actual harm intended toward me or Rowan.

He smiles in that sad way that tells me something's wrong. "I heard from the deputy out in Dublin. He located your dog sitter. No word from Rowan."

I do the only thing I know to do: continue on with the case. "Take a look at this." I enlarge the thumbnail picture of Sambino.

Davis looks down over my shoulder at the computer screen. "Well, look who it is," he whispers. "Our little vampire buddy." Davis shakes his head. "We need more. Sambino's lawyer will only say he has an interest in photography and Klosenova's a hero of his." He absentmindedly picks at his pinkie nail. "Keep searching. If he's blogging, he's probably commenting on other sites." He dry-washes his face with his hands. "Meanwhile, just got word that Kaitlin got out on bail. I have an officer looking into who paid the bond."

As I reach for the doorknob of his office, Davis calls me back.

"God, Davis." My jaw aches from my worried clench. My fingers knead the drum-tight muscles in my temples. "Where is she?"

"Well, I know where she's not." He waits for me to look up at him. "A city park employee called in an abandoned SUV and arranged for a tow in Stow, not far from here. We ran the plates."

"Any signs of struggle?"

Davis shakes his head. "Nothing there to suggest any problems. We have three uniforms searching the park and surrounding area. Her bags are all in the car untouched."

"What about her phone?"

"In the cup holder between the driver's and passenger's seats. Only the keys are missing."

"And Rowan." The words come out much louder and shriller than I mean them to, and my hands tremble. I bite down hard to keep my teeth from chattering.

Davis slips into comfort mode, giving my shoulders a squeeze. "We'll find her, Luce. I promise you." We stand this way together, facing one another, for a few breaths before he adds, "Colby Sanders is on the way."

I throw my hands up and turn away from him.

"I'll do everything I can to keep you on the case. Okay? Luce?"

My back's to Davis and I've fallen into that nervous habit again of untying and retying my ponytail.

"We'll find Rowan. You have my word."

My head spins with details of the last place that I saw Rowan and all possible dangerous scenarios. I'd dropped her off at the front door of the hotel. "The security recordings."

I push past him on my way out of the office door.

"We checked the hotel. They only show Rowan's return from our morning meeting and then at checkout."

"I need to see them." My coat's on, keys in hand, and I'm headed toward the exit with or without Davis.

"Hold up, Agent," he says. "I'm coming with you."

Hope. It's funny how such a small little word can whittle its way into the most concealed crevice, drip its lightness into the most congested tunnel. It's that tiny zing that slips into our darkest hour and relentlessly teases with the prospect of resolution, renewal, and forgiveness. During my first three One True Path meetings, hope was the thing that showed up at the eleventh hour just as silent as a nuclear holocaust.

It happened with those glances Marci gave me, those looks that connected us. I'd secreted them away inside a tiny corner of my heart. While the pastor droned on about the consequences of our sins, I thought about the way that butterfly of hope had landed so gracefully on my shoulder. The thinnest of wings still thrummed from flight and whispered into my ear: *Hold on, Lucinda. Hold on.*

Marci didn't do anything, really, other than be present at those group meetings. I studied closely every move she made, every rise of her chest with breath, even how long it took her still-damp hair to dry. Marci equaled hope in mere presence. Why else would God have put this girl so near if not to send me a message? I only knew the teachings of the few church services my father had taken me to, the promises of fire and brimstone for any misstep in life. Perhaps Marci was God's way of testing me. If so, I failed miserably. But deep in my gut I knew this wasn't so.

I always called my intuition my God-speak, and my dad always nurtured it. If I could only quiet myself enough, I reasoned, if I could only be patient enough, the voice was there—it had always been there. I found that God's voice sounded quiet and sweet, nothing like the loud brash and clatter of out-of-tune musical instruments in the pastor's lectures and preaching. No matter what I called the voice, I realized in those early days of that summer, it didn't always talk. Sometimes it simply pointed out images to me, like the golden hue of sunsets or the flutter of a nearby blue jay, and hope settled on me.

Now, on the way to the hotel, I wait for a feeling of what to do next, for the ghost of my father to appear and guide me, for the voice to help. I drive Davis to the Ridgeway Inn while his scanner crackles dispatch and locations of officers all over the county. Although he says all the right words, it's clear that Rowan's disappearance has rattled Davis. He's talking so fast, his words slur together.

I do my best to tune out Davis and to quiet myself. It feels like my heart might burst out of my chest and I cannot stop my feet and legs from jumping. Still, I do my best to listen for a message that tells me all will be okay.

The voice never comes. Neither does my father.

CHAPTER TWENTY-FOUR

Alison, the Ridgeway Inn's owner, lives on the premises in an attached apartment. Davis and I wait as she corrals her overgrown, burly German shepherd into a back bedroom. We follow Alison's thick blond ponytail to the kitchen. She grabs us bottles of water from the refrigerator, her soft, fleshy body hidden within layers of sweatpants and a hoodie. The kitchen sink drips, drips, drips to avoid the slow freeze of the water lines.

Alison joins us at the table with her laptop. Her pleasant, moon-round face looks over at me. "I'm not sure what you're hoping to find, Agent. The other officers went through these recordings only a few hours ago."

"Do the cameras record twenty-four-seven?" Davis asks.

"They do in the summer and fall," Alison says, "when the tourists are all here to see the changing leaves and to go hiking or camping. We get very few visitors this time of year. This whole deal is a fluke." She points out her kitchen window to the media vans parked everywhere. "I hate what's happening in this town, but the business has been great." She opens a web page and turns the screen so I can watch it load.

"We use a company that stores the recordings online," she says. "Keeps the insurance company happy. We can access them through their website. You'll have to forgive me, I'm slow at this. We've never needed to get to any of the recordings before today."

Her thick fingers maneuver the keyboard through passwords and different screens until she's finally in. "The other officers found that the parking-lot camera didn't record, but we have the hall."

"What's wrong with the lot camera?" I ask.

"Not sure. We had no idea there was a problem with it."

Davis and I exchange glances over the convenience of the camera outage. Given that Rowan presumably got to her car and loaded her belongings, the parking lot was most likely the point of attack. Rowan left in the middle of the day, though, and I've only witnessed the lot when it's been teeming with news media and bored reporters. Someone must have seen something.

I fast-forward through hours of recording until I locate exactly when Rowan and I left for the police station, her laptop tucked underneath her arm. The recording shows Rowan returning from the station alone, and I'm able to zoom in on her as she fumbles with the keycard and nearly drops her bag in the process. At 9:04 a.m., Rowan disappears into the hotel room. At 1:52 p.m. Rowan emerges with her two bags and easel. She sets her duffel in the hall while she pulls the room door closed behind her.

Rowan freezes on the screen facing the closed door. It's not as though she's forgotten anything, she simply isn't moving. The camera zooms in as far as the program will allow, but Rowan's face is too grainy to make out her expression. Then, almost as suddenly as she stopped, she bends over for her things and walks down the hall. It's easy to see why the officers missed it. To someone who doesn't know Rowan, her movements might seem like only a glitch in the film, a pause for a deep breath, nothing more. But I know her too well. The fumbling, the pausing—that's not like Rowan. It's something more.

Rowan's intuition rivals mine when it comes to her awareness of people around her and their intentions. So it begs the question: If Rowan had sensed some sort of danger, what caused her to go ahead with her plans to leave? If she had been concerned, why didn't she contact me?

"There's nothing here," I say to Davis, fast-forwarding through the remainder of the recording. There is no other movement at my hotel room until 3 p.m. when the cleaning crew enters. Nothing more happens until 11:57 p.m., when I return to the room.

I have no valid reason to check my room again. After all, I slept there last night and noticed nothing unusual. It is out of desperation and an effort to quiet my worry that I leave Davis to look once more for anything Rowan might have left behind. The recording nags; it won't let me go. I've missed something.

Inside my hotel room, the curtains are pulled tight and the sunless room still feels heavy with sleep. I check all the drawers in the dresser. I search the desk and under the bed and in the bathroom. Only the heater answers as it clicks on, blowing air against the armchair in the corner of the room.

Rowan left her black hoodie balled on the seat of that armchair. When I grab the sweatshirt to check the pockets, her laptop greets me from the seat. The lid of the laptop is closed, the computer in sleep mode. Its black lid meshes perfectly with the dark fabric of the chair. Hidden under the sweatshirt, the laptop would have been easy enough to miss.

The computer powers on to the page Rowan last viewed, the very last image of the *Crossed* series, number seven. The screen holds the Klosenova image, zoomed in to only the model's pale bare shoulders and face. Her eyes are closed with her chin resting on her right shoulder. The model looks as though she is perched on some sort of overhang. A cliff, maybe. Winter has stripped the foliage from the branches that surround the woman, and the sky looks gray, thick, and brimming with snow. It could possibly be a photograph taken at night. I scroll back up to the model's face and pull out of the close-up view. The full photograph depicts the naked model lying across the top of a boulder. The layers of the rock are visible and the photograph is taken from an angle that shows the model is on a pedestal of rock as some sort of an offering. Her arms are spread wide with her legs together, and the long mess of her curly hair covers her naked breasts, much like Botticelli's *Venus*.

The wild mass of curls. The slim build. The fine bone structure. If I didn't know every expression of Rowan's face from my life with her, every indention and smile line, I could be convinced this model is Rowan. I click back to the previous image, photograph number six. This particular model has short dark hair along with pale skin and is positioned amongst winter foliage.

Picasso hasn't killed out of order. Yet. He has dutifully followed Klosenova's numbered prints. It is possible he has killed a woman we haven't found yet, a woman who matches image number six. Then he will have moved on to the final photograph.

My breath grows quick and shallow. Suddenly light-headed, I sit down hard on the corner of the hotel bed until my world rights itself.

Rowan.

It's 4:30 p.m. Just enough time.

❖

The original Stonehenge in England remains a mystery to most anthropologists, but many agree that the site had been used for different types of rituals. Remnants of animal bone indicate lavish feasts from gatherings of celebration while the different orientations of the stones to the sun signal some sort of calendar. The shape of Stonehenge is significant, the circular plan that gathers energies and blessings for all those who enter. Just like the original, Marci used her Stonehenge within the limestone quarry for her own forms of celebration. It even held her in the final ritual of life: death.

I don't know how many years Marci had escaped into the accepting, cool cavern of Stonehenge. When did she discover the distant burrow in the back edge of the cave? How long had she been squirreling herself away from the adults in her world? The hushed, velvety stones held all her secrets, her dreams, and once I came along, her desires. Inside that earthly crevice, we united—a bond built on acceptance of one another even when it seemed like everyone in our lives based their love for us on the changes we first needed to make.

At the entrance of the quarry, the remnants of the day fade fast beyond the wooded terrain. Hunched against the stab of cold, it is the anxiety to find Rowan that warms me at my very core. A quick pang of guilt shoots through my chest at the thought of Davis, who most likely is still waiting with Alison for me to return from my hotel room. Davis would have insisted on an approved, full-team search of the quarry. I need to go in quiet, and I need to go in alone. If Rowan isn't already dead, the full team complete with tracking dogs would only spook Picasso, endanger her life. I only have the heavy-duty flashlight from my console, my service weapon with a full round, two extra rounds tucked inside a coat pocket, my cell phone, and the small pen knife on my key chain.

Plunging into the mouth of the forest, my heavy boots cave through the top layer of ice and sink into the deep snow. This motion of sinking and pulling a boot out only to do so all over again is agonizingly slow. Panic clenches my chest. I don't have time for this! I try to run and my feet move much too quickly, throwing my balance into confusion. When a forked limb suddenly appears centimeters from my forehead, I can't stop. The hard smack from the jutting branch wallops me flat. Heart inside my throat, I finally hear the voice I've been waiting for: *Slow down. Listen.*

With the wind knocked out of me, I obey. I lie down in the snow to gather my bearings, my scattered breath. Gentle snowflakes flutter down on me, catching against the ridges of my eyelashes. Somewhere not far away, a woodpecker battles against a tree trunk and black crows caw. Inside that hushed quiet of the trees, in the impending darkness, something within me takes over. Memory fuses with my body—I'm sixteen again. My feet know the trail to Stonehenge. I've been here a thousand times in my dreams since Marci's murder. Standing once again, I shut off my mind and let my body memory take over.

The rocky ridge that overlooks the deep bowl of the Midwestern mini-canyon is at least a half mile away. From there, Stonehenge is roughly another quarter mile. Each step of my foot has been here before, I remind myself; each fall of my breath has filled this air. Dark or not, freezing or not, this space will accept me once again. I revert back in time until I'm spinning inside that miniscule but tenacious rut between wake and sleep. When I was sixteen and came to visit Marci in Stonehenge, I used to clock myself to see how fast I could race from the entrance to her.

My record comes back to me. "Six minutes, three seconds," I say out loud. "Beat it."

❖

Marci! I call out and listen for my voice to echo back. *Marci!* Only the familiar sound of the woodpecker responds. *I'm here*, it says. *I've always been here.*

Is it the nature of being young or just first love that is so palpable, vibrant, and electric your body can vibrate while sitting still and damn near take off with just the sound of your lover's name? *Marci. Marci.*

Sometimes when I ran inside the quarry, I thought of Chaz. I imagined him sneaking off to meet with a lover. I already knew who— the boy from the basketball team with lanky limbs and a chiseled chin spotted with a baby beard. I was always curious as to how Chaz got away from his father's suspicious eye. Did he slip out through the bedroom window in the middle of the night? Or did he lie about how many practices the team really held? Did he and his lover have their own hidden place? These were the types of secrets even Chaz and I never told one another.

Marci! I say it over and over and over until I burst through the thicket of trees beside the collection of boulders near Stonehenge. The coolness of earth mixed with the metallic smell of blood slaps me in the face. Or is it a memory? I drop to my bony knees.

I was so sure I'd find Rowan. Kneeling at the site of Marci's death, I bury my face in my hands to hide the tears that squeeze from my eyes. Stonehenge's silent dankness nearly chokes me. My chest thumps hard with the run and I smack my fists against the frozen limestone floor. The symmetry of Picasso returning to the location of his first kill only makes sense. I'd convinced myself that Rowan would be here waiting for me, very much alive, sketching away in her book. *Silly, Luce*, she'd say. *I'm drawing!* And then we'd laugh together, and head out along the trail for a lovely winter stroll back to my car to live happily ever after.

If only.

Night has fallen. I step outside the cave. The sky is painfully clear, the moon a sharp crevice amongst the spray of bright stars. The clarity feels frozen with the subzero temperature. It feels like if I could reach up high enough, I could grab hold of a ball of ice instead of a burning star. Leaning against the bumpy limestone wall, my eyes slowly adjust to the darkness. Snippets of what I imagine happened after I left Marci's body that day mix with my present knowledge of how a crime scene is processed. I can hear the rescue workers crashing through the woods, their medical equipment boxes bouncing against their knees, a much younger Ainsley as he kneels over Marci's body looking for signs of evidence, the painstaking search of the rocky terrain for any sort of clue. Marci hadn't been dead long when I found her—at most thirty minutes. But someone was still there. Waiting. Watching. Biding his time until I made a move.

Blood. I remember there was so much blood on my hands from the blow to the back of Marci's head. Wringing my hands now, I can still feel the sticky warmth of her blood, the way it covered my skin, the way it marked me with its cruelty. First kills are usually messy, I know this now; rarely does the murder go down the way the killer fantasized it would. Marci's was no different. I interrupted his sick game. His rage at my interference must have been nothing short of fierce.

I edge closer to the lip of the ravine. Thirty feet or so below, the deep water that flows in the warmer months is iced over, solid in spots. *Rowan, where are you?* Turning to make my way back along the trails to my truck, I resolve to bring the entire team into the quarry for a search. That's when I see it from the corner of my eye. Only a glint at first. Out past the bottom of the ravine, on the opposite side of the water. A flash. It's the head of a torchlight moving away and following the frozen waterline.

There is no quick way down to the base of the ravine without alerting Picasso. If I jump from the stony ledge, I'll slam into the limestone of the ravine walls and land against the rocky bed of frozen water that would at the very least break my legs. Instead, I follow the glow of light in search of a quicker way into the ravine. Running low to the ground with my knees bent, I'm in tracker mode, my senses sharply honed inside the dark. I can't risk that Picasso will see the flash of my light the same way I've seen his.

After I call Ainsley for backup, I turn off the cell, afraid a ring or ding or buzz, or the glow of the screen, might give away my location. Through our patchy connection, Ainsley reamed me for sneaking out solo. "Davis is searching everywhere for you." he growled into the phone and added that if he found me first, *he'd* be the one to kill me. I can't wait, but at least the team is on the way. I know these woods, but so does Picasso. He's proven that with the careful plots of each grisly installment of his own *Crossed* series.

The thin ledge of a path narrows and my footing threatens to toss me over the edge into the ravine a few times. The patches of icy snow mix with an uneven stone route that catches me off guard and slows me down. Picasso's glowing light dims. I can't let that distance get any wider.

A trail toward a clearing suddenly presents itself and I abandon the path along the ledge of the ravine. My plan? To make up lost time on a well-worn jogging course that leads to the bottom. I've lost sight of the light below, but I know his pace which will allow me to cut him off at the far end of the quarry. With my flashlight on the lowest setting and tucked under my sweater, the dimmed gray just enough light to see a few steps in front of me, I full-on sprint now, no longer unsteady on my feet, tearing through the top icy layer of snow with each footfall. My legs and breath fall into a steady rhythm as the path leads me down to Picasso.

I explode onto the expanse of the quarry's Staircase. In spring, rivulets of water run down the falling, layered limestone. The solid layer of ice on top of the limestone threatens to toss me down. But the toe of my boot catches on the edge of something solid—I've misjudged the space between steps and trip. I stumble to gain my balance, but it's no use. I'm moving too fast to stop. Tumbling forward, I shoulder roll along the gnarled bedrock and stumps, cursing every smack of my body along the way.

I land with a hard thud of my back against the base of an enormous elm, listening and feeling for injuries to my body. It's only after I catch my breath and pull myself up that I recognize a soft whimper in the dark.

"Rowan?" The flashlight has gotten tangled within the folds of my shirt and coat. Digging out the torch, I sweep the light across the landscape. "Rowan, is that you?"

"Help me!" Rowan's voice trembles from somewhere above me.

With the eerie, wide sweep of my light, I find Rowan at the top of the staircase. I scramble up the limestone layers to get to her, slipping on the ice. It's the sight of Rowan that knocks the breath, and damn near the strength, out of me.

Rowan lies bound to the earth, naked, on her back with her arms sprawled out to the sides and her legs together—Picasso's makeshift cross of a body. White plastic binding strips bind Rowan's wrists to enormous roots of an oak tree. Her ankles are zip-tied together and he's placed a heavy rock on top of her shins to hold her legs down. Rowan's skin already has a bluish hue, her nipples a deep violet. Her entire body quakes with a violent shivering that knocks me into action. She's going into shock. Her whimpers beg me to help her.

Crawling to Rowan's side, I search my pockets for anything sharp to cut the zip-ties. Truck keys! The utility knife on the keychain. I scan the tree line for any sign of movement while I saw back and forth through the thick plastic ties at her wrists. "Are you hurt?"

"My ankle. I can't feel my feet or hands." A quivering sob chokes up inside her. "He hunted me."

"Hunted?"

"He told me he'd kill me if he caught me. He carried me here and tied me up."

"Does he have a gun? A knife?"

"A huge gun."

Rowan knows next to nothing about guns. Her notion of a huge gun could be a shotgun or some sort of rifle. Frustration burns in me until the small knife from the keychain finally breaks through the tie at her left wrist. Rowan sits up quickly, wringing her near-frozen fingers around the bruised skin.

"How did you get out here?" I move down to her legs and lift the enormous stone from her legs. Rowan's right about her ankle. The left is about twice the size of the other with no signs of the swelling receding.

"A young woman stopped me in the hotel lobby after you dropped me off. An art student who saw my work and wanted to have coffee before I left town. And…I don't know. I can't remember. Somehow I ended up with the man in these woods."

Kaitlin. I saw away at the ankle binding. Rowan's missing memory suggests Kaitlin roofied her.

"Ow." Rowan's hands shoot down to cover her swollen ankle.

"I'm sorry." I unzip my coat and slide out of it for Rowan. If I can't move her, she'll freeze. It's quite possible that frostbite has already set in to her fingers and toes. Helping her into the coat, I zip it all the way to her chin.

"They're working together. What are we gonna do?" Rowan cries, pulling her hands up inside the sleeves of the coat.

"What does he look like?"

"He's completely covered in black, even one of those face masks that robbers use. I couldn't see any part of him."

I try again with the knife to break the remaining zip tie, but the jarring is too much for a shattered ankle. Thank God I was smart enough to put on a few layers of clothing this morning. Kneeling beside Rowan, I pull off my sweater and wind it around her thighs and knees. The thick fabric hardly covers the freezing pale skin of her legs.

"What about you?" She points to my thin long-sleeved T-shirt.

"I got my trusty hat." I pat the bomber on my head. "I'll be okay."

Powering my cell phone on, I call for help. "They're here, Davis. Rowan's at the top of the Staircase," I tell him. "Bring EMS. She's got a broken ankle." The connection is so spotty the phone loses reception before I can tell him Picasso is armed and working with Kaitlin.

"Keep calling Davis." I leave the phone and my keychain with the pocket knife for her. "Use the light of the phone to signal them when they get close, instead of your voice. Keep working at the binding."

I lean forward and give her a quick kiss on the cheek. "Don't hesitate to use this knife. Go for the eyes. And the balls."

Her hand grips mine. "Stay with me."

"I have to end this thing." I squeeze her cold hand and then pull away.

"Promise me. Please." Rowan begins to tremble again.

I look down at her. "You have my word. I'll come back for you."

White clouds of my exhalations trail behind me in the frigid night air. The tips of my eyelashes and the tiny hairs inside my nose have frozen, and the skin around my eyes burns with the icy blast. My mind churns possible scenarios as my heartbeat rushes inside my ears. I understand why he has bound Rowan alive. She is waiting her turn.

She is meant to be the seventh victim and Picasso can't bring himself to do the kills out of order. Somewhere out here in the quarry, victim six has most likely been killed and Rowan is next. In order to get the photographs to match Klosenova's, he'll have to use special lenses for his camera. The flashes will have to be timed just right. All of the technical difficulties with night photography will slow Picasso down and grant our team some extra time.

The bottom of the ravine is maybe fifteen feet below me now. The trail could possibly have been the longest way down. But, I remind myself, it led me to Rowan. I weave out of the heavy forest toward the ledge. I have to go back to the original path and move down that way. There is no more time to waste. The bed of the ravine stretches quite a few miles and it eventually meets up with the Mad River. There are all sorts of theories of the ravine's origins, but the most popular is that the semi-canyon of the ravine has been whittled away over the years from the steady water flow from the large Mad River. I stand a few seconds at the limestone edge. My eyes have adjusted somewhat to the darkness and I scan the landscape for any sign of light or movement. Crows *caw-caw* from somewhere nearby and then fall back into the silence.

I see it again—the flash of light, a shimmer much closer than I've anticipated, down to my left. I spin on the balls of my feet to head that direction when the heel of my left boot slides on a patch of ice. My feet scramble through snow to take hold of something solid. The icy edge gives way. I tumble and bounce against the jagged edges of limestone, rolling over winter-hardened earth. I land hard and flat on my back against the snowy ice along the edges of the frozen water, exactly where I've been trying to get all along. The absurdity of it almost makes me laugh until the back of my head erupts in maddening pain. I've smacked it hard against a jutting stone and the world suddenly goes black.

CHAPTER TWENTY-FIVE

Everything blurs white. I manage to prop up on a shaky elbow, but it slips out from under me on the ice. A woman moans not far from me along the water's edge.

"Whoa, Hansen." Bear-sized hands take hold of my shoulders. "You took quite a fall."

Rubbing my eyes, I squint to make sense of the shape looming above me. "Ainsley." Thank God—someone to help. "Where's the team?" My fingers trace the growing egg of a knot on the back of my head. No blood, but swelling can be just as dangerous.

"Davis called for search and recovery. I got to thinking on my way over here about an old dirt access road on this side." He thumbs back. "It's used as a launch and parking area." He points up the bank. "Look who I found down here." Kaitlin lies curled on her side against the frozen earth, completely naked.

Ainsley sweeps his flashlight over the hillside and then around Kaitlin. "She's bound. He's drugged her, so she's groggy and weak. Best to leave her until we catch Picasso." He looks down at me. "We have to get off this ice and under cover." He reaches down for my hand and nods toward the bank. "Let me help."

The knock to my head has left me light-headed; everything looks larger and slower than it really is. My hypersensitive ears hear every rustle of movement. Kaitlin kicks out her skinny legs every few seconds, her arms pulled back and tucked under her head. Shaking my head, I try to clear my thinking. Kaitlin. Victim number six. She's got the dark hair, albeit dyed, and she's childlike in stature. But if Kaitlin's meant to mimic number six, where is Picasso and why hasn't he already killed her?

"Luce? Take my hand."

With Ainsley's help, I'm able to stand. My balance is off, though, and my boots are no contender against the slick ice. Together we manage to get to the bank and onto sure footing. "Have they found Rowan?"

"I followed two squads out here. Davis broadcast her location. I'm sure by now they've got her."

I breathe in relief. "She's number seven."

"Yes," Ainsley says. "Why else would he take her?"

"Kaitlin's the one who lured Rowan into his trap."

Ainsley doesn't respond, only continues to push through the undergrowth and snow ahead of me. Fighting to keep my balance, it's like I'm trying to walk inside a spinning kaleidoscope, never certain of my footing against the bank. When the radio crackles on Ainsley's belt, I stop and take a step back from him. One by one, officers from all over the quarry call in their locations as they make their way toward the bottom of the ravine. Ainsley never reports his position. The hairs on the back of my neck suddenly prickle.

Ainsley thought of the access road when no one else did. He was the first man down the ravine and alone. If Kaitlin was meant to be number six, she would have been killed immediately so Picasso could move on to number seven. I seem to have a way with timing. Is Ainsley the masked man Kaitlin and Sambino are assisting with the murders? Did my fall interrupt his kill?

"I saw a light down here along the water's edge," I tell Ainsley, hesitant now. "Didn't you?" I fake a stretch and my hand creeps up to where my shoulder holster should be. The entire holster is gone. A gaping tear in the back of my shirt leaves the exposed skin beaten and scraped raw from the fall.

"Which way was the light going?" Ainsley stops and waits for me to catch up. "The first thing I saw was you falling down from that limestone ledge."

I take another step back, then another, and stand where the icy water's seam meets the land.

"Hansen?"

"What's going on, Ainsley? Where's my weapon?"

Ainsley turns to face my wide stance. He watches me watching him. "Jesus! You think I'm the one with the light down here?" He reaches into his pocket and holds up his car keys and jingles them. "I got here in my Jeep, Hansen. I didn't come with the cavalry."

"Where's my weapon?"

"How the fuck should I know? You just fell down a rocky cliff, for Christ's sake!" He reaches for his waist and grabs his radio. "I've already called in our location. Why do you think everyone's making their way down here?"

"Give me your gun." My voice comes out much calmer and steadier than I expect it to. My head's beginning to clear.

"Hansen." He says my name as if he's very tired. He bends over and sets the radio on the ground between us.

"The gun, Ainsley."

Angry now, he rips the gun from his holster as though he's about to throw it at me. "Take it."

"Set it next to the radio."

Once he drops the weapon, I scramble for it and hold Ainsley at gunpoint.

"We're wasting time with this bullshit. We're completely exposed here."

I hold the aim of the gun on him. "Radio in we need help," I demand. I don't know what to believe. I want to trust what Ainsley is telling me but he is the only person I see inside the ravine with a flashlight. I have to play it safe. "We're not moving until someone else from the team gets here."

Ainsley groans, but he picks up the radio and holds in the talk tab. "Davis?" he calls into it. "Hansen's—"

Without warning, a loud *whomp* yells through the night from somewhere above and behind me. The whoosh of the crossbow sizzles past my right ear and lodges its shaft deep within Ainsley's lower abdomen. The impact of the arrow knocks him flat on his back. Instinctively, I drop down beside him. Only the sounds of my quick breath and his jagged groans surround us. I wait for a few seconds in the silence. Then I'm up and pulling Ainsley with all my strength between two enormous oak trees along the bank. Once behind the oaks, I can make out the shadowy figure near the spot where I fell. And I see the red eye, the dot-like glow of the crossbow's target. The controlled movement of that light from side to side tells me he's searching to secure us within his crosshairs.

I unlock the safety of Ainsley's gun, learning the feel of his weapon in my hands. It's heavier than mine, wider. My small grip fumbles with the wide handle. Small hands or not, my shots have to count—the killer has the advantage by shooting at us from above. Ainsley and I are merely squatting ducks behind this tree. The moment I move, our location will be blown.

Ainsley writhes in pain and the words spill out of my mouth without a second thought. "Please God," I bargain, "keep Rowan and Ainsley safe and I'll do whatever you want of me. Please." The final plea comes out jagged and hoarse. Then, out of nowhere, a wave of calm strikes me. The voice. *It has to be now.* Holding the gun close to my chest, I take a deep breath.

In one motion, I roll my body around the trunk of the tree and fire up at the limestone ledge. Explosions of rock and dust rumble down the cliff. The next arrow whizzes past me as I squeeze off another round, this one narrowly missing Picasso. His footfalls crash as he retreats to the inner realm of the forest.

Ainsley is still alive. His flashlight lies in the snow. The spread of its yellowish gleam puts an eerie glow on the scene before me. Bubbles of blood run over the corner of his mouth with each jagged breath. The blood vessels in his neck throb chaotically. Silence closes in around us after a company of birds perched high above finish squawking. Ainsley is sprawled on his back, the arrow's end juts from his lower belly.

Nearby Ainsley's radio spits out Davis's voice. I scramble for the radio, which is difficult to find in the flashlight's shadow. Finally I grab hold of it from a snowbank near the water's edge. "Ainsley's down! Shooter's on the move with crossbow." I scan the area wildly for any sign of movement. In the distance, the wail of emergency sirens calls to me.

I kneel beside Ainsley. "You're doing fine," I whisper. "Cole, look at me." I tap his cheeks until he opens his eyes, rolling and unfocused beneath his fluttering lids. "Stay with me. We're going to get out of this mess, I promise."

Ainsley's eyes grow wide behind his crooked glasses. He struggles to tell me something while he gestures to his gun in my hand. At first horror rockets through me: *Absolutely not. I will not shoot you.* But as he continues to struggle to call me closer, I understand he has something much different in mind. His lips whisper against the ridges of my ear. "Two," he mouths with barely any sound.

I get it: only two rounds left. "What about the other rounds?" But Ainsley fades fast, his skin cold with the sweat of the body fighting for life. An answer wouldn't have changed the reality.

There is the rustle of earth, the snap of winter-frozen branches behind me. Pistol aimed, I turn to locate the movement. Picasso stands there, at most only about seven steps away from me. The tip of the crossbow's arrow isn't pointed at me, but directly down at Ainsley's heart.

"He's still alive. Do what I say and he might stay that way. No promises." He waits for my nod. "Drop the weapon."

I do as I'm instructed. The black mask has been rolled up to his forehead, his glasses the identifying marker against his pale skin. There is only one reason he'd let me see his face. He intends for no one to get out of this quarry alive.

"Mr. Eldridge, there's still time to turn this around." The centered calm from my years of training falls into place. It never ceases to amaze me how easily I can retreat into my professional role even with the hot danger that pulsates through me. Rote and ingrained in me, it's like reverting to the role of student.

Chad Eldridge shifts the crossbow from Ainsley to me. Standing face-to-face, he tosses a fisted cloth at me that I catch on reflex.

The fabric opens like a blooming flower in my hands. It's the faded plaid of Marci's shirt I know all too well—the button-up I'd been so certain she wore the day I found her dead. The cloth is stiff in places, blackened with Marci's long-dried blood.

"Put it on."

I slip into the snug short sleeves and leave the buttons open. I imagine for a second that I can smell Marci on the shirt, feel her touch with the caress of the cotton, and it's like she's folding her arms around me. I'm safe inside the protection of her.

A much younger Eldridge had been in the forest that day in July 1989; he'd been no older than eighteen or so. He watched me find Marci. Once I left to call for help, he returned to her body. He came back for the plaid shirt—the trophy. Remnants of my nightmares come back to me in flashes. The slim hips. I'd gotten away from Picasso then by jumping into the quarry. He didn't follow me into the quarry, I'm certain of it now. He's terrified of water. I step back onto the quarry's icy covering. Then I take two more steps back toward the center of the quarry.

"Stop," he warns.

I take two more large steps. The ice has significantly thinned beneath my boots. I hear the water's heavy movement deep below. Picasso doesn't follow and my confidence spikes.

Anger boils over inside, tunneling up my throat and erupting out at him. "You let me go that day." My eyes fill with tears. "Why didn't you kill me, too?"

"I would have if it wasn't for the stunt you pulled. Don't take another step."

I dare him. I take another step back and suddenly there is a tremendous burn in my right shoulder before the sound of the arrow's release can register in my mind. Hot liquid runs down between my shoulder blades. My fresh blood soaks into the plaid shirt mixing with Marci's. Dropping to my knees, my hands shoot up to the feathered edge of an arrow that peeks out from under my collarbone. The stake has lodged itself through and through.

"I have no intention of ending this any way other than how Klosenova wished. All our traveling"—Eldridge looks around us for any movement—"but he never really left this place."

The searing pain in my left shoulder throbs. For a second, I think I may pass out. My entire body breaks out in a sheen of sweat and the muscles of my legs could give out at any second. I'm panting, my breath is shallow, my vision darkens around the edges. Suddenly there is the voice: *Think of Rowan. Think of Marci.* They both need me now as much as they ever have. I struggle with my mind to quiet the pain. "You traveled with him."

"All over." Eldridge inches closer. His expression is stone-still, his voice deliberately calm and controlled. "Klosenova killed my mother in seven different photographs for her sins before finally taking her life."

A wave of pain ignites my shoulder when I try to move my arm and my words stumble on its attack. Where the hell are Davis and the team? "Your mother was a lesbian."

Eldridge winces at the word lesbian. "It's so easy for women," he says. "You should know—out there flaunting your love of other women."

Eldridge slips his gloved hand into the breast of his coat and pulls out long silver scissors. He opens the blades wide, then slices them back together.

"My father, that's what Klosenova was to me. For both of us," he says, "it wasn't just about the photographs but the exposure of sin— that instant flash of recognition that highlights the nasty truth for all to see. It was his way to publicly display punishment for breaking God's word."

The scissor blades swipe open and snap closed again. In the glint of the metal's shine, I understand. Kaitlin's not number six. It's me.

And he's going to cut my hair short to match the model. He couldn't kill Rowan until he had me. Kaitlin's meant to be the final act—she's the replica of Klosenova's murdered wife Alada. Kaitlin may have denounced homosexuality and joined One True Path, but it's her sexual history with women that has attracted Eldridge. Still, I'm the one Picasso's been waiting for—everything hinges on my death. He needs me to begin the final slaughter. And he needs me alive for his ritual. This gives me the upper hand; I hold the power.

Eldridge grabs for my wrists and the harsh movement rocks my shoulder into screaming pain. I surprise him by falling forward into him, my cheek landing flat against the snow-topped ice. Time slows to a trickle—I see everything: Ainsley's pistol from the corner of my eye, Kaitlin curling into a tight fetal position on the quarry's bank, and Ainsley, who rolls onto his side within a pool of his own blood with his eyes open. Our gazes lock while Eldridge works behind my back, pulling zip ties from his pockets, a fumble of a feat with his thickly gloved hands and my refusal to comply. He's never dealt with a conscious victim, I realize, only ones who are roofied. This gives me another edge.

I watch as the area around Ainsley's eyes softens and he mouths words to me that I can't make out. I question him with a look back. *What are you trying to say?* Instantly Ainsley pushes himself up with nothing other than sheer will and begins to crawl toward Eldridge. A scream erupts from him.

I understand the words Ainsley has mouthed to me: *Go for the pistol.*

Eldridge throws my hands down before my wrists are completely bound. He raises the crossbow from his shoulder and shoots Ainsley directly through the heart. By the time Eldridge turns back to me, I've gotten the pistol and I'm up on my feet with the weapon pointed square at his chest.

"It's time, Lucinda." Eldridge grips the bow in his right hand. "You must take your place before God. It's all ready."

I don't doubt that Eldridge has the location laid out perfectly, the headstone and branches modeled just right. But it isn't going to be me posing dead for him against that headstone. "It's over, Eldridge. Hear the sirens?" Their wails scream through the cold morning from every direction.

"You got away from me once, but not again. This is my one true path."

"There is no one true path! Can't you see that? There is no one right way of being."

His eyes widen as if this somehow will help to fight off the words I've just spoken. He screws up his face and scoffs. "Drop the pistol," he growls, but there's a hint of uncertainty in his voice. My refusal to comply with the zip ties has shaken his confidence—everything has to be just right and I'm not making it easy for him. After all, everything relies on me to create the perfect scene for photograph number six. His OCD won't allow him to kill out of order. Another surge of confidence rockets through me.

"I couldn't figure out how you got close enough to those girls to drug them. I have to hand it to you, Eldridge. Kaitlin was the perfect lure. A beautiful, nonthreatening girl with an artistic flair to maneuver inside the lesbian community. We would all be putty in her hands. Let me guess: she kept coming around the funeral home to see Nick. So when your oldest daughter began looking up to Kaitlin as a role model, that was the final blow."

Eldridge's eyes flame at the mention of his daughter, the one on the edge of womanhood. He couldn't stand to see his daughter idolize what his own mother had been. The fear that Eldridge held deep inside regarding his daughter's sexuality must have been something fierce.

I don't want to kill Chad Eldridge—I really don't. It would have been a far greater punishment for him to sit in a jail cell for the rest of his life, obsessing over where he and the crime scenes went wrong. But when he raises the bow with the arrow and cocks it at me, I fire directly at his heart. He explodes backward with the force of the bullet, dead before his back even hits the ground.

Grabbing the bow, I gain control of all the weapons and drop to my knees at Ainsley's side. For what it's worth, he looks peaceful, a slight smile on his lips, as though he always knew we'd take Picasso down together. In the breaking dawn, I hold Ainsley's bear claw of a hand in mine. After several seconds, I kiss his warm cheek good-bye.

Inside Ainsley's pocket are his Jeep keys on that Swiss Army knife keychain filled with pictures of his great-niece. Voices filter through the west end of the ravine. Eldridge was brilliant to use the crossbow; fired shots would only ricochet noise throughout the entire quarry and announce his location. My gun blast was the noise that led the cavalry to us. Uniformed silhouettes charge toward me and scatter about to deal with Ainsley, Eldridge, and Kaitlin. In the chaos, I scramble up the ravine bank to the lot where Ainsley said he parked, my thoughts only of Rowan.

❖

The funny thing about hope is that it can be found in the smallest circumstance that pushes us on for its next intoxicating dose. My hope comes in a series of events this early morning under the dawn light. First, I find Ainsley's Jeep parked exactly where he said he left it, not far from the river's bank. I couldn't have mistaken the vehicle for anyone else's—two bumper stickers call out to me as clear as Ainsley's voice: *Back up! These colors don't run* and *Proud Republican on board!* I've never been so happy to see those right-wing slogans in all my life. When the engine rumbles, I jam my right boot down on the accelerator. The back end of the Jeep fishtails until the tires finally grip the dirt road beneath the snow.

My real hope, though, comes that morning in the sky. I drive up, up, up the bank toward Willow's Ridge and the hospital, for Rowan. It is within the spread of clouds and morning's pink glow that I catch sight of something I never thought I'd see: a glimpse of God. My version of God, anyway, that presence who has never left my side. There within those swirls of golden colors and feathery textures of morning sky is Marci Ann Tucker, still sixteen, those sea-navy eyes smiling down on me. Suddenly something inside me folds open like a lotus flower that finally releases its bloom to whatever nature holds. Gratitude takes hold of me, that breathtaking realization that I am not alone.

Marci's leaving. With my next breath I finally break through the water's thin, elastic sheath that has quietly and patiently shielded me for so long. Water drains from my ears and hair, drips from my face and shoulders. As the water loosens its embrace and puddles at my feet, I can now let Marci go. I watch in the rearview mirror as plumes of exhaust twirl behind the car in the cold air, and I press that Jeep on toward Rowan like I could bust right on through that burning horizon.

EPILOGUE

Friday, March 7

Weaving through the rows of gravestones, three wreaths of fresh flowers drape over one of my arms while Rowan's hand clasps the other. It has been years since I visited the grave site. The cold spell has passed, bathing the outskirts of Willow's Ridge in warm sunlight that works hard to get rid of all the dirty snow and ice left behind. Rivulets of water run down the edges of the drive for the nearest sewer. Spring will come, the sunlight promises. Spring will finally come.

Rowan lets go of my hand and walks ahead to examine a large monument, an eagle on the verge of taking flight. There is a skip in her step, a lightness as her A-line belted coat twirls around her knees. It's the same coat she was wearing the day we met, a geometric pattern that features every color under the sun. It will be some time before she recovers fully—physically or emotionally—from the ordeal, but it could have been so much worse. For both of us.

"Here, Ro." She stands at my side and we take in the weather-worn stone before us.

Careful not to step on the hallowed ground, Rowan kneels beside the length of the grave, her hair a tumbling river of curls scattered about her. As she speaks, she rests her right palm on the ground. "Marci Tucker. I've waited a long time to meet you."

The Tucker family had chosen an intricately designed Irish Catholic cross for Marci's headstone. I kneel at the stone, letting my fingertips trace the engraving:

OUR LOVING ANGEL,
WATCH OVER US WITH A PEACEFUL HEART.
MARCI ANN TUCKER
AUGUST 18, 1973–JULY 27, 1989

"Marci," I whisper, using my gloved hands to wipe away the dead leaves that have collected, the dirt and splatters of dried rain and snow on the stone. "I've missed you so much." I work slow and steady, my eyes blurred with tears. When I finish cleaning the cross, I scoop away some of the remaining snow from around the stone. Soon, as the sun moves across the sky, Marci's grave will be in the full light and will finally let go of these clinging pockets of snow and ice. My Frye boots sink into the spongy brown grass as I ring one of the wreaths over the top of the cross. Out of nowhere I hear the high lilt of Marci's laughter, and the image of her smiling face fills my mind. *A circle*, she says. *You remembered!*

Rowan wraps a strong arm around my shivering shoulders, her quiet presence grounding me.

"You can finally rest now," I tell Marci. "You are safe from Eldridge. And this"—I hook a thumb beside me—"is Rowan. You'd love her, Marce. She's made me so happy." I can almost hear Rowan's smile spread from ear to ear. Soon she stands and moves away from the grave to give me a minute.

I kiss the tips of my fingers, holding them a moment to my lips while I picture Marci's blue eyes once again. Then I touch my fingertips to the ground over the area I imagine Marci's face to be. "I love you, Marci. Always have. Always will." The gentle breeze picks up my words and carries them through the trees. "You'll always be my first love. I've missed you so much that sometimes I thought my heart might split." I speak softly to the stone. Tears spill onto my cheeks. "We got him. It's finally over."

Marci's Irish cross pendant hangs from my neck and I hold it tight inside my fist. Once her case was solved, all of her belongings were released to the Tuckers. The missing journal was located tucked away inside the Tucker's attic with mementoes of their dead daughter. Ainsley had released it to her parents so that no one would see Marci's fantasies about girls. Still, I couldn't believe it when Martin Tucker came through my door while I was recovering from the arrow wound in the Willow's Ridge Hospital.

"It's been a long time," he said, almost apologetically. "I didn't recognize you at the restaurant that morning." He stood at my bedside. The emotions tangled his words on his tongue until he could only say, "Thank you."

After a moment, he spoke again. "My mom and I want you to have something." He reached into his pocket and pulled out Marci's cross. The chain collapsed in my hand as Martin slowly set it in my open palm. "We had the original chain fixed."

"I can't. It was a gift to her from your mom. She should have it."

"Mom wants you to have it, Luce. Marci would want you to have it." I couldn't take my eyes from his face, from those navy-blue eyes he shared with his sister.

Now, I reach into my jeans pocket and pull out the limestone pebble I'd taken from Stonehenge the day I promised Marci I'd find her killer. With the edge of my red flannel, I polish it clean and tuck the round stone into a corner of the cross gravestone. Then I place my Marci rock beside it. My pocket feels lighter without the limestone chunks, and the bubble-filled stones are where they now belong. I will those holes and the layers of limestone to hold only happy times at Stonehenge, snippets of our laughter and sliced images of the love we shared inside that cavern. I sit until it is time. My time to finally say good-bye.

❖

We walk, Rowan and I, hand in hand across the cemetery, up the drive to the gazebo that overlooks all of Willow's Ridge. "I'm so proud of you," Rowan says. I can't find the words to explain to her what it is like to have the weight of over twenty years lifted away. The bones of my past have been unearthed, exposed. Instead of feeling the shame I thought I would, I only feel stronger.

We always want to know *Why?* when a murderer is caught. Why did he choose the victims he did? Why did he have the urge to kill? My training tells me we need those answers to learn from the experience and put closure on it. But with Chad Eldridge, I only have some of the answers, not nearly enough explanation. Kaitlin survived unscathed and awaits a trial on four counts of murder as well as a charge of obstructing an investigation and desecration of a corpse. She'll face the charges alone. Since her arrest, she's told police that she'd been sleeping with

Eldridge for over two years. This statement shows me just how much we cannot trust a word Kaitlin says; everything we have found points to Eldridge's sexual dysfunction that would have made it impossible for him to have sex. There is no doubt in my mind, however, that there was some sort of emotional relationship between them.

While my shoulder healed and I visited the hospital for physical therapy, people asked me why I didn't go ahead and shoot Kaitlin, too. Her involvement outraged people, this twenty-year-old woman with so much life ahead of her. How could she trick these innocent victims and drug them so they could be led to their deaths?

I can't speak for Kaitlin or why she did what she did. I can only say that she learned the One True Path teachings and had been a participant as well. That's where she met Chad Eldridge. I've always found there's a strong tendency in humans to recognize our own behavior in another and purely despise it. Maybe she thought killing off lesbians around her would scare off her own sexual temptation. Maybe she thought she could kill her sexuality by killing others. All I have is a bunch of maybes when it comes to Kaitlin. Still, every time I think of Kaitlin and Sambino, I only see the grand betrayal they pulled on the local gay community. If we cannot trust each other for safety and compassion, who can we trust?

Eldridge's biological father, the owner of the funeral home in Willow's Ridge, divorced his mother when Chad was two. Chad moved with her to Chicago, and by the time he was three, his mother had remarried the photographer, Klosenova. He completed *Crossed* while traveling, taking many photos in different towns, dragging Chad and his mother along with him. All reports state that Klosenova wanted to live in the quaint town of Willow's Ridge but felt he could not because of his wife's ex, who'd built a solid anchor in the town with his funeral home.

Before he started the *Crossed* series, Klosenova caught Chad's mother with another woman. He let that image simmer. He let her try to make it up to him. Once he finished the series, though, he shot her dead. Klosenova was arrested for the murder and Chad was sent back to Willow's Ridge to live with his father above the funeral home. The very location where he eventually brought his victims and injected them with a mixture of roofies and vitamin K. Sambino got the blood—that's all he ever wanted from the whole deal. For that desire, he'll serve at least fifty years behind bars.

I couldn't help but think Eldridge would still be out killing if it hadn't been for Emma Parks's strength and the young kid out four-wheeling that morning. The rumbling sounds of the bike spooked Eldridge, made him run and not finish with Emma Parks. Was it simply luck? Or something much more?

We also uncovered that Eldridge had been an active supporter of One True Path, donating large amounts to the national group every year. He provided the Jamesons the funds to move their meetings out of their basement and into the strip-mall space. He never got over his mother's sexuality—not a single photograph of her was found within his belongings.

Why Marci? This is the question I most want an answer to. What did she ever do to catch his attention?

"He must have been watching," Rowan said. "Waiting and watching in the forest. He saw you together. God, Luce, if you had been there on time to meet Marci, he would have killed you both." I escaped his twisted form of justice twice now, two blessings I couldn't let myself forget.

Near the top of the hill, through the statues and soldiers, we cross a line of old graves that leads to where Captain Davis took me two months ago. Freshly turned earth lies beside Tim Ainsley now; fresh bunches of flowers and planters cover the graves of Tim and his father. Cole's funeral was a hero's ceremony for a fallen officer. I'd taken part, even been a pallbearer for the man who saved my life with his own. One of the American flags from the ceremony still remains at the side of Cole's gravestone.

"Why did he do it, Ro? Why did he give his life for me?"

I don't really expect an answer from her, but she has one when her arm wraps around my waist. "He understood," she says.

"Understood what?"

"Life. The danger you were in. That his wounds were severe. He saw you, so able and healthy and with so many years ahead. It was an offering, really, an offering to his profession or a higher power so that both of you wouldn't die inside that quarry." Rowan kisses my cheek.

I place the remaining two wreaths of flowers on Cole's and Tim's graves, hidden among the mounds of others, while Rowan walks a few steps away.

I kneel at Cole's side, the way I had with Marci. The tears swim in my eyes again when I think of the good man below me, the one I doubted and fought with so fervently those last couple of days of the investigation. There's nothing left for me to say except: "Thank you a million times over."

When Rowan and I finally make it back to the truck, the sun has settled over the lot, spreading its warmth like a comforting blanket. Rowan pulls herself up and sits on the hood. "The sun!" She squeals, throwing her arms out to her sides, tossing her head back. "It really does exist in Willow's Ridge!"

I laugh and step toward Rowan, using my hands to spread her knees apart. As I pull her close, Rowan wraps her legs around my waist, clutching me in a strong hug. She buries her face against my neck, nuzzling close. We hold each other for quite some time, clinging to each other the way lovers do who've almost lost each other.

"Let's go home," Rowan says. When I say nothing, Rowan leans in for a kiss. "Think the kids have missed us?"

I laugh. "Actually, the real question is, do you think Dan is still talking to us after this enormous stint of dog sitting?" Rowan lets out a howl of laughter. She jumps down and opens the truck door.

I stand for a second longer and breathe in the quiet comfort of the graveyard. I can sense its welcome to the end of the storm, inviting the change, the growth of new life. I hear it whisper in the space all around me, *Change is finally coming.*

"You ready?" Rowan calls to me for a second time through the hushed glass of the windshield.

I consider Rowan's smile, her eagerness to get on our way. Sometimes I wonder why she is still by my side even after the threat to her life and my steadfast, though diminishing, Berlin Wall. She tells me this is love. She tells me this is what we do for those we love. I hope someday I'll get to the place where I can actually give back the full-throttle love Rowan so deserves. Maybe people really are like the consistency of limestone, just as Marci told me so long ago—able to change and shift with our surroundings and experiences.

Most of all, though, we survive.

About the Author

Meredith Doench's short fiction and creative nonfiction have appeared in literary journals such as *Hayden's Ferry Review*, *Women's Studies Quarterly*, and *Gertrude*. She earned a Ph.D. in creative writing from Texas Tech University and served as a fiction editor at *Camera Obscura: Journal of Literature and Photography*. She teaches writing and literature at a university in southern Ohio. *Crossed* is her first novel.

Books Available From Bold Strokes Books

The Chameleon's Tale by Andrea Bramhall. Two old friends must work through a web of lies and deceit to find themselves again, but in the search they discover far more than they ever went looking for. (978-1-62639-363-9)

Side Effects by VK Powell. Detective Jordan Bishop and Dr. Neela Sahjani must decide if it's easier to trust someone with your heart or your life as they face threatening protestors, corrupt politicians, and their increasing attraction. (978-1-62639-364-6)

Autumn Spring by Shelley Thrasher. Can Bree and Linda, two women in the autumn of their lives, put their hearts first and find the love they've never dared seize? (978-1-62639-365-3)

Warm November by Kathleen Knowles. What do you do if the one woman you want is the only one you can't have? (978-1-62639-366-0)

In Every Cloud by Tina Michele. When Bree finally leaves her shattered life behind, is she strong enough to salvage the remaining pieces of her heart and find the place where it truly fits? (978-1-62639-413-1)

Rise of the Gorgon by Tanai Walker. When independent Internet journalist Elle Pharell goes to Kuwait to investigate a veteran's mysterious suicide, she hires Cassandra Hunt, an interpreter with a covert agenda. (978-1-62639-367-7)

Crossed by Meredith Doench. Agent Luce Hansen returns home to catch a killer and risks everything to revisit the unsolved murder of her first girlfriend and confront the demons of her youth. (978-1-62639-361-5)

Making a Comeback by Julie Blair. Music and love take center stage when jazz pianist Liz Randall tries to make a comeback with the help of her reclusive, blind neighbor, Jac Winters. (978-1-62639-357-8)

Soul Unique by Gun Brooke. Self-proclaimed cynic Greer Landon falls for Hayden Rowe's paintings and the young woman shortly after, but will Hayden, who lives with Asperger syndrome, trust her and reciprocate her feelings? (978-1-62639-358-5)

The Price of Honor by Radclyffe. Honor and duty are not always black and white—and when self-styled patriots take up arms against the government, the price of honor may be a life. (978-1-62639-359-2)

Mounting Evidence by Karis Walsh. Lieutenant Abigail Hargrove and her mounted police unit need to solve a murder and protect wetland biologist Kira Lovell during the Washington State Fair. (978-1-62639-343-1)

Threads of the Heart by Jeannie Levig. Maggie and Addison Rae-McInnis share a love and a life, but are the threads that bind them together strong enough to withstand Addison's restlessness and the seductive Victoria Fontaine? (978-1-62639-410-0)

Sheltered Love by MJ Williamz. Boone Fairway and Grey Dawson—two women touched by abuse—overcome their pasts to find happiness in each other. (978-1-62639-362-2)

Searching for Celia by Elizabeth Ridley. As American spy novelist Dayle Salvesen investigates the mysterious disappearance of her ex-lover, Celia, in London, she begins questioning how well she knew Celia—and how well she knows herself. (978-1-62639-356-1).

Hardwired by C.P. Rowlands. Award-winning teacher Clary Stone and Leefe Ellis, manager of the homeless shelter for small children, stand together in a part of Clary's hometown that she never knew existed. (978-1-62639-351-6)

The Muse by Meghan O'Brien. Erotica author Kate McMannis struggles with writer's block until a gorgeous muse entices her into a world of fantasy sex and inadvertent romance. (978-1-62639-223-6)

Death's Doorway by Crin Claxton. Helping the dead can be deadly: Tony may be listening to the dead, but she needs to learn to listen to the living. (978-1-62639-354-7)

No Good Reason by Cari Hunter. A violent kidnapping in a Peak District village pushes Detective Sanne Jensen and lifelong friend Dr. Meg Fielding closer, just as it threatens to tear everything apart. (978-1-62639-352-3)

Romance by the Book by Jo Victor. If Cam didn't keep disrupting her life, maybe Alex could uncover the secret of a century-old love story, and solve the greatest mystery of all—her own heart. (978-1-62639-353-0)

The 45th Parallel by Lisa Girolami. Burying her mother isn't the worst thing that can happen to Val Montague when she returns to the woodsy but peculiar town of Hemlock, Oregon. (978-1-62639-342-4)

A Royal Romance by Jenny Frame. In a country where class still divides, can love topple the last social taboo and allow Queen Georgina and Beatrice Elliot, a working-class girl, their happy ever after? (978-1-62639-360-8)

Bouncing by Jaime Maddox. Basketball coach Alex Dalton has been bouncing from woman to woman because no one ever held her interest, until she meets her new assistant, Britain Dodge. (978-1-62639-344-8)

Same Time Next Week by Emily Smith. A chance encounter between Alex Harris and the beautiful Michelle Masters leads to a whirlwind friendship and causes Alex to question everything she's ever known—including her own marriage. (978-1-62639-345-5)

All Things Rise by Missouri Vaun. Cole rescues a striking pilot who crash-lands near her family's farm, setting in motion a chain of events that will forever alter the course of her life. (978-1-62639-346-2)

Riding Passion by D. Jackson Leigh. Mount up for the ride through a sizzling anthology of chance encounters, buried desires, romantic surprises, and blazing passion. (978-1-62639-349-3)

Love's Bounty by Yolanda Wallace. Lobster boat captain Jake Myers stopped living the day she cheated death, but meeting greenhorn Shy Silva stirs her back to life. (978-1-62639334-9)

Just Three Words by Melissa Brayden. Sometimes the one you want is the one you least suspect…Accountant Samantha Ennis has her ordered life disrupted when heartbreaker Hunter Blair moves into her trendy Soho loft. (978-1-62639-335-6)

Lay Down the Law by Carsen Taite. Attorney Peyton Davis returns to her Texas roots to take on big oil and the Mexican Mafia, but will her investigation thwart her chance at true love? (978-1-62639-336-3)

Playing in Shadow by Lesley Davis. Survivor's guilt threatens to keep Bryce trapped in her nightmare world unless Scarlet's love can pull her out of the darkness back into the light. (978-1-62639-337-0)

Soul Selecta by Gill McKnight. Soul mates are hell to work with. (978-1-62639-338-7)

Shadow Hunt by L.L. Raand. With young to raise and her Pack under attack, Sylvan, Alpha of the wolf Weres, takes on her greatest challenge when she determines to uncover the faceless enemies known as the Shadow Lords. A Midnight Hunters novel. (978-1-62639-326-4)

Heart of the Game by Rachel Spangler. A baseball writer falls for a single mom, but can she ever love anything as much as she loves the game? (978-1-62639-327-1)

Prayer of the Handmaiden by Merry Shannon. Celibate priestess Kadrian must defend the kingdom of Ithyria from a dangerous enemy and ultimately choose between her duty to the Goddess and the love of her childhood sweetheart, Erinda. (978-1-62639-329-5)

The Witch of Stalingrad by Justine Saracen. A Soviet "night witch" pilot and American journalist meet on the Eastern Front in WWII and struggle through carnage, conflicting politics, and the deadly Russian winter. (978-1-62639-330-1)